"Will you make me beg, Esme?" Varian asked, so very softly. He slipped his hand about her waist. "I've missed you dreadfully."

"Don't." She didn't try to push him away. Yet she couldn't bear to be made helpless. And in his arms she was lost.

"I know what I am, Esme," he said. "But you gave yourself to me, and now I need you. Beyond bearing, and so, beyond conscience." His hands tightened on her waist. "And I shall win you all over again, this night, however I must. Without scruple."

"Loretta Chase makes a masterly historical romance debut with a thoroughly captivating tale featuring two irresistible characters . . . and an abundance of high wit . . . *The Lion's Daughter* is a keeper."

Mary Jo Putney, author of *Silk and Secrets*

"A writer of exceptional expertise, Ms. Chase leaves an indelible mark on the romance genre. Sure to become a cherished classic and all-time reader favorite, this dazzling foray into high adventure and romance will steal your heart completely away."

Melinda Helfer, *Romantic Times*

The Lion's Daughter

Loretta Chase

AVON BOOKS NEW YORK

THE LION'S DAUGHTER is an original publication of Avon Books. This work has never before appeared in book form. This work is a novel. Any similarity to actual persons or events is purely coincidental.

AVON BOOKS
A division of
The Hearst Corporation
1350 Avenue of the Americas
New York, New York 10019

Published by arrangement with the author
Library of Congress Catalog Card Number: 92-93072
ISBN: 0-380-76647-7

First Avon Books Printing: October 1992

Printed in the U.S.A.

RA 10 9 8 7 6 5 4 3 2 1

Prologue

Otranto, Italy
Mid-September 1818

Jason Brentmor put away the note his sister-in-law had given him. His glance swept unseeingly across the blue Adriatic, glistening in the early autumn sun, and around the stone terrace of his brother's *palazzo* until he met Diana's blue gaze. Then he smiled.

"I'm relieved to learn my mother hasn't gone soft in her old age," he said. "Doesn't waste a word, does she? You'd never know she hadn't laid eyes on me in twenty-four years. To her, I'm still the reckless boy who gambled away his inheritance and ran off to live with the barbarous Turks."

"The prodigal son, rather," came Diana's amused response.

"Indeed. I've merely to creep to her on hands and knees and beg forgiveness, and I and my half-breed daughter will be restored to the bosom of the Brentmors. What on earth did you write her, love?"

"Only that I'd met up with you in the spring in Venice. I also enclosed a copy of my new will." Diana gestured toward the elaborate chess set that stood on a table near her chaise longue. "The set was yours once. Now it shall be Esme's dowry."

"That was my wedding gift to you," he said.

"I'd rather had *you,*" she answered. "But we spoke

all our regrets in Venice, didn't we? And we had three glorious weeks to make up for it."

"Oh, Diana, I do wish—"

She looked away. "I hope you will not become maudlin, Jason. I really cannot abide it. We've both paid a high price for our mistakes. Still, we had Venice, and you're here now. The past is done. I don't want our children to go on paying for it, as though they existed in some ghastly melodrama. Your daughter needs a proper home and a husband—in England, where she belongs. The set's been appraised. It will bring her a large sum."

"She doesn't need—"

"Of course she does, if you want her to marry happily. With the dowry and your mother's backing in society, Esme may take her pick of eligible bachelors. She's eighteen, Jason. She can't remain in Albania to be shut up in some Turkish harem. You said as much yourself. Now, just take her home and make up with your mama, and don't argue with a dying woman."

Jason knew she was dying. He'd suspected it by the time he left Venice; otherwise, he'd not have attempted a second visit to Italy so soon. In the interval, his golden-haired Diana had faded to a wraith, her graceful hands so sadly frail, the blue veins throbbing weakly under nearly transparent flesh. Yet she was determined to appear strong. Proud and stubborn, as she'd always been.

He moved away from the stone railing and, looking away from her still beautiful face, took up the black queen from the chess set. The minute gems of the elaborately carved Renaissance costume sparkled in the sunlight. Though the chess set was supposedly more than two hundred years old, it was complete and in fine condition.

"Thank you," he said. "I'll take Esme back as soon as I can."

"Meaning?"

"Meaning I can't just yet," he said. "But soon, I hope." He met her reproachful blue gaze. "I have obligations, love."

"More important than those to your family?"

He put back the queen, then moved to Diana's side

and laid his hand gently on her shoulder. He hated to disappoint her, but he couldn't lie to her, either. "The Albanians took me in when I had nothing," he said. "They gave me a loving wife who bore me a strong, brave daughter. They gave my life a worthy purpose, gave me a chance to do some good. Now my adopted country needs my help."

"Ah," she said softly. "I hadn't thought of that. Your life's been there for more than twenty years."

"If it were just the usual thing, I'd not hesitate to leave. I know I've put it off too long, and that's hardly fair to Esme, as you say. But Albania is on the brink of chaos at present."

She looked up at him.

"There's always unrest," he explained. "Lately, though, the uprisings show a pattern, as though they were being orchestrated. I've captured a store of English weapons—stolen, it turns out, and smuggled. There's definitely someone behind it, someone of considerable cunning who, unfortunately, appears to have an equally adept supplier."

"A conspiracy, Uncle Jason?"

Jason and Diana turned toward the doorway, where her twelve-year-old son Percival stood, his green eyes glowing with excitement. Jason had forgotten about the boy, who had discreetly withdrawn more than an hour ago with the excuse of trying on the Albanian costume his uncle had brought him.

"Gracious, how dashing you look," said his mother. "And how well it fits."

Indeed, the snug trousers with their distinctive braiding fit perfectly, as did the short black jacket Percival wore over the loose cotton shirt.

"I had it made to Esme's size. It's what she usually wears. She's a terrible hoyden, I'm afraid." Jason ruffled the boy's dark red hair. "Do you know, at the moment, you might pass as her twin. Same hair, eyes—"

"Your hair and eyes," Diana said.

Percival moved away and, with typical boyish disregard for life and limb, jumped onto the terrace wall. Far below him, the sea lapped lazily at the jagged rocks of the shore.

"Only I was never so scrawny," Jason answered, smiling. "It's not so bad for a boy, but most exasperating for Esme. Because she's so small and slight, others tend to forget she's a grown woman—and she objects very strongly to being treated like a *child.*"

"I wish I could meet her," said Percival. "I like tomboys. The other sort of girls are so ghastly silly. Does she play chess?"

"I'm afraid not. Perhaps, when we return to England, you'll teach her."

"Then you *are* returning, Uncle? I'm most pleased to hear it. That's what Mama wishes, you know." Perched on the wall, his legs dangling over the side, Percival squinted against the sun at the faint line of peaks just visible on the opposite shore: Albania's coast. "Every fine day," he went on, "Mama and I come out to wave to you and Esme, and pretend we can see you waving back. Of course, we don't tell anyone, do we, Mama? Not even Lord Edenmont. He thinks we're waving to the sailors."

"Edenmont?" Jason repeated incredulously. "Not Varian St. George, surely? What the devil was the fellow doing here, Diana?"

"He lives here," she said with a faint smile. "You know of him, then?"

"I got an earful in Venice. He was one of Byron's circle. Left England to escape his creditors—and proceeded to cut a swathe through the contessas, not to mention—" Jason recollected Percival's presence. He perched himself on the chaise longue and whispered fiercely, "The man's a parasite, a libertine, a wastrel. What do you mean '*lives* here'?"

"I mean he lives upon my husband."

"A parasite, as I said. Hasn't a groat to his name—"

"Then obviously he must rely upon others. I think of Lord Edenmont as ornamental ivy, supporting itself upon an otherwise vulgar and boring public building—that is to say, Gerald, and others like him. Varian is very ornamental. He is darkly beautiful in that brooding way so fatal to feminine sensibilities . . . and sense."

She glanced at Jason's face and a ghost of a laugh escaped her. "Not to mine, darling. All I feel for him is pity and, occasionally, gratitude. If Baron Edenmont has sunk to playing footboy to an ailing woman and nursemaid to her precocious son, that is the baron's misfortune. Percival and I are glad of the company, are we not dear?" she said in more carrying tones.

"He's a terrible chess player. Otherwise he's quite intelligent," Percival said judiciously. "Besides, he amuses Mama."

Jason took her hand. "Does he?"

"More important, he's kind to Percival," she whispered. "But my son needs *you,* Jason. Gerald loathes him. I fear when I'm gone—"

"Papa's coming!" Percival cried. "The carriage has just come around the turning." He scrambled down from the wall. "I'll run down to meet him, shall I?" Without waiting for a reply, he grabbed his uncle's hand, shook it, and dashed away.

Jason knelt beside Diana. "I love you," he said.

Her frail arms went round his shoulders. "Go now," she said. "Don't let your brother find you here and spoil it for us. I love you, darling, and I'm so proud of you. Do what you must—only try, will you, to hurry back to England with Esme?"

Jason swallowed and nodded.

"Don't be sorry," she said firmly. "Think how lucky we were to have our time together in Venice. You've made me happy, truly."

His eyes misting, he embraced her. He didn't ask for forgiveness, because she'd already given it. And he didn't say goodbye, because he couldn't bear it. He simply kissed her one last time, then left.

Not wishing to worry his mama, Percival didn't tell her he'd become a spy. Never in his twelve years had he encountered a man he could truly admire—until he met his Uncle Jason. From respect to hero worship was but an instant's leap—a leap Percival made the moment he heard his uncle speak of uprisings, smuggling, and conspiracy. With some vaguely formed notion of secretly passing on valuable information to his uncle, Percival began to skulk about Otranto or—when inclement weather or late hours confined him indoors—his own house, where he eavesdropped shamelessly, searching for clues.

Like most persons who look for trouble, Percival found it.

Three nights after Jason's visit, the boy stood on the narrow wrought iron balcony outside his father's study window, peering through the slit between the drapes. Since the window was not quite closed, Percival could hear the conversation clearly.

His father's visitor may well have been Greek as he claimed, but he was not a merchant, and he had most certainly not come to play chess, as Papa had pretended. What Mr. Risto wanted was an immense quantity of British rifles and smaller quantities of other sorts of weapons and ammunition. Papa replied that smuggling such merchandise was becoming more difficult, and Mr. Risto answered that his master was well aware of this. Then he emptied out a good-sized bag of gold coins onto Papa's desk. Without batting an eyelash, Papa scribbled something on a piece of paper and, after explaining the code's meaning, gave it to Mr. Risto. But Mr. Risto shook his head and said it wouldn't do. It seemed he didn't entirely trust Papa to keep his part of the bargain. This made Papa very angry.

Mr. Risto wanted a token of good faith, and nothing but the chess set would do. Papa answered that the chess set had been in the family for generations and was worth several times the value of the weapons. Furthermore, he was deeply affronted by this sudden mistrust after months of doing business with Mr. Risto's master, Ismal. The debate continued until, finally, Mr. Risto said he'd settle for one chess piece. When Papa objected, Mr. Risto began to throw the coins back into the bag. Very vexed, Papa snatched up the black queen, unscrewed the bottom, twisted up the piece of paper, stuffed it inside, and gave it to Mr. Risto.

Mr. Risto promptly became cordial again, took Papa's

hand, and promised to return the chess piece when the merchandise reached Albania. Then the two men left the room.

British weapons. Smuggling. Albania. This, of course, was quite impossible, Percival told himself as he stared blindly into the vacant study. He'd dreamt the whole thing and was at this moment sound asleep in his own bed.

Percival succeeded in convincing himself that what he'd seen and heard was all a dream until the following afternoon, when his father had the entire household searching for the black queen, which he claimed had inexplicably disappeared.

Chapter 1

Otranto, Italy
Late September 1818

Varian St. George stood at the terrace wall and gazed across the water. The sea breeze lolled lazily about him, scarcely ruffling the gleaming dark curls at his forehead. Like a sea of blue flame under the fiery autumn sun, the Adriatic inched toward the faint line of peaks on the opposite shore. In his fancy these were mountains of ice the sea strove to melt and draw into its depths. Always the blue flames clawed at them, yet they stood, impervious, as impenetrable as the vast Ottoman Empire they guarded.

Lord Byron claimed the world's most beautiful women could be found there. Perhaps this was so. Yet it seemed an overly long way to go, even for Aphrodite herself. Certainly, Varian had no need to seek so far for beauties. Women sought the twenty-eight-year-old Lord Edenmont endlessly, and he felt certain there must be quite enough women in western Europe to suffice even the greediest of men.

This evening, for instance, he had an appointment with the dark-eyed wife of a banker, and that was as far into the future as Varian needed or cared to think. The result of the meeting was hardly in question. He would pretend to believe the signora's virtuous protestations for about an hour or perhaps less—depending upon how long she liked to play these scenes. Then they would do exactly as they'd both intended to do in the first place.

Lord Edenmont's mind, at the moment, was not upon the signora, but the family which had fed and housed him all summer.

Lady Brentmor's ashes had been scattered over the Adriatic a week ago. Holding her son's hand, she'd quietly passed away on the day the household had been frantically searching for a valuable chess piece.

Though Varian had been told she was incurably ill, her death had shocked and distressed him. Despite her increasing frailty, she had never truly seemed an invalid. Now he suspected she'd lived these last months on sheer strength of will, and that entirely for Percival's sake. Still, she hadn't kept the truth from her son. It was the boy, in fact, who'd explained Lady Brentmor's rules to Varian very early in their acquaintance.

"Mama says she's not afraid to die," he'd told Varian. "What she *can't* abide, though, is for everyone to be gloomy and anxious about her. And I do believe she's right. If we're sad, we make her feel sad, and it's ever so much healthier for her to feel cheerful, isn't it?" Giving Varian a gravely assessing look he'd added, "I wasn't quite prepared to like you at first, but you make Mama laugh, and you read with a great deal more expression than Papa or I. If you like, I shall teach you how to play chess properly."

Thus, simply because Varian amused Lady Brentmor and provided distraction from her pain, Percival was prepared to like him. Varian found this touching, since he knew the boy thought him a hopeless idiot. The boy, however, considered his father an even greater idiot and clearly didn't like him, which Varian felt was proof of both superior intelligence and taste.

Having apparently discovered long ago that his father detested him, Percival returned the favor by politely disregarding his sire. The boy possessed his mother's affection, which had been enough for him. Until now.

Not that Percival's unhappy family situation was Varian's problem. He'd never been fond of children, especially precocious adolescents like Percival. He did not want to pity the boy, or even like him. Unfortunately, he reminded Varian of his younger brothers. Percival possessed both Damon's genius for getting into scrapes and Gideon's talent for soberly and logically explaining them away.

Now and then, when Varian thought of the siblings he'd abandoned, he experienced a twinge of something like regret. Lately he felt the same disagreeable twinges on Percival's account. With Lady Brentmor's death, Sir Gerald had begun belittling and berating his son relentlessly. This behavior would have been unpleasant enough in any circumstances. Coming immediately upon the loss of an adored mother, it was unconscionably cruel. Still, the world was a cruel place, wasn't it?

Varian took out his pocket watch. Ordinarily, he didn't rise from his bed before noon, but yesterday he'd taken Percival out of Sir Gerald's way, on a long ramble through the Castle of Otranto, then the Cathedral. Exhausted, Varian had made an abnormally early bedtime, and woke at dawn as a result.

He told himself it was just as well. He'd join Sir Gerald at breakfast and announce his plans for departure. Perhaps he'd try Naples next. Not that he had enough money to get there. Still, he had traveled through half of Italy with no funds. He possessed an ancient title, a handsome face and figure, and a devastating charm. These, he'd early learned, were nearly as useful as ready money.

Luckily for Varian St. George, the world was filled with social climbers like Sir Gerald, who, despite the title his father had bought, was a tradesman still. Like so many other jumped-up Cits, however, he was a snob. By dining with an aristocrat or two now and then, he created the illusion that he traveled in elite circles. It was never difficult to find a hard-up aristocrat willing to consume a free meal.

Varian, more hard-up than most, was willing to consume a great deal more. He'd even condescended to become a house guest. He ate Sir Gerald's food, drank his wine, slept in his luxurious guest chamber, and permitted the baronet's servants to wait upon him. In return,

Varian allowed Sir Gerald to drop his ancient name as often as he wished.

It was a pity to give up so convenient a berth before one was obliged to. Sir Gerald would be returning to England soon, anyhow. To leave now would hardly improve Varian's lot . . . and certainly not Percival's, drat him. What would become of the boy after Varian—his only friend, apparently—was gone?

Resolutely banishing Percival's plight to the further recesses of his mind, Varian headed for the breakfast room.

Durrës, Albania

From a distance, the Durrës house seemed a ramshackle heap of stones piled upon a ledge overlooking the Adriatic. It was smaller than their previous abodes, comprising but two tiny rooms: one to live in, one to store supplies in. To Esme Brentmor, it was a beautiful house. In all her peripatetic life, this was the first time she'd lived upon the sea.

The Adriatic was not as richly blue, perhaps, as the Ionian, but then, it was not so tame. In summer, the Etesian breezes roused it. In autumn and winter, violent southerly gales drove themselves to furious frenzies, trying to tear the house apart. In vain. Though the crooked little structure seemed about to tumble to pieces at the next light breeze, it was as solid as the ledge upon which it stood, defying gales and blistering summer heat with equal aplomb.

The sea brought them fresh fish nearly all year round. A short distance from the ledge, Esme's garden thrived in surprisingly fertile soil. It was the first she'd been able to tend for more than one season, and the most generous in supplying maize, alliums, and herbs. Even the chickens, in their own irritable way, were happy.

At the moment, Esme was not. She sat cross-legged upon the hard ledge, her eyes on her folded hands as she conversed with her very best friend, Donika, who was leaving the next day for Saranda, to be married.

"I shall never see you again," Esme said gloomily. "Jason says we must go to England soon."

"So Mama told me—but you'll not leave before my wedding, surely?" Donika asked in alarm.

"I fear so."

"Oh, no. You must ask him, please. Just another month."

"I've asked already. It's no use. He's made a promise to my English aunt, who is dying."

Donika sighed. "Then nothing can be done. A promise on a deathbed is sacred."

"Is it? *She* held nothing sacred." Esme hurled a stone into the water. "Twenty-four years ago she broke her betrothal vows to him. Why? Because one time he got drunk and made a foolish mistake—as any young man might. He played cards and lost a piece of land—that's all. But *she* told him he was weak and base, and she wouldn't marry him."

"That was not kind. She should have forgiven him one mistake. *I* would."

"She did not. But he's forgiven *her*. Twice this year he's gone to visit her. He tells me it was not her fault, but her parents' doing."

"A girl must obey her parents," said Donika. "She can't choose a husband for herself. Still, I don't think they should have made her break a sacred vow."

"It was worse than that," Esme said angrily. "Not a year after she drove my father away, she wed his brother. She was of a noble family, and wealthy, and you'd think Jason's family would have been appeased. They were quick enough to take *her* in, but my father they made an outcast forever."

"The English are very strange," Donika said thoughtfully.

"They're *unnatural,*" Esme returned. "Shall I tell you what my English grandfather wrote when he received the news of my birth? The words are burned in my heart. 'It was not enough,' he said in his hateful letter, 'that you disgraced the Brentmor name with your reckless debauchery. It was not enough to gamble away your aunt's property and break your mother's heart. It was not enough to run away from your errors, instead of remaining, like a man, to make amends. No, you must compound our shame by joining the ranks of Turkish brigands, marrying one of these unspeakable barbarians, and infecting the world with yet another heathen savage.' "

Donika stared at her in horrified disbelief.

"In English, it sounds even worse," Esme grimly assured her. "This is the family my father wishes to take me to."

Donika pressed closer and placed a comforting arm about her friend's thin shoulders. "It's hard, I know," she said, "but you belong to your father's family—at least until you're wed. Perhaps it won't be for long. I'm sure your father will find you a husband in England. I've seen some Englishmen. Taller than the other Franks, and some quite handsome and strong."

"Ah, yes, and I'm sure their kin are just dying to welcome an ugly little barbarian into the family."

"You're *not* ugly. Your hair is thick and healthy, filled with fire." Donika smoothed the wavy dark red locks back from Esme's forehead. "And your eyes are pretty. My mama said so, too. Beautiful, like evergreens, she said. Also, your skin is smooth," she added, lightly touching Esme's cheek.

"I have no breasts," Esme said glumly. "And my legs and arms are like sticks for kindling."

"Mama says it doesn't matter if a girl's skinny, so long as she's strong. She was skinny, too, yet she bore seven healthy children."

"I don't want to bear children to a *foreigner,*" Esme snapped. "I don't want to climb into bed with a man who can't speak my language, and raise children who'll never learn it."

"In bed, you won't need to converse with him," Donika said with a giggle.

Esme threw her a reproving look. "I should never have told you what Jason said about how babies are made."

"I'm glad you did. Now I'm not at all frightened. It doesn't sound very difficult—though perhaps embarrassing at first."

"It's also rather painful at first, I think," Esme said, momentarily distracted by the titillating subject. "But I've been shot twice already, and it can't be worse than having a bullet dug out of your flesh."

Donika threw her an admiring glance. "You're not afraid of anything, little warrior. If you can face marauding bandits, you should have no trouble with even your English kin. Still, I'll miss you so much. If only your father had found you a husband here." She looked toward the sea and sighed.

"As well wish to find a mountain of diamonds. The fact is, I make a far better boy than a girl, and a better soldier than a wife. A man must be very old and very desperate to want me, when he could have a plump, pretty, *docile* wife for the same price."

Donika tossed a stone into the water. "They say Ismal wants you," she said after a moment. "He isn't old or desperate, but young and very rich."

"And a Moslem. I'd rather be boiled in oil than imprisoned in a harem," Esme said firmly. "Even England, with relatives who hate me, would be better than that." She considered briefly, then added, "I never told you before, but I was afraid once that it would happen."

Donika turned to her.

"When I was fourteen, visiting my grandmother in Gjirokastra," Esme continued, "Ismal and his family were there. He chased me through the garden. I thought it was a game, but—" She paused, flushing.

"But what? But what?"

Though there was no one else about to hear, Esme lowered her voice. "When he caught me, he kissed me—*on the mouth.*"

"Truly?"

Esme shook her head from side to side in the Albanian affirmative.

"What was it like?" Donika asked eagerly. "He's so handsome, like a prince. Beautiful golden hair, and eyes like blue jewels—"

"It was *wet,*" Esme interrupted. "I didn't like it at all. I knocked him down and wiped my mouth and cursed him soundly." She looked at her friend. "And he just lay there on the ground and laughed. I thought he was crazy, and I was so afraid his grandfather would make an offer for me and I would have to marry this crazy boy with his wet mouth and live in his harem . . . but nothing happened. Or if it did, Jason must have said no."

Donika laughed. "I can't believe this. You knocked down the cousin of Ali Pasha? You could have been executed."

"What would you have done?" Esme demanded.

"Screamed for help, of course. But it would never occur to you to call for help. You don't just think you're a warrior. You think you're a whole army."

Esme turned her gaze to the sea. Any day now it would carry her far away from all she knew and loved . . . forever.

"My father is no unwanted suitor, no enemy," she said quietly. "I can't fight him. When at last he confessed he was homesick, I felt so ashamed for arguing with him. I've complained to you, only to unburden myself, but you mustn't mind it. I know what I must do. He won't leave without me, and I love him too much to try to make him stay. I'll make the best of it, for his sake."

"It won't be so bad," Donika comforted. "You'll be homesick at first, but once you're wed, with babies of your own, think how happy you'll be. Think how rich and full your life will be."

Her gaze upon the pitiless sea, Esme saw only emptiness ahead. But her friend was, miraculously, in love with the man her family had chosen for her. No more self-pity, Esme resolved. No more gloom. This was Donika's happy time, and it was unkind to spoil it.

"So it will," Esme said with a laugh. "And I shall teach my babies Albanian, in secret."

Otranto

"I must ask a favor of you, Edenmont," Sir Gerald said as Varian was pouring his second cup of coffee. "I'd hoped to leave soon for England, but my responsibilities order otherwise. I want you to take Percival to Venice."

"Certainly, I should like to oblige," Varian murmured politely, "but—"

"I realize it's a great deal to ask," the baronet interrupted, "but I haven't much choice. I can't look after the boy at the moment. it's too complicated and tedious to explain, but it suffices to say there are certain delicate negotiations—that sort of thing—and one can't have the lad about, making a nuisance of himself."

Varian gazed impartially at his coffee cup.

"It wouldn't be for very long. I expect to take him off your hands in a month or so."

A *month? Or so?* Varian dropped in another lump of sugar.

"Naturally, I would assume all expenses," said Sir Gerald. From his breast pocket he withdrew a bank draft, which he laid beside Varian's saucer.

Varian eyed it with all the composure with which he regarded a winning card hand, his gray eyes as unreadable as smoke.

"For out-of-pocket expenses," his host said. "Of course, I shall see to your passage and write to engage suitable lodgings en route, and in Venice."

"Venice," said Varian, "is very damp this time of year."

"Well, you needn't hurry. It hardly matters to me whether you dawdle along the way to see the sights, does it? Certainly I'll send a manservant with you, and pay his way as well. Choose whomever you like."

Passage paid, a fortune to spend on the way, and a servant. For a man with one pound, three shillings, sixpence in his pocket, the offer was—as it was intended to be—irresistible.

Varian looked up from his cup to meet his host's impatient gaze. "As I mentioned, Sir Gerald, I should be happy to oblige," he said.

Tepelena, Albania

Ali Pasha, the wily despot who ruled Albania, was old, fat, and sick. Periodically, he suffered fits of madness.

These drove him to acts of savagery so sadistic that even the Albanians, inured to the brutality of a world in which human life was held very cheap, found them worthy of remark.

That the populace remained loyal, for the most part, and even boasted of his triumphs, was evidence not only of their stoicism, but of their acute political perceptiveness. There were plenty of monsters about ruling the downtrodden masses of the Ottoman Empire. Ali, however, was the only monster the Sultan could not make his slave. Consequently, the Sultan could not make the Albanians his slaves. They answered only to Ali—when they condescended to answer at all—and he was no outsider, but an Albanian, one of their own. He couldn't even be bothered to learn Turkish. Why trouble himself when he wasn't going to listen to the Turks anyhow?

Like the Albanians, Jason Brentmor took the broad view of the Machiavellian Vizier. Aware of Ali's courage, his military and political acumen, and weighing the advantages against the man's many character flaws, Jason still felt that Ali Pasha, the Lion of Janina, was far preferable to any available alternative.

After more than twenty years' close association, Jason knew Ali very well. As he left the Vizier's palace, Jason wished his friend did not know *him* quite so well. Naturally, as a British subject, Ali had said, Jason was free to leave Albania whenever he wished, but . . .

Well, what Ali's long "but" boiled down to was, "How can you abandon me at a time like this? After all I've done for you?"

"He's quite right," Jason told his comrade, Bajo, as they rode out of Tepelena that afternoon. "And he doesn't know the half of it. If the rebels succeed, Albania will be plunged into chaos, and the Turks will sweep in easily to crush your people. Ali doubts the uprisings will lead to anything, but he doesn't want any trouble now, when he's trying to get the Greeks to join *his* revolution."

"If the Greeks join, under his lead, we'll be able to overthrow the Turks," said Bajo. "But Ali's old. I fear there won't be time."

"He's lived this long. He might live to be a hundred."

Bajo looked at him. "You didn't tell him, then, of your suspicions about Ismal?"

"I couldn't. Ali's been too preoccupied with his grand scheme to notice that we've more than scattered unrest on our hands. If he learns a conspiracy's afoot—and his own cousin behind it—"

"A bloodbath," Bajo finished succinctly. His gaze softened into compassion. "Ah, Red Lion, you must deal with it yourself, if you wish it to be done without great slaughter."

Jason sighed. "I realized that in about a quarter hour. I had plenty of time to think it through while pretending to listen to Ali's brilliant plans to throw off the Turkish yoke." He paused for a moment to glance about him, but the landscape was deserted. "I shall have to pretend to be killed," he said quietly.

Bajo thought this over, then shook his head in agreement. "Very wise. If Ismal wishes to succeed, he must get you out of the way. If he believes you're dead, he won't need to be so cautious. Meanwhile, you can go where you like and do what you must without troublesome spies and assassins bothering you."

"That's not the only reason," Jason said. "I think Ismal is too cunning to try to kill me outright, at least this early in the game. It's more likely he'll try to tie my hands—and the best way to do that is to take Esme as hostage. He's been moaning about his desperate love for her just a bit too much lately. I suspect he means to abduct her and make it look like an act of passion. *That* Ali will readily believe; he's stolen women and boys enough, merely because he fancied them."

"I see great advantages to your death," Bajo said. "She'll be no use to Ismal then, and he'll leave her in peace."

"I don't mean to risk even that. I want her out of Albania," Jason said firmly. "I've thought it over, and what I propose is a cruel deception, but I see no alternative. Esme must believe I'm dead, or she'll never leave without me. You must make certain she believes it, and get her on her way to England. I'll give you money and the names of some people in Venice who can be trusted to take her to my mother."

"Y'Allah, Red Lion, what a thing you ask of me. To tell the child you're dead—and then make the grieving creature go away? She's very stubborn, this girl of yours. How am I to make her go to strangers, foreigners?"

"Don't give her any time to think," Jason answered sharply. "If she gives you trouble, knock her on the head and tie her up. It's for her own good. Better some hours' discomfort and a few weeks' grief than rape or murder. I want my daughter to be safe. Don't make me choose between her and Albania. I love this country, and I'd risk my life for it . . . but I love my daughter more."

Bajo shrugged. "Well, you're English, after all." He threw Jason a smile. "I'll do as you ask. She *is* a superior female, worth two good men, I've often said. And once she's safely away, I'll return to help you. I suppose you want me to go now?"

"Not just this minute. I need to be killed first. We'd better do it further north. I must fall into the river, and be swept away—or into a deep gorge. We don't want anyone hunting for my body, now, do we?"

Chapter 2

Bari, Italy

"'Who soon had left her charms for vulgar bliss,' " Percival quoted. "What does it mean?"

Varian paused in the doorway, a towel in his hands.

Percival had begged to visit the fish stalls today, which he claimed had existed on the Bari breakwater since before Roman times. The area certainly stank as though it had existed—and not been cleaned—since the beginning of time. There Varian had watched the boy consume a bucket of oysters and another of sea urchins, followed by a half bucket of clams. Though Varian had not partaken of the feast, the stench of shellfish had permeated them both equally. This was the third bath he'd taken, and at last the odor seemed to be gone.

He gave his hair a final rub with the towel, then tossed it behind him and entered the sitting room. He sniffed dubiously as he passed Percival, but their servant, Rinaldo, had scrubbed the boy raw. Not a hint of fish remained.

Percival repeated the line from *Childe Harold*. "I take it 'vulgar bliss' is a euphemism," he said. "Does Byron refer to women of ill repute? I can't think what else he could mean. But why leave the one he loved for a tart, when he's supposedly sick of tarts? And why call it 'bliss' when he's so unhappy?"

"I'm not certain I ought to explain it," Varian said as

he dropped into an overstuffed chair by the fire. "I suspect your father would not approve your reading Lord Byron."

"Indeed he would not," Percival answered, looking up from the book. "But Papa isn't here, and you are, and you are not in the least like him. Mama said you were like Childe Harold, actually, and so one must conclude you are best able to explain his state of mind. He seems a most morose sort of hero. That is, if he spends his life in pleasure, how can he be unhappy?"

"Perhaps he's repenting his sins."

"I thought wicked men did that only when they were old and decrepit. Gout, I understand, has reformed a great many rogues."

"Perhaps Childe Harold suffers from toothache," said Varian, leaning back comfortably. He was relieved to find Percival once more his usual self. The boy had been unnaturally quiet and well-behaved all the way to Bari, a sad ghost who gazed dully out the coach window for hours and passively did whatever Varian asked. The shellfish had evidently enlivened Percival's disposition. Certainly his digestion hadn't suffered. At dinner, the lad had consumed enough to bloat an elephant. Where the devil did he put it? He was the scrawniest boy Varian had ever seen outside a slum.

"Did you sin with Signora Razzoli?" Percival asked, after a moment. "Rinaldo says you were her *cavalier servente*, but that is an idiomatic expression, isn't it? When you visited her house, did you—"

"We conversed," Varian said. "She is very well-read. And it is vulgar to gossip with servants, Percival."

"Yes, that's what Grandmama says, but it's ever so interesting. Servants know *everything.*"

"I expect your grandmother will be happy to have you and your father back in England."

The boy obligingly followed the conversational detour.

"Well, she makes the best of it, Grandmama says, since she hasn't anyone else. Uncle John—but they all called him Jack—was the eldest. He died before I was born, though. And Uncle J—" Percival hesitated, then closed his book and pulled his chair closer to Varian's. In low, confidential tones he concluded, "They pretend Uncle Jason's dead, too, but he isn't."

"Your mama's brother?" Varian asked. He knew Sir Gerald's elder brother had succumbed to influenza ages ago. He'd heard of no other Brentmor siblings.

"Papa's younger brother," Percival explained. "He ran away years and years ago, and they've always pretended he was dead, they were so angry. But he's not. He's alive and . . . and he's a *hero.*"

"He must be a very discreet sort of hero," Varian said. "I've never heard of him."

"Have you heard of Ali Pasha, the ruler of Albania?" Percival tapped his finger on the book cover. "That's why I'm reading this. Lord Byron tells all about Ali Pasha and the Albanians, and that's where Uncle Jason is. He's lived there all this time, and they call him the Red Lion. That's for his courage and his red hair. It's the same color as mine—and quite rare in Albania, I believe."

"I beg your pardon, Percival, but I do read upon occasion, and am familiar with the poem. I recall no mention of the Red Lion. Where did you read about this fellow?"

Percival wrinkled his brow. "But I'm sure I never said I *read* about my uncle."

"Then how do you know so much about a relative everyone pretends is dead?" Varian gave the boy a searching look.

Percival squirmed a bit, then sat back in his chair, his expression thoughtful.

"Perhaps it was a dream," Varian suggested.

"No. It wasn't a dream."

"A fairy tale, then."

"No. It's quite true." Percival bit his lip. "I can prove it," he said. "If I may be excused for a moment?"

He ran to his room, leaving Varian to stare uneasily at the fire. Moments later, the boy was back, bearing a pile of clothing. He draped the pieces over his chair: woolen trousers with elaborate braiding, a black, gilt-embroidered jacket, and a voluminous cotton shirt.

"Uncle Jason gave them to me," Percival said. "It's what the Albanians wear—or some of them. He said he didn't think I'd want the kilt until I was older. Mama said I wasn't to show them to anyone, because Papa would find out. But *you* wouldn't tell Papa, would you?"

"Tell him what?" Varian asked, though he had a suspicion what the answer was.

"That Uncle Jason came to see us." Percival picked a minute piece of lint from the jacket and smoothed a crease in the shirt.

In half an hour, Varian had most of the story. Jason had made two visits: one long stay in Venice while Sir Gerald was away, seeking a villa in southern Italy, and one brief visit a few days before Lady Brentmor died. From innocent remarks Percival made—in between extolling his uncle's endless virtues—Varian guessed that Jason Brentmor had been more than a brother-in-law to Diana.

Varian could hardly blame her for infidelity to a husband like Sir Gerald. Nor was he shocked that the lover was her brother-in-law. On the contrary, the news was welcome. Varian had suspected her life was unhappy, even apart from her illness. He felt an odd relief that someone had made her happy for a while.

"Well, I'm delighted you had a chance to meet this splendid uncle," Varian said when the tale was done. "However, it grows late, and you ought to make an early bedtime if we're to tour the Church of St. Nicholas tomorrow." Varian had his own tour planned for this night: a leisurely exploration of the charms of a certain dark-eyed lady he'd encountered at the Castle of Bari.

"But I haven't told you the terrible thing I did," Percival said, his green eyes downcast.

"I am hardly the father confessor," Varian answered with a tinge of impatience. "So long as you don't dissect your various specimens upon the table at mealtimes, or fill my bed with your rocks, your sins are of little moment—"

"I gave him the black queen," Percival said in a choked voice. "By accident, I mean. But if Papa finds out he'll—he'll send me to school in India. He's threatened that hundreds of times, but Mama wouldn't let him."

Varian had risen, preparatory to carrying Percival over his shoulder to bed if need be. Now he sat back down. After endless searching, the black queen had finally been presumed stolen, and Sir Gerald had mentioned offering a thousand pounds for its return. Varian could not believe his ears. He gazed at Percival with narrowed eyes. "You *what?*"

"I meant to give Uncle Jason my rock—the one with the green streaks and the little knobby—"

"The rock's unique characteristics do not appear pertinent," Varian interrupted.

"I beg your pardon, sir. Quite right. They're not—well, not at present, I agree. The fact is, we were in the study. How we got there is not pertinent either, I believe?" Percival asked, looking up hopefully.

"Not at present."

"Well, that's a relief, because—"

"Percival."

"Yes, sir, indeed. To put it as succinctly as possible: I bumped into the chess table and knocked some pieces over. In my agitated state—for Papa would be most—" He caught Varian's eyes and went on hurriedly, "Well, I must have wrapped the black queen in Uncle Jason's handkerchief by mistake, because later I found the rock was still in my pocket. When Papa told us the queen was gone, I knew what had happened. But I couldn't tell him, could I?"

If the queen was in Jason's possession, then it was in Albania by now, hopelessly beyond the reach of a penniless nobleman.

"I suppose not." Varian rose once more. "I'm sure you're emotionally drained by this confession, Percival, and most anxious to rest."

Percival gazed at him consideringly. "Actually, now I've confessed, I feel obliged to *do* something."

"Yes. Go to bed."

"What I mean is, we could get her back. That is to say, she *is* worth a thousand quid to Papa and"—he flung his arm eastward—"she's just over there, you know."

" 'Over there' is the Ottoman Empire. Don't be absurd, Percival. Unless your uncle chooses to return it, the queen is gone for good."

"It takes only a day or two to sail there," Percival said. "Uncle Jason lives right on the coast. We wouldn't have to go *into* the country. Just stop at the port, as scores of ships do every day, from everywhere."

"We?" Varian repeated. "If you think I'm hiring a vessel to travel to *Albania* with a twelve-year-old boy, his father's sole heir—"

"Papa would pay you the reward, and you know he gave you plenty of money for travel expenses and we've got lots of time."

"No, Percival. Go to bed."

Percival went to bed, but not until hours later, and Lord Edenmont, having altogether forgotten the dark-eyed lady, sat up until dawn watching the fire dwindle into smoldering embers.

Staring unhappily into the darkness, Percival told himself he was very lucky Lord Edenmont was not as perceptive as Mama. She would have grown suspicious when she saw how much he'd eaten. She knew he overate when he was particularly agitated.

He'd gorged today because he knew he must tell Lord Edenmont a falsehood about the black queen. He had to. Stolen weapons were on their way to Albania, and no one but Uncle Jason could be entrusted with the information, especially since Papa was involved. Unfortunately, one couldn't write to Uncle Jason. He'd said that powerful men in Albania had spies who regularly intercepted other peoples' letters.

Which meant he must be told in person. Which meant deceiving Lord Edenmont. Which had made Percival feel just like a criminal.

It hardly counted that people said Lord Edenmont was wicked—even that Uncle Jason thought so. His lordship had *always* been kind to Mama, and agreeable to Percival himself. He wouldn't be agreeable ever again, Percival thought regretfully, when he learned the truth. But that would happen only if his lordship took the bait. Perhaps he wouldn't.

The room's blackness was just beginning to fade when Percival heard Lord Edenmont enter the adjoining bedchamber. Closing his eyes, Percival told himself one *shouldn't* feel sorry about trying to do one's duty, especially when hundreds of lives might be saved. Besides, one couldn't expect Lord Edenmont to remain about forever. Sooner or later they'd reach Venice, and his lordship would go away. On the other hand, if all went well, Uncle Jason would soon be on his way to England with Cousin Esme. That would more than make up for losing Lord Edenmont's company. They'd be together. A family, just as Mama wanted.

This reflection quieted Percival's distress, rather as his mama's voice might have done. Moments later, while the rising sun darted gold sparks across the Adriatic, he fell asleep.

Tepelena, Albania

Ismal, the beautiful prince with the golden hair and blue jewel eyes, reclined upon his divan and gazed thoughtfully at the ornate chess piece in his hand. "Jason is not leaving?" he asked Risto.

"Ali has convinced him to stay and help quiet the unrest."

"That's disappointing. He's already captured an important store of weapons. We can't afford continued interference."

"You want him dead, master?"

"That would be politically unwise. The Red Lion is too well-loved, even by those who support our efforts to oust Ali. I can't risk being suspected of his murder. Fortunately, I was prepared for this annoying setback." Ismal smiled at his devoted servant and spy. "You did better than you knew in persuading the Englishman to give you this bit of 'collateral.' "

Risto bowed his head. "I'd hoped to bring you the entire set. It would have been a fine addition to your treasures. Besides, Sir Gerald's prices are excessive," he added disapprovingly.

"I want modern British weapons, and he's the only dependable source," Ismal answered with a shrug. "But what a fool he was to put anything in writing, even in code. His hand is too distinctive."

"He believed me a stupid barbarian, master. He did not trust me to remember the details correctly."

"Most convenient." Ismal stroked the black queen's head. "I kept the message, in case it might be of use. Now I think it will be of great use." Looking up at his servant, he went on, "I want a party sent to abduct the Red Lion's daughter—immediately. Jason will know he must accept the bride-price for her, and once she's mine, he won't dare move against me."

"He may go to Ali."

"I doubt he'd risk her life in that way. But let him." Ismal turned the chess piece in his hand. "See that this is in Esme's possession when she's taken. If Jason dares to make difficulties, why, I shall say he's a traitor, and the chess piece will be my proof. I'll advise Ali to consult the British, who'll have no difficulty tracing the queen to the Red Lion's brother. No trouble either, showing that the brother wrote the message. Ali knows the Red Lion has been to Italy twice this year, to visit his family. Both my cousin and the British will conclude Jason and his brother are selling stolen arms for their own profit. Both governments will be most displeased."

His blue eyes glittered as he handed Risto the chess piece. "Now perhaps you see, Risto, how very powerful the queen can be—to a player who knows how to use her." Then he laughed.

Durrës

Esme woke the instant she felt the hand upon her shoulder and sat bolt upright. The room was still dark. "Papa?" she said to the black shape beside her. Even as she uttered the name, she realized the man wasn't Jason.

"It is I, Bajo," the figure said.

A chill of anxiety seized her. "Where is Jason?"

There was a long pause, then a sigh. Even before Bajo spoke, her heart was pounding.

"I'm sorry, child."

"Where *is* he?"

"Ah, little one." Bajo laid his hand on her shoulder. "It is bad news, little warrior. Be strong. Jason has been shot."

No. *No!* Her heart screamed, but her tongue was silent. Her hands tightened on the blanket and she bit her lip, refusing to shriek and weep like a weak female.

"We were . . . ambushed . . . in the straits of Vijose," Bajo said. "They shot him in the back, and he fell over the cliff, into the river far below. I thank God it was so. A quick death—and the river swept him away so the filthy assassins could not carry his head to their lord in triumph."

Jason. Her strong, brave, loving father. Shot in the back like a thief . . . the icy torrent dragging his body, dashing him against the cruel rocks . . . Esme closed her eyes and gritted her teeth, and willed the racking grief into rage.

"What assassins?" she demanded. "Who owes me blood?"

"Nay, little one. The Red Lion's daughter does not seek blood," he reproached. "The killers are dead. I saw to that. But we've no time for talk. Jason's murder was only the beginning, and you are in great danger. Make haste," he urged, pulling her from the bed.

Esme yanked free of his grip and found she was shaking. With an effort she made herself stand upright. She always slept fully dressed in her male costume, her long gun within easy reach. One of Bajo's cousins invariably kept watch outside, even when Jason was home, but she didn't want to be caught unprepared if the town were suddenly attacked.

"Why haste? Where are we going?"

Bajo picked up her head covering and thrust it into her hands. "North. To Shkodra." He lit a candle, then hustled about the room, gathering up belongings and tossing them into a sack. Hardly aware of what she did, Esme pulled on the woolen helmet and tucked her hair up inside it, all the while staring at Bajo.

While he packed, he went on talking nervously. "We were hurrying home because Jason feared Ismal was planning to abduct you. Now there's no doubt of it. Of course he'll lie—blame the murder on bandits. And Ali will be too devastated to notice or care that Ismal steals a mere female in the meantime." Bajo paused. "This is why we must make haste. Don't even think about revenge. If you delay, you invite your own shame. You can't wish to be concubine of the man who killed your father."

"I'll tell the Pasha of Shkodra," Esme said. *"He'll* help me. Ismal owes me blood."

"The Pasha will help you out of the country," Bajo answered. "That's all. That's what Jason intended, and we'll do as he wished."

He met Esme's horrified gaze, then quickly looked away.

"No," she said, her voice choked. "You're not sending me to *England?* Alone?"

Bajo hauled the sack over his shoulder and moved to the door, where he paused. "It's a hard thing, I know, little warrior, but the choice is plain. Either you show courage in this, or become Ismal's slave . . . and your father will have died for nothing."

Later, she told herself. Later, she'd have time to think, and she'd find a way.

Without another word, Esme collected the few things Bajo had missed, thrust them into her small traveling pouch, grabbed her rifle, and followed him out the door.

Minutes later, they reached the Durrës harbor. It was nearly dawn, but the shore was so thick with fog that the first tentative rays of light were dull spots of pink in the heavy grey blanket. Bajo's boat was moored discreetly some distance from the main pier. As they neared the shore, Esme made out the outlines of a larger ship, one of the *pielagos* which so often called here. Rarely at this time of year, however, for they were ill-equipped to withstand the autumn gales.

A moment later, she discerned figures approaching in the mist. Though they came on foot, she tensed and glanced at Bajo.

"Foreigners," he whispered.

The next instant confirmed this, as the wind carried to her ears a hodgepodge of Albania, Italian, and English.

"No . . . *zoti* . . . the boat, I beg you . . . master . . . kill me."

As the figures neared, their voices became more distinct, and Esme heard the boyish tenor reply in cultivated English accents. "Nonsense. My uncle lives in this town."

"Please, young master, only wait—"

"Here are some people. We can ask them."

The pair was almost upon them. Though they seemed harmless enough, Esme let her bundle drop to the sand and took a firm grip on her rifle. Bajo, his stance alert, stood near, his rifle ready as well.

"Tongue-got-yet-ah," the boyish voice called out.

He was only a child, an English child, with accents like her father's.

"Tungjatjeta," she cautiously answered the greeting.

Encouraged, the boy hurried up to them.

"Come away," Bajo whispered to her. "We have no time."

"He's *English,"* Esme answered. In the next instant, she wondered if her ears had deceived her, for the boy's garb closely resembled her own. He even had a pouch slung over his shoulder. Then, as he came closer, she felt certain she was dreaming. The weak light glinted upon hair the color of her father's. She backed away as the boy stopped short, his gaze upon Bajo's rifle. His fat, timid companion cowered several feet behind him.

"Oh, dear, we seem to have alarmed them," the boy said. "How does one—" He cleared his throat. "Koosh sha-pee—ah—ah—Jason? I mean, it's quite all right. He's my uncle. Jason. My jah-jee. The Red Lion, you know—"

"Xhaxha?" Esme repeated, stunned. Jason—this child's uncle? Incredulous, she stepped closer, all else

forgotten as she stared at him. Her father's hair, her father's eyes . . . hers, as well.

Beside her, Bajo lowered his rifle. "He looks like your brother," he said.

The boy was staring at Esme with equal astonishment.

"Who *are* you?" she demanded in English.

He stepped nearer, his gaze fixed on her face. "You speak English. Good heavens, you look—but Uncle Jason said she—you *are* a 'she,' aren't you?" His face reddened. "Oh, dear. How rude of me. I am Percival Brentmor, Jason's nephew."

"Jason's nephew," Esme repeated numbly.

"Yes. How do you do?"

Esme felt an insane urge to giggle. Or cry. She didn't know which. She was aware of a rumble, far away. But perhaps she was merely dizzy. Her ears seemed to be ringing.

"Percival," she said, her mouth dry. "Jason's nephew."

"Yes. Are you—are you Esme?"

The rumbling grew louder. Bajo had turned away. He must have heard it, too.

Esme glanced from him to the lad who called himself Percival, Jason's nephew. The boy was speaking rapidly, but she scarcely heard him. Her concentration was fixed on the building thunder. Not a storm. Riders.

Bajo raised his rifle.

"Go back," she commanded harshly in English, pushing the boy away. "Go back to your ship—quickly, child. *Now!*"

"What is it? Bandits?"

"Go back!" she shouted. "*Run,* damn you!" She gave him another, harder push. This time he got the message and backed away. His alarmed companion was already running for the ship. The boy gave Esme one bewildered glance, then followed.

The pounding hoofbeats raced toward them, and Bajo was screaming at her to run. But the riders, coming from the east, were heading straight for the boy, who was still far from his own ship. If she and Bajo ran for their boat, her cousin would be caught in the crossfire.

She had barely thought it when the dull thunder broke into a roar and a dense, black cloud swept down from the road onto the beach. In the thick fog, they were a whirling mass of dark shapes—a score of horsemen at least. Ignoring Bajo's frantic commands, Esme raised her rifle and fired, drawing their attention to her. Answering shots flew over her head.

She raced toward an overturned boat on the beach, and saw other forms approaching. Bajo's comrades. A bullet whizzed past her. She dove for the shelter of the boat and hurriedly reloaded.

The explosions outside jolted Varian from a sound sleep and brought him almost instantly to his feet. A glance about the cabin showed no sign of Percival. Varian yanked his shirt over his head, jerked on his trousers and boots, snatched up his pistols, and raced to the deck.

On the shore, the light-streaked fog shrouded a writhing mass of horses and men and a cacophony of war cries and rifle fire. He scrambled onto the pier and dashed toward the battleground.

"Percival!" he bellowed.

As he leapt from the pier to the sand, he heard a high-pitched cry and turned toward it. A half dozen riders were bearing down upon one slight figure running clumsily across the sand. A feeble ray of early sun broke for a fleeting instant through the haze and lit a crown of dark red hair.

His heart thundering as loudly as the deadly hooves closing in on the boy, Varian aimed and fired. He saw a horse crumple to the ground, even as he aimed and fired his other pistol. With shaking fingers, he began to reload. There was a deafening noise close by, then something crashed. A lightning bolt of pain shot through him . . . then darkness.

Gently, Esme wiped away the sand from the unconscious man's face. It would be more efficient simply to empty the bucket over his head, but that might wake him too suddenly, and the blow he'd suffered would cause sufficient pain as it was.

The ship rocked, and the water sloshed in the bucket beside her, splashing her trousers. They were soaked already, though, scratchy with sand and salt. Still, that was a negligible discomfort, her only physical one. Some of the others had not fared so well: two of Bajo's cousins were dead, and several friends wounded. Townsfolk had quickly taken up the latter and would care for them.

They'd not yet collected the six marauders' corpses when Bajo had ordered her to the *pielago*. He'd thrown the Englishman over his shoulder and, deaf to her arguments, had seen them both safely aboard and ordered the captain to sail south, to Corfu. Then Bajo had set off to rescue the boy . . . her cousin.

Esme glared down at the haughty face beside her knees. What fiend had led the man here, of all places, with a young boy—unguarded, unarmed?

Actually, the Englishman's face was that of a fiend, albeit a coldly beautiful one, she thought, gazing at the dark, curling tendrils that straggled over his high forehead. Her wary scrutiny traveled slowly over black, high-arched eyebrows and black lashes, down the long, imperious nose, and past the full, sculptured mouth to the clean, angular jaw. An arrogant face. Petro, the dragoman who'd been with the boy, had said this man was an English lord.

Esme's glance moved to the hand that lay over his flat belly. Long fingers, the nails manicured and clean but for a few grains of Durrës beach imbedded there. Not a callous, scar, or scratch marred their elegant perfection. She looked at her own tanned hands, hard and strong, then at her stained, gritty trousers. Her belly tightened with anxiety. It was the way she always felt when she encountered her father's countrymen: the same sense of inadequacy, the same tense anticipation of their barely masked distaste and scorn. Some looked right through her, as though she were invisible, and sometimes that was worse than the more open condescension. She knew they viewed her as little better than an animal.

Those she had met before were only soldiers. This man was a lord. Even now he seemed to sneer at her.

His eyes, she decided as she returned her gaze to his face, would be cold and hard as stone.

It didn't matter, she told herself. His opinion was of no consequence. She threw the rag into the bucket, angrily wrung it out . . . then paused, her hand inches from his face as his mouth worked soundlessly and his eyes slowly opened.

Her heart skittered like a frightened mare. Gray eyes, but not like stone. Gray smoke. As they focused with painful slowness, the rigid countenance softened into life, and she drew the cloth away, her hand trembling.

It *was* the face of a dark angel. For one giddy moment, she thought it was Lucifer himself, just hurled down by a wrathful Almighty.

"Percival," he murmured. "Thank G—" He blinked. "Who *are* you?"

The low, hoarse voice was smoke, too, enervating as opium. Esme drew a sharp breath and told herself to *wake up*.

"I'm called Zigur," she said.

Chapter 3

The boy's resemblance to Percival was startling: the same feline cast to vividly green eyes, the same small, straight nose and assertive little chin. He even related the dawn's events in the same patiently logical way, though more succinctly than Percival would have done. Had Varian been his usual self, Zigur's cool self-possession would have amused him, for the boy could only be a year or two Percival's senior—fifteen at most. But Varian's head was pounding, his muscles shrieking, and the tale, in any case, held no humor.

"My father, Jason, is the uncle of the boy, Percival," Zigur was explaining. "This morning, I learned my father had been killed and that men were sent to take me for their master's pleasure. In the confusion at the harbor, these men took my cousin by mistake."

Zigur pushed back his thick woolen headgear slightly, and Varian saw that the hair beneath, like the eyes, precisely matched Percival's. Then the boy's meaning sank in. In these realms, Varian had heard, children of both genders were commonly abducted and raped. Percival was in the hands of pederasts.

Varian must have looked as sick as he felt, for Zigur added hastily, "You have no cause for alarm, *efendi*. It was me they wanted. With Jason dead, I have no kin to avenge the insult. Me these villains might take as easily as one collects a pebble from the shore. But my cousin is English, and Ali Pasha wants your government's help to extend his domains. The villains know, as all Albania knows, that to offend any Englishman is to invite Ali's cruelly painful revenge. When the abductors discover the boy is English, they will leave him in one of the villages to the south, where my father's friend, Bajo, will easily find him."

"These men killed Jason," Varian said, sitting up hastily. He instantly regretted it. An explosion seemed to tear his skull apart. He sank back down. "And they attacked *me.* That's two Englishmen in a matter of days."

Zigur's face tightened into a harsh mask. "Jason's kin disowned him long ago. He is considered an Albanian. Naturally, there must be blood payment for his murder, but it is not your feud, *efendi.* As to you—they struck only to get you out of their way. Had they meant to kill, your severed head would now be lying upon the Durrës shore."

Zigur hesitated, then placed a small, cool hand on Varian's forehead. "You are warm, but not feverish," the boy said. "Do not agitate yourself. We sail to Corfu, where you will find British soldiers to escort you to Ali in Tepelena. There you will find my cousin Percival safe, I promise. Ali will protect him as though he were a great, rare diamond, and your British friends will make sure the Pasha does not demand too high a reward for his hospitality. The matter is easily settled. Would to God all else were so simple," he muttered as he reached again for the damp cloth.

Later, Varian would wonder at his own docility. At the moment, however, he existed helplessly in a nightmare of shock and pain. He possessed neither the will nor the strength to make the ship turn back. Even if he did, what would that accomplish? He might be on the moon for all he knew of this place and its inhabitants. He must trust Jason's young bastard because, quite simply, Lord Edenmont hadn't the first idea what else to do.

Esme had smelled the storm in the air by late afternoon. When she went above at sunset, she saw the awareness reflected in the crew's eyes. The ship was not built to withstand turbulent weather. Money, she'd learned, had tempted the captain to make a voyage so close to the start of the stormy season. Now, clearly, he regretted his greed.

"We can't continue," he told her. "Warn the English baron we must make for land."

Esme somberly eyed the coastline. Nothing resembling a port stood here, she knew, and the light craft already shuddered at the assault of wind and roughening sea. In the distance she saw lightning crackle.

"It's no good telling him," she answered. "His head is broken and he understands nothing. You expect difficulty." It wasn't a question.

"If I can't maneuver close enough, we'll have to get him on a boat," the captain answered unhappily. "I'll send two reliable men to take you to shore."

She calculated. A small boat ran less risk traversing the shallow waters. If they took it now, they'd reach land before the storm broke. Petro would be useless, of course. He'd begun wailing and praying hours ago. Fat, lazy, and dirty, he was the poorest excuse for a dragoman she'd ever encountered. While his origins were undeterminable, it was plain enough that he was inept in at least five of the seven languages he lay claim to. Nonetheless, with two sturdy sailors to help, she could manage.

"Let it be now," she said calmly. "Neither you nor I want a dead English nobleman on our hands. Your ship may survive the storm. If the lord remains aboard, I doubt he will."

As it turned out, the Englishman barely survived the short trip to shore, most of which he spent retching over the side. Still, he made no complaint—unlike Petro, who shed tears enough to sink them while he tore at his hair and wailed at Allah and Jehovah and all the saints by turns for mercy. Undistracted by their passengers, the two Italian sailors steadily plied their oars, leaving Esme to keep a lookout for obstacles and make sure the landlubbers didn't tumble into the sea.

When they all reached solid land at last, the Englishman sank to the ground, while the others gazed haplessly at the desolate landscape. All around them lay a flat stretch of wasteland, empty of any sign of human habitation. But there would be something, Esme knew. Some shelter. She might camp here comfortably enough—she'd slept in the open before, even in rain. Unfortunately, her patient needed a roof over his head, lest he contract a fatal chill, and that she didn't need. He'd already caused complications enough.

"Help the Englishman," she told the sailors as she took up her long gun and swung her leather bag over her shoulder. "You, Petro, take his bag and hold your tongue. We must go eastward a ways, and we have no time for dawdling and lamentations."

When Varian finally awoke from what he fervently hoped was only a nightmare, the sun had risen. Or he assumed it had. Through the open doorway he saw gray, not coal-black. It was still raining, relentlessly, and a small lake had formed in the entrance, with sister ponds beneath the two narrow slits that passed for windows.

Twice he closed his eyes, only to open them to the same appalling scene. The hut's stone walls were dark and slimy, and the blanket he lay upon was damp and rough. His head pounded as though all the fiends of Hades beat upon it, his mouth was gritty with sand and salt, and his hollow belly knotted in hunger. "Bloody hell," he groaned.

A small, cool hand touched his forehead. Startled, he turned to meet a sober green gaze. He hadn't realized Zigur was crouched beside him.

"You still have no fever," the boy said. "That's good. We could not make a fire, and I feared you would take cold, but you are sturdier than I thought."

"My head is splitting into a thousand pieces," Varian gritted out. "I lost my last meal on that wretched boat, and I don't even remember when that last meal was. I'm wet and filthy and—"

"Then you must be grateful you don't have chills and fever as well. As I am, since my bag of remedies is still upon the ship. A chill is not such a bad thing, if properly tended," he explained, oblivious to Varian's exasperated gaze. "But what is to be done without garlic and restorative herbs?"

Slowly and painfully, Varian raised himself up on his elbows. He saw that Zigur's blanket lay next to his own on the tiny square of relatively dry dirt floor, and wondered bitterly what vermin had emigrated thence in the night. He was certain the boy's clothes had not been washed since the long-ago day he'd first donned them. Varian wished Jason had devoted a bit less time to his little bastard's language lessons and a bit more to personal hygiene.

"I take it then," he said, "that your magic cures, along with the ship, are at the bottom of the sea. It only wanted that, of course."

"No. The rest of us were up at daybreak. We saw the ship afloat, but badly damaged. Lightning, I think, for they'd lost their mast. Petro has gone with the two sailors to bring back what we need. I regret to tell you that this must be a long stay. I suspect they must replace the mast altogether. That, and the other work"—he spread his hands—"in this season, it will be weeks before the vessel sails again."

"Weeks? You mean we're *stranded* here?" Varian's despairing gaze wandered about the miserable, filthy, *disgusting*, hovel. He saw two snails inching up the wall.

The boy settled himself into a cross-legged position and, with an annoyingly patient expression, explained. "This is the mouth of the River Shkumbi. The region near the coast is all marshland, with but a few poor villages. To travel by land we need horses, and the nearest place to hire them will be to the east, about twenty English miles."

"You've got to be joking. No horses for twenty *miles?*"

"You are not in England or Italy. Mine is a poor country, and horses are precious. What fool would keep stables in a great swamp? You cannot hire so much as a mule here."

"You can't be telling me I'm stuck in this hovel for weeks." Varian shook off his horror. "That's impossible. We'll send someone for horses, or another ship."

"And if fortune smiles upon you, they'll accomplish the mission in less than a month." The boy studied his grimy little hands. "As you wish, *efendi*. You are a great English lord. To walk is beneath your dignity. Besides, the journey will spoil your handsome boots."

Varian glanced down at his muddy, salt-stained boots, then eyed the urchin suspiciously. "You don't think much of English lords, do you?"

"I beg your pardon, oh great one, if I offended," Zigur said, his eyes still downcast. "It is my ignorance. I am rarely in the company of princes."

"You're an impertinent little wretch, and you needn't waste that false humility on me. Despite this infernal lump on my head, my faculties are functioning." Fighting his protesting muscles and the lightning bolts inside his head, Varian sat up. "You think I'm a great joke, don't you? If you'd been the one with his skull cracked, you'd not be feeling so damned superior just now."

"If the Turk had struck me the blow he dealt you, I'd be dead," the boy replied with the faintest of smiles. "Your head is wonderfully hard, *efendi*."

Gingerly, Varian touched the throbbing lump near his ear and winced. "All English lords are thickheaded. Didn't you know that?"

The boy's smile widened, transforming his face, and for the first time, Varian saw a countenance quite distinct from Percival's, though like it in many ways. The mouth was different, wide and overfull, the features altogether more delicate. This child, in short, was beautiful. At this moment, Varian could see how the boy might appeal to a man with that sort of appetite, though the understanding was purely intellectual. Depraved as he was, Lord Edenmont had always confined his carnal desires to adult women. The idea of children being used for pleasure thoroughly nauseated him.

Banishing the image of Percival or this poor by-blow of Jason's at the mercy of some gross Saracen lecher, Varian returned Zigur's smile. "It's true I don't bear illness and pain uncomplainingly," he said. "It's also true I'm terrified of spoiling my lovely boots. But I'd rather not rot in the middle of a swamp, either, thank you. If you've got a sensible alternative, then out with it."

* * *

Esme lay awake beside the Englishman half that following night, assuring herself she was doing the right thing. She'd told the truth about the ship, as Petro and the others had confirmed when they returned. She didn't want to linger for weeks in this wasteland any more than the Englishman did. She wanted to see her cousin safely out of Albania as quickly as possible, so she could take up her life. The faster they reached Tepelena, the sooner this would happen. In the present circumstances, journeying the hundred or so miles south by land offered the speediest alternative.

Besides, if they waited to sail, she'd end up in Corfu among the British, and Bajo would be there to force her to go to England. She'd been too numb with shock to argue with him yesterday morning in Durrës, or even to think. Since then, she'd had plenty of time to reflect.

She thought of her father, who'd been killed on her account. Never again would he tease her and laugh with her. Never again would she stand proudly beside him while he boasted of her to his friends—his daughter, the little warrior. Never again would she hear his gentle voice, always filled with love, even when he scolded. Her loving father, who only wanted to return with her to his own people, had been shot like a dog . . . because of her. With him, her life would not have been entirely empty, no matter where she went. Without him, she had nothing, only grief . . . and no one to share it with.

All through the long day she'd shut it away, raised a fortress around her aching heart, and done what must be done. Through that interminable day, her rage had grown, until she thought she must go mad. She could not run away, could never hope to find peace when her heart cried for revenge. Bajo was wrong. He had not killed her father's murderer. Ismal was still alive. There was only one course for the Red Lion's daughter: blood for blood.

It would not be difficult. She would see her cousin safely away, then accept Ismal. With Jason dead, Ismal must pay Ali her bride-price, and it would be a high one. But she would cost Ismal more than jewels and coins, and when she took the life from his young body, her honor would be wiped clean. She in turn must pay for that, she understood well enough—either with her life or in the bed of one of Ali's current favorites. She was not afraid. So long as she cleaned her wretched soul with revenge, she could endure whatever Fate dealt her thereafter.

Beside her, the Englishman stirred restlessly and moaned. She'd made light of his injury, to rouse his spirit, yet she knew the pain must be dreadful. She knew as well he was deeply anxious about Percival. Still, this lord would have no lump on his thick head and no reason to be anxious, if he'd only stayed where he belonged. On the other hand, she quickly reminded herself, the Englishman's errors had delayed her departure. This terrible mess he'd made had given her an opportunity.

Esme glanced over her shoulder at him. No wonder he groaned. He'd turned to face away from her, and the tender place on his head rubbed against the rough blanket. She sat up and carefully coaxed his unconscious form onto his other side. The low groaning stopped. She lay down once more, her back to him.

She had just begun to sink into sleep when she became aware of a wall of warmth along her backside. In his sleep, the Englishman had edged onto her blanket. She was about to retreat when he moved, mumbled something, then flung his arm over her.

Esme gasped, her heart thumping crazily. Cautiously she took hold of his arm and tried to lift it away. It was like trying to lift a stone pillar. He shivered and nestled closer still, his arm tightening around her. A blanket of heat enveloped her.

Esme rarely thought about cold, was accustomed to accept and ignore it. Yet the man was unwell and the hut chilly and damp. His body sought warmth, that was all. She told herself there was no harm, and closed her eyes. For all her brave resolutions, she felt miserably alone, and sorrow made her cold within. To be held so was comforting.

She was just drifting to sleep when he murmured unintelligibly, and his hand slid up from her waist, over her shirt, and closed over her small breast.

Blind panic shot through her. She clawed at the hand and kicked wildly as she wriggled to get free.

"What the—"

His hand clamped round her wrist, and in the next instant, Esme found herself flat on her back, the Englishman crouched over her. When she tried to scramble away, he dropped on top of her, pinned her hands to the ground on either side of her, and thrust his legs between hers before she could jam her knee into his groin.

For a moment, Esme was too stunned to move. Never in her life had any adversary gained such speedy control. She'd thought this man effete, a lazy weakling. But he was terrifyingly quick—and disconcertingly efficient. Still, he was panting, his curses coming in growling gasps. The oaths didn't bother her. She knew curses in five languages. What bothered her was the hard weight of his rigid body and the numbing sensation of helplessness. But not for long, she told herself. He was injured, after all, and she was not.

"English *swine,*" she growled, kicking angrily at his legs. Her flailing foot struck Petro, who'd been snoring obliviously on the other side of her. He bolted up in terror.

"Help! Help!" he screamed in Greek, as he scrabbled wildly at the blankets. "Robbers! Murder!"

"Shut up, you idiot," the Englishman snapped. "Light the lantern. It's not robbers, dammit. It's a girl!"

It took Petro forever to light the lantern—which stank to high heaven. In that time, Varian had relieved the little fiend of his weight, and her headdress. Not that he needed to examine her more closely. He recognized a female body when he felt one, and he'd fully awakened to find his hand curled over a very small, very firm, but unmistakably feminine breast. He'd dreamt he was sleeping with a woman, and woke to find that he was. A girl, he silently amended, his gray gaze upon the shining mass of dark red hair. A girl who'd probably reached puberty about the day before yesterday.

She was sitting cross-legged, glaring at him. Varian's hands itched to spank her. He didn't like being made a fool of. He liked still less narrowly escaping murder twice in forty-eight hours. A moment's delay and he'd have found her knife in his ribs. Yet furious as Varian was, he was not completely insensitive. If she wasn't Jason's son, she was surely his daughter. Her name was Esme, a Saxon name, and there way no denying her uncanny resemblance to Percival. All of which meant that she'd just lost her father, which was reason enough to be overwrought. Furthermore, the liberties he'd unconsciously taken with her young body must have terrified her.

"I'm sorry I was so . . . violent," he said tightly. "But you took me by surprise, and I thought I was being attacked."

The green glare changed to an expression of pure scorn. "*You?* It was not *my* hands roaming where they had no place to be."

"I was *asleep!*" he snapped defensively. "How the devil was I to know where my hands were?"

"So it is," Petro eagerly agreed. "Why should he caress one he thought a boy? The master does not care for boys. So everyone knows—"

"I wasn't *caressing* her, damn you. I was asleep and—"

"You put your hand on my breast!" she accused. "You think I am a concubine, to make no objection? I only tried to get away—and you act as though I tried to murder you. And then it is not enough to subdue me in that shameful way, but you must take off my clothes."

"I took your knife, so you wouldn't kill me, and I took off your *hat*—or whatever that medieval monstrosity is," he returned, tossing the woolen rag to her.

"It does not matter what it is. You had no right. Had I menfolk by, they'd have killed you for the insult."

She jammed the ugly woolen helmet onto her head and shoved her thick hair up inside it. Varian saw her hands were shaking. He'd frightened her badly. The poor child must have thought he'd meant to rape her.

"I beg your pardon," he said. "I'm not altogether rational when I'm awakened suddenly. But you did deceive me regarding your gender. It was only natural to imagine you were up to some dangerous trick. Theft, murder—how was I to know?"

"So it is," Petro said. "So I thought myself. Foolish, very foolish," he chided, "for a little girl to make herself like a boy. And sinful to tell lies."

"How can you be so ignorant?" she exclaimed. "There is a man after me whose accomplices seek a red-haired girl—and will again seek me when they learn my cousin is a boy. The task isn't difficult. How many red-haired Albanians do you think there are?" she demanded. "I've never heard of any but me."

She turned her accusing gaze to Varian, who was growing acutely uncomfortable. "It is not the best disguise, I know, but Bajo and I did not plan to linger about long enough to allow close scrutiny," she went on. "Had the men not spied my cousin, they might have turned away to look elsewhere. And I might have escaped."

Varian could hardly argue with that. It was his fault she'd not been able to escape, his fault Percival was in the hands of perverts.

"I agree I'm responsible for this whole ghastly mess," he said. "Considering how stupidly I've behaved, I oughtn't be surprised at your reluctance to trust me with your secret."

This seemed to placate her somewhat, for she answered less belligerently. "I thought we would all be safer if you did not know. You might treat me differently, or accidentally say something—and others might notice, and I would be discovered."

That, too, made sense. For all her youth, she had a level head on her shoulders. Varian's mouth eased into a rueful smile.

"Percival said his uncle was not only brave, but astute," he said. "It would appear you've inherited those qualities as well as his looks."

The defiance faded from her intense green eyes, and sorrow clouded them.

"I was son and daughter to Jason." Her voice was just a shade unsteady. "He taught me all I know. Four languages I speak well, and Turkish enough to curse." She swallowed. "I am an excellent marksman, both with rifle and blade. I can take care of myself—and both of you as well. You will find there's no need to treat me differently, just because I'm a female."

Varian must have looked exceedingly doubtful—how could he not, gazing at this elfin creature with her great green eyes?—because she raised her chin and stiffened her posture. "I am not a weak and nervous female, to make a great fuss about a small mistake. I shall forget the insult to my person and take you to Tepelena—if you will forget my small offense in deceiving you."

"That's very . . . generous of you," Varian said, "but—"

"There's nothing to fear," she interrupted impatiently. "I am a fighter, with the scars to prove it. There," she said, pointing to her arm. "And there." She slapped her thigh. "But the men who shot me are dead. 'Little warrior' my people call me. You can ask in Rrogozhina—anywhere—and they'll tell you."

"Shot?" Varian repeated. A chill trickled down his neck.

"Oh, yes." She pushed up her sleeve to show the scar. Her slim arm was smooth and delicate, much whiter than her strong, sun-bronzed hands.

"Don't," he said sharply. "I believe you." Lord, what sort of swine would put a bullet into that fragile wisp of a body? He felt ill.

"Does your head trouble you, *efendi?*" she asked, concerned. "Your face has gone white. Perhaps you should lie down."

Dizzy with the effort to make sense of her, of everything, Varian lay down willingly. No use trying to reason with her tonight. Her mind was disordered by distress. Even her solicitousness bordered on panic.

Still, it was touching the way the girl tucked him in, as though he were a feeble child. She must have decided he was about as dangerous as one, too, for she resumed her place beside him and ordered Petro to move to the other side, that his lordship might share their warmth.

She continued solicitous the following morning until, seeing her packing to travel, Varian gently pointed out that they weren't going anywhere.

Her face hardened to stone. "Because you do not trust a female to guide you?"

"A young girl," he corrected. "It's not you I mistrust, but—"

She didn't wait to hear more, simply took up her bags and marched from the hut. Despite Petro's shrieks of panic, Varian was tempted to let her go. The alternative, he was certain, was to tie her down.

The trouble was, letting her go off alone was tantamount to murder—after she and her friends had saved his life. Plague take her. Varian gritted his teeth and stormed out after her.

Chapter 4

Ali's mouth would probably water when he saw *this* one, Esme reflected as they neared Rrogozhina two days later. Though the Vizier's court boasted some of the most beautiful youths in the Ottoman Empire, the English lord would make them look like trolls. Tall and well-formed, he carried himself with all the arrogant assurance of a sultan, even while they trudged through slimy marshland, the torrents beating relentlessly at them. His insolence was bound to win respect, for in these realms the meek inherited only abuse. His looks, furthermore, would surely make more than one courtier weep.

His skin was as fair and smooth as a pampered concubine's, yet his beauty was purely masculine—an irresistible combination to many men. But they'd yearn in vain.

The English lord, Petro had told her, was addicted to women. Though the man's licentiousness was common knowledge, the Italian women had flocked to him like flies to manure. Of course, the gossiping Petro had boasted, the lord selected only the most beautiful and sophisticated of those who so shamelessly offered themselves to him.

The dragoman had shared this information while his master slept. If Esme meant to travel with them, she must help keep an eye on the master, Petro warned, lest he make advances to virtuous Albanian women and get them all embroiled in a blood feud.

"He'll hardly find the other sort on the way to Tepelena," Esme had answered. "We're not likely to meet up with courtesans in these parts. Just tell him he must wait. Ali will give him as many as he likes."

"No, *you* must tell him, for he never listens to me. He says he cannot understand my English. You will tell him, and explain so cleverly, as you did the other night. Never have I seen him so angry. I thought he would beat you. But you scold and he only smiles and listens."

The Englishman was not smiling now. His gray eyes were fixed on the humble village ahead, and his face had set into taut lines.

"Rrogozhina," she said. "I told you we would reach it well before dark."

"You said it was an important town. I count six houses—or hovels. It's hard to tell where the mud leaves off and architecture begins."

"I told you the site marked an important *crossroads,*" she said. "Two branches of the ancient Romans' Via Egnatia meet here, one from Apollonia and one from Durrës."

"Then the Romans have fallen sadly behind in upkeep. Even had Caesar Augustus possessed the visionary powers of the god he claimed to be, I would defy him to discern so much as a path, let alone two great roads in this godforsaken sea of mud. For two days we've crawled through it. Two days to cover twenty miles—to reach a cluster of muddy little huts which, as far as I can see, were abandoned by all human inhabitants about six centuries ago."

"You were expecting Paris, perhaps, *efendi?*"

"I was hoping for something connected, however distantly, to civilization."

Esme experienced a powerful desire to connect her boot with his backside, but told herself he was like a spoiled child and didn't know any better. Also, being childish, he was relatively easily managed. If he were not, they'd yet be huddled in the cramped shelter by the mouth of the Shkumbi.

Fortunately, he needed her far more than she needed

him. In England he may have been a powerful lord; in Albania he was helpless as a baby.

Efendi, she'd called him, as a joke, from the first. It was a title of respect, yes, but for a learned man, a scholar or cleric. She might have called him a pile of offal, for all he understood or cared to understand. Y'Allah, but these English lords were ignorant provincials—and proud to be so, evidently.

"I shall not tell you," she said now, "not to make such remarks to the villagers, for you are an English gentleman, and Jason told me a true gentleman is courteous."

"I am not a gentleman. I am an animate piece of mud, crawling with fleas."

"Yet I will warn you not to flirt with the women."

His head turned slowly toward her. "I beg your pardon?"

"You are not deaf. Don't flirt with the women, if you wish to depart Rrogozhina in one piece. If we come across a whore, I shall tell you so, but it's most unlikely we will. Albania has many more men than women, and the women are guarded jealously. A Moslem, for instance, may pay as much as a thousand piastres for his bride. An important investment. Please keep this in mind."

He glanced ahead at the mass of structures, lumpen forms in the gray rain, then back at her. "Certainly I will. Thank you for the warning. How dreadful if I should run amok among Rrogozhina's hordes of fair maidens."

"There is no need to be sarcastic," she said.

"I should like to know," he said, "what put it into your head that I'd flirt with every female who crossed my path."

Petro, at present, trailed miserably many yards behind them. Even though he couldn't possibly hear, Esme was reluctant to reveal her source. She didn't want the master to know she'd gossiped with his servant.

"Because you look as though you do," she said. "I should be interested to watch you flirt sometime, for surely it would be amusing, but I must wait until we reach Tepelena, I expect."

"*Watch* me?"

"Flirt," she clarified. "I am certainly not curious about the rest. That is a private matter."

"Esme," he said, "do you have any idea what you're talking about?"

"Yes. Jason told me, because I had no family to shelter me. He felt it was best I understood these matters, lest my ignorance be used against me."

"I see."

"Are you shocked?"

"No, only . . ." Pausing, he turned fully toward her. She halted as well, wondering why he looked so troubled.

"What of your mother's family?" he asked. "Your mother herself?"

"She died when I was ten. Jason and I moved about a great deal. He was always needed somewhere. My grandmother lives in Gjirokastra, but the others are all dead."

Now Jason as well, she thought, and the ache sped swiftly from her heart to catch in her throat. She resumed walking. "That was all long ago," she said tightly. "Let us speak of something else."

As it happened, they'd no time to change the subject Varian had so thoughtlessly introduced. Their approach speedily attracted notice, and in minutes all of Rrogozhina rushed out to welcome them.

There was a great deal more to the village than Varian had guessed. He was quickly surrounded by a crowd of men, on whose fringes stood another crowd of women and children, all of them talking at once and never uttering a word he could understand. Nor could Petro, evidently, who complained that the dialect was impossible.

Varian's head pounded and his ears rang. He was tired and hungry, and so filthy he wanted to crawl out of his skin. Had Esme not taken charge, he might well have sat right down in the mud and wept.

As she'd predicted, the villagers took no notice of the ragged boy Esme appeared to be, and nearly trampled her as they swarmed about Varian. She doggedly elbowed her way back to his side, however, and in minutes had fully obtained their attention.

Less than an hour later, thanks to her, Varian was lowering his aching frame into a large wooden laundry tub filled with steaming water.

The tub stood in the central washing room of a cluster of connected cottages. These belonged to the extended family of his host, Maliq. Beyond, in the kitchen, Varian heard the chatter of women's voices as they prepared a feast to honor his lordship. Closer to hand, in the small passage just outside the doorway, Petro stood, dutifully brushing his master's clothes.

Most of Varian's wardrobe remained on the ship. None of the crew had proved insane enough to accompany them for any price, and three people, on foot, could only carry so much. Which meant that Varian possessed exactly three changes of linen, one coat, one heavy cloak, and two pairs of trousers.

Though accustomed to changing several times a day, Varian had thought he'd manage adequately for the day or two it would take to reach Tepelena. It was not as though he expected to attend soirees on a regular basis. He had never dreamed the journey would involve several tons of mud and enough crawling creatures to fill Westminster Abbey.

He was soaping his neck and contemplating the tragic condition of his expensive shirts when Esme burst through the doorway, stopped dead, then hastily backed out.

Petro's roar of laughter rang through the passage.

"Son of a jackal!" she shouted. "Why didn't you stop me?"

"A thousand pardons, little one," came the chuckling answer. "I thought you were in a great hurry to wash his back."

"That is not amusing," she snapped. "Also, you are a very poor servant to let someone interrupt your master at his bath. Have you no respect for his modesty?"

"Modesty?" Petro echoed. "Y'Allah, half the women of Italy have seen his—"

"Petro," Varian called out sharply.

Petro hastened to the doorway.

"Yes, master?"

"Shut up."

"Yes, master."

The passage fell deadly quiet.

Varian quickly finished his bath, threw on the immense robe his hostess had left for him, and called them both inside.

Esme entered and, without looking at him, gathered up the towels he'd thrown on the floor and draped them over the tub handles. Then she sat down upon the floor in her usual cross-legged position and studied her hands.

Petro stood cringing by the door.

"You will apologize, Petro, for your tasteless prank," Varian said. "Even now, our young friend must be devising ways to get even, and I had much rather not be caught in the middle, thank you."

Petro promptly dropped to his knees before her and commenced banging his head on the floor in an exaggerated salaam. "A thousand thousand pardons, little one," he said abjectly. "May I be forever cursed, may my limbs rot and fall off, my—"

"Don't be ridiculous," she snapped. "It is not as though I have never seen a man without his shirt before." As Petro hastily rose and resumed his dignity, she looked up at Varian, and a faint tinge of rose washed her cheeks. "All I saw were your shoulders and that was hardly for a moment, and—"

"And it's a very *deep* tub," Varian said.

The rose deepened. "So it is. Also, my mind was altogether elsewhere, I promise you, or I should never have rushed in upon you in that mannerless way. Did I not order the bath myself? But I forgot, because—"

"Because you were in a great hurry to tell me something, I think." Varian crouched before her. "What was it?"

She gave a quick glance at the doorway, then turned back to Varian and whispered, "Esme has been killed."

"I beg your pardon?"

"Rrogozhina had word days ago of the abduction. That

is why they all rushed out to welcome you, and why they fall all over themselves to make you comfortable.''

''So it must be,'' Petro agreed. ''I was much amazed to see all the women come out, with the little ones.''

''But days ago?'' Varian asked. ''That's impossible. How—''

''In Albania, word flies through the air, like the birds,'' she said.

''Aye, master,'' Petro eagerly put in before she could continue. ''They cry out from one mountain to the next. A great, ear-breaking shriek it is. And such faces they make—''

''Never mind that. What about your—about Esme being killed?'' Varian asked her.

''Bajo sent word, in the manner Petro tells you: that Jason was murdered and an English lord's son taken by bandits,'' she explains. ''But Bajo also reported that Esme was killed in the villains' attack. Do you see how clever he was? By now word has surely reached the villains who sought me—that is, Esme—and—''

''And so there won't be any more abduction attempts.''

''Now you've no need to be uneasy,'' she said confidently. ''All is as I told you—even better. No one will guess I am not who I pretend to be, and the people will make your way easy. Further south they are doubtless looking for Percival, or have already found him and are keeping him safe. Also, by now the villains must surely be fleeing both Ali's and their own master's wrath.''

About this time, some thirty miles south of Rrogozhina, several unhappy villains were arguing in harsh whispers while a twelve-year-old boy slept nearby. Half the party felt he should simply be abandoned where he was. Even now, Ali Pasha's men might be on their trail. The other half argued that the boy merely represented an unfortunate mistake. If he came to harm, however, even Ismal could not protect them. Besides, the child had given no trouble—except when anyone touched his leather bag. Since it proved to contain only rocks, of no value whatsoever, they concluded he was a trifle unhinged by the recent excitement.

"Only a mile west is the abode of a priest," Mehmet pointed out. "We can leave the boy with him."

"Aye, you need a priest badly enough," said Ymer. "That game piece the master gave you is cursed. Since we got it, there has been nothing but trouble. We go to the house, the girl is gone. We hasten to the shore, and half of Durrës waits, armed. Two of my cousins are killed, and we carry away an English boy, a lord's son, by mistake. Now the Red Lion is dead, and his daughter, and we will be blamed for everything. Ali will kill us by inches."

The mention of curses made the group uneasier still.

"Bury it," one suggested.

"The evil will remain," said another. "Best to give it to the priest, and the boy as well."

"Ismal will be furious. The little chess piece was to be returned to him."

"In the girl's possession, fool! The girl is dead, and Ismal cannot expect us to take it back to him now. Ali will roast us on a spit!"

"Best to hide in the mountains—and go *now* if we wish to keep our heads."

While the others continued debating, Mehmet rose and crept to the sleeping boy, opened the leather pouch, and dropped the black queen, thickly wrapped in a rag, among the rocks.

Returning to his companions, he said, "I'll take the child to the priest, because I wasn't paid to kill little boys, merely to steal a female. Sooner or later, someone will take the boy to Ali for safekeeping, or to the British in Corfu. Perhaps Fate will lead the chess piece back to Ismal. If not, it wasn't meant to be." He shrugged. "If the thing's truly cursed, it's best out of his hands."

Several hours later, Percival lay upon a hard pallet in the humble abode of an Albanian priest. The dying fire's feeble glow created shadowy shapes in the dark room. The window showed only a slit of black, no glimpse of a star.

On the pallet opposite, the priest snored raucously. The irregular series of snorts, growls, and wheezes was symptomatic, Percival thought, of the nasal obstruction Mr. Fitherspine, his last tutor, had suffered. The sound was so normal that one might almost believe the last few days were just a dream. Only they weren't, and wishing otherwise wouldn't solve anything.

The priest had cried when he told Percival that Uncle Jason and Cousin Esme were dead. Percival hadn't. It had all been too strange: the young priest telling the awful news in Latin—for they had no other language in common—while tears trickled down the sides of his bumpy nose. Percival would not cry now, either. If he gave way to tears, he'd give way altogether. He needed to think.

Drawing his leather pouch close, he took out the object he'd dared do no more than touch while the priest was awake and resolutely unwrapped it. There. The black queen. Proof he hadn't dreamed. The bandit *had* put it in his bag . . . after an angry conversation with the others, of which Percival had understood only one word: Ismal. He was sure, because he'd heard it several times.

He crept toward the hearth and unscrewed the chess piece. And stared . . . because the slip of paper was still there. Bewildered, he took it out and, in the faint light of the embers, studied his father's message.

The code was ludicrously simple. It merely turned the alphabet around, substituting "Z" for "A" and so on. Then the words turned into Latin. Ungrammatical, but clear enough. The ship was the Queen of Midnight, delivery in Prevesa, early November.

That was about all Percival understood. He didn't know why his papa had put anything so incriminating in writing. Or why Ismal hadn't destroyed the note—unless he'd never got it. Above all, Percival wondered why on earth the bandit had stuck the queen in his leather pouch.

As though it mattered. Whatever the explanation, it must be ugly because those men were ugly, and other ugly men had killed his uncle and cousin.

Percival dropped the paper onto the embers, then hastily snatched it back, brushing off the sparks. Angrily he rubbed away the tears welling in his eyes. Uncle Jason would never do such a cowardly thing. He'd been killed trying to save Albania from the man to whom this message had been sent. Someone needed this information, and that someone would never believe a twelve-year-old boy without proof. It was Percival's duty to pass on all the evidence . . . and let the world know his father was a base smuggler, a criminal—oh, heavens, perhaps even responsible, albeit unwittingly, for his own brother's murder?

"Oh, Mama," Percival whispered, gazing down unhappily at the black queen. "What on earth am I to do?"

Chapter 5

Neither Maliq nor his company sighed or salivated over the English lord at supper. After all, they were not dissolute denizens of a corrupt court. Though gracious and hospitable, they had too much pride to fawn all over him.

Which wasn't to say they weren't curious. While Rrogozhina saw many visitors in the course of a year, a foreigner was a rare species, and this exotic newcomer was, in addition, tall, graceful, and handsome. They found his physiognomy, attire, and behavior thoroughly fascinating, though they had the dignity not to show this in any blatant way.

At least the men didn't, Esme corrected herself as she followed him to his chamber and saw two plump, pretty girls peeping out at him from a doorway, their mouths hanging open. When he turned to bid them good night, they giggled and retreated. Fools, Esme thought disdainfully. If only they knew what a depraved, idle piece of worthlessness he was.

At supper, Esme had been obliged to introduce him properly to the company. When they had first arrived in the village, he appeared so tired and ill that formalities were left for later; first, the English lord must be made comfortable. Not until supper did she realize *she'd* never been honored with a formal introduction. Three nights she'd slept beside him, and she didn't even know his name. *The English baron, the lord.* That's all she'd heard from Petro and the captain—as though the man's true name was too holy to be spoken aloud.

"Tell them your name," she'd whispered harshly as the women carried in the food. "I don't know it."

In quick, clipped syllables, he'd tossed out a long, ridiculous set of names: Varian Edward Harcourt St. George, Baron Edenmont of Buckinghamshire, England. Then he'd given her the most obnoxiously smug smile, as though defying her to remember it all. Though she'd wanted to slap him, Esme had turned to her host and gleefully supplied a translation, at the end of which she heard several smothered chuckled in the audience.

"What the devil did you tell them?" he'd whispered, making her ear tickle.

"St. George is *Shenjt Gjergj,* a saint they all recognize," she said. "I told him a baron was something like a *bej,* and a shire was one of England's *pashaliks.*"

"What's so hilarious about that?"

She shrugged. "Perhaps it was your Christian name. I said it was from Latin. Varian," she said, pronouncing it with the wide vowels and burr of Albanian. "Fickle, it means."

"Later," he warned, "I shall *spank* you."

Nonetheless, he'd laughed, and the company with him, and someone had said his laughter was like music.

Though she much doubted his lordship had the temerity to spank her, Esme was not eager to be alone with him. She trailed him into the chamber and pulled the door hanging closed behind her. She'd only make sure he had all he needed, she decided. Then she'd be quit of him for the night.

The room was small. All the same, by country village standards, it was luxurious. Few houses had more than two rooms. Maliq's encompassed six, and this must have been fitted up to accommodate visiting dignitaries. Instead of *sofas*—the boards built against the walls to serve as couches and beds—the tidy space boasted one large bunk and a substantial hearth. They'd given the Englishman not only the softest cushions and thickest blankets, but privacy, a rare commodity.

Two large pitchers filled with steaming water stood by

the hearth, and a kettle hung from a chain over the fire. A twinge of envy pricked her. She'd washed her face and hands earlier, all the while acutely conscious he'd hardly consider that sufficient. Petro hadn't needed to tell her how fastidious the master was. She had a nose and eyes, didn't she? She'd seen how clean his shirt was, and could not remember when her own had gleamed so dazzlingly white.

Still, Esme would never dream of imposing on strangers. She knew what it was to haul buckets home from the village well or nearest stream and heat kettle after kettle of water. Since she was supposed to be a boy—Petro's nephew—at present, she must leave that work to the women, and she hadn't wanted to add to their burdens.

"You'll have peace and comfort now," Esme said, glancing about the room. Her gaze lingered one yearning moment upon the pitchers of hot water and the precious cake of scented soap adorning an embroidered towel. "They're all going to bed. No one will trouble you until daybreak, and I'll be back then to interpret."

He sat down on the edge of the bunk, brought one lean, muscular calf up to rest on his knee, and tugged at his boot. "You won't be *back,* since you're not leaving," he said. "I won't have you sleeping with Petro and all those men, and you can't go with the women."

"I had thought you would prefer your privacy." She watched uneasily as he tossed away the boot and yanked at the other one.

"I prefer to have you nearby," he said. "When you're out of sight, I find myself imagining every sort of disaster. I would rather not lie awake all night in that state. It's no reflection on your gender, I assure you. If you were Percival, I'd feel exactly the same. Recollect what happened when *he* took off on his own."

"It is not the same," she answered. "For one, my cousin and I are not at all alike, except outwardly. For another—"

"Esme, you can argue until Doomsday if you like, but the long and the short of it is, I shall not sleep a wink tonight if you leave."

Which meant that tomorrow he'd be tired and cross, and she would be to blame. Esme set her mouth, strode to the bunk, snatched a blanket, and threw it onto the floor near the hearth.

"I didn't mean you had to sleep on the floor." He rose from the bunk. "Naturally, you may have the bed."

"I shall sleep on the floor," she said firmly. "My bones are not so tender as yours."

He smiled. "Perhaps not, but yours aren't very well padded."

"They are *younger* and more flexible," she answered witheringly.

"You find me decrepit?"

Esme flicked one resentful glance up and down the length of his perfectly proportioned body. "That is not what I meant. Just because you are a grown man, and strong, does not mean your endurance is greater. I should sleep contentedly upon the floor, whereas you will surely lie awake half the night in great cold and discomfort. I advise you to enjoy the soft bed while you might."

"But I'm determined *you* should enjoy it," he said. "I've fully made up my mind to be chivalrous." His smile broadened into a teasing grin. "Shall we commence a war of wills, madam? Shall we see who is the more obstinate?"

"I am not—"

The rest came out in a choked oath, as Esme found herself swiftly caught up in his arms and deposited upon the bed. She instantly bolted to her feet, but his hands clamped down on her shoulders. Instinctively, she retreated from the hard column of his body and felt the edge of the bed press against her thighs. "Do not think you can vanquish me so easily, *efendi,*" she declared. "If you do not release me and move out of the way, you shall feel the weight of my boot on your noble foot."

Defiant words, it turned out, were no match for two firm hands. Scarcely had she finished speaking when her bottom landed on the bunk. Before she could bounce up again, he got hold of her foot. Esme tumbled backward, and while she struggled to regain her balance, he pulled off first one boot, then the other.

"Stomp on my feet now, if you like," he said, still holding her ankle prisoner, "but you shall not spoil my lovely stockings, little wildcat."

"Silk," she sneered, despite the unnerving awareness of the long fingers clasping her ankle. "Only a concubine would wear silk upon her feet."

He studied the thickly hosed foot he held. "Much pleasanter than scratchy wool, I assure you. If you're a good girl, perhaps I'll send you silk stockings from Italy for your trousseau. Your stockings are still damp," he added. "That's unhealthy."

She tried to jerk free, but both wool socks came off with the same swift ease as the boots. Her heart pounding, Esme concluded that he must have had a great deal of experience relieving women of their clothing. And why the devil would he not release her? You'd think he'd never seen feet before, the way he stared.

Her cheeks burned with embarrassment. Her feet were not so very dirty, but then, not so very clean, either. Not like the clean, soapy smell of his head. In the glow of candle and hearth, his black hair glistened like jet beads.

"Your feet are so tiny," he said in soft surprise. "Small, fine bones, like a bird's." His finger lightly traced a muscle to her ankle, and the thread of warmth he drew there spread upward to her knee and made her tremble.

He looked up, and it seemed for a moment as though the air between them vibrated, like the strings of a mandolin. In the room's amber light, his clean-shaven face gleamed smooth as polished marble, but his gray eyes had darkened, grown strangely intent. A lock of black hair tumbled to his eyebrow, and she wanted to brush it back. The wish made her feel weak, and wistful.

"Let go of me," she said in a tiny voice she didn't recognize.

"Oh." He blinked, and the shimmering warmth vanished from his eyes. "I'm sorry." He released her. "I forgot . . . that is . . . you have lovely feet." His voice, too, sounded strange.

Her heart battered confusedly within her chest, like a

moth beating at a window. "My feet are dirty," she said tightly.

"I beg your pardon. I didn't think—Well, I suppose no one bothered much about you, did they?" He stood up. "If you'd like to wash, I'll step out of the room for a bit."

Without waiting for her answer, he left. After a moment's hesitation, Esme darted for the pitchers. With furious speed, she stripped to the skin, then savagely scrubbed herself from top to bottom. There wasn't enough water to wash her hair, so she untangled it as best she could with her fingers, then wove it into a single braid to keep it out of her face.

When she heard his returning footsteps, she was just pulling on her shirt. She grabbed a blanket and wrapped it around her. "I am not yet dressed," she called softly.

"Just as well. Our host's nephew or cousin or grandson or whatever has donated a clean shirt for you to sleep in." The door curtain parted slightly, and he tossed the garment inside.

Blushing hotly, Esme snatched it up and hurriedly threw it over her head. It fell well past her knees.

"I—I'm decent now," she said, suddenly feeling foolish. She had no need of his approval. What did it matter to him if she was clean or dirty? She was an ugly little savage, his guide and interpreter, that was all.

Outside the door, Varian hesitated. There was plenty of room elsewhere. Perhaps he should let her have the chamber to herself. She was far away from the men. She'd be safe enough. Except that he didn't like to leave her alone. She was too much alone in the world . . . and too young.

He should not have teased her. Though young, she was not entirely a child, and he most certainly wasn't, either. He was no older brother who might tumble her about in innocent horseplay. Varian St. George had left innocence behind long ago. All the same, he'd been shocked to find himself stroking her foot—and a heartbeat away from worse. That small, bewildered voice . . . She must have seen it in his eyes, or sensed it.

It didn't matter, he told himself. She didn't, couldn't *know*. He'd pretend nothing had happened. Nothing had. It had all happened in his mind, which obviously had snapped. Hardly surprising in the circumstances.

He flung back the curtain, entered—and nearly stumbled.

Esme stood before the fire, her stance stiff and defiant and her color very high. If she'd any inkling what the firelight revealed beneath the lamentably thin nightshirt, she'd probably turn purple. He ought to tell her. That was the gentlemanly thing to do. And he'd do it, in a moment—but, oh, Lord, was there ever anything so sweet? The slight swell of her taut young breasts, and a breath of a waist rounding ever so subtly into slim hips and firm, slender thighs and . . .

In short, she was a nymph whom Artemis herself had surely fashioned.

Belatedly, Varian saw her growing edgy under his ogling. Gad, he hoped he wasn't so obvious as that. "You're so . . . tiny," he said.

"Papa said the women of his family were late to mature." She lifted her chin. "I will grow."

Varian thought he'd like to be there when she did. Aloud he said, "Certainly. You've lots of time." He moved to collect a pillow and two more blankets from the vast heap on the bunk.

"One of my friends grew two inches between her first babe and her second," she said defensively.

"One of your *friends?*" He turned to her, unconsciously clutching the cushion to his belly. "How young do Albanian girls wed?"

"Twelve, thirteen, fourteen." She shrugged. "They're often betrothed at birth and wed when they're old enough to bear children. But Jason would not do so with me, because it was not his country's custom."

"Good heavens, I should say not." Varian tossed pillow and blankets atop the one she'd laid out by the hearth. "Girls in England wait until they're eighteen to go on the Marriage Mart—at least among the upper orders. Even then, I much doubt they're sufficiently adult to become mothers."

Her gaze grew thoughtful. "Yes, I expect they're much sheltered," she said. To his relief, she moved away from the fire and toward the bunk, the contemplation of which drew her full mouth down into a frown.

"You will be cold on the floor," she said, her gaze still upon the bed.

"My dear girl, last night I slept in a leaking tent in a typhoon."

"But you had a body on either side to keep you warm."

This, Varian thought, was not the time to remind him. It would be a deal cozier to share the bed with her, but tonight he hadn't Petro as chaperon, and tonight, of all times, he *had* experienced disquieting feelings about a very young, innocent girl. Suppose this should trigger another lascivious dream and liberties similar to or even greater than those he'd taken a few nights ago in his sleep? Then, at least, she had been fully armored in her rough woolen garments. Now there was as good as nothing between his depraved hands and her innocent flesh. No, he would *not* think about that.

"I'll be sufficiently warm here by the hearth," he said. "Really, Esme, I don't want the bed. I want you to consider it as—as amends, you see. For my rudely tumbling you about a while ago," he hastily improvised. "And—and because I've been such a pestilential traveling companion, and will likely continue so."

She turned and looked at him, the faintest hint of a smile on her otherwise grave countenance. "The bed is my revenge, *efendi?*"

"Exactly."

With a low chuckle, she climbed onto the bed and comfortably established herself in her customary Buddha-like pose. "In that case, I shall enjoy it to the fullest. It is very soft," she added.

Varian sighed and pulled off his coat. "I expect it is." He unwound his neckcloth and dropped it on the floor.

"You are most untidy," she said. "Also, your neck will get cold."

"Would you rather I strangled myself? And do you mean to sit there and watch me disrobe?"

"I did not know you intended to disrobe *altogether*. You will be very cold," she said. "Also, it is immodest to undress without putting out the candles first."

"*Also,* it is a tedious business to find one's buttons in the dark. Can't you just put your head under the covers? Unless, that is, you wish to admire my manly beauty," he added provokingly.

This did not fluster her as he'd expected. She regarded him coolly for a moment, then equally coolly, drew up the blankets and lay down with her back to him.

"Petro was right," she said scornfully. "You have no modesty at all. Also, you are vain. Not that I am surprised, when I see how the women become like drunkards when they look at you." She yawned. "Still, if you wish to prance about the room naked, that is your affair. Perhaps the activity will keep you warm."

"What an elegant picture you paint," Varian said, grinning in spite of himself. "The twelfth Baron Edenmont dancing about in his birthday suit like a—like a—"

"A faun," she supplied. "Or a satyr. Or perhaps like Eros. But no, you are too old for that—"

"Eros will do nicely. At least you attribute to me some sort of godlike quality—"

"He was *blind.*"

Varian gave up and, laughing to himself, put out the candles. When he came, still smiling, to the last—the one nearest the bed—he paused to look at her. She lay curled on her side, snuggled deep beneath the blankets. The candlelight drew fiery threads in her hair. A part of him wanted to stroke her hair. Another part wanted, absurdly, to tuck her in. He did neither.

"Good night, madam," he said.

"*Natën e mirë, Varian Shenjt Gjergj,*" she answered.

The Albanian words fell upon his ears soft as a caress. Varian hesitated a moment, then resolutely turned, put out the candle, and headed for his lonely pallet on the floor.

Chapter 6

Though Lushnja was supposedly a mere ten or so miles south, Varian's party was unable to reach it by sunset. The nearest bridge across the Shkumbi was some miles west of Rrogozhina. They crossed minutes before the ramshackle structure was swept into the river.

Once that horror was behind them, they faced a pathless wasteland. The rains having obliterated the road, they had to detour farther east, close to the low hills. Trapped on the fringes of this marshy coastal plain, the small group progressed by inches. In the downpour, even with horses, they advanced no more rapidly than they had done previously on foot.

At present, however, Varian barely noticed his physical surroundings. His mind was fixed on other matters, such as the men who formed his escort. A less reassuring lot was difficult to imagine.

Esme had insisted they were good, reliable fighters. Certainly they appeared fierce enough: tall and sinewy, their mustachioed countenances dark and leathery under the hoods of filthy cloaks. Their rough manner and low, terse speech was scarcely calculated to win an Englishman's trust, however.

In their midst, Esme seemed smaller and more vulnerable than ever, terribly in need of protection. That they didn't seem to suspect she was a female was in no wise comforting, given the practices common in these parts. Varian thought the men watched her too closely. He had a strong suspicion what was in their minds, though she clearly didn't.

It was in his thoughts too much for comfort. Admittedly, she was a lovely child. He'd recognized that even before he'd discerned the alluring subtlety of her nymph's body. Her sun-burnished complexion was smooth and soft, her full, ripe mouth softer yet, begging to be kissed. But that was the whole trouble. She was a *child,* and Varian St. George had no taste for children, and therefore no business thinking about her mouth or any part of her.

Only he couldn't stop thinking about it. Repeatedly his mind thrust before him the disquieting moment when he'd caressed her foot and gazed into the beguiling green depths of her eyes, and felt the first treacherous stirrings of desire.

Alarming as it was, Varian assured himself, the attraction was easily explained. He'd not touched a woman in weeks. This, coupled with a miserable journey in filthy weather through a hellish terrain, had disordered his mind. He perceived Esme as a woman because he wanted one, and she was the only female at hand.

Nonetheless, a temporary celibacy would not kill him. He was a gentleman and, while admittedly dissolute, certainly possessed sufficient honor to keep his hands to himself. Unfortunately, he much doubted the same could be said of the men escorting them.

When at last they stopped for the night and the Albanian men began to set up camp, Varian took her aside.

"I think it will be best if you continue sharing my tent," he said.

Seeing rebellion smolder in her eyes and the stubborn jut of her chin, Varian added, "Arguing with me is a waste of breath. You'll only tell me how illogical and foolish I am. But being so, I'm not likely to heed a word, am I?"

"If you are foolish," she said with exaggerated patience, "how can you know what is *best?*"

"I said I *thought,* not that I knew," he answered even more patiently. "Perhaps what I think is idiotic, but my dear girl, it's the best I can do."

She considered this, her meditative expression a comical replica of Percival's when puzzled by a geological specimen.

"I see," she said after a moment. "It is much like last night. You have some deranged belief that you must guard and protect me. You see danger here, where it is not, just as you saw no danger in Durrës, where it was. Y'Allah, you are so confused. I begin to think your mother dropped you on your head when you were a babe."

Varian kept his face straight. "One ought to be patient with the mentally unbalanced."

"For my patience with *you,* I should be made a saint," she retorted. "All while we travel, it is either complaint or sarcasm. As though your disapproval will change the weather, or magically rebuild the roads the rain has washed away."

He had been grumpy, Varian realized. Being displeased with himself, he'd expressed displeasure with everything else.

"I'm dreadfully spoiled," he said. "I've lived a sheltered life, I'm afraid, and an idle one. Traveling in your country is hard work, and I've never even done a day's *easy* work in my life."

"Aye, and such a man thinks he can protect *me.* Never have I heard anything so crazy." She began to move away.

Varian lightly caught her arm to stop her. "Crazy or not, I want you to stay away from the others," he said. "If they observe you closely, they'll surely discover you're not what you seem. We'll eat together in my tent, and there you'll spend the night. It's the only sensible thing to do."

She shook her head.

"Esme," he whispered harshly, "while I may be spoiled, I am *larger* than you, and I am quite serious about this."

"I understand, *efendi.*"

"Yet you refuse?"

She hesitated, then nodded and clicked her tongue.

What in blazes was the problem? As he was trying to

devise a more convincing approach, he caught the glint of amusement in her eyes.

"May I ask what you find so humorous?" he asked. "Is a flea crawling up my nose?"

She nodded. Though he'd felt nothing, he instantly let go of her to brush at his nose.

"Four days in my country and you never noticed this simple thing," she said. "When we shake our heads, that is 'Yes.' When we nod, that is 'No.' Did you not say yourself we were backward? So it is." She laughed, mightily amused at her wit.

"I see you mean to make me the butt of your jokes the whole long way to Tepelena," he said. "I must resign myself to playing the fool—and I a great English *bej* of the *pashalik* of Buckinghamshire. I can only hope a *bej* is some sort of nobleman, and not the Albanian word for jackass."

This, too, tickled her, and as she dashed away to collect her belongings, she was still laughing.

Their supper was the most amiable they'd shared so far. Evidently still amused by the earlier exchange, she wasn't so quick as usual to take offense at every word. This night they dined on fowl, rice, olives, bread, and a malodorous cheese, but Varian made no complaint. He knew he'd behaved disagreeably during the day and had best not try her patience further. She might throw a temper fit and storm off to her countrymen.

Fortunately, a few swallows of the poisonous grape whiskey they called *raki* made the rest go down more easily. Brewed, apparently, in the infernos of Hades, it was a demonic liquid fire, more potent even than Italian *grappa*. The men gulped it down with their meals as though it were spring water. At present, the raucous song and laughter outside told Varian they were drunk, and Petro drunkest of all, no doubt. All the more reason to keep her away from them, Varian told himself righteously.

"What are they singing?" he asked.

Esme had cleared away the remains of their meal. She

stood now by the tent opening, the flap in her hand as she gazed out. The rain had dwindled to a drizzle.

"It is the tale of Ali Pasha's conquest of Prevesa," she said. "He's crazy sometimes, but a good general."

The tenor voices seemed to wail a funeral chant. That must be the Eastern influence, he thought, with its preference for the minor key.

She let the flap fall back into place and moved toward the center of the tent, to the rug where he reclined against a low stack of blankets. "Do you want me to translate it?" she asked as she dropped gracefully into a cross-legged position opposite him.

"Not if it's about warfare. I'm a man of peace. A lazy idler, as I told you."

"Njeri i plogët," she said. "Sluggard man. Lazy bones."

To his ears, the Albanian language sounded guttural and harsh, as thick and rough as their blankets. When uttered in her low-pitched voice, however, the rough syllables became rich and breathy. Last night, the caressing sound of her quiet good night had nearly undone him.

The memory made him restless. "Teach me," he said.

She raised her eyebrows. "It is an ancient language, you know, much inflected. Like Latin, but harder to pronounce. The consonants will strangle your tongue."

"I'm not afraid," he said. He gave up his lolling pose to sit upright and cross-legged, as she did. "It will occupy me until bedtime. Moreover, it will give you an ideal opportunity to make me appear ridiculous."

"I may die of laughter, *efendi.* Then you'll have only Petro as interpreter."

"No, I'll be dead, too, throttled by my own tongue."

"Very well. I warn you, though, it will be difficult." She considered briefly. "Perhaps no declensions at first, or you may begin weeping." She held up her strong little hand. *"Dorë*—hand. There is definite and indefinite. *Dorë, dora.* But I suppose you cannot hear the difference?"

He gave her a blank look.

"It is not important," she said patiently. "No one will expect you to be a scholar. Say it the best you can."

"Doh-lah," he responded gravely.

"No, no. Not 'l,' but 'r.' " She obligingly burred the 'r,' parting her mouth slightly to demonstrate.

Varian was fully capable of mimicking the sound, and knew he shouldn't play games with her. On the other hand, how could he resist, when she so ingenuously offered her luscious mouth for his perusal?

A child's mouth, said a reproachful voice in the back of his head. He didn't listen.

Varian St. George had never heeded nagging internal voices in his life, and was ill-equipped to begin now. What conscience he owned existed in hopeless decrepitude. A mere glimpse of temptation was sufficient to stifle it.

"Doh-dah," he said.

She gazed at him with the stoical resignation of a tutor confronted with a mentally deficient child. She sought simpler nouns, naming objects in the tent, but nothing was simple enough. Varian listened and watched attentively, then murdered every word.

Determined to teach the thickheaded Englishman, Esme moved closer to allow him better study of the movement of lips and tongue as she formed the syllables.

"Kokë," she said, pointing to her head. "Those are like English sounds, are they not?" She touched her straight, delicately shaped nose with the tip of her finger. *"Undë."*

Eyebrows, eyes, cheeks, ears, mouth—she recited them one by one, as patiently persistent as any evangelist intent on a sinner's salvation. So near, so invitingly near. He wanted to touch her, to trail his finger along the silky gold of her cheek.

"Gojë," she said, pointing to her mouth. "Come, it is not so hard."

No, her mouth was soft and full and moist. *Come,* she'd said. *"Kokë, syrtë, undë,"* he said softly, perfectly. He leaned closer. He wanted that mouth, and it was all in the world he wanted or knew at that moment.

"Gojë," he whispered. His lips brushed hers—the lightest caress of a kiss, yet something crackled in him, like fear, and he drew back, startled.

Not nearly so startled as she. Her green eyes opened wide in astonishment. Then her face blazed scarlet. Her hand shot out and whacked the side of his head so hard that his ears rang and his eyes watered.

"That was not amusing." She began rubbing her mouth vigorously.

As he gingerly massaged the side of his head, Varian decided he'd never met with a more deflating—or appropriate—response. He'd been slapped before, on the rare occasion, though not nearly so hard. Never, however, had one of his kisses been wiped away with such utter revulsion.

Still, what did he expect? How had he dared to soil her innocent mouth with his? Damn, and how could he not, being what he was, and finding her so . . . enchanting? Which she was, astonishingly enough, despite her ragged, *hideous* boy's attire and that godawful woolen helmet.

At the moment, however, Varian's most urgent problem was how to pacify her. Admittedly, he'd experienced a moment of insanity, but he was fully in control now. The men outside, on the other hand, were drunk.

"You didn't find Petro's behavior yesterday amusing, either, yet you didn't give *him* a concussion," Varian pointed out in aggrieved tones.

"*He* did not insult my person," she said icily.

"I assure you, Esme, I meant no insult."

"I know. You meant only a joke. You pretended you could not say the words—"

"You played a joke on me a short while ago," he interrupted. "Perhaps I wanted to get even."

This gave her pause. It was very curious—and convenient, certainly—how easily she accepted revenge as an excuse. Varian only wished she wouldn't weigh his case with precisely that sulky expression. He wanted to kiss the pout away, or tickle her, or do something . . . which would only offend her dignity further and no doubt result in his immediate demise. Really, you'd think he was twelve years old. Perhaps this was a case of premature senility, the result of years of dissipation and—

"Very well," she said. "I made you appear foolish,

and so you did the same to me. Still, I will warn you to keep such revenge to words, *efendi*. Otherwise, on the way to Tepelena, we may find ourselves in a blood feud. To insult another's person is to strike a blow," she explained, "which likely will be returned. One time, one of us may be tempted to strike a fatal one."

Lord love the girl. She saw no difference between being kissed and having her ears boxed. Vain, had she called him? He'd not be for long, in her company.

"I quite agree," he said. "I did overstep a bit with the kiss. Fortunately, you took your revenge quickly, so I will not have to lie awake all night, wondering what ghastly way you'll find to get even."

"No, and I shall not have to lie awake devising sufficient ghastliness." She paused, and turned her head slightly, listening.

Outside, there was only the faint sibilance of the drizzle.

"The others have gone to sleep," she said. "We'd best do the same."

As he helped her arrange the blankets, Varian noticed with some surprise that she placed hers next to his, just as though nothing had happened. Clearly, she did not assume the "revenge kiss" implied her virtue was in any danger. In that case, the words of reassurance he'd contemplated offering would have quite the opposite effect, and alarm her needlessly.

He may have kissed her, but that was so brief you could hardly call it a kiss, and certainly he wouldn't attempt to ravish the girl while she slept. He would not *touch* her, he told himself. In fact, he'd stay awake until she fell asleep, then move his blankets some distance away so he couldn't touch her, even unconsciously. Gad, at this rate, not a shred of indecency would be left to him, he thought ruefully.

Esme woke to darkness and the not entirely unfamiliar sensation of weight upon her. A long arm curled round her waist, and a long, lean body pressed along the length of her back. She had wrapped her blanket about her like a cocoon, and no part of his flesh touched hers, yet she was as acutely aware of every masculine bone and sinew as if she were naked. The images she conjured up made her face hot, and she stirred uneasily.

He mumbled something into her neck, and the arm pressed her closer. Then abruptly, it jerked away, and the heavy warmth of him vanished, too. He thrashed at the blankets. "Bloody hell," his voice came, a growling whisper.

She turned and found he was sitting up.

"I woke you," he said.

"I was awake," she said to his shadowy form. "It is nearly dawn."

"Have I been crushing you the whole curst night?" He sounded angry.

"You are large, but you are not an elephant. I am not crushed."

Only embarrassed, she added inwardly. To be held so was more than warming; it made something inside her rush and pound, like a flock of swallows beating their wings. She'd felt that when his lips had touched hers: a terrible sweetness, come and gone in an instant, and afterward the flurried throbbing within. She should have felt nothing, and so was dismayed with herself.

"I'm sorry," he said. "I didn't—I didn't insult you, did I?"

"No."

There was a long pause. Then he said in more normal tones, "And I trust you didn't insult my person, did you, miss?"

"No! What do you—" Her face burned. "Oh, it is a joke."

"Or wishful thinking," he muttered. He caught his breath, then went on. "That is to say, I distinctly felt something bite me, and I rather hoped it was you because—"

"You wished me to *bite* you?"

"Because otherwise it was some other creature that bit me. There being a great many of them and only one of you, the latter odds were less disheartening, you see."

"Then perhaps you should not sleep so close, *efendi*.

I think the fleas find you more appetizing, and so mine may travel to you,'' she added guiltily.

"I don't mean to sleep so close. It just seems to happen. I suppose you find me very troublesome.''

The air in the tent carried a faint, fresh promise of morning, and the heavy darkness was receding, leaving a somber veil of gray light in its wake. He sat with his knees drawn up and his arms loosely crossed upon them. Even in the gloomy shadows, he seemed a work of sculptor's art, too beautiful to be mortal flesh and blood. He was indeed troublesome, she thought. Her mind should remain fixed on her duty, on a father's murder to be avenged, but this man called her mind away to fasten on him instead.

''Yes,'' she said.

''You won't believe this, Esme, but normally I'm most agreeable company. It's one of my few talents. I can make myself agreeable to just about anybody.''

He hesitated, then went on in light tones, ''Otherwise, I'd surely have starved to death by now. You see, all I've got to my name *is* my name. That and a skill for pleasing is what feeds, clothes, and houses me.''

She turned a disbelieving gaze upon him.

''It's quite true,'' he assured her. ''Like my untitled brothers, the fleas, I'm a parasite. But a charming one. I never bite, for instance.''

''I believe you can be agreeable,'' she said. ''At least to the women, or you would not have had so many.''

''I should like to know exactly what Petro has been telling you. I'm sure it's a hideous exaggeration—''

''He said you were addicted to females, and that they all throw themselves at you shamelessly, and so you've had your pick of Italy's most beautiful women. I understand Italy has many such,'' she said expressionlessly.

''I have not been a monk, precisely, but—''

''Therefore I am not surprised you can be charming. I was surprised only that you are poor.'' Esme did not want to reflect further upon the series of mouths he'd kissed—and not in joke—or the voluptuous bodies his smooth, long fingers had caressed—and not recoiled from.

"I am penniless," he said. "*That's* no exaggeration."

"Then it is one thing we have in common," she said. "I doubt it raises your opinion of me, however."

"My opinion is of no consequence."

"If it weren't, I shouldn't be going to all this bother to tell you what a pleasant fellow I really am. I wish you would pay attention, Esme, and stop distracting me," he complained. "There was a point I wished to make, about two centuries ago, before you detoured into my promiscuity.'

"I beg your pardon, *efendi.*" Folding her hands, Esme gave him her full attention—and found it very difficult to suppress a smile. With that aggrieved expression on his face and his black hair tousled every which way, he looked like a sulky schoolboy.

"I was trying to explain" he said reproachfully, "that I'm not naturally bad-tempered. It's the fleas and the dirt. Even those I could endure stoically enough if I could be assured of regular, hot baths and fresh changes of clothing. But to sleep in the same filthy clothes I traveled in all day, then to wake and spend another filthy day in the same foul garments, while the vermin continue to feed and breed upon me—well, it does make me wild."

She did smile then, though she looked away. "Ah, Varian *Shenjt Gjergj,* you call yourself penniless, yet I cannot imagine such a life as you live. Hot baths whenever you wish, and always clean clothes. I doubt even the most pampered of a rich man's concubines knows such luxury. If this is what you are accustomed to, it is not surprising that our journey makes you cross. I shall try to be more understanding in the future."

"You think I'm childish, all the same," he said. "Shall I tell you what it's like, and let you judge whether it's childish to want such things?"

"As you wish," she said with a shrug. "It is too late to go back to sleep. The others will rise soon."

"Then let me charm you. Let me paint you a picture." He unfolded his long body to lean back on his elbows, and closed his eyes.

Then he began to speak, his voice soft and dreamy as he described a luxurious room, the floors laid with rich carpets . . . coals glowing in the hearth . . . an enormous copper tub, smooth and deep, filled with steaming water. There was soap, sweet with the scent of herbs and flowers, and a maidservant gently washing her. There was Esme, luxuriating in the scented warmth . . . then rising from the water like Aphrodite . . . soft, thick towels enveloping her. He painted Paradise, but it was more than a painting. The words and his dreamy tone seeped into her very soul and made her ache with longing.

She didn't realize she'd closed her eyes until the low, smoky sound of his voice abruptly ceased. Opening them, she found him staring at her very strangely, the smile gone. She flushed and looked away.

"Oh, Lord," he murmured. Then he scrambled up and strode out of the tent.

Chapter 7

Ignoring the men staring at him in sleepy astonishment, Varian stomped toward the river. En route, he nearly collided with Petro, who'd emerged from behind a bush, hastily arranging his trousers.

"What is wrong, master?" he cried as Varian thrust past him.

"Nothing."

"But you are angry, master. Is it the child? Y'Allah, what has the little wretch done now?" Petro asked, trotting alongside.

"I'm not angry," Varian ground out. "I'm going to have a wash, and I don't need an escort. Go make yourself useful, and try to boil some coffee that doesn't taste as though it were spewed from a cesspit."

"A wash?" Petro shrieked. "In the river? You will freeze your privates, and they will drop off like pieces of ice."

"Go make the coffee, drat you, and leave me in peace."

Petro uttered a soulful sigh, then shrugged and turned back toward the camp, doubtless to inform the company that his master had taken leave of his senses.

He would not be far wrong, Varian thought. Certainly the master no longer recognized his own mind. When the Turk had struck his head, some rotting mental door to the blackest part of Varian's soul had surely come unhinged. Because only the most corrupt and depraved of men could lust for a child.

He'd promised himself he wouldn't touch her, yet he'd wakened with Esme's slight body crushed to his, and his own rigid with wanting. Even when he sat talking normally, it wasn't normal at all. The whole time he'd contrived excuses for himself: she wasn't *really* a child, not by her country's standards; she was old enough to wed and bear children, therefore old enough to be bedded.

He knew that wanting her was wrong, and all his twisted reasoning wouldn't make it right. All the same, her low, soft voice was right, and that whisper of a body had felt right enough in his arms. And so he'd chattered nothing but drivel, more excuses, and hated himself because he couldn't stop making them.

He'd felt, Varian reflected in frustration, like a schoolboy, infatuated with a girl who'd as soon knock him down as look at him. He'd behaved like one, too, trying to coax tolerance from her, or, dammit, even *pity*.

Which had backfired nicely, hadn't it? To speak of bathing, of all things, and burn that image in his mind: her slim, untouched body stepping from the bath into his waiting arms . . . her skin, naked and wet against his . . . her soft, ripe mouth offering up its innocence to his.

He groaned and sank to his knees at the river's edge. Closing his eyes, he plunged his hands into the frigid torrent and gasped at the shock. Determinedly, he drenched his face. It wasn't enough. He needed a punishment he'd recollect with dread the next time this filthy lust got hold of him.

Varian set his teeth and began to pull off his clothes.

"I think he has gone mad," Petro said sadly as he took the blankets from Esme. She'd sent the protesting dragoman back after his master, and Petro had reached the stream in time to see his lordship emerge naked and shivering from the icy water.

"He complained of the dirt and fleas," she answered, betraying none of her own anxiety. "Besides, he's English, and they have strange customs."

Not until the party was well on its way, and Petro safely out of hearing range, did she express her feelings to his lordship.

"Why must you do such a stupid thing?" she scolded. "Did I nurse you for nothing? Is the journey not hard enough for you? Must you make yourself ill? The streams are cold enough in the height of summer. Now they will stop the blood in your veins, and your limbs will fall off."

"Actually, I found the experience most . . . invigorating," he answered. "My blood still tingles."

"You are a crazy man. And I warn you, if you become sick, I shall not nurse you again. I shall stand by your deathbed and *laugh.*"

"Don't be cross, love. The sun has condescended to shine today, and your scowl will frighten it away."

Esme hastily subsided, though not for fear of driving away the sun. It was the careless endearment that stopped her tongue. When he said her name, the whispery sound seemed to call to her very being. This was worse.

Love. It called back the touch of his mouth upon hers and the hot pressure of his body against her back. Those recollections brought a tremble of sensations within her that left her disoriented and wistful, like one waking from a bittersweet dream.

Esme was not given to self-delusion. She suspected what her trouble was, and could not be altogether amazed. Petro had said his master had a way with women. Moreover, she doubted any female could spend so much time in the company of such godlike beauty and remain unaffected, worthless and dissolute as this particular deity might be. His face and form, unfortunately, betrayed nothing of his weak character, nor did the smoky sound of his persuasive voice. When one admired a handsome palace and longed to live there, Esme reflected, one did not think of the rats scurrying about in its bowels.

She was no saint and, being female, must have some feminine susceptibilities. This she understood. Yet it didn't mean she approved, or wished to encourage her frailties. There was no place in her life for such foolishness.

Besides, it was mortifying. How he'd laugh if he guessed what his ugly, scrawny little interpreter felt. Had she been a beauty, tall and voluptuous . . . but she was not and never would be. For that, she should be thankful. Since he'd never find her desirable, her virtue would never be tested. She'd enough cause to blame herself, enough reason for sorrow. She certainly didn't need to heap shame upon grief.

They rode on in silence for an hour or more, and Esme felt his gaze upon her several times. She resolutely kept her own eyes upon the treacherous path ahead.

"Are you angry with me?" he said at last.

"Yes," she answered. "I should not be, because you cannot help being what you are. All the same, it is most trying. You have a gift for making difficulties for yourself."

"Good grief, you're not still upset about my swim in the river?"

"I do not know what is to be done with you," she said. "You are like those little children who seem to spend all their time devising new ways to hurt themselves. Since I cannot swaddle you up or tie a leash about your waist, I am convinced you will be dead by the time we reach Tepelena, no matter what I do. Then Ali will blame me. If he's in an amiable mood, he might merely have me shot from a cannon. Otherwise, I shall probably be roasted upon a spit, or torn limb from limb. Whatever he chooses, it is bound to be humiliating. One rarely dies with dignity at his hands."

"I see. It's not my survival that worries you, but your own."

"Of course your survival concerns me." she answered coldly. "You are a guest in my country. I am obliged to see to your safety and comfort."

"But except for that, you don't give a damn about me."

"What is the use, when you do not give a damn about yourself? I do not pursue hopeless causes."

His sharp intake of breath was clearly audible above the hoofbeats."

"Well, that wasn't pleasant," he said. "The truth rarely is, I understand. Not that I'm much acquainted with truth, personally, but . . . Drat it, Esme, you don't even know me."

She almost felt sorry for him. She'd never imagined anything she said would penetrate his arrogance. "This is true enough," she said after an uncomfortable moment. "I know only what I observe. Perhaps there are extenuating circumstances."

He considered. "Perhaps. Perhaps not. It's just that—oh, never mind. 'Extenuating,' " he went on more lightly. "Your English vocabulary is remarkable."

"My own language is more beautiful," she said, "but sometimes yours offers a greater choice of words."

"I should think that the case always. You can choose among several words to convey exactly the nuance you wish."

She nodded and clicked her tongue. "You don't know my language, and so you don't understand. In Albanian, one conveys the nuances, as you say, in tone, expression. It is more subtle. It has more feeling."

"That may be so. Regrettably, I have found its speakers remarkably *un*feeling."

Esme felt a nasty prick of conscience. She ignored it. Her conscience was an idiot to respond to the plaints of a spoiled, selfish libertine. "That is not reasonable. In Rrogozhina, my countrymen treated you like a prince. What more do you want?"

"Your countrymen have been unremittingly kind and gracious," he said. "Perhaps I should have been more precise. I meant *you.*"

"You find me unfeeling?"

He shifted uneasily in the saddle, and his mount snorted in annoyance. "That's not quite what I meant. You've looked after me very kindly, indeed, and I do appreciate—that is, you did save my life . . ."

Esme waited, but his lordship produced no further enlightenment. "Then I do not understand what you are complaining about," she said haughtily. "When you discover what it is, I shall be honored to hear."

They reached Lushnja at midday, and it was there Varian first encountered the harsh reality of Albanian tribal justice. Two men had recently quarreled, and one had murdered the other. The murderer had fled, and the chiefs of his tribe had set fire to his house and land. Another blood feud had begun.

Though Esme had assured him guests were safe from attack, Varian refused to linger in the town. Even the promise of a hot bath could not tempt him.

"It's barbaric," he told her as they passed the charred field. "A man must be punished for murder, I suppose, but why punish his wife and children as well by burning their property?"

"Others will look after his family," she said stiffly. "They at least will not be thrown into dungeons for their poverty. My father told me that in England a man and his whole family may be imprisoned merely because they are penniless."

That struck too close to home. Lord Edenmont himself belonged in debtors' prison. As to his own lands, he'd needed no torch to devastate them.

All the same, he'd rather quarrel with her than endure more hours of cold silence. Varian was unused to coldness, unused, certainly, to such open contempt, and it upset him far more than he could have guessed.

He didn't know how to fight it. All his attempts to defend himself sounded querulous . . . and only made him appear more childish than ever. It was mortifying that Edenmont, who could coax warmth from the stoniest ogre of a dowager, could not elicit a glimmer of softness from this adolescent girl.

This was how low he'd sunk: wanting to make her berate him, mock him—anything but that chilly disregard.

"True," he said. "But we English place a high value on money. This is what distinguishes us from less civilized nations," he added provokingly.

"You English recognize only one civilization—your own," she returned. "Albania built fine temples and created great art while your ancestors lived like animals in mud hovels and caves. The Romans sent their noble sons here, to Apollonia, to be trained as warriors, and these men sailed across the seas to conquer the savages of your little island. Time after time nations have come and tried to rule us, yet they could not mold us to their will. They could not even mold our language—not the Greeks, nor the Romans, nor even the Turks. Four centuries they've ruled us, and still the only ones who speak Turkish here are the Turks themselves. How long did the Normans need to convert your people to French? A week?" she concluded scornfully.

"That's simply because we're so enormously hospitable. And not nearly so obstinate. Of course, your people may have retained the one language simply because they were *incapable* of learning another."

"How can you be so ignorant? I speak four languages excellently, and even in Turkish I can communicate."

"But you're half English."

She threw him a murderous glance.

"Is that the evil eye Petro speaks of?" Varian asked. "It's quite good, I must say. If I weren't so hardened in wickedness, it should stop my tongue for a fortnight."

"You have been provoking me deliberately," she accused. "Why? Do you *like* to hear me scold?"

"Yes. You make such wonderful speeches. I wish I could let you take my place in the House of Lords. You'd enliven the proceedings considerably."

Esme in England. The prospect boggled Varian's mind. What would they make of her, this ferocious nymph? Add a few years—Esme at eighteen, perhaps—and place her at Almack's among the glittering, bored lights of society. What then?

Then, Varian had small doubt, at least a few perceptive men would discern what he did. Though she was unlike anything they knew, and possessed virtually every quality most disapproved of in females, they'd glance once into her passionate green eyes and forget utterly everything they'd ever believed about women.

She was looking away from him, her high-boned cheeks tinged with pink.

"I see," she said. "You are amused. I make a fine court jester."

"The jester, may I point out, was usually the only member of the court who dared speak the truth."

"Aye," she answered wearily, "and they all laughed, just the same."

They stopped to make camp just before sunset and, for the first time, his lordship made himself useful. He assisted not only in unloading the horses, but in setting up the tents and collecting fuel for the fire. Esme thought he was more in the way than helpful, but the men didn't seem to mind his incompetence, though they were obviously amused. He seemed amused as well. Esme heard a great deal of laughter, interspersed by Petro's translations—inept, no doubt.

She was not allowed to join them. His royal highness had pointed to one spot near the horses where she was to remain until their tent was in place, unless she wished to suffer some perfectly ghastly punishment.

The threat was unnecessary. Esme fully understood why she must keep away from the men. If they discovered her gender, they could easily, though unintentionally, misspeak in the wrong company. A single words—a feminine pronoun instead of masculine—could arouse suspicion, and one could never be certain where Ismal's spies were.

Nonetheless, Esme found she could not wait calmly. She had never been good at waiting, and now she felt so restless she could scream. It was his lordship's fault. He made her tense and unreasonably angry and, driven by anger, she found herself behaving exactly like the uncivilized heathen he thought her.

How many times had she insulted him? A hundred, at least. Yet it was his fault, too, for provoking her, and treating her like a helpless child, and nearly falling off his horse in amazement every time she showed the smallest sign of intelligence.

Extenuating. You'd think it was the most obscure and complicated word in twenty languages. And to say English was precise—when he could not produce a string of words in that curst language to explain himself.

Also, he'd said she was unfeeling. She, wracked with grief for a murdered father. She, anxious—for all her assurances to everyone else—for her young cousin.

Should she have wept and worried the whole day? Or perhaps his lordship would prefer to hear her boast of her plans for revenge, and the certain death she was headed for. Or maybe she should moan pathetically that she was all alone in her own country, and the few who cared about her at all planned to send her away to a foreign land and a family that despised her.

Aye, she had plenty of feeling to show, were she weak-willed enough. Should she tell him, too, that he only made everything worse?

From the clearing beyond came his low-pitched drawl and another burst of laughter from the men. Esme kicked a stone. There he was, charming them all, as usual. And here she was, driven to distraction, because the sound of his voice drew her entire being to him, and she could not stop it, for all her will.

She sent another stone flying into the thicket and wished she could find some greater damage to inflict. She wished she had Ismal's neck in her hands at this moment, for she could have wrung it as easily as if it were a chicken's. It was *all* his fault, every bit of it, up to and including this devil of an Englishman.

"Are you trying to pave a road for me singlehanded? How very thoughtful, ma'am."

Esme turned hastily. She'd not heard him approach. "I was bored," she said, dropping her gaze to the ground. "Better to kick stones than living targets."

"Do you want to kick me so badly?" he asked. "What have I done now?"

"You've made me stay in one place, all by myself, while you go and amuse yourself with the other men. I wait alone and listen to you laugh, and no one tells me the jokes."

"Of course not. They're not fit for a young lady's innocent ears. Besides, you wouldn't understand them." He paused. "At least, I hope not."

Her head went up. "They told wicked stories and you would not let me hear?"

"It doesn't matter what kind of stories. You know why you have to keep away from the men, Esme, so there's no need to look at me in that murderous way."

"You might have given me something to do," she grumbled. "To wait idly, with no company, is tiresome."

A lazy lure of a smile curved his wicked mouth. "Forgive me," he said. "I had no idea you were longing for my company. How cruel of me to deprive you."

To her consternation, Esme felt her cheeks heat. She raised her chin. "Indeed, *efendi,* my beautiful god. You have broken my heart. I think I shall run to the river and drown myself."

Her spine straight, she began to march past him. His hand shot out and lightly caught her arm.

Esme looked down at his long, smooth hand, then up into his face, and her heartbeat quickened.

"I was only teasing," he said. "I know you'd rather the Devil's company than mine."

"I think that is much the same thing," she answered tartly. "You may let go of me. I cannot run away. I have no place to go."

"I'm sorry." He slid his hand down her arm, where it lingered a moment to leave a tingle of warmth. Then, finally, he released her. "Shall I tell Petro to keep you company tonight? I can't leave you by yourself."

Petro—that fearful old woman—her guard? How dare he? Yet Esme knew why. His almighty lordship didn't want *her* low company.

"You think I need *him?*" she cried. "What is wrong with you? Only tell me where to sleep and I shall make my bed there. Here, if you like. What have I to fear? Kidnappers—when I'm *dead?* Wild beasts? There are none hereabouts. And besides, I have my rifle and my knife and—"

"And you're a female," he interrupted, "so it's no good telling me how capable you are of defending yourself. I'm an Englishman, recollect, and it's against our rules to leave women to fend for themselves. You shouldn't even be traveling with me without a chaperon, but I can hardly get you one when you're supposed to be a boy." He sighed, then started back toward the tent.

After a moment's hesitation, Esme followed.

"You make a great piece of trouble about nothing,"

she said as she trailed him into the tent. "You agitate yourself for no reason. If this is the English way, I must tell you it is stupid and crazy. My father reared me to protect myself, not be sheltered and coddled by others. I am not a babe, and it is offensive to be treated like one."

His back was turned to her, and he was pulling off his cloak. He flung it to the ground and swung round to face her. "I do beg your pardon, madam," he said. "How do you wish to be treated?"

His tower of a body vibrated with anger. Only a fool would provoke him further. Esme's brain told her to *shut up,* but she was beyond heeding it. "As I appear," she snapped. "As a boy. Even a boy of twelve, like my cousin, is considered a man, not a helpless infant."

He advanced and, in a flash, yanked off her headdress and threw it onto the cloak. Her tangled hair fell loose against her shoulders, and she immediately felt undressed. She started to back away, but his hands clamped down on her shoulders. Not so strong a grip. She might easily break free. She didn't want to, and hated herself.

"You can't change your gender with a hat," he said. "You're *not* a boy, and all the wishing in the world won't make you one. You are a wretched, quarrelsome female, and you are plaguing me to death. I'm trying to behave like a gentleman—why must you make it so curst impossible?" His hands moved from her shoulders, up her neck, to cup her face. "Why, Esme?"

She didn't know. Within, a vast impatience consumed her. She'd always been so levelheaded, above vanity, yet looking into that beautiful, dissipated countenance, Esme wished desperately she were beautiful as well, that she might dare to touch him . . .

She closed her eyes. If she couldn't see, she wouldn't weaken.

"Oh, don't," he whispered, so near his breath caressed her skin. A tiny shiver ran down her neck. Nearly in the same instant, she felt the soft warmth of his mouth touching hers. A shower of sparks darted through her, a delicious feeling of gladness.

Instinctively, she touched his sleeve, to keep him there.

Miraculously, it worked. The warmth sank down upon her, and his lips clung to hers like morning dew upon a budding rose. For one long moment, she felt as beautiful as a rosebud, all her being opening in pleasure as a flower opens to a warm spring dawn.

He scarcely held her, his hands lightly cupping her face. Esme felt only the lightest pressure as his lips moved gently over hers, but that was an aching sweetness which swelled within her while he lingered . . . as though it were delicious to him, as though he savored what he tasted there.

But that was impossible. All he could feel was curiosity. Though she was another species to him, she was a female, as he'd reminded her so angrily. Being addicted to females, he must, naturally, investigate even this pitiful specimen. He must toy with her and discover if she was like other women.

Esme pulled her head back, and his eyes opened in sleepy surprise. "That is enough," she said shakily.

"No, it isn't." His voice was soft and thick as velvet. His hands gently threaded through her hair, and his gaze, warm smoke, drifted slowly from her mouth to her eyes and back again.

"Enough to satisfy your curiosity," Esme answered firmly, stiffening her posture. She ought to break free entirely, because his body was much too close, making her want, so weak she was, to lay her head upon his chest. Yet the tension she sensed in him made her cautious. She'd provoked him moments ago, and he'd found a devastating method of bringing her to heel.

"I'm not at all curious," he said. "I understand you well enough, and never has comprehension been more vexing. You don't want me to look after you. You don't want me to understand you. You don't even want me to like you. You most especially don't want me to like you as a woman. Well, I don't want to worry about you, or understand you, or like you in any way." His hands slid slowly to her shoulders. "But nothing goes as we want, does it? Gad, how long is it since we first collided, Esme? Less than a week? Does time pass so slowly here, or is it something in the air?"

Esme did break away then. His words may not be entirely enlightening, for all the immense English vocabulary he possessed. Her intuition, however, filled in the gaps. She understood what he told her, though she could scarcely believe it. He felt what she did, or something like it. But it meant nothing, she told herself. A whim. A man's need, perhaps. Nothing more.

She moved several steps away and pushed her heavy hair back from her face. Her head wrap lay near his feet. She wanted its protection. She felt too exposed. Nonetheless, she was not inclined to retrieve it.

"You and I have many troubles in our minds, *efendi.*" She spoke in her most reasonable tones, her gaze upon the ground. "The way is difficult and slow, and these problems, as well as our differences, agitate us. Confined together with our troubles and differences, it is no wonder we feel so much . . . vexation. I think, at times, you will drive me mad. It is not surprising that you feel the same."

"Oh, indeed." His voice was tight, and she felt the angry tension growing again. "I kissed you in a fit of temporary insanity, I suppose."

"Aye," she said. "And I must have been in the same state to permit it."

"That's a relief. At least you weren't humoring me. My vanity is already in tatters. Thank you ever so much for sparing me a shred at least."

His vanity? *His* feelings? What of her? Did he think she was made of wood?"

"What do you want me to say, *efendi?* Tell me. I'm not practiced in such matters. Should I tell you I was swooning with desire?"

"Yes, dammit! *I* was!"

She caught her breath, and her gaze shot to his.

"I was," he repeated more quietly. Then he snatched up his cloak and turned away. "Disgusting, isn't it? As though you hadn't a low enough opinion of me already."

He thrust the tent flap aside and left.

Chapter 8

After sending Petro to the tent to keep Esme company, Varian punished himself in the brutally frigid stream. Then, as an extra dose of self-chastisement, he ate with the men. This turned out to be a surprisingly light penance. They'd established something like rapport earlier, when he'd helped set up camp. Communication wasn't completely impossible. One of the men—the youngest—knew a few words of English. Varian had picked up a word of Albanian here and there, and hand gestures helped. When at a loss, they resorted to drawing primitive pictures in the damp dirt with sticks.

The labor of trying to comprehend and make oneself understood provided some distraction from his troubling thoughts. Yet when the meal ended and the men began to sing, Varian found his gaze turning repeatedly to his tent. Doubtless the men sang war songs, but the music sounded like longing to him.

He rose. *"Natën e mirë,"* he said.

Agimi, the one who spoke a bit of English, held up the *raki* flask. "Take," he said. "Warm. Good. You need."

Varian smiled. They'd warned him most politely and patiently against bathing in the rivers. Too cold. Bad for the chest, they insisted. Also, it made "Zigur" most angry. Agimi had clutched his head and shaken it from side to side, indicating that the child's scolding made one's head ache.

Varian took the *raki.* "Thank you," he said. *Falemin-derit."*

Agimi shrugged. *"S'ka gjë."* It's nothing. "You need."

Perhaps he did. What Varian needed most, though, was an apology, and he'd not yet composed a satisfactory one.

Esme was playing *vingt-et-un* with Petro when Varian entered. She did not look up.

"Ah, master, at last you come!" Petro cried, throwing down his cards. "May I go now?"

"I should think you'd want to play the game through," Varian said. "Don't you care whether you win?"

Petro scrambled to his feet. "With this one, there is no winning. She gives me the evil eye and all my luck goes away." He scowled at Esme.

She gazed coolly back at him. "Then go out and kill a snake," she said, "and cut off its head with silver. When the head is dry, wrap it up with a medal of *Shenjt Gjergj,* and take it to a priest to be blessed."

Petro pulled out the cord he wore about his neck. On it dangled a rock of some sort. "I have a charm against evil," Petro said. "A piece of the heavens, from a falling star. But your witchcraft is too strong."

"Everyone knows meteorites are good only against gunshot, you superstitious old woman," she said. "But you make do because you are afraid to kill a snake." She shrugged. "It is no great matter. Tomorrow I will kill one for you."

"And one for me as well?" Varian inquired.

"I did not give you the evil eye, *efendi,"* she muttered as she gathered up the cards. "There is no such thing."

Petro gasped. "Do not say so. The eye will fall upon you."

"If I believed in such foolishness," she returned angrily, "I would declare that it fell upon me a week ago—when you crept out upon the Durrës shore with my cousin."

"Ungrateful child! Had we not come, they would have taken *you,* and then—"

Varian clamped a heavy hand upon Petro's shoulder. "Go away," he said, "until I call you back."

"*Back,* master? You will not leave me with her again?" Petro pressed his hands together in supplication. "I beg you, lord, not again. I am cut in a thousand places from her tongue."

"If you didn't irritate her, that wouldn't happen," Varian said. "Go join the men for a while. But don't get drunk, or I'll cut you in another thousand places with my horsewhip."

The dragoman left, muttering resentfully in what sounded like Turkish.

Varian set down the *raki,* hesitated a moment, then sat down opposite her, Indian style, as she did. His trousers, he thought wryly, would never recover.

"I've come to apologize," he said. "I've not been a gentleman."

Esme shuffled the cards, tapped them into perfect alignment, then set them down before her. "That is true." She placed her hands on her knees. "Still, the apology is welcome."

"*Besa?*"

She glanced up, her enormous green eyes lit with surprise.

"*Besa,*" he repeated. "Truce, is it not?"

"Yes," she said. "No . . . no, I must say my part as well, or I do not truly pledge truce." Her gaze dropped to the rug. "You said before that I made it impossible for you to be a gentleman."

"That was—"

"No, let me finish." Her hands tightened on her knees. "You find it so difficult because I am not a lady. I know. Jason told me so often. I can never be a lady by your people's standards. I am not one by my own people's, either. Other Albanian girls are not like me. They have better manners, much better. I am not always pleased with myself. I do and say many things I later wish I had not. Only later, too late, when it's done. I have great will, yet I *cannot* will my temper. Never. Also, many times, I cannot will my patience . . . and sometimes, other feelings. My grandmother said I have a demon inside me. I do not believe in demons, yet that is truly how it feels."

She clenched her fist and pressed it to her heart. "Here. A fiery demon. That is how I am. It cannot be helped," she concluded sadly as she took her hand away.

It was a confidence, and the confession had not been easy for her. From the start, when she'd refused to show any emotion regarding her father's murder, Varian had understood that the Red Lion's daughter locked her feelings securely inside her. Now, when he'd offered only the smallest of apologies, she'd opened up a corner of her heart to him. His own twisted guiltily.

Varian wished he could shelter this girl in his arms while he assured her she was not to blame, not at all. He realized he was leaning toward her.

"I see." He unfolded his legs and leaned back on one elbow, to widen the distance between them. "That explains everything."

She shot him a wary glance. "Does it?"

"Oh, yes. Very simple. A cliché, actually, though I'm mortified to admit it. I am a stupid, lazy moth, fluttering about aimlessly. You are a little firebrand, constantly bursting into flame. The stupid moth catches sight of the bright, lovely flame, and without a thought for consequences—though he's old enough to know better—rushes right at it. Then he gets his wings singed and, like the mindless imbecile he is, berates the flame."

Esme mulled this over, taking up the cards, shuffling them, putting them down again. Watching her deft hands, Varian recalled her tentative touch upon his sleeve. No, he mustn't think of that, or his mind would turn again to the rest. He wanted peace, the truce he'd sought, because he wanted to remain with her this night, honorably.

"I'm not a good man," he said. "My character is odiously weak. If there's a wrong done, it's more than likely I've done it quite on my own. I'm selfish and thoughtless. I've always been. If not, I should never have brought Percival here."

"Why did you bring him, *efendi?*"

Varian stared at the cards. He still hadn't told her. He'd neatly avoided it, unwilling to face her withering ridicule. For a chess piece, a *toy?* He could hear her say it, hear the contempt in her low voice.

"We came to get a chess piece," he said. Instantly heat flooded his face. He—Edenmont—was blushing. Well, he ought to. As he forced himself to meet her gaze, he saw her eyes widen. Then, of all things, a smile.

"I am sorry," she said. "I am very sorry, Varian *Shenjt Gjergj,* that your mother dropped you upon your head so *many* times."

"It wasn't *entirely* my doing," he said. "Your cousin has a fiendish knack for making the most outrageous matters seem perfectly reasonable."

"He is twelve years old." She shuffled the cards.

"He is not. He's fifty if he's a day."

She placed the cards before him. "Cut."

"Do you mean to tell my fortune?"

"No. I mean to beat you at *vingt-et-un,* my lord, while you tell me of this chess piece."

Though Esme beat his lordship only once, they passed the night peaceably enough, and it was very late when he summoned Petro at last. Despite the earlier threat of horsewhipping, the dragoman entered none too steadily.

His master, however, only uttered a few sharp words before giving up. "He's no better than I at tolerating hardship," he muttered. "Liquor is the only comfort he has at present. Why shouldn't he get drunk? I wish *I* could."

Esme noticed that he made his bed as far from hers as the tent's confines would permit. That was best, she told herself. If his lordship felt a man's need, he might well wish to ease it with whatever was at hand, even herself. This was one of the ways men differed from women, Jason had said, even those of otherwise good character. It was a demon many men seemed to possess.

This man may have compared her to a lovely flame and himself to a helpless moth, Esme reflected, but that was his need speaking.

"When lust takes hold of a man," Jason had warned, "he'll say anything, do anything, and there are men who can seduce with words only. Sometimes guile can be as dangerous as force. Properly armed and prepared, you've a chance of eluding an attacker. Even you, small as you are, might fight him off successfully, as I've taught you. But what will you do, little warrior, when a man sighs and tells you you're breaking his heart?"

That was too ludicrous to contemplate.

"I shall laugh," she had answered confidently.

"That may anger him."

"Then he will attack, and I shall be prepared."

Naive. Abominably so. This man had kissed her, and she hadn't raised a hand against him. In his man's heat, he'd spoken of desire, and in the pit of her belly, a woman's heat had throbbed in answer.

It was best he slept far from her.

Besides, Esme needed to think about what the baron had revealed. The business of the black queen baffled her. If her cousin had given Jason the chess piece, why hadn't her father mentioned it? Jason had shown her his mother's curt note and the kinder one to Esme from his sister-in-law. Why should he keep the chess piece a secret? That made no sense. Percival must be mistaken, and the English lord had made a grave error of judgment, to travel to Albania on a boy's mere say-so.

Still, Lord Edenmont did have an understandable motive. He was penniless, he'd reminded her, and in Italy he could live on a thousand pounds for many months.

"And then?" she'd asked.

"Oh, I would worry about 'then' when it became 'now.' "

Esme looked into his future, and worried for him now.

They might have passed the next day peaceably as well, had Lord Edenmont not made another trip to the river in the morning. When he returned, his hair in shiny damp waves, Esme was so furious that for perhaps the first time in her life she was beyond speech. She simply glared at him and stalked away. They rode toward Poshnja in rigid silence.

They reached the town just after noon. They planned to stay the evening, so that his lordship might manage a hot—or at least warm—bath to soothe his fastidious soul, while they replenished their supplies.

Only a small party greeted them this time, which was odd. Equally intriguing was the agitation Esme sensed in the village. She quickly dismounted, and collared a boy who was gawking at Lord Edenmont as though he'd ridden direct from the moon.

"What's happened?" she asked. "Where are all the men?"

The boy came out of his daze long enough to explain that Poshnja was battling bandits. In broad day, just before the English lord's party arrived, a band of men had swept down and relieved the villagers of some livestock and a great deal of grain. They'd even stolen some loaves of bread which had been left upon a ledge to cool.

Esme released the boy and glanced about her. Agimi and some others of the escort were talking excitedly with an old man. His lordship, though, didn't seem to notice. He was too busy glaring at Petro, whose interpretive skills were evidently failing to please. Esme perceived how the muscles of his chiseled aristocratic countenance tightened and hardened with vexation as he turned his head, looking for her.

When he located her at last, he looked at her for a long moment, then smiled and raised his shoulders in a gesture of helplessness. Her mouth wanted to return the smile. Her pride wouldn't let it. Chin aloft, Esme went to him, to translate their host's welcoming speech and Lord Edenmont's gracious response.

All this time, their Albanian guards were conducting business of their own. While Hasan, the village elder, led his lordship indoors for the obligatory pampering and cosseting, half of Lord Edenmont's men were leaping back upon their mounts.

Well, one could hardly expect them to sit idly about, drinking *kafe* and smoking their pipes, while thieves took the food from their countrymen's mouths. So Esme explained when she gave Lord Edenmont the news . . . half an hour later, when she felt certain the men were well away.

"You saw them go and didn't tell me?" he demanded

in a harsh whisper. "I know you're not speaking to me, but you might have informed me of that, at least."

"I could hardly tell you in the midst of Hasan's greetings," Esme answered as their hostess set down a tray before him. "Besides, you could not have stopped them."

"If they were doing what they believed was their duty, I wouldn't wish to stop them," he said. "I only wish I might be informed—that someone might make at least a *pretense* of consulting me."

"What sort of sense would they expect from a man who bathes in a freezing river, not once but twice in six hours?"

"I saw Petro pick a louse from his head. What would you have done?"

"I should have thrown *Petro* into the river."

He glared at her, then laughed. When Hasan looked inquiringly at her, Esme explained that the English lord laughed with pleasure to see so many kind faces and so much good food.

The men returned several hours later, while Varian was shaving—with blessedly hot water. It was Petro, not Esme, who brought the news. Esme had not yet forgiven him for this morning's ice bath. Well, she didn't understand, thank heaven. Otherwise, she'd probably drown him herself.

Varian squinted into his small shaving glass. What he wouldn't give for a proper mirror, that he might discern more than a square inch of skin at a time. He tried to recall whether there had been any looking glasses in the houses he'd visited. Perhaps these were rare in the villages. He wondered if Esme had ever seen her own countenance, or merely murky reflections in a pond or a bucket.

"Did they capture the thieves?" he asked.

"One they killed," Petro answered. "Two others were shot, but escaped. They have brought back the animals and the grain. But the bread is gone, and Agimi's arm must be cut off."

"What?" Varian turned so quickly, he nearly sliced off his ear.

"The bullet went deep, and at a strange angle, and did not come out the other side."

"He was shot?" Varian threw down his razor. "Damn. I *knew* this would happen. Where is he? Have they summoned a doctor?"

"What doctor? Here?" Petro shook his head. "There is an old man, wise in these things. He says the arm must be taken off before the poison goes to the heart."

"Bloody hell." Varian pulled on his coat. Poor Agimi. How old was he? Little more than a boy—eighteen, nineteen, perhaps. But these things happened. How many young men had lost limbs fighting Napoleon's armies? "I hope to God he's not conscious. Where is he?"

"In the next house. The little witch has gone there, and she howls like a dying cat and will not let anyone near him."

Varian rushed from the room.

Esme was not howling when Varian entered the tiny house, though her voice sliced like a whip as she berated the men, a score of them, who shouted back, furious as she. Yet she stood defiantly by Agimi's cot, knife in hand, and the men, incredibly, hung back.

Varian swiftly threaded his way through the crowd. As he neared the cot, the room quieted to a low rumbling.

Esme looked up at him, her eyes twin green flames. "They shall not," she said, "no matter what you say. The first one who comes near, I will kill. And the others I will kill after, one by one."

"Will you murder me, too?" Varian asked, stepping nearer.

"You, too, if you let them commit this outrage." She nodded at Agimi, who gazed dully back. "The wound is not so bad as it appears. I have had two such. I can take out the bullet and heal his arm, but they have no faith in me. They will not help me. They heed only that babbling old man there," she said, gesturing with her knife at a small, gnarled Methuselah who trembled in a corner, mumbling to herself.

Varian turned his gaze back to Agimi and to the filthy, oozing hole in his muscular arm. "The old man may be senile," he said gently, "but the wound is ugly. I had friends at Waterloo, tended by surgeons, and it was often so. Better to lose part of a limb than to die."

"I am alive," she snapped, stamping her foot. "I showed you the scar on my arm, where I was shot. Do you think I lied? That it was merely boasting? *Twice,"* she said. "The arm that held a bullet now holds a knife. I stand on the leg where another bullet stung. Where should I be now, if others had made a cripple of me, as they mean to do with him?"

The vision her words conjured up triggered a chilling wave of nausea that made the room whirl giddily about him. Varian inhaled slowly, and the room swung back into focus. "Very well," he said. "What do you require?"

Her shoulders sagged slightly in relief. "I need a great, blazing fire, so I may clean my knives and tools in the flames. I need *raki* to cleanse the wound. Send someone for my bag. The tools I require are in it, as well as the medicines: pine resin, green bark from elder twigs, and white beeswax. I shall need some good olive oil as well, and clean sheep wool."

"A salve?" he asked, surprised.

"Yes, it is very good. An old man in Shkodra taught me—he who took the bullet from my arm. It weakens the poison and aids the flesh to heal. That is why my scars are so small."

"How do I tell them to listen to you?"

"Dëgjoni," she murmured.

Varian turned to the group. *"Dëgjoni!"* he said sharply.

Esme looked about her at the uneasy faces, then, her voice clear and sure, rattled off her commands in Albanian.

The men looked from her to Varian.

Varian was about to nod when he remembered. He

shook his head in the Albanian affirmative. "Yes," he said. "*Po.* As Zigur says."

The tall Englishman stood by her while Esme tended her patient. She wished she'd not insisted on Lord Edenmont's remaining, for it was plain that of the two, his lordship suffered most. When she gently slid her thin knife into the wound, his face went white as ashes. Still, he held onto Agimi, his smooth aristocratic hands firm on the young man's shoulder. Agimi endured it all silently. He had refused the laudanum she'd offered, preferring *raki* instead. She hoped the liquor numbed him sufficiently. She couldn't tell. He kept his blue gaze pinned to the ceiling and his lips pressed tightly together.

"Dammit," the baron muttered. "I'm ready to cast up my accounts, and he doesn't even groan."

"He is *Shqiptar,*" Esme said softly. "Son of the eagles. Strong and brave." She murmured soothingly in her own tongue while she probed, then smiled when she located the bullet. "Ah, as I thought. It will come out easily."

The room was quiet. His lordship had managed to persuade the others to leave. Only Mati remained, to help keep Agimi still.

Esme eased the bullet free, then, with the precious tweezers Jason had bought for her, caught it and dropped it into the bowl in her lap.

She heard Lord Edenmont's muffled oath.

"We shall pierce it," she told Agimi, "and you shall wear it about your neck and laugh when you tell them your story: how here in Poshnja, they wanted to cut off your arm just to get this little bullet."

Agimi smiled wanly.

She poured more *raki* into his wound. His mouth tightened, but he made no sound. "Your arm is very drunk, indeed, Agimi. You had better let it sleep." He shook his head weakly. Then she applied the salve and covered it with the wool, which she fastened with strips of cloth. "Let it sleep," she repeated. "Close your eyes, and be patient with your drunken arm."

"It is done," she said, looking up at Lord Edenmont.

His face was gray. He looked far worse than Agimi. She handed him the *raki*.

He took one quick swallow, then passed the flask to Mati.

"You need not remain," she told his lordship. "I'll stay and look after him. The dressing must be changed in a few hours."

"You most certainly will not. You're exhausted. Tell Mati or one of the others what to do. They can summon you if there are any problems. You're coming back with me," he said huskily.

He gathered up her tools and medicines, and placed them carefully in the leather pouch. "You're going to have a long, hot bath, and something to eat and drink. And then you're going to tell me where the devil you learned to perform surgery."

Chapter 9

"These are not my clothes." Clutching the blankets to her chest, Esme frowned at the garments Varian had heaped upon the woven straw pallet where she sat. At the moment, she wore only an overlarge shirt. Varian's shirt. His last *clean* shirt.

"They're donations," he said. "Trousers, shirt, vest. Oh, yes, and a frock," he added, tossing a red woolen gown onto the pile. "While you were yelling at them, they figured out you were a girl. That partially explains why the men were so reluctant to let you operate on Agimi. After I sent them away, they had a good, long discussion about you. Someone must have noticed the color of your eyes. You were *glaring* at them, recall. The concluding evidence was this," he said, lightly touching her hair. "When our hostess collected the coffee cups, she found a strand of red hair on the tray."

He sat down on the edge of the pallet. "I didn't realize you were molting, Esme."

"I *knew* I should have shaved my head," she muttered. "But there was no time."

"Well, it's too late now," he said quickly. If Esme decided she must shave her head, then Esme would do it, and he might as well protest to the stone wall, for all the good it would do him. And they said the English were obstinate.

"In any case, the revelation seems to work to my advantage," he went on. "As soon as they deduced you were the Red Lion's daughter, they were filled with sympathy for my plight. What does *kokëndezur* mean?''

She flushed. ''It means rash. A hothead.''

''They seemed proud of you, nonetheless. They said you're fearless, a lion like your father. They said you're highly intelligent as well.'' Varian paused. ''They said that's why Ismal wants you as his wife.''

Her mouth tightened.

''Rumor has it he wept at the news of your death,'' Varian continued. ''I was unaware this man was in love with you.''

''Is that what they say?''

''Oh, yes. Petro couldn't believe his ears. He made them repeat their remarks several times, to be sure he hadn't misunderstood. He told me Ismal is very rich, very powerful. A most desirable spouse. Wed to him, you would live in the greatest luxury.'' Varian looked at her. ''I take it this Ismal is rather elderly, however?''

''He is young,'' she said. ''Two and twenty, I think.''

A young man, closer to her own age. Much closer, Varian thought with a twinge of irritation.

''But an ugly brute, no doubt,'' he said.

''He's considered very handsome. His hair is fair, pale gold, and his eyes are like blue jewels.''

Nonetheless, Varian assured himself, the man must be a brute. A great, hulking creature, with a neck like the trunk of an oak. And huge, clumsy hands.

He felt edgy and ill, and very, very weary. It was not enough that she must drag him through the most godforsaken wasteland this side of Siberia. It was not enough to spend all his days and half his nights tense with anxiety for Percival and sick with longing for her. It was not enough that she leap into battle against twenty men, insulting and humiliating each and every one of them—including her own escort—then leave Lord Edenmont to restore peace. He'd stood by her side while she worked on Agimi, because she'd asked him to, and he didn't want her to think he'd no confidence in her skill. He'd wanted to avert his gaze from the ugly wound, but hadn't dared, because she would think him weak.

None of these purgatories was enough. Now the whole

town must know who she was, and within hours—thanks to their accursedly swift communication methods—her enemy would have the news. An enemy, it turned out, who was young, rich, handsome, powerful, and surprisingly well-liked. That should not amaze him. These baffling people even admired that monster, Ali Pasha.

Her uneasy voice broke into his thoughts. "You wonder," she said, "why such a man should go to the great trouble of killing my father and trying to abduct me."

"I wonder about a great many things," Varian said.

"I don't understand, either. He might choose from hundreds of women for his harem. Women brought up to wear the veil. Beautiful women whose blood is not mixed. Still, if Ismal imagined he must have me, it would have been enough merely to steal me. Jason did not believe in blood payment, and he could not take me back to England once my virtue was gone. Here, the man is the guilty one, and must make amends. There, the woman is shamed."

In her case, it would have been far worse, Varian thought. Even had Jason actually wed her mother, English law recognized no marriage rites but those of the Anglican Church. Esme would still be considered, technically, a bastard, and society would leap eagerly upon the technicality. Illegitimate and despoiled, she'd be a pariah.

"That, unfortunately, is accurate," he answered. "In the circumstances, Jason would be obliged to consent to the marriage."

"As Ismal knows. He's been educated abroad. He's well aware my father could do little against him. There was no need to kill Jason," she said tightly. "I would have gone willingly, had I known his life was in jeopardy. Many women must endure worse husbands than Ismal, for smaller reasons. It would not be so terrible a sacrifice for me."

It seemed terrible to Varian, to imagine this fiery young nymph stifled in a harem. Still, women endured worse, he knew, even in England. Among the upper orders, families formed alliances for land, money, political power. Sons as well as daughters were merely pawns.

Even when they chose for themselves, love rarely entered their calculations.

Yet Varian was certain this girl would have wed Satan himself to protect her father. What sort of man had Jason been, to have spawned such a daughter, to have merited such a love?

"I suppose you might do worse," he said. "Besides, you'd be sure to have the mighty Ismal running at your beck and call in a matter of hours."

She made a moue of distaste. "I have no wish for a slave. I meant only that I could contrive as other women do, and find happiness in my children. If God is generous, I may have many."

Varian blinked. "You want to be a *mother?"*

"Yes. What is so shocking about that?"

"What's so shocking?" he echoed. "Good grief, Esme, your entire existence is one ghastly shock after another. You've got men shooting at you, trying to abduct you, and English lords falling unconscious at your feet. You haul foreigners from shipwrecks and drag them, singlehanded, through a swamp the size of Australia. A few hours ago, I watched you challenge half a town to battle and saw your knife pointed at my own heart. Where in blazes do you expect to find time to bear children?" he demanded. "What poor devil is going to hold you still long enough to get one on you?"

"I didn't mean *now,"* she said patiently.

"I'm vastly relieved to hear it," he said. "Being the only poor devil in the immediate vicinity, I was, naturally, alarmed. Not that I shouldn't like to oblige, my dear, but I'm afraid you've worn me out."

Her face blazed crimson. "I did not mean you!"

"Oh." Varian looked away. "Yes, that does ease my mind. Because if you had meant me, and you had meant now . . . Well, we know how it is when you make your mind up to something, Esme. If twenty strong men couldn't change your mind today, how is one weak-willed, exhausted fellow to gainsay you this night?"

She opened her mouth, then closed it. The crimson subsided and her expression grew thoughtful. "You are provoked with me,'' she said. ''That is why you make immodest jokes.''

''There is that.''

''I made a great turmoil for you,'' she went on contritely. ''Now they know I'm not dead, you worry that Ismal will send his men after us again.''

''Among other concerns.''

''I am sorry,'' she said. ''But it is done, *efendi.*''

''I know.''

''You should not trouble yourself. Ismal will not dare attack us now.''

''No, certainly not. It won't be anything I might reasonably expect. It will come from nowhere, some unimaginable horror.''

''You worry too much,'' she said. ''You make deep lines in your forehead.''

''My hair is turning gray,'' he said. ''I can *feel* it.''

''No, it is not.'' She shifted her position, to make room for him, then patted the rough pillow beside her. ''*Hajde.* Come.''

Varian stared at the small hand resting on the pillow. ''I beg your pardon?''

''Put your head down,'' she said. ''I will make the lines go away, and your worries as well.''

Varian felt a halfhearted tremble of anticipation, but that was all. He was truly worn out, body and spirit. She may have done all the work, but being a helpless bystander had proved far more taxing. She was in no danger from him tonight, and knew it.

Varian lay down and closed his eyes. Only for a moment, he told himself. Then he must leave.

''I will tell you about the mountains,'' she said softly. Her cool hands stroked his brow. ''Beautiful, reaching to the heavens, where the eagles soar, our fathers.''

Her fingers began to knead, and tiny streams of pleasure sped through him.

''Cool and clear, the water rushes down, bathing the white mountain side, laughing as it goes.''

His mind cleared and cooled, too, though he was warm under her touch, and the warmth sank into his aching muscles.

"Your hands are beautiful," he murmured.

He felt a pause—half a heartbeat—before she continued stroking, kneading, soothing.

"It rushes to meet the forest below," she went on, "where the breeze laughs among the fir trees and wakes the songbirds."

Her voice faded to murmuring pines, far away. It was her hands that made soft music, while Varian slipped deeper into a darkness like velvet, a darkness that enveloped him with a warm gladness, astonishingly like peace.

Esme watched him sleep, his finely sculptured features touched by ghostly shadows in the flickering light of the single oil lamp. She ought to put the light out. She ought to leave, make her bed elsewhere in the small room at least. She could not lie beside him this night. She dared not. With one act of generosity, he had shattered her defenses.

She'd needed him—though she'd have cut her own throat before admitting it—and he'd come. He'd stood by her, against half the town, though he owed her nothing, not even loyalty.

He'd stood and watched while she tended the ugly wound, though the sight must have sickened his sensitive nature, unused to hardship, violence, ugliness. But so it had been from the start. She'd shown him nothing else.

She should not have made him take this journey with her. He didn't understand her people. To him, Albania was nothing but ugliness and brutality, and she had made him endure it.

Esme looked down at her hands, which were trembling. Beautiful, he'd said. Yet they were brown and hard. Good hands for work, for fighting, but not beautiful. Never.

What would he think if he ever learned why she was taking him to Tepelena, why she subjected him to so much trouble? What would he think if he guessed that the hands he called beautiful would soon be stained with a man's blood?

Dear God, let him never learn the truth. Above all, let

this man never guess how his generosity had gouged her heart and poisoned it with shameful wishes.

The oil lamp sputtered and smoked, and the air of the room seemed to grow heavy, an oppressive mass that throbbed with the pounding of her heart. Esme wanted to flee, far away, where she could breathe easily again, her spirit light, without burden.

That was impossible. Nevertheless, she could and must escape his lean body's beckoning nearness. She had only to rise and cross the room. She reached to draw the blanket over him.

He stirred and breathed a sigh. His eyes opened, dark gleaming pools, and his mouth curved into a sleepy smile.

"Your hands are beautiful," he said softly. Then he caught her trembling fingers and brought them to his lips.

His mouth brushed her knuckles, and her pulse raced in answer.

No. Her lips formed the words, but no sound came out.

No, again, as he turned her hand over, and once more, no sound. She must speak, or admit her shame, but she was shamed already, for she couldn't utter the simple word.

His lips sank into the softness of her palm, and Esme caught her breath as pleasure pierced her, sharp as a stiletto. Then again, and again, as he trailed tiny, lingering kisses to her wrist and found at last her betraying, throbbing pulse. A moment only it was, yet surely he'd need no more to read her heart's clamorous message. At last his mouth released her, and the tingling shocks subsided. She told herself to move away, far away, but his intent silver gaze pinioned her.

"I need you," he whispered, and in the space of a heartbeat, he reached out and pulled her down to him.

Her small body sank against his without struggle, though she'd full reason to resist—and quickly. She knew his strength and his swiftness. She knew as well how his touch made a shambles of reason, and scattered right and wrong to the wind.

Without protest or struggle, she'd go speedily to her disgrace, all the greater because she knew what he was and what he sought. But her heart leapt in gladness when his hands caught in her hair and pulled her face to his. She knew she'd be lost, that dishonor hastened toward her. But his wicked mouth was a breath away, and Esme wanted it so badly she could weep.

She closed her eyes, and he swept her into a long kiss that made the world reel crazily. His smooth fingers drew trails of tingling warmth along her skull, and her thoughts scattered like sparks from a crackling hearth. His hard body pressed its heat to hers, and her tense muscles yielded like metal to fire and forge. His tongue coaxed and, obedient to his gentle urging, Esme parted her lips.

The cool taste of his flesh within her was a shock, but only for an instant before a rush of dark pleasure swamped all else. His tongue coiled about hers, and the taste was like a wicked secret. It was sin she tasted, and sin was a delicious drunkenness. It was treacherously sweet, an insidious poison that seeped to her soul. This was evil she tasted, the wickedness of his heart. Though he was as beautiful as a god, Esme knew this was not paradise he took her to. Here danger thrummed in the darkness. Yet it seemed she'd hungered for this all her life.

His mouth left hers to draw fire trails along her cheek and tease at her ear, then on, to kiss the throbbing pulse at her throat. Esme caught her breath, and her eyes flew open. But a wicked secret seeped into her skin where his mouth touched it, and the secret sped through her, making her forget all else. Languorous pleasure streamed through her, and she sighed. Yes. This. His mouth whispering evil to her flesh . . . a path of tiny kisses, tongues of fire along her shoulder . . . the rustle of linen as the shirt slipped down, down, and was gone . . . the cool night air upon her exposed skin. But the air soon warmed to languorous smoke, rich with his masculine scent. His smooth fingers slid, achingly slow, down her naked breast, and her heart raced in answer: *Yes. Touch me. Make me beautiful.*

She became beautiful, soft as velvet, for a dark god held her and transformed her with his caress. She wanted to be beautiful, always, wanted more. Her body strained toward his, yearning to be melted and changed. She would liquefy in his hands, and he'd mold her into a goddess.

He drew back, though she could still feel his breath upon her as he gazed at her. "You're so beautiful." His voice was rough.

Yes. He'd made her so. Esme wanted to tell him. She couldn't. She wasn't Esme any more, but molten liquid, a hot stream of pleasure coiling about him. Her fingers curled round his neck and crept into the silky waves of his hair.

He shuddered, drew her closer, and pushed his knee between her legs. His hands slid up her thighs, then he sank against her once more, and his tongue traced a slow, curling path to the sensitive peak of her breast. His warm mouth drew upon her tender flesh, draining her, only to flood her with rapture that made her moan. The stream of pleasure swelled into a beautiful, wild sea. She wrapped about him tighter still, pressing her thighs against his, demanding more, impatient now with gentleness.

His hands dragged hard down the length of her body, while he murmured words she couldn't understand. Then he rolled her fully onto her back and sought her mouth. Again and again his tongue plunged and coiled within her, and she surged like a great wave, yearning to break upon the shore. Higher and higher she surged, only to find no release. She didn't want it to stop, yet she'd surely die if it didn't.

His restless hands found her breasts again, her waist, then slid lower, toward the intimate place between her legs. She understood it must be so. She had to be his, and must yield all her secrets, all her self. Yet when she felt his touch upon that most private of places, fear stabbed her. She drew back instinctively—for an instant only—but he paused.

His breathing was labored, and his long sigh shaky. He rolled away from her, onto his back, leaving her chilled . . . and alone. Then rose all the shame desire had so thoroughly subjugated while he made love to her. Her face burned.

A long moment passed.

"Good God, Esme," he said at last, his voice hoarse. "You weren't leaving it up to me, were you? Did you think it would ever occur to me to stop?"

"I was not thinking." Her own voice was thick as well. She felt as though she'd been fighting ten armies singlehanded, though she'd never fought at all. "How is a woman to think when you do such things to her? Once you begin, it is impossible to be sensible. Impossible." She fixed her humiliated gaze upon the ceiling. "I could not stop you. I did not wish to stop you. I am ashamed to say this, but it is the truth. If you wish to dishonor me, I cannot prevent it. You make me as stupid as a *sheep.*"

"Don't say that." He turned toward her. "You can't leave it up to me." He grasped the back of her head to make her face him. "You can't."

"You can't leave it to me," she said shakily. "Not when you look at me so, not when you touch me. I am not made of wood, Varian *Shenjt Gjergj,* and I am not a child. Nor is this a child's game you play. It is a man's game, one I am certain you always win. Must you win it with me?"

His hand strayed to her shoulder, then trailed lightly down over her breast, to her waist. She caught her breath, but that was all. How could she push his hand away when it made her desperate, made her ache for him to complete what he'd begun?

"Yes," he said, "but not against your will." His hand moved to her belly and rested there. Heat washed through her and sank to throb in the private place he'd touched moments ago.

"Against my will?" she murmured. "Ah, Varian, you are so foolish."

Esme tugged at his shoulder, to bring him closer, but he didn't seem to understand. With a gasp of impatience, she pulled him to her and shamelessly pressed her mouth to his. He made the faintest resistance, then, with a sigh, succumbed.

Their tongues met and coiled, and Esme took his kiss even more greedily than she'd done before. She knew where it would lead. She wanted it. She wanted to be driven again into the dizzying darkness, but farther than before. Much farther. She touched him now, as he'd done to her. He trembled and moved restlessly under her caresses, his breathing shallow, hurried. His body answered her touch as hers had done his. Half in wonder, half in triumph, Esme let her hands wander freely and grew giddy with power when she heard him moan.

He pulled back slightly. "Stop it."

Oh, no. Not yet. Esme slid her hand down the opening of his shirt, to the waist of his trousers. He grabbed her hand and pressed it to his chest. His heart thundered like a crashing sea.

"No," he groaned. "You don't know what you're doing."

"Then show me."

"No." He broke away abruptly and hauled himself up to a sitting position. "No. I've shown you a great deal too much. Damnation." He looked at her. "Don't ever, *ever* do that again. I'm not Sir Galahad, dammit. It just about killed me to be noble once—but twice—in a few minutes—in the most aggravating circumstances?"

"You should not have touched me again," she said. "I told you how it was."

"You didn't have to *demonstrate!* Do you have any idea what you're doing to me?"

"What you do to me?"

He flinched as though she'd slapped him. "I didn't mean . . ."

He stared bleakly about him. "But I did, didn't I? Not against your will, I said. That was bloody chivalrous of me." His gray gaze, bitter now, returned to her. "I'd better leave," he said.

Chapter 10

The day after the bandit left him with the priest, another huge man came and took Percival away. His name was Bajo. According to the priest, Bajo was Uncle Jason's most trusted friend. He'd been following the bandits, waiting for a chance to get Percival safely away. Last night, Bajo had stood guard outside the priest's house. Though he was a great bear of a fellow who spoke in growls, Percival felt entirely safe in his company.

After a very wet, long journey, they reached Berat—a largish village stuck to the sides and top of a mountain—and went to stay with a man named Mustafa.

To Percival's relief, the old man understood some English, though he spoke to Percival mainly in Greek. While they talked, Mustafa's mother, Eleni, plied Percival with food. Then the kind old lady took him away and put him to bed.

Percival slept through the night, most of the following day, and a good part of the day after. He was so miserably weary he might have slept away another week if, on his fourth day in Berat, the news hadn't come.

He'd just finished picking at his supper when the two men entered the small bedchamber, and a smiling Mustafa announced that Cousin Esme was alive and with Lord Edenmont in a village called Poshnja, about forty miles north of Berat.

Even while he was digesting the wonderful news, Percival was aware that Bajo didn't seem pleased.

"Bajo says he knew Esme was not dead," Mustafa

said after a brief exchange. "He spread the lie so that she would not be pursued. He's sorry for deceiving us, but with spies everywhere, he had no choice. But word is out now. In a few more hours, all Tepelena will know."

Bajo growled something else.

"He is vexed with your cousin," said Mustafa. "He ordered her to remain with the ship. Not only has she disobeyed, but she has been most indiscreet." He explained that one of Esme's escort had been wounded, she'd raised a fuss on his account, and it appeared she'd remain in Poshnja until the man recovered.

No wonder Bajo was cross. Now that people knew Cousin Esme was alive—and still in Albania—she was in danger again.

"Good heavens!" Percival jumped up and grabbed his pouch. "We'd better go after her—before Ismal tries—"

Mustafa waved him back down. "Do not vex yourself. Ismal is closely guarded in Tepelena, for Ali is greatly annoyed with him. Ismal is too busy preserving his own neck to trouble your cousin. He has blamed the abduction on overeager followers, who acted on their own. It is said the ringleaders confessed under torture. Of course, it is only coincidence that these men were very wealthy, with beautiful wives," Mustafa added drily. "Their possessions, naturally, are now forfeit to Ali."

Percival couldn't believe his ears. "Ismal's only under guard? Does this mean he's still under suspicion? Is he awaiting trial? It wasn't just abduction, after all. That is—well, surely the two events were connected. I mean, Uncle Jason's murder. That couldn't be a coincidence. Ali can't believe that. *No* one can believe that."

"You do not understand these men," Mustafa said patiently. "Ismal can be most persuasive. Also, to murder Jason is not in character. Even I cannot believe Ismal would act so incautiously. I loved your uncle, and my heart, too, cries for revenge. Yet neither reason nor feeling points to Ismal."

Bajo said something, to which Mustafa answered sharply, which led to a long debate. Meanwhile, Percival tried to sort out what he'd just heard.

Evidently they believed Ismal hadn't any motive for murdering Uncle Jason. Even Ali must believe that, if he hadn't executed Ismal already. Which meant that Percival Brentmor might well be the only person in Albania who knew what Ismal was up to.

There was no doubt this was the same Ismal mentioned in Otranto, and the other night by the bandits. He sounded just the sort of man who might succeed in overthrowing Ali Pasha: influential, devious, and terribly clever. Ali must be warned before it was too late and Albania erupted into bloody revolution.

Belatedly, Percival realized Mustafa was speaking to him. He stammered an apology.

"Bajo must be on his way," Mustafa repeated. "We agree it is best that you remain with me. Your cousin and the English lord are headed to Tepelena, thinking to find you there. But they will stop here first, for Berat is on their way. From here, you may easily travel west to Fier, thence to the coast. There you can get another boat, either to take you to Corfu—which is under British control—or directly to Italy. There is no need to continue to Tepelena."

Percival fought down his panic. "You mean, I shan't get to—to meet Ali Pasha?"

Mustafa glanced at Bajo. "That would not be wise. The sooner Esme is out of the country, the better."

Bajo was already rising, clearly eager to be gone.

Percival thought quickly. If anyone knew about the conspiracy Uncle Jason had been trying to unravel, it must be Bajo. Surely he could be trusted with information about Ismal. But how to tell him? He understood only Albanian. Mustafa would have to translate . . . but maybe he shouldn't know about the matter. Bajo hadn't even told him Cousin Esme was alive. Because of the spies. Everywhere.

Just as the large Albanian turned toward the door, Percival bounced up again. "Please sir, is he going to Tepelena?"

"Aye. He must explain to the Vizier what has happened."

"Please then, would you ask him to wait? Oh, dear,

I don't mean to be a bother, but I must—that is, may I have a bit of paper and pen and ink?''

Mustafa stared at him.

Percival realized he was wringing his hands. He hastily composed himself. ''I do beg your pardon—but he's in such a hurry—and I do hope he doesn't mind—but I really *must* write to Ali Pasha—and express my—my regrets that I can't see him . . .''

Fortunately, Percival hadn't to hold his breath very long. The discussion was mercifully brief.

''Bajo agrees it is an excellent idea,'' said Mustafa. ''Ali will be most disappointed not to meet you, but a note in your own hand will please him. It may ease his temper somewhat, which will spare Bajo a great deal of distasteful flattery and appeasement.'' He patted Percival's shoulder. ''You are a thoughtful and courteous boy. Come, I will take you to my study, where you may write your note in peace. Bajo and I will bide our time with a cup of *kafe.*''

Nearly an hour later, Percival rejoined the men. His hands *almost* steady, he gave Bajo two folded notes.

Percival turned to his host. ''Please tell Bajo that the one I've marked with his name is a present for him. It's a riddle I made up for Uncle Jason, but—but I should like Bajo to have it. I've nothing else to give him in thanks. I hope he finds it interesting. And please tell him I wish him success in—in all he does.''

The translation brought a rare smile to Bajo's stern mouth. He responded that Percival was like Jason in more than looks: not only brave but generous of heart.

With that, and a hearty handshake, the big man took his leave.

Though Agimi declared to one and all that he was strong as two oxen and fully capable of the journey, Esme declared otherwise.

That took care of that, Varian thought resignedly. It was a great pity Madam had not been about some years ago to lay down the law to Bonaparte. England and her allies would have been spared a deal of trouble.

She had certainly neatly disposed of his lordship,

hadn't she? *You can't leave it to me. Not when you look at me so, not when you touch me.* It was the cruelest temptation any man could face. She'd offered herself . . . if he wished to take full responsibility for ruining her.

She could not possibly know how fiercely he'd wanted her at that moment. What Varian had felt before was nothing to what he felt once he knew she wanted him.

He was sick with it.

He wanted to kill her.

He wanted to kill everybody, and most especially Percival, because if it had not been for that wretched boy, Varian would never have clapped eyes on her.

Lord Edenmont did not, however, kill anybody or even give utterance to a cross word—except to Petro—during the remaining interminable four days they spent in Poshnja. Instead, he took a lesson every morning in the river and tried to exorcise his frustration with activity. With his host and Petro, Varian visited every house of the village, where he spent hours telling anecdotes about his native land and his countrymen, especially Lord Byron, of whom all had heard.

When he grew sick to death of Byron, Lord Edenmont played the role of lord of the manor and offered his woefully limited advice regarding defenses, architecture, and agriculture. His father had drummed—and occasionally thrashed—some farming wisdom into him, which Varian, when interrogated by his hosts, scraped out from the dustiest recesses of his mind.

He even submitted his tormented body to physical labor. To their very great astonishment—and embarrassment—the English baron helped Hasan's sons repair their mill, which had been severely damaged in the recent storms. In the process, another storm burst without warning upon them, and Varian was drenched through before they found shelter. The morning on which they were to leave Poshnja, he woke with a burning throat and a beastly headache.

Esme took one critical look at his ashen face and announced they could not depart until he was better.

Varian turned away from her, threw his traveling bag

over his shoulder, tore his cloak from the hook, and marched from the house.

''You are not fit to travel,'' she cried, hurrying after him. ''It begins to rain again, and you will take a very bad chill, and—''

''I'm not spending another *minute* in this place,'' he declared.

Setting her mouth, Esme stomped off toward her horse, leaving Petro to communicate to Hasan the baron's thanks and farewells.

When they stopped for their midday meal, Varian's throat was swollen enough to make eating a torture. He drank *raki* instead, which made him sick to his stomach. By the time he climbed back onto his mount, his entire body was shaking.

Berat lay only five more miles ahead, five treacherously steep, downhill miles in a downpour. Grimly, Varian rode on, shivering one moment, burning up the next.

The hours passed like decades. He scarcely saw Berat. It was all haze. He heard voices, was aware the group had stopped, and halted his horse. He looked down, and the ground yawned miles below him, then swayed, treacherously.

An earthquake, he thought. Of course. Why not?

Someone cried his name. Esme's voice. Varian turned his head, searching for her, and the world tipped sideways, then sank away and left him falling into the heavens.

Varian opened his eyes to a thick gray fog. He blinked but couldn't focus. It must be a dream: a white mountain side, a rushing stream, and evergreens. No. The somber green was her eyes. They shouldn't be so dark as this, not so afraid. Esme was never afraid.

''I'm sorry,'' he said. Croaked. Was that horrible sound *him?*

''Aye, *now* you are sorry.'' She laid her cool hand upon his brow. ''Only because you are hot with fever and miserable. If you were not so sick, I would beat you.''

He smiled. It hurt. His lips were parched.

He felt himself sinking again. Esme brought her arm round his back and raised him, while she nudged cushions underneath to prop up his head. The room shifted dizzily, then slowly slid back into focus.

A moment later, the most ghastly aroma rose to his nostrils. Varian glanced down. A spoon. He groaned and turned his head into the pillow, then winced as a great claw squeezed his skull.

"It is not poison," she said. "A broth, of garlic and chicken. Swallow it, or I shall call Petro and Mati to hold you down while I *make* you swallow it."

"Yes, Esme," he said meekly, as he turned back to accept the reeking spoonful. Yet he hated having her feed him, hated feeling helpless, like a child. Too often she made him feel like a child. Except when he held her in his arms. He couldn't even lift them now.

"I'm not a child," he said.

"When I am ill, I am a little baby," she said, administering another dose. "Cross and impatient. Once, I threw a bowl of soup at my father's head, then wept with vexation when he laughed."

"I can't imagine you ever being ill."

"It was when they took the bullet from my leg, and I was made to lie abed for weeks. Two years ago."

Varian closed his eyes briefly. He'd felt the scar upon her thigh that night . . . when his hands had explored nearly every part of her. He'd wanted to kiss it. He wished he'd been there two years ago to look after her. He wished she'd thrown the bowl at him. He couldn't tell her. He couldn't explain, even to himself.

"But you will try to be more cheerful," she went on, "for I have good news. My cousin Percival is here, and he is well and eager to speak with you. Later, though. I told him you must rest."

"Percival? Here?"

"Yes. Bajo found him, as I told you he would, and brought him here, to this very house, where Mustafa has taken very good care of him. But you must hurry and grow strong, for the boy has no one to talk to except me, and he makes my head ache."

"I must hurry and get strong," Varian said, "so that I can give him a birching."

"Be quiet. Eat. I will tell you a story."

He accepted another spoonful, then another, while she told him of her life. Her voice low and musical, she spoke of the years she'd lived in the north, near Shkodra. Another pasha ruled that area, and it was thought safer than Ali's territories, which at the time were in bloody turmoil. There, in the harsh mountains, Esme said, the stern Canon of Lek prevailed, laws handed down over generations, from the time of the hero Skanderbeg in the fifteenth century. Blood feuds raged all over Albania, and violent revenge was a common response to injury. In the north, however, the rules were intricately defined and strictly carried out. It was a hard place for women, she told him, but the land was beautiful.

For five years she'd lived in the region of Shkodra, the longest her father had lingered anywhere. Not that he truly lingered. He left her with friends while he traveled the length and breadth of Ali's domains, doing what he could to help bring order and persuade the fiercely independent tribes to unite. Before Shkodra, she'd spent two years in and around Berat. Before that, three in Gjirokastra, where her mother had died—though they continued to visit often afterward, because Esme's grandparents lived there. Korçe, Tepelena, Janina. But these she said she didn't remember well. Janina not at all, for she'd been an infant. Jason had met her mother, a young widow, there. One of Ali's spoils of war, she was given in reward to Jason for services rendered. She was the only woman Jason accepted from Ali. Her name was Liri.

Varian absently swallowed what must have been a cauldron of odiously pungent broth while he listened. It was not just that the tale of her life took his mind off his physical misery and the great claw tearing at his head. He listened because this was Esme's life, what had made her what she was, and he was greedy to know. She had secrets. He wanted to learn them all.

At last she put the relentless spoon away. Varian breathed a sigh of relief.

"I am sorry you didn't like it," she said. "Yet I am glad you were brave enough to take it anyway. Now your body is filled with the strength to fight your illness."

"My body is filled with garlic," he said. "I *reek* of it."

"Yes, it will sweat through your skin, taking the illness with it. Now you have only to sleep."

"I'm not sleepy," he said.

"I tell you this long, boring story of my life and you are not sleepy?" She peered at him. "But you are," she said. "You blink and blink to keep your eyes open. Close them." She stroked the tight place between his eyebrows.

"I want to look at you," he said.

"There is no need to watch me. I shall not go away and make new trouble for you. Do not be anxious."

But Varian was. He knew the fever and headache muddled his mind, but he was afraid to close his eyes, because he might wake and she'd be gone. Then how would he find her again?

All the same, there was no withstanding the gentle pulsing between his brows, no resisting the waves of cool peace streaming through the tight muscles of his face. The claw eased its grip and the world grew soft and thick as velvet, cool and dark. He felt himself slipping, but some part of his mind, sweeping down this sweet river, snagged on a recollection. Time . . . years . . . count them. Five years in Shkodra, two in . . . where? Another place. Other places. How many years? He couldn't remember. His mind went dark and he sank.

Within three days, Lord Edenmont was recovering very well, yet Esme continued to nurse him diligently. He was not overly demanding. He took his medicine with a minimum of complaint and ate whatever she gave him. Otherwise, he slept, mostly. That left her little to do, yet she remained with him and kept her hands busy helping Mustafa's mother, Eleni, by mending clothes, picking through beans, carding wool. Esme did not want any more private conversations with her cousin, and this was the only polite way to avoid them.

Often, Percival kept her company, but while Lord Edenmont slept, the lad had to sit quietly. He did this surprisingly well for a boy. Sometimes he'd take out a half dozen rocks from his leather pouch and study them, occasionally making notes on the paper Mustafa had given him. Most often, though, the boy would sit reading one of Mustafa's books.

Percival tried not to be troublesome, but even in the brief intervals they'd been alone together, he'd said enough to disturb Esme deeply. His heart was set on taking her back to England with him. This was painfully clear, though he said it was what his mama had wanted. When he spoke of his mother, Esme's heart ached for him.

Percival said little about his father, yet here as well she needed few words and only a glimpse of his eyes to understand his father was not a loving one. How could he be, to leave his only child in the care of an irresponsible libertine?

That left the boy only an unforgiving old witch of a grandmother who had refused to write even one kind word to Jason, the son she'd not seen in more than twenty years. The boy had no one. He was desperate enough to make do with Esme, but it was Jason he truly needed, and Jason was dead.

Esme looked at Percival and saw her father's image. She looked at the boy and saw loneliness. When the boy looked at her, she knew he thought he'd found a sister.

He was bright, even amusing, and gentle natured. She wished she could be a sister to him. They'd do well together. There was a bond. She'd felt it in the first five minutes they were together in Berat: kinship, and something else. A sympathy.

But Fate had decreed she must hurt him, and there was no way to prepare him, no way to break it to him gently that she would never accompany him to England. He must go on his own way alone, just as she must carry her burden alone. Yet even as she grieved for Percival, Esme told herself the grief was salutary. It reminded her of her duty.

For a while—too long a while—she'd let a shameful

infatuation take precedence over duty. No more. From now on, all her mind would be fixed upon revenge. Merely killing Ismal would not be enough. He must suffer hideously, body and spirit, before he died. His blood for Jason's, aye, but he must pay as well for the injury to her cousin, who'd needed Jason even more than she had.

Esme allowed herself to think of nothing else as the days stretched into a week. She evaded her cousin's efforts to get close to her and told her conscience it was better this way. She watched Lord Edenmont grow stronger, heard the teasing irony creep back into his voice, and steeled her heart against him as well. She could not allow herself to feel anything for either of them, or give anything of herself. She had her own destiny to follow. They would soon be gone. It was better this way.

Chapter 11

Walled in by mountains, Janina climbed the eastern slope of the Hill of St. George, to command a breathtaking view of the Lake of Janina. Between hill and lake stretched a promontory that rose as it jutted out into the waters. This narrow, rocky quadrangle formed the foundation of the vast fortress that housed one of Ali Pasha's palaces as well as the city's prison, official buildings, cemetery, mosques, and the miserable dwellings of the Jewish population. A drawbridge connected the citadel's lone gate to the small esplanade—a site of executions—which led to the *pazar,* the marketplace.

Janina's *pazar* represented, physically as well as economically, the town's lowest point, its crooked, filthy, ill-paved streets crowded with shops. Beyond the shops, the streets straggled on to the very edge of the lake, where the poorest classes lived. In this quarter, Jason Brentmor, too, had been living in quiet anonymity these last weeks.

After his supposed death, he'd disguised himself as a peddler and headed south, where discontent was building to fever pitch. The complaints he heard en route were familiar. An official of Ali's would be robbed, or pelted with refuse, or suffer some like insult, and a group of innocent locals would be blamed. The punishments ranged from extortionate fines to maiming and execution. When the locals loudly objected to the injustice, the official—goaded, no doubt, by the same vipers who had actually caused the trouble—would respond with greater brutality. As a result, scores of southern towns and villages were seething.

On his way south, Jason had listened sympathetically to the villagers' grievances, while counseling patience. Finally, he'd sent a trusted friend to the Vizier in Tepelena to urge Ali to replace his officials and pacify the people. There was no assurance Ali would do so. Even if he did, it would probably be too late.

A few agitators and a supply of weaponry could instantly whip outrage into open rebellion, as had happened every time before. Given the present level of frustration, the weaponry must be expected soon. Timing was everything. Jason guessed it was a matter of weeks. The weapons would surely come to one of the southern ports. But which one?

It was the same question he'd been asking himself for weeks. Pushing his supper away, Jason moved to the narrow window. Five days of unceasing rain. Mid-October already. Time was running out, and Bajo still hadn't come.

For all one knew, the south could surge into bloody revolt in days . . . with Esme and Percival caught in the midst of it. Jason had heard about Edenmont's arrival with the boy, and the ensuing events, but there was nothing he could do. A frantic dash north might, at best, be a waste of valuable time. At worst, it might endanger friends as well as kin. Jason had no idea what steps Bajo or other comrades had taken. His interference—even if he managed to interfere without being recognized—could undo whatever good others had done. He couldn't take the risk, though it ate at him to wait, as helpless in this matter as in the other.

His only comfort was that Ali hadn't blamed Ismal for the Red Lion's death and taken bloody revenge. That would have promptly triggered revolt in the north as well as the south. Jason had counted on Ali's greed and Ismal's cleverness to avert that catastrophe. Local gossip confirmed he'd judged correctly.

"Ismal claims it was the work of misguided men, overeager to curry favor," one old man had told him. "I do not know who killed Jason, only that Ali was happy to blame those Ismal accused, in order to have their riches and women. Some say Ismal should have been executed, because his followers would not act without his encouragement. I answer that Ali will not kill the goose who lays the golden eggs. Ismal may do as he likes, for he knows he may easily appease Ali by feeding his greed."

How much longer, though, would Ismal continue to appease his cousin? Jason swore to himself. What the devil did it matter? At present, both Esme and Percival were in danger. He was bitterly berating himself for hanging uselessly about Janina when he heard a pounding at the door and a rough, familiar voice calling his assumed name.

Minutes later, the weary Bajo sat at the low table, making quick work of the fish stew and maize bread Jason had had no stomach for.

Bajo took a swig from the wine bottle and wiped his mouth with his sleeve. "I should have done as you advised and knocked your daughter unconscious," he said. "Though I fear that would have been futile. It's clear the Fates conspire against us, for I, who'd give my life for you, haven't stepped once since I left you without stepping wrong."

Despite this ominous opening, Jason was prepared to wait patiently until his friend had eaten. But Bajo needed to unburden himself at least as much as he needed to fill his belly. While he ate, he talked.

The story which distressed Bajo so much eased Jason's anxieties considerably. Esme surely had reached Berat by now. She and Percival might even be on their way west to the coast—well protected by Maliq's men—or already upon a ship. She'd be traveling with a cousin fully prepared to like her and eager to fulfill his late mother's wish to send the girl to England. So Jason reassured his friend.

"I'm certainly not worried about Edenmont raising difficulties," he added. "He may not care a damn what becomes of Esme, but he cares a great deal about his own soft hide. He's probably frantic to be gone, and he'll have to take her with him, like it or not. Both Mustafa and Percival will see to that."

"So I've prayed, Red Lion," said Bajo. "But I fear I've made a great mistake in my haste to rejoin you." From the ammunition pouch at his waist he withdrew a piece of paper. Laying it on the table before Jason, he described his last meeting with Percival.

"I'd no time to look at it until after I left Ali," Bajo explained. "Since then, I've heard many things, and each night as I studied that paper, I grew more amazed."

Jason stared at the paper for a long while. It was not a riddle. Percival had drawn a boat with a black crown in one of its sails. There was a bit of black above, with a few stars. Within the hold, the boy had sketched a rifle. Beneath, in Greek characters, he'd written 'Prevesa.' Below that was the numeral one, followed by a question mark, and the numeral eleven. At the bottom of the page was a black heart, and beneath, the word 'MALIS'.

"This is incredible," he muttered. Yet all the facts he possessed and all Bajo had said obliged Jason to believe it: his twelve-year-old nephew had sent the answer. Prevesa, a southern port, was the smugglers' destination. The numbers must indicate early November, some two or three weeks hence, as he'd guessed. The crown and the night must signify the ship's name. Very useful. The British authorities might be able to identify and stop the vessel well before it reached Prevesa.

He raised his head. "I should have realized Percival had an urgent reason for coming to Albania. He'd overheard me telling his mother something of our problem, you see. I can only conclude that somewhere in Italy he overheard another conversation and decided I must be informed. When I turned out to be dead, he passed the information on to you."

"All I could think was that the boy had visions," Bajo answered. "This message tells all, even to the traitor's name: 'Malis' for 'Ismal.' And all so cautiously done, Red Lion. Not a word of this before Mustafa. No hint in the letter to Ali—for Fejzi, who's trustworthy, translated it in my presence."

"The letter to Ali was just an excuse to get writing materials quickly, before you could leave. Percival knew better than to warn Ali in a letter because Ismal might have been by when it was read.'' That extraordinary boy of Diana's had thought of everything.

''Still, your nephew has dangerous knowledge. I should never have left him in Berat.''

''If you'd taken him to Tepelena as you'd originally planned, Esme would have had the perfect excuse to go there as well,'' Jason pointed out. ''Then we'd have reason to worry. We both know why she left the ship and headed for Tepelena.''

''I know, Red Lion,'' Bajo said wearily. ''The little warrior wants Ismal's blood.''

''Now she has no excuse to go anywhere near him. Mustafa will see that Edenmont takes her and Percival west and out of the country as soon as possible.''

''All the same, I should have stayed in Berat and made certain.''

Jason clicked his tongue. ''If you had, I wouldn't have this. I might have gone on looking for the answer for weeks, most likely in vain.'' He crumpled up the note and tossed it onto the fire. In seconds, nothing remained of Percival's message but a few bits of soot, drifting upward on the smoke of the fire.

Turning back, Jason met Bajo's troubled gaze.

''Tomorrow we must start out for Corfu,'' Jason said firmly. ''We've got to notify the British authorities, find the ship, and track down Ismal's agents. Esme's surrounded by men determined to get her out of the country, men Ismal has no reason to fear. He only wanted her in order to control me, and I'm dead, recollect. All his attention now is fixed on southern Albania. I want to keep it there. Let him watch while this monster he's so laboriously created is dismembered, part by part. We can do it now, Bajo. Percival has given us the key.'' Jason smiled. ''He'll be terribly disappointed if we don't use it.''

Chapter 12

"Are you quite sure you don't want to come?" Percival asked for the tenth time. "Cousin Esme said the walk would do you good."

Varian stood at the doorway of Mustafa's house and let his gaze travel up the narrow path Percival, Mustafa, Mati, and Agimi were proposing to follow.

Mustafa's home stood in the upper reaches of the Mangalen quarter—a village that hugged the base of the rocky hill above the left bank of the River Osum. Its limestone houses crowded tightly along narrow, twisting streets.

There was far more to Berat, however. Above, a grim fortress crowned the precipice. Several churches as well as the palace of Ibrahim—official Pasha of Berat and currently Ali's prisoner in a Gjirokastra dungeon—lay within its walls, many of whose stones had been laid in remotest antiquity.

Antique or not, Varian was not about to tax his recently recovered body with a long, virtually perpendicular hike up the mountainside.

"What your cousin meant," he said, "is that it would do *her* good to watch me plummet from some crumbling stone down to the river, where my brain would be dashed to pieces upon the rocks."

"Good heavens, I'm sure Cousin Esme would never wish such a thing, and even if she did—that is to say, merely as a supposition—I doubt she'd put it in such a roundabout way. She is not at all indirect in her speech.

But, of course, that's not what she meant. It's not logical that she'd nurse you for a whole week if she wished you ill. Obviously—"

"She was trying to lull me into a false sense of security," Varian murmured.

"I beg your pardon, sir?"

"Nothing." Varian met the boy's puzzled gaze. "I was just being fanciful. I'm not delirious, Percival, I promise you. Run along. Don't keep the others waiting. I prefer the role of spectator."

Percival considered briefly. Then he gave a shrug and ran along. In a short while, Varian lost sight of the four figures, for they were soon swallowed up by the clustering white houses.

Berat was lovely in its way, Varian mused, with its limestone houses imbedded in the gray rock like rough white gems. Mustafa had said the place was more than two thousand years old. It had survived centuries of battle, conquest, destruction. Crushed, rebuilt, crushed, rebuilt again, it yet stubbornly clasped the rugged peak in fierce embrace. Like the people, Varian thought.

The sky had cleared in places today, though ponderous masses of gray clouds surged and rolled in the chill wind. This was not an English sky. Here the heavens seemed farther away, the clouds wilder. Even the great rock, thrusting up from the rolling landscape with the ancient fortress as its crown, seemed animate. One sensed some tumultuous presence, as though the ancient gods truly dwelt here. Even amid this quiet landscape, one sensed the storm throbbing at its heart.

It was the place, Varian told himself, and something in the air. He was simply caught in it, under its influence, like an opium eater. When he left, he'd be free.

He leaned against the door frame and closed his eyes. When he'd wakened from the oppressive fog of fever and wracking pain, he'd felt surprisingly clearheaded and strong. He'd smiled, and Esme had smiled in answer. But hers was a smile as impenetrable as Berat's unforgiving mountain. Though kind, gentle, and diligent in his care, she was shut away behind an empty smile and evergreen eyes that told him . . . nothing.

Varian had thought at first the change was because of Percival, who hovered nearby constantly, and talked. As the days passed, though, each more slowly than the one preceding, Varian had come to understand that Percival wasn't the reason.

Varian had also understood—and comprehension had come slowly, in a series of small, chill shocks—that nothing he did or said had any effect on her. It was as though he only imagined he spoke or acted, while Esme perceived but an inanimate lump, existing only to be arranged and examined, like one of Percival's rocks.

The sensation made him anxious, then angry, then miserable, and now, resigned, he supposed. Miserably resigned. It was hopeless and ought to be. It was better this way, really. What had he expected?

He heard footsteps and opened his eyes, but it was only Petro coming up the stony path from the *pazar*, panting and muttering to himself. Some weeks before their arrival, one of Ali's officials had passed through, along with a large entourage, and taken all the best horses. Mustafa had heard today that the horses had been returned at last, and Petro had gone with one of Mustafa's relatives to secure them for the journey west. The fat dragoman had wanted an excuse to avoid work, as usual.

"Did he get them?" Varian asked as Petro came to a wheezing halt before him.

"Aye. Good ones, though not so good as those which carried us to this cursed place."

"Esme advised us to send them back to Maliq. He needs them."

"Aye, and halfway to Fier, she will say someone needs these, and she will make us go by foot, and I shall fall by the way and die, and be glad, for it will be the end of my sufferings." With a loud moan, Petro sank down upon the stone bench beside the doorway.

"Don't be ridiculous. She'll hardly subject her young cousin to a forced march over the mountains."

Petro eyed him gloomily. "There is no knowing. She is not right in the head. I see it in her eyes. A wicked spirit lives there, and she is surely cursed. All was well with us until we came upon her in Durrës. In an instant—not five minutes—calamity fell upon us, and since, one calamity after another. Always you do as she says, and always, trouble follows—at the River Shkumbi and in Poshnja and here as well, for you fell gravely ill."

Not right in the head. Was that—no, gad, he was listening to this fat, superstitious sot.

"At present, I mean to do as *I* wish," Varian snapped. "Which is, I trust, amenable to your wishes as well—to leave Albania as soon as possible."

"I do not wish to leave with *her,*" the dragoman whined. "Let her go her own way and take her curse with her."

"The man who rescued Percival wanted us to take her to Corfu. It's the least we can do," Varian answered impatiently.

Then what? Percival had some fancy he was taking Esme back to England with him, which was ludicrous. One could hardly present the girl to Sir Gerald. That didn't bear thinking of. One needn't think of it, Varian told himself. Mustafa had said Jason had friends in Corfu. They'd take care of her. It had all been arranged. Esme couldn't stay here, that was certain. All that awaited her in Albania was violence and, if her would-be lover succeeded, degradation and slavery.

"She does not wish to go," Petro said. "She will make trouble. I feel it. I see it in her eyes. Her cousin speaks, and she smiles and answers softly, but her eyes . . ." He shuddered theatrically.

It was a waste of breath to argue with him, and Varian didn't know why he bothered. He was master here, after all. "Are you chilled?" he demanded. "Perhaps you want some exercise. Why don't you start packing? If we've got horses, there's no reason we can't start tomorrow." Varian pulled his cloak closed and, ignoring his dragoman's dark looks and darker mutterings, strode off down the path toward the *pazar*.

Varian had never before ventured anywhere in Albania without an interpreter. He was in no mood, however, for Petro's lachrymose drivel. Agimi and Mustafa were with

Percival, and Esme had taken herself off to the still-room. She was making a concoction of some sort for Eleni, who suffered from swelling in her knuckles. At any rate, it was quite clear that the last thing the girl wanted was Varian's company.

In the marketplace, he encountered one of Mustafa's friends, Viktor, who in rough Greek invited the lord to take a cup of *kafe* in a nearby coffee shop. A few others joined them and, the conversation proving amiable, Varian lingered at the *kafinet* more than an hour. Though his own Greek was as inept as Viktor's, it was sufficient for comprehension, and the time did not pass unpleasantly.

All the same, by the time he'd swallowed his third cup of thick Turkish brew, Varian was edgy. After a polite leave-taking, he decided to settle his nerves with a longer walk.

This section of the main road was unusually quiet for the time of day. Apart from himself, the only other moving object was one of the buffalo-drawn carts he'd seen before in Berat, carrying wood, hay, and other homely necessities.

Though the cart was some distance ahead, this was the nearest Varian had been to one, and what he observed was not calculated to inspire confidence. The wheels, poorly secured to the axles, wobbled like drunkards, threatening to reel loose and collapse into the muddy road. Varian tensed as the cart neared a narrow turn, where the road gave onto the steep riverbank.

The driver proved cautious, however, slowing his wagon nearly to a standstill as he reached the curve. At that moment, a slight, ragged youth climbed up from the bank and called out to the driver, who answered cheerily. The boy flung two leather bags onto the cart, then leapt in after them.

In stunned disbelief, Varian watched the child burrow under the hay. Then he spat out an oath and charged after the vehicle.

He caught up in minutes, grabbed the board at the rear, and hurled himself aboard. In the next instant, the cart struck a rut, Varian lost his balance, and toppled into the hay.

A woolen-encased head poked up from the mound beside him, and he caught a glimpse of startled green eyes. As Varian started toward her, Esme threw a mass of straw at him, then dashed for the back of the cart. He reached out and grabbed her leg. She staggered, her arms flailing wildly, then fell backward and landed hard upon him before he could roll out of the way.

She couldn't weigh more than six stone, but her head struck his right shoulder with force enough to crack one or the other, he was sure, as the pain ricocheted up his neck and down his arm. He'd no time to catch his breath, though, because she was trying to struggle up. He flung his aching arm over her, heaved her to the other side, and rolled on top of her. She stilled instantly.

Varian glared at her. Her woolen helmet had slipped down over her eyes. He yanked it off and threw it out of the cart.

The vehicle had rumbled to a stop, and the driver was shouting. Varian ignored him. "We're getting out," he told her. "Do you need a clip on the jaw, or will you come peaceably?"

"Don't hit me," she gasped. "I'll come."

Varian rolled off her, grabbed the bags, and flung them into the road.

She sat up, rubbing the back of her head, her green eyes wide with misery as she gazed about her. Varian jumped down from the cart and held out his hand. Esme stared at his hand a moment, then, tight-lipped, climbed out unaided. As her feet touched the ground, she swayed and caught at the cart for support.

Varian picked her up, carried her the few feet to the side of the road, and deposited her upon a large white rock.

The driver said something in Albanian and laughed. Esme's color deepened to scarlet.

Varian dug into the inner pocket of his coat and pulled out a coin. Throwing Esme a warning glance, he approached the driver.

"Faleminderit," he told the driver. "I'm sorry for your trouble." He held out the coin. The Albanian hesitated a moment, then nodded and clicked his tongue.

"Oh, yes, you must," Varian said. "Buy yourself some *raki.*"

The driver looked from Varian to Esme, smiled, shrugged, and took the coin. After another incomprehensible speech, he drove away.

Varian picked up the leather pouches and marched back to the rock. He dropped them at her feet.

His entire body pounded with outrage. His chest was tight with it, and it beat in his ears, making the tranquil landscape about him throb as well, like a great, hammering sea. He looked at her.

In the sullen afternoon light, her hair glinted deep copper sparks. Yet it was a rat's nest of tangles and bits of straw and several knotty tendrils stuck damply to her face. She'd dug out her worst, oldest garments, or, more likely, traded some beggar for these.

Had he lingered another few minutes at the coffee shop, she'd have got clean away. He should have let her go, to the Devil if she wanted. He wasn't responsible for her. He didn't want to be responsible for anybody. Percival he'd been paid to look after, and couldn't do even that simple task properly. How was one to look after her? What was one to *do* with her?

Varian looked about him, at the river glistening in the fitful light, and at the tiny village on its opposite bank. Hills completely enclosed the narrow valley. In Berat, even from the citadel, one could see nothing of what lay beyond.

Varian didn't want to see, didn't want to think about what lay beyond, ahead. All he wanted from tomorrow was to get away. Only he wouldn't. Even far away, Esme would haunt him. He spun round to face her.

"What the devil is wrong with you?" he demanded. "Where in blazes did you think you'd go? How far did you think you'd get—a girl, alone and penniless? How far before your would-be lover tracked you down, or you stumbled into the hands of others less loving?"

"A great deal is wrong, Varian *Shenjt Gjergj,*" she said. "Keep me, and you make it worse. I cannot go to Corfu with you." Esme raised her head. Her cool green gaze was steady. "You of all people must see that. You are a man of the world. You know your world. You have seen mine. You know me as well.''

He clenched his fists. He wanted to shake her. A moment ago, he'd offered to strike her. He could not recall when he'd ever felt so desperately angry. Or angrily desperate. He knew he was a fool. He knew he was behaving like a brute, yet he couldn't stop it. Even while he told himself to calm down and *think*, the fury rose in his throat, nearly choking him.

''Then go, damn you!'' he shouted. ''Go to the Devil. Get yourself raped—killed. What is it to me, you little lunatic? All who care about you—men older and easily wiser than I—are ready to move heaven and earth to get you to Corfu. But you think you know what's best, don't you? Never mind that you'll break Percival's heart. Never mind that a few weeks' travel with you is the only happiness he's got to look forward to for the next ten years. He's just a twelve-year-old boy who doesn't know any better. And the rest of us are just a lot of stupid men, irrational, illogical, *blind,* because we want you to be safe.''

''Listen to me,'' she said. She put out her hand. ''Take my hand, Varian. Be a friend to me, and listen.''

He was afraid to touch her. His rage would weaken, and he didn't want to feel what lay within it. He turned away and stared blindly into the distance.

''Please, Varian. Will you destroy my life without giving me a hearing?''

He could have borne her angry reproach and all the lashing fury she was capable of. This too quiet plea he couldn't. The shell of rage cracked, Varian saw himself, and shame washed over him.

She had looked after him, attended him patiently, made his way as comfortable as she could. In return, he'd tried to ruin her. He'd soiled her innocent mouth with his polluted kisses, corrupted her innocent flesh with his filthy hands. He wanted her still, more than ever. He'd stopped her escape not for her sake but for his. In his twisted mind, Esme had become his property. He needed her, and so, she must stay with him.

Varian exhaled a defeated sigh and turned to her. He

took her small hand in both of his and crouched before her. "I'm listening," he said.

"My father is dead," she said, her voice expressionless. "Of my English kin, that leaves Percival's father and grandmother. They do not want me. They may have tolerated me for Jason's sake, but they would not have taken me in. They might accept a genteel young lady as his daughter, but even Jason could not make me one. Do you think I am mistaken in this, Varian?" she asked quietly. "Tell me truly."

He wanted to lie. He couldn't, not under that steadfast green gaze. "No."

"Perhaps someone, even my young cousin, may persuade them to charity. That is bad enough in any case, but in England, among foreigners—I do not think I could bear it. It is my fault, perhaps. I am too proud."

"Yes. Proud."

"Here, in my own country, I have no kin but my grandmother in Gjirokastra. I can go to live with her, but she is old, and when she dies, I shall have no home, no kin. I will become Ali's property, to dispose of as he wishes. So you see, my best hope is to get a husband."

"Oh, Lord." Varian knew what was coming. Already his mind had frantically scrambled down every path, seeking a solution. He knew what it was. There was only one answer. A sick dread settled upon his heart.

"I am going to Ismal," she said.

"Oh, lovely." His voice was taut. "The man who killed your father."

She clicked her tongue, the Albanian "tsk" that negated and dismissed in an instant. "Even Mustafa does not believe that. I have thought on it long and hard, and find I cannot believe it, either. I told you some of my thoughts in Poshnja. It makes no sense to me, to anybody. Bajo alone blamed Ismal, but I believe Bajo would have said anything to make me leave. He thought of nothing but my father's wish to take me to England. He did not think how Jason's death changed everything. It is much the same with my poor cousin. He wants to fulfill his mother's wish—a kind one, if Jason had lived, even if she had lived. But they are gone, and their wish is gone, impossible.''

Varian bowed his head. He wanted to argue, but all he could offer were sweet assurances, to bury the bitter truth. If he took her away, she'd be miserable. To live in exile would be hard enough in the best of circumstances. To be exiled among people who'd despise or pity her, in a world where she could never belong? Her spirit couldn't bear it. Esme was fearless. Physical danger didn't alarm her. The life awaiting her in England, though, would surely kill her, and she knew it.

He felt her brush a lock of hair back from his forehead, as she'd done countless times when he lay ill. Always he wanted to kiss that hand in gratitude, because its magic touch dissolved pain and trouble. Now it burned his skin like acid, and the poison streamed through his blood, a searing river of jealousy, frustration, and fear.

He saw a fair-haired stranger with blue jewel eyes who'd wanted her badly enough to steal her . . . her hand, brushing back that golden hair . . . her voice, low and soft, telling this young prince of the white mountainside and the fir trees and the rushing river . . . her supple body, roused to passion in the arms of a young man of her own kind, who'd murmur love words in her own tongue.

It was right, wasn't it? To Varian the vision was loathsome, yet it was Esme's only hope of happiness. He wanted her. He needed her. That was all. He'd nothing to offer but promises, and those must be lies, because whatever he felt, always, was for the moment. Nothing lasted, least of all desire.

''Will you help me?'' she asked. ''Will you let me go?''

''Yes,'' Varian said, raising his head at last. ''No.''

Chapter 13

They stood by the side of the road for more than an hour, arguing. Yes, Varian would help her. No, he most certainly would *not* allow her to go alone to Tepelena.

Forcing herself to remain calm, Esme tried to explain how reasonable and safe her plan was: she'd worked out her route carefully; she knew what she was doing.

It was no use. He wouldn't listen. If she wouldn't return willingly to Mustafa's, his lordship coldly told her, he would pick her up and carry her—kicking and screaming, if necessary.

In icy silence, Esme returned with him to the house, then stormed to her cousin's room. She found Percival studying the rocks he'd collected that day.

Reluctant to spoil the boy's excitement about his discoveries, Esme dutifully inspected the heap of stones.

"We'd best hire a couple of donkeys," she said. "Your own pouch will never hold all these. You might build a fortress with what you've gathered in Berat alone."

"They're much too small to build with," he answered patiently. "But I do mean to make an organized display, with notes on every specimen. Perhaps in the library at the country house. The estate was Grandfather's," he explained, "so it's Papa's, but Papa hates it, and lets Grandmama live there. He can't sell it, you see, because the property's entailed."

Here Percival launched into a dissertation on primogeniture. Only with great perseverance did Esme succeed in leading him back to his plans for the rocks.

When she was gone, she would think of her young cousin. She didn't want to reflect upon his lonely existence. She wanted to envision him happy, organizing his rock collection and making his voluminous notes about them. Then he'd grow into a man with children of his own. He'd show them the stones of Albania and tell of his adventures, and of the Red Lion and the cousin who looked like him. He'd not forget her, not Percival. By the time he was a man, he'd surely have forgiven her for deserting him. No, more than that. He'd understand then, and thank her in his heart for sparing him.

"They belong in a library, don't you think?" he was saying. "Because rocks are like books. What they're made of tells you about their history. Now they're part of my history as well. Of course, I shall have to keep them in boxes until I'm grown up, because Grandmama doesn't—"

"Hush." Esme held her hand up. "Someone's come."

"I don't hear anything."

She'd sensed it minutes before, though she'd not really heeded, for it was only a vague awareness, far beyond Percival's voice and her own troubled thoughts. She heard clearly now: heavy footsteps, and the murmur of voices.

"Good heavens," said Percival. "What acute hearing you must have, to be sure. I just now—but it's like Durrës. You heard the men coming well before I did." Then his eyes opened very wide, and Esme saw a flash of panic there.

The voices were distinct now. Lord Edenmont's, clipped and irritated, though she couldn't make out what he said. Another voice soon rose above the rest and launched into grandiloquence.

Percival started to get up. Esme grabbed his arm, and he sank back down.

"What's wrong?" he whispered. "Something's wrong, isn't it?"

He must sense the tension in her, just as Esme sensed the trouble itself. Not that one needed especially acute perceptions. Authority had its own sound, an arrogance one heard in a man's footfall as well as his voice. She had felt its approach and heard it clearly when it invaded the house. There was but one authority in these realms. The voice only confirmed, allowing her to put a name to the speaker: Fejzi, one of Ali's secretaries.

"Something must be wrong," she answered, speaking her thoughts aloud, scarcely aware of the boy near her as she concentrated on the voices. "There was no reason for them to come, not in such numbers. A dozen at least—no, more—perhaps a score. Ali's men." She paused a moment as another voice launched into fulsome speech.

Nearby, she heard an odd, choked sound. Turning to her cousin, she found he'd gone white.

"Oh, dear." He grasped her hand. "Oh, dear, oh, dear."

"What?"

He stared at her with glazed eyes. "Oh, dear. It's my fault. It's *him.*"

"Who? Risto?" she demanded, for that was the new voice. One of Ali's men, but also one of Ismal's associates. "You know him?"

The hand clutching hers had grown cold and damp. "He never saw me," the boy said. His voice was shaky. "I'm positive. Oh, dear."

"Saw you when? What is wrong with you? There is no reason to be frightened. They'd not harm you." Esme released his hand and moved closer to put her arm about his thin shoulders. He trembled. "Come, Percival. You are a brave boy. You're not afraid of a lot of stupid courtiers."

"Yes, I am. I think—oh, it's most embarrassing, but I do think I'm going to be *sick.*"

In an instant, she'd hauled him to his feet. In the next, she was pushing him through the door, then pulling him down the narrow passage leading to the small courtyard at the rear of the house. As they descended the stairs, she saw no soldiers loitering about. Whatever their reason for coming, it hadn't motivated them to surround the house. That was reassuring.

Percival's near-hysterical state was not. He was not an hysterical sort of boy. He'd endured an abduction and called it an exciting adventure. He never screamed in the night, plagued by terrifying dreams. He never seemed uneasy or tense or anxious. He was, Esme felt certain, composed of the same stoical fiber as herself. If he was frightened, then he must have good reason.

Y'Allah, but even in this state he would not forget his wretched rocks. He'd snatched up his pouch as she dragged him from the room. Now he clutched at it while he leaned against the low garden wall and gasped for air.

"Oh, thank heaven," he said, after his chest had finally stopped heaving. "It would be mortifying to cast up my accounts in front of a girl."

"Percival, they may call for us at any moment," she said sternly. "Have you something to tell me? What is wrong?"

He bit his lip and looked down at his feet, then at the stairs to his right, then at the curved gateway before him, then down the stony path to his left, then, finally, at her. "I think I've made a dreadful mistake," he said, "I'm—oh, it's no use to be sorry, is it? I'm always sorry after, but then it's too late, isn't it? Oh, I do wish Papa had sent me to school in India. I never thought he was particularly sensible, and Mama did say the climate would kill me, but for once Papa may have been right. Except that maybe India wouldn't be far enough away, and I daresay one school is much like the rest. But perhaps they're the only ones who'd have me. Being so far away, you see, they may not have heard. I assure you, the pig was for a scientific experiment, and how was I to know that one mustn't place a lighted candle near—"

"Percival, you are babbling," Esme said sharply. "Stop it this instant."

He bit his lip and hugged the pouch tightly, apparently oblivious to its stony contents, which were bound to leave bruises.

"You are hurting yourself," she snapped. "Put the curst bag down." She reached out to take it from him, but he spun away so quickly that Esme lost her balance. Making a clumsy grab to pull her up, Percival lost his own footing. They tumbled to the cobblestones in a tangle of arms and legs, the bag slipping from his grasp and its contents spilling about them.

Percival was on his knees in an instant, scrambling to gather up his rocks. Cursing under her breath, Esme started to pull herself up to a sitting position. She swore loudly, for something hard and angular jabbed her bottom. She shifted away to snatch up the offending object. Then she paused, staring at it.

A tiny crowned head poked out of a ragged cloth wrapping. Percival gave a low, anguished groan but remained kneeling where he was, his green eyes fixed on the shrouded object in her hand. Esme swiftly unwound the rest of the fabric.

"A most unusual rock," she said.

Percival sat back on his heels.

She studied the small, regal figure. "It looks like a chess piece."

"Please," he whispered miserably. "Please don't tell. *Anybody.*"

"You tricked Lord Edenmont," she said. "You told him you'd given it to Jason, but you had stolen it yourself."

"I didn't—that is—"

"You knew he needed money."

"Everyone knows that," her cousin answered defensively. "Papa bribed him to take me to Venice."

"And you bribed him to take you to Albania instead. Why?"

Percival squirmed, his eyes darting anxiously about. "I can't tell you. You'd never believe me anyhow."

"Very well." Esme rose. "I shall go to Lord Edenmont and give him this chess piece he wanted so badly."

The house behind Percival was filled with Ali's men. One of them was Risto, the tool of the evil Ismal. It didn't take a genius to deduce that Ismal had something to do with their arrival. From which one might reasonably conclude that Ismal had got hold of the message to Bajo and knew that Percival Brentmor had tried to betray him.

As soon as he'd thought it, Percival had panicked, convinced Risto had come to kill him. It had taken only a few minutes to recognize his error. Ismal was too clever and devious to murder a twelve-year-old English boy, especially when there was a much simpler way to keep the boy quiet.

Cousin Esme. All Ismal had to do was lure her to Tepelena. Then Percival wouldn't dare utter a word against him. And once Ismal got her to into his clutches, he certainly wouldn't let go. Ever.

The worst was that Cousin Esme would probably jump at the chance to go to Tepelena. Percival knew she didn't want to go to England. He was sure, in fact, she'd tried to run away earlier. From a window he'd watched her return to the house with Lord Edenmont, both looking as though they'd been wrestling violently in a muddy field, and both furious.

Now she was proposing to run back to his lordship, waving the black queen in his face. With Risto there to see it.

Percival stood up. "I did steal it," he lied. "I hadn't any choice. Uncle Jason told me about a conspiracy to overthrow Ali Pasha. A few weeks ago, at the Castle of Bari, I overheard Risto arranging with another man to ship smuggled weapons to a man named Ismal, in Albania. I tricked his lordship into coming so that I could warn Uncle Jason."

Despite the patent incredulity on her face, Percival went on to describe the secret message he'd given Bajo, and what he'd just deduced: Ismal had intercepted the message and sent men to lure Esme to Tepelena, to make her his hostage.

"Spies. Conspiracy." Esme gave him a pitying look. "You have too much imagination. You heard some men talking of rifles or pistols—which men often do—and in your mind you discover a great conspiracy. It is not a terrible thing to be fanciful, cousin. Perhaps you will become a poet one day."

"It wasn't imagination," Percival protested. "I heard it. Risto's voice. I'd know it anywhere. His Italian was terrible, and his English even worse."

"You heard something, and your clever brain embroidered it," she said. "But this was long ago. Now you cannot distinguish between what you truly heard and the evil you imagined, and so you frighten yourself. Ismal is too clever and cautious to attempt a hopeless rebellion. He knows how clever Ali is. Men have been trying for years to overthrow the Vizier. They always fail, and always pay dearly—along with all their friends and kin."

She gave him back the chess piece. "I will not tell his lordship what you have done. I owe him no loyalty. Besides, it is most amusing how cleverly you tricked him. Now I see how foolish I was to try to deal openly and honestly with him. I must take my lesson from you."

Percival stood a moment in mute indignation, watching her hurry up the stairs. Then, as he recollected what she was hurrying toward, panic seized him. He dashed up the steps, calling to her to stop, but she wouldn't listen, only darted down the passage, straight to the door behind which disaster waited.

Even while he shrieked at her, Esme was pushing the door open. Without pausing to think, Percival burst in after her—and collided with Lord Edenmont.

As he staggered back, stammering apologies, Percival saw that his lordship had got Esme by the arm. She wore a particularly unfriendly expression. His lordship didn't notice. He was bending his own unfriendly expression upon Percival.

"Take your cousin," he said in a low, definitely unfriendly voice, "and go to your room, Percival. *Now.*"

"Certainly, sir. Immediately, sir." Percival politely offered his arm to his cousin. "Cousin Esme?"

She clicked her tongue.

Percival's heart sank. The room had grown very quiet, and everyone was watching them. 'Everyone' included about twenty men, some of them as big as Bajo.

"My Lord Edenmont, if you please." A short, fat man wearing a dirty yellow turban stepped out from the crowd. "It is because of the Red Lion's daughter that I have come. My master wished me to convey his message to her directly."

Lord Edenmont said something under his breath.

Though Percival couldn't make out what it was, he could guess. He was rather exasperated with Esme himself, though at the moment what he mostly felt was terror.

Releasing Esme's arm, Lord Edenmont said, "Miss Brentmor will remain. Master Brentmor, however, will return to his room. Agimi. Mati. See that he stays there."

A true hero would have stood his ground. Percival wanted to be a true hero, but his stomach wouldn't let him. He saw Risto staring at him, and the horrid feeling of sickness welled up. Percival hurried out the door and on to his room, Agimi and Mati following close behind him.

Once safely inside, he lay down and tried to make himself breathe slowly and calmly. It took a very long time for his stomach to settle. He couldn't stop trembling, though. He'd made a ghastly error of judgment in telling Cousin Esme. She didn't believe him. And she was probably going to make Lord Edenmont so angry that he'd be happy to let the men take her away. Forever.

Percival stared hard at the ceiling. It was all his fault. He should never have given Bajo that message. He should have considered his cousin's safety. Now it was too late.

He crawled from the bed, got down on his knees, closed his eyes tightly, and prayed as hard as he could.

But he'd prayed for Mama, hadn't he, and for Uncle Jason, and God wouldn't listen. God had *never* listened before, not once. Why should He start now?

Percival jumped up and began to pound frantically on the bedroom door.

Varian flung the door open and entered Percival's room. He had heard the pounding and sent one of the men to quiet the boy, but the boy wouldn't be quieted. Percival had threatened to bash his skull against the door if he couldn't speak to Lord Edenmont.

"I'm here," Varian said curtly. "What the devil is this tantrum about?"

"You can't let them take her, sir," Percival said, rubbing his reddened knuckles. "No matter how angry you are. You can't."

"Indeed. She says I must and you say I mustn't. Do I look like Solomon to you, Percival?"

Varian moved to the narrow window, which offered a thin slice of darkening sky above the red-tiled roofs. "Sit down," he said. "I've something to tell you. You won't like it any better than I do. There's a great deal in life one doesn't like yet must accept all the same."

"But, sir—"

"*Sit.* And listen." Varian glared at him. Percival hastily crossed to the wooden *sofa* and sat.

In a few terse sentences, Varian summarized Esme's view of her situation and what she felt must be done about it.

"Well, yes, of course," Percival said impatiently. "That's all quite obvious. Naturally, she'd think so. But she *is* a girl."

"Most astute of you to notice. What's that got to say to anything?"

"Well, she's *wrong*. I don't mean to say she's not intelligent. She is. But she's a girl, you see, and naturally she'd think marriage was the only solution. Also, being a delicate member of the weaker sex—"

"*Delicate?*"

Percival gazed gravely at him. "The feminine constitution is delicate, sir, and you must recollect she's recently suffered any number of shocks to her tender sensibilities."

"Tender? Sensibilities? Your rocks have more sensibilities. There's not a delicate bone in her . . . Damnation." Varian turned abruptly to the window.

"I know she *appears* strong," Percival said, "and altogether rational. But I assure you, she isn't. When the men came, she nearly swooned, and I was obliged to take her out to the courtyard for a brisk walk in the fresh air. Then she became hysterical—"

"Percival."

"Indeed, she must have, sir, because she was carrying on about *curses*, of all things. She said she was a curse to everyone, and that everyone she loved got killed, and I'd be killed, too, if she stayed with me. She said the best thing she could do was marry her worst enemy, because she could get rid of him without lifting a finger. Then she laughed and ran back into the house. So naturally I felt obliged to run after her. I was concerned she might injure herself. It was obvious she was not in her right mind."

She is not right in the head.

Varian swung round to face the boy, who composedly met his suspicious scrutiny. "You expect me to believe that your cousin is a candidate for Bedlam?"

"Oh, no, sir. I hope I didn't imply she was *insane.* The symptoms would be much more obvious, I should think. Even you would notice. I meant only that the strain of recent weeks has been too much for her, and being a female, and therefore delicate, she's unable to think logically."

Varian winced. He'd certainly contributed to unhinging her, hadn't he? Yet how calm she had been, even after he'd dragged her from the cart and berated her in the most hurtful way he could think of. He'd expected her to scream back accusations, tear him to pieces with that razor tongue of hers. She'd not behaved normally, had she? Not normal for Esme, that is. Too quiet, too coldly quiet. Was it because she'd slipped into a twisted world of her own? Was that why she had been so chilly and distant all this last, interminable week? He eyed Percival warily.

"Do you know," Varian said, "I am convinced that between you and your cousin I shall not have a particle of wit remaining."

Percival bowed his head. "I'm dreadfully sorry, sir."

"I let you convince me to come to this madhouse of a country, and I have let her persuade me repeatedly to courses of action against my better judgment. Today I made her a promise, which you now indicate I can't keep. I promised I'd help her remain with her own people. I *promised,*" he repeated angrily.

"Yes, but it doesn't count, does it, if she was lying? That is to say, she didn't *mean* to lie, I'm sure. Very likely, she didn't even realize she was lying. I mean, you might consider her an amnesiac, mightn't you, in a manner of speaking? When she recovers, she'll probably have forgotten the whole thing."

"It's not that simple, my boy." Varian exhaled a sigh. "There are twenty-two men in the other room, sent by Ali Pasha to escort us all to Tepelena."

Esme ruthlessly shoved her elbow into Petro's fat gut and pushed past him into Lord Edenmont's bedchamber.

"Are you mad?" she demanded. "You cannot take that boy to Tepelena."

His lordship paused in the act of pulling off his boot. "Ah, I might have known," he said. "I can only be grateful you held your tongue before the others." He looked past her to the doorway, where Petro groaned, clutching his belly.

"Go away, Petro," he said, "and be thankful she didn't aim for your privates."

The door slammed shut, cutting off a stream of Turkish curses.

Varian yanked off the boot and tossed it next to its mate. Then he gave Esme a long, slow survey that made her face unpleasantly warm.

"Most gracious of you to change for supper," he murmured. "But I daresay you decided you had frightened them sufficiently with your first explosion upon the scene. Twenty-two strong men nearly fainted dead away at the sight of you."

Esme winced inwardly. She'd never thought what a hideous spectacle she must have looked, her hair filled with straw and dirt and her scrawny frame lost in the too-large goatherd's garments. She'd traded the red frock she'd got in Poshnja for the clothes. Percival hadn't made any remark, and so she'd forgotten her ghastly appearance—until she burst in upon Ali's men and saw their mouths drop open.

"I did not come to listen to your ignorant jokes," she said. "I came to see if you had taken a fever, for surely you must be delirious to accept Ali's invitation. You cannot take my cousin there."

"No, my dear. I'm taking *you* there, as I promised.

Percival is simply a necessary adjunct. I can't leave him here."

"You said you would not let me go alone. I shall not be alone. I shall have twenty-two men to escort me."

"More like thirty," he said. "Ali's men, plus myself and Percival, plus Agimi and Mati and the rest of our escort. If, that is, they decide to accompany us. I left it up to them."

His calmness was not encouraging. Esme tried another tack. "Varian, please—"

"Don't even think of wheedling," he interrupted in that same maddeningly calm voice. "I've had quite enough of the Brentmor brand of managing for one day, thank you. Go to bed. We'll be making an early start tomorrow."

She wanted to strike him. She wanted to dash his thick English skull against the stone wall. She told herself to wheedle anyhow, but rage and panic ruled her tongue. "You great, reckless fool! You cannot take Percival to Tepelena!"

He lifted one dark eyebrow a fraction of an inch, but his gray eyes remained blank as stone.

So had he been when she burst into the roomful of men earlier. He'd sat, listening to Fejzi repeat Ali's invitation and relay the Vizier's condolences upon the loss of her father, and never once had Lord Edenmont's cool expression changed. He was every inch the English lord, incurious, unmoved, his face a polite mask. When the others had finally done with their endless speeches, he hadn't troubled to respond to their flattery, or even express his gratitude for the honor proffered him. Instead he appeared bored, and answered coldly that he would inform them of his decision after supper.

His insolence, predictably, earned their respect. He behaved like a sultan who condescended to endure the ennui of being pestered for favors, and they treated him accordingly. He could have bade them to the devil, and they'd have had to accept it. He was a lord and a British subject besides. All the same, he'd bowed to Ali's wishes in the end. Esme still couldn't believe he could be such an idiot.

He didn't deign to answer now, only continued to regard her in that supercilious way. He made her feel very small, every inch a barbarian. She lifted her chin.

"You cannot take Percival to Tepelena," she repeated. "I shall not permit it."

"Don't be tiresome, child. Go to bed."

"I am not a child!" she cried, stamping her foot.

"You're behaving like one."

Esme marched across the room to him. "Must I do all your thinking for you? Do you understand where you are going? Ali's court is dangerous, intrigue everywhere—corruption, debauchery. To such a place you wish to take my young cousin?"

"If it's all right for you, I don't see why it isn't for him. He is a male, after all, not possessed of delicate feminine sensibilities." Varian unwrapped his neckcloth and threw it aside in his usual careless, lordly way.

Esme automatically retrieved it and began folding it while her mind worked feverishly for the words and tone to pierce this stone wall of indifference.

His sharp oath startled her. He got up and tore the neckcloth from her hands. "Drat you, Esme, don't do that! Stop picking up after me! You're not my bloody servant!"

She stared up at him.

He stared back, and the air about them throbbed with tension, as though a storm threatened in the surrounding hills. The storm was all in his eyes, though, dark as a lowering sky.

His hands caught in her hair and pulled her head back, and his mouth crashed down upon hers, hard enough to make her stagger.

He had seemed so coolly composed a moment ago, but she understood now it was only seeming. His mouth was hot and punishing, and his hands dragged angrily through her hair. She felt a surge of relief, then a surge of shame for it.

Esme tried to shut him out, but his onslaught was too sudden. His fierce kiss was a lightning bolt that crackled through her and left her will in ashes.

All the suppressed longing of the last week rushed

through her and heated into need. She grabbed the lapels of his coat and held on tight, as though she feared he'd escape.

The kiss lasted but a moment, and when his mouth released her, she nearly cried out in frustration. He slid his hands to her shoulders, then down, to clasp her arms, but more gently. She didn't want gentleness. She wanted to be crushed and conquered. She wanted to be driven beyond conscience and reason.

"Little liar," he said. "You want me."

It was no use. Esme closed her eyes tightly, then slowly bent her head until it touched his chest.

"You ought to know better." His voice had softened. "But I don't want you to. I won't let you."

"Everyone wants you," she told his coat sadly. "You cannot help it. When Ali sees you, he will weep, and half his courtiers will weep with him, and all the women. I shall be sick."

He laughed, then tipped her head back to gaze intently into her eyes. She wanted to look away but couldn't, and felt a blush steal up her cheeks.

"I think you're trying to turn me up sweet," he said. "You do it surprisingly well for such an obstinate little wildcat. In other circumstances, I suspect you might do whatever you like with me. But not this time, Esme. If you want to give yourself to me tonight, I won't say no. I'm cad enough to take whatever you give. But it will change nothing. Tomorrow we can go south, or we can go west. Either way, though, we go together."

Esme jerked away. "Y'Allah, but you are impossible. Do you think I am trying to bribe you with my body?"

"I think you'd do anything to bend me to your will."

"I? It is you who fight unfairly. When you cannot argue sensibly, you must try to subdue me with embraces." She eyed him up and down, resentfully. "You *know* you can make me witless."

He smiled. "Then at least we struggle on equal terms. You reduce me to a babbling idiot. Am I not entitled to do the same to you? You're the one who fights unfairly. You want to go to Tepelena, desperately, to unite with your golden prince. Yet you don't want me and Percival there to witness your joy. What is it you're hiding from us, Esme? What is it you don't want us to see?"

She caught her breath. She knew he wasn't altogether brainless. She'd never dreamed, however, his wits could be so quick. Or had Percival told him that pack of nonsense about a conspiracy?

But Percival couldn't have. Varian would never have consented to go to Tepelena with a child who babbled of revolutionary plots. Perhaps Esme should tell him herself . . . but then he'd not let her go, either.

She was trapped. "I've nothing to hide," she answered tightly. "It was my cousin I feared for. But you are right. He's not a babe. He will not die of shock to see a den of iniquity. More likely, he will take notes, and when you return him to his kin, they will blame you for corrupting him. But what do you care? I tell you of the court's depravity, and it only whets your appetite, I suppose. Your mind is filled with the harem, and you know Ali will give you women. I should have realized. You've been too long without a whore. Well, it is nothing to me. I shall find my own pleasure there as well—with my golden prince."

She turned and stalked out.

Chapter 14

Though the punishing rain continued, the entourage reached Tepelena in four days. They might have reached it even sooner, but Fejzi insisted on easy stages. Each day they halted well before sundown, to be quartered with the wealthiest citizens of the area. No more camping out in the muck. No more shaving with icy water. No more stale bread.

Each night they feasted and afterward slept on thick bedding in warm chambers. When Varian woke in the morning, he'd find his linen freshly laundered, his coat and trousers well brushed, his muddy, stained boots polished, and fresh towels and hot water awaiting his morning ablutions.

His slightest whim was fulfilled in an instant. He was treated with unremitting deference. Petro, who was certain they accompanied Esme to their doom, subsided into gloomy but generally silent servility.

Even Percival behaved himself. He did not fall off his horse, or into a river, or out of a window. He was a paragon of docility, showing no interest in anything or anybody but his cousin, whom he stuck to like a leech. And she was so quiet and obedient it made Varian's flesh creep.

By day Esme rode with Percival, closely guarded by soldiers. At night she was shut away with the Moslem women. Being a mere boy, and an apparently undernourished one at that, Percival was allowed to be shut up with them, so they might dote upon him and stuff him with sweetmeats.

Lord Edenmont, meanwhile, had to sit for hours and burn his gullet with *raki* and smoke rich tobacco until his head swam. Ali's representatives treated him like visiting royalty, and he soon found royalty a wearisome business.

He could not sleep properly and blamed it on the rich food, drink, and tobacco. Because he slept badly, he woke in a foul temper. By the time they reached Tepelena, he wanted to kill somebody—anybody—and preferably with his bare hands. He viewed the small, unprepossessing town with disfavor and Ali's recently rebuilt palace with loathing.

He hadn't read Hobhouse's account of his travels with Byron in Albania, though it had been published well over a year ago. Varian had, however, heard Byron's own account. The view he now beheld accorded in most particulars.

The palace enclosed two sides, and a tall wall encompassed the other two of the court they had just entered. It was filled with heavily armed soldiers and richly accoutred horses. At the corner furthest from the palace, animals were being slaughtered and dressed—yet another indigestible feast in the making.

The rest of the group would lodge elsewhere, while Varian, Percival, Esme, and Petro were to be quartered in the palace itself. They followed Fejzi up a flight of wooden steps and down a long gallery, thence into one of its two wings, which housed several apartments.

The chamber Varian entered was a shock, given the general run of Albanian habitations. It was a large room, lined with the usual perimeter of *sofas*, but these were covered with silk. The floors were thickly strewn with rich carpets and the walls hung with lavishly printed fabric.

"Your sleeping quarters are above, my lord," Fejzi explained. He indicated a low entryway that led to a set of narrow wooden stairs. "Please make yourself comfortable. Refreshment will be here momentarily.

Meanwhile, I must take the girl to the harem. It is not seemly—"

"Miss Brentmor does not go to the harem," Varian said frigidly.

"Certainly not," Percival piped up. He took Esme's hand.

She didn't shake him off, as Varian expected, only stood quietly, her face expressionless.

Fejzi's posture stiffened. "Your indulgence, my lord, but it is the rule. We do not permit the females to wander shamelessly about, as the infidels—" He paused, then went on contritely, "I beg your forgiveness, oh great one, but all must bow to the law."

"A woman submits to the law of her male kin. He's standing next to her, and he says she's to remain. Do you mean to insult Master Brentmor the instant he reaches the palace to which Ali has invited him?" A full five inches taller than the chubby secretary, Varian gazed coldly down his nose at Fejzi as though the height were as many miles.

Fejzi hesitated, plainly torn. He appeared, in fact, scared to death, but whether of Varian or of Ali's wrath one could not tell. Finally, he bowed his head. "As you wish," he said. He salaamed himself out of the apartment.

When the secretary's hurried footsteps had faded away, Varian looked at Esme, who had still not uttered a sound. "Nothing to say? Aren't you going to berate us for insulting your countryman and affronting Moslem dignity?"

She shrugged. "It makes no matter. I shall enter the harem soon enough. Better as the bride of a prince than an orphaned nobody."

"You're *welcome*," Varian said icily.

Green fire flashed back at him. "I beg your pardon, oh great light of the heavens. A thousand, thousand thanks for preserving me from the unspeakable perils of the harem: three hundred bored women and their deadly eunuch companions."

"Three hundred?" Percival echoed. "Good heavens!" He looked at Varian. "What is a eunuch?"

"Lord Edenmont's destiny," Esme snapped, "if he chooses to make a habit of flouting Ali's commands."

"Yes, but what is—"

"A man," she said, "who has—"

"Petro!" Varian shouted, though the dragoman stood no farther than the door.

"Aye, master?"

"Take Percival upstairs and see that he gets a proper wash and changes his clothes. He's crawling with fleas."

Before Petro could move, Esme grabbed Percival's shoulder. "A man, but not a man, because—" In a flash Varian clapped his hand over her mouth and pulled her away.

"Take the boy upstairs!" he bellowed.

Percival didn't wait to be taken. He shot Varian one panicked look and dashed to the entryway and on up the stairs. Petro hastily waddled after him.

When they had disappeared, Varian took his hand away, marveling that she hadn't bitten him.

"I'll thank you to refrain from enlightening the boy regarding the filthy practices of this misbegotten country," he said.

"It is Mohammedan practice, and there is no reason my cousin should not know. You chose to bring him here. Did you think you could keep him deaf, dumb, and blind to what is about him? Now look what you've done. You howl like a monster and frighten the child out of his wits. And to what purpose? Petro even now satisfies his curiosity, in ghoulish detail, I expect. Better I had explained."

"There'd be no need to explain," Varian ground out, "if you hadn't brought up the curst topic in the first place, you sarcastic little know-it-all. You wanted to make a fool of me in front of your cousin, didn't you? You wanted—"

It struck him then what was wrong. She wasn't in a temper at all, only pretending to be. That's why she hadn't bitten him. In a rage, Esme was incapable of thinking, only acting, instinctively.

"You *want* me to banish you to the harem," he said

in a dangerously quiet voice. "You have been *deliberately* goading me."

The color drained from her face, and she backed away.

"What vexes me most," he went on, "is that you know precisely how to do it. Until our paths crossed, no one had ever caused me to lose my temper. There's scarcely a human being in England, France, or Italy who's heard me raise my voice. I've never deluded myself I was a good man. I had thought, however, I was a civilized one. By God but you bring out the worst in me." His voice rose. "What in blazes *are* you? What demon spawned you?"

There was an agitated knocking at the door. Varian strode across the room and wrenched it open. It crashed against the wall, and Fejzi winced.

"A thousand pardons, oh bravest of princes," he said shakily. "I would not for worlds disturb you, but I am the slave of my master and must do his bidding."

Christ, he must have *run* to Ali and back. "What does your master want?" Varian inquired tightly.

"I am to assure you no harm will come to the Red Lion's daughter. She is as dear to his highness as if she were his own, for she is Jason's flesh and blood, who was like a brother to him. All this last week, the Vizier's wives have with their own hands sewn garments for the girl. If she does not come, they will weep grievously, and the other women with them. This the master cannot abide, for the tears of females are so many daggers in his affectionate heart. He asks you to indulge the women, that there may be peace in the harem."

Indulge the women, indeed. Manipulative devil. Still, it was the custom of the place, Varian told himself. More important, it was where Esme wanted to be.

He exhaled a sigh. "The Vizier is a genius, truly, if he can keep peace among three hundred women. I can't do so with only *one.*" He shot Esme a murderous glance, then shrugged. "Take her if you must. But don't blame me if the harem breaks out in revolution."

Fejzi dared a feeble smile. "Ah, well, she is the Red Lion's daughter." He turned to Esme. "Come, little warrior. You will not make war in the harem, will you?"

She uttered an impatient "tsk" and moved to the door.

"I'll wish to see her again later," Varian said, forcing his gaze back to Fejzi.

"I shall convey your request to his highness."

"It isn't a request."

Fejzi's smile faded. "As you wish, my lord."

Ali leaned back on his *divan* and laughed, his round belly shaking like pudding. "A face and form like Apollo and the temper of Zeus. I heard him shouting and wondered if he'd kill the wench before you returned."

Fejzi's smile was thin. "He is abominably insolent, highness."

"Aye, I watched through my telescope as you approached. I saw it in his bearing. And other things, of course," Ali added, fixing Fejzi with his piercing blue gaze.

"The Lion of Janina sees everything."

"When I see for myself. You'd rather I settled for rumors or the clumsy explanation of that thickheaded oaf, Bajo. You all must think I'm in my dotage. All I hear these last days is how beautiful the English lord is. More beautiful than Byron, they say, and no cripple, either. When they don't speak of the lord, then it's the boy. Surely Jason's son, they whisper, a red-haired youth with old, wise eyes. These wonders come to my realms, and I'm not to clap eyes on them but hustle them away to the coast?"

"No, highness. That would be unthinkable," Fejzi said resignedly.

Ali slowly raised himself to a sitting position and swung his legs to the floor. Dropping his hands on his thick thighs, he eyed Fejzi reproachfully. "Today I watched the Englishman ride into Tepelena in all his bold arrogance, and I laughed with pleasure. A moment ago, I laughed again, to hear of his fury with the little spitfire. How long has it been since I laughed, Fejzi? For how long has my heart lain like a stone coffin within me? Three weeks it's been since my Red Lion was cut down, an Englishman brave as a Shqiptar. Scarcely has this happened when another Englishman arrives with a red-haired boy, Jason's kin. It's a sign from heaven."

"Or from the other place," Fejzi muttered.

Ali's expressive face eased back into a smile. "So it may be. I fear no devil. Am I not everlastingly surrounded by them—and my cousin the prettiest devil of them all?"

He looked away, toward the window, where the sky was darkening. "Tonight I play with two beautiful devils. One fair, the other dark. Well, we'll see. The game will be interesting."

Chapter 15

The Vizier was shorter than Fejzi, and fatter. He'd probably been handsome once. His complexion was fair, his forehead broad above the bushy brows, his nose well-shaped. With his great white beard and twinkling blue eyes, one might easily take him for somebody's jovial grandpapa.

Ali Pasha proved to be lively, talkative, and amazingly good-humored. His was the sort of disarming manner that could lead the most cautious men to betray themselves. Even Varian was tempted to succumb. But a charmer himself, he recognized quicksand when he saw it. He knew that throughout the exchange of elaborate courtesies he was being minutely examined . . . and all too accurately sized up.

Fejzi interpreted during supper. The man's linguistic abilities were superior to Petro's but not nearly as good as Esme's. She had full command of English vocabulary and used it with both assurance and, too often, unnerving accuracy. Fejzi, however, could scarcely keep up with Ali's rapid speech, and the Vizier grew increasingly impatient during the lengthy meal.

Finally, declaring they would take their coffee and sweets privately, he waved his courtiers from the room.

Before he, too, departed, Fejzi softly told Varian, "I am to fetch the boy now. His highness did not wish the child to be gawked at and made uncomfortable by the court, but he does desire to see and speak with him. The girl comes in a moment, to interpret for you." He gave

Varian his thin half-smile. "It is not seemly, but she is skilled in languages, and Ismal—" He hesitated, looking to Ali.

The Vizier gave another impatient wave of his hand. Fejzi hastily left the room.

"Ismal speaks English well enough, but his hearing fails him sometimes," Ali said in slow Greek. "I want no misunderstanding. Fejzi is slow, and when frightened, stammers and stutters. Most annoying."

"What has he to be frightened of?" Varian asked.

"What do you think?" Ali looked toward the entryway. "What do *you* think, little warrior?"

Varian's head swiveled in the same direction, and a heavy fist seemed to drive into his solar plexus.

He saw undulating waves of dark fire streaming over Esme's slim shoulders and down upon the sea-green silk bodice. His glance slid swiftly down the silken gown to her tiny waist and the supple curves of her hips.

Swallowing a groan, he hastily looked away, and hoped his countenance didn't betray him to the old man watching with such fiendish interest. All the same, at the moment, it was an effort to recollect that Ali existed. Even while Varian looked politely to the Vizier, all his concentration was fixed on Esme.

He felt her approach, saw a shimmer of green silk as she moved past him, the dress whispering against her slim body . . . where his mouth wanted to be, and his hands. Heat set his loins aching. Gad, he was pathetic. The girl donned a frock, and he went to pieces.

The rustling of silk seemed to thunder in his ears as she paused a moment, then sank down on his left, onto a cushion.

Ali said something else, and this must have vexed her, for Esme answered tartly in a rapid stream of Albanian. Varian tensed. She was trying to get herself killed, the sharp-tongued little witch. But Ali only raised his eyebrows in exaggerated shock and laughed.

Varian mustered the courage to look at her. Her face was flushed and her green eyes flashed militant sparks.

"What was that about?" he asked. His voice sounded weak, strained.

"Nothing. A lewd joke, unworthy to be repeated. He's heard disgusting gossip, that is all."

Varian wanted to pursue the matter, but a servant entered, bearing a heavily laden tray. A moment later, Percival appeared, his face white as a sheet, though otherwise remarkably composed, considering he had just entered the private chamber of an acknowledged madman, a monster whom even the Sultan feared.

The monster stared at the boy a long, tense while. Then his blue eyes filled with tears. He put out his hand and, after a brief hesitation, Percival took it.

Ali said something, his voice broken.

Esme clicked her tongue. *"Jo,"* she corrected sharply. "Not his son, you dirty-minded old man," she muttered in English. *"Nip.* His nephew." She threw Varian an accusing look. "I knew this would happen."

"Still, the resemblance is remarkable," came a new voice behind Varian. It was low and musical, the English only lightly accented.

All Varian's senses bristled, as though the silken male voice were a glove striking his face in challenge. He didn't deign to turn his head. He understood now why he'd been seated with his back to the door. Ali was positioned to catch every expression at each new entrance—the first, unguarded reaction. Varian would not give him the satisfaction again. He waited until the speaker entered his line of vision and, even then, chose to keep his attention upon Ali until the man was seated, his eyes level with Varian's.

These were deep sapphire eyes, slanting upward slightly above high cheekbones. These were clear, apparently guileless eyes in a smooth young countenance whose fairness any English lady would envy. He wore no turban, and his hair was long, the color of cornsilk. He introduced himself. He didn't need to. This was the golden prince: Ismal.

Esme had said he was two and twenty. He appeared no more than eighteen, a slim youth with a proud, elegant bearing and all the grace of a dancer. No, a cat.

Ismal had garbed himself in the Turkish style: a gold silk tunic with a sash of blue the precise color of his eyes, over matching silk trousers. He needn't have bothered. Ismal could have worn a flea-bitten hide, and he'd still be beautiful, cultivated, and noble to the bone. For a moment, he made Varian feel like a peasant, and a barbarian to boot. But only for a moment. Humility, after all, was not an article in great supply among the St. Georges.

Varian returned the young man's gracious greeting with excruciating courtesy, his face unreadable, his insides churning with hatred and blind, mindless jealousy.

He spent the next quarter hour trying to maintain his composure, trying to think rationally, past the roiling rage in his mind. But thinking was impossible. He was too aware of the richly garbed bodies on either side of him, too aware of their voices, their scents: one light and teasingly feminine; the other darker, exotic, and clearly masculine. Through the rustle of silk, Varian could scarcely make sense of the conversation about him.

He heard Ali's voice rising in inquiry . . . Percival's, answering stiffly at first, then with increasing assurance until he was chatting eagerly . . . and between them, smoothly interpreting, Esme's voice, low and soothing as a cool stream on a sultry day.

Then Ismal spoke, and Ali answered at length.

Esme touched Varian's arm, and the contact jerked him out of the haze so abruptly that he blinked. His companions came into sharp focus. They were all watching him.

"Ali gives Ismal permission to address you directly," she said. "You are to stand in the place of Percival's father, the head of my English family, and speak on our behalf. Ali says my cousin is intelligent, but such matters cannot be resolved by children and women." She met Varian's puzzled gaze for one tense moment, and he read in her eyes what she wouldn't add aloud: Remember your promise.

Varian stiffly turned his attention to Ismal, whose expression grew solemn.

"I'll not tax your patience with endless roundabout speeches, my lord," said the golden prince. "I admit freely it was my own followers who so villainously sought to steal the Red Lion's daughter, but I tell you as well that I never commanded it. Never. I have denounced those who ordered the deed, and will happily preside over their lackeys' executions when they are found."

Percival made a queer, choked sound, but Ismal appeared not to notice.

"It is also claimed—and this is cruelly unjust—that I ordered the Red Lion's death. This is a vile lie, which all reasoning men recognize. Why should I cut down the sire of the girl I seek as my bride?" His feline blue gaze flickered to Esme, then back.

Varian felt his fingers curling tightly against his palms. He settled them back upon his knees. "It's not the customary way of wooing," he said. "At least not in England."

Ismal's mouth curved with amusement. He'd probably broken a thousand hearts with that lazy cat smile.

"You please to be droll, my lord," said the golden prince. "Even in Albania, it is a most irregular way to go about winning a girl's heart."

Wonderful. A wit, in addition to everything else.

"I'd not kill Esme's father, even were he my worst enemy, for she loved him and must look upon his murderer with vengeful hate."

When Esme translated this for Ali, he made a jovial comment.

Ismal's smile widened. "Ali remarks that vengeful wives are uncomfortable creatures to have about. He has no doubt the little warrior would slit my throat if she believed me guilty. Such a state of mind in a bride is poor encouragement to a groom's ardor."

Varian looked at Esme. She sat composedly beside him, her hands folded, her eyes demurely downcast while she translated for Ali as though they discussed agriculture, rather than her father's murder and her own future.

Vengeful hate. Slit his throat.

No.

She wouldn't.

The hairs on the back of Varian's neck bristled all the same.

He glanced at Ali, unaware of the silent question he asked until he saw the Vizier's answer, a barely perceptible motion of his head. Side to side: *Yes*. Was it possible? Did the genial old fiend suspect what he did—and worse, know the answer?

Varian returned Ismal's smile with one equally disarming. "You appear far too intelligent to do such a foolish thing," he said. "Nor can I believe a man the Almighty has so highly favored need take such desperate measures to secure a woman."

Ismal calmly accepted this rubbish, his eyes as trusting as a babe's.

"Frankly, though, I can't understand why you'd want her at all," Varian went on blandly. "You appear not the least deluded regarding her *violent* character."

The green silk gown rustled as Esme shifted her position. She muttered something, too low for Varian to catch, then briskly translated Varian's remarks for Ali, who chuckled.

"I have no taste for a docile wife," Ismal said. "The little warrior is fierce and brave, and stirs my blood as no other woman can. So it has been since we were children. She knows. She knows how she has tormented me." He shot her a soulful look, but Esme kept her attention upon her hands.

So demurely feminine. So sweetly shy under her would-be lover's passionate gaze . . . while she was no doubt reviewing in her twisted little mind how she'd kill him.

"Four years ago," Ismal went on, "when she was fourteen, I begged her father for her hand in marriage. He said she was too young, and I must wait."

Four years ago—when she was *fourteen?* Then it all came back, stunningly clear. She had told Varian of her life—a year in Durres, five in Shkodra, two in Berat, and so on and so on. Her life. *All eighteen bloody years of it.* Why the devil had he never simply asked? Why had he tortured himself all this while when a simple question would have relieved him—of that particular guilt at least.

But Varian knew why. He'd been afraid he'd learn she was even younger than he'd guessed.

"Yes, Jason would say that," Varian agreed composedly. "English girls mature more slowly, I believe, than those in other parts of the world. Esme herself admitted she was slower than most."

"She is no longer too young, my lord. I have wanted her many years. Now, because she is alone, I feel responsible for her as well. When my noble cousin told me you were coming to Tepelena, I rejoiced, for I would have an opportunity to make amends for all the insults she and her English friends suffered that evil day in Durrës. I might try, at least in part, to wipe away my shame and sorrow for all that has happened in my name."

Ismal's approach to repentance was briskly businesslike. He would pay two hundred English pounds in bride-price to Esme's uncle. This was about twenty times the going rate, Esme coolly explained, women being accounted, generally, less valuable than horses. Fines must be paid as well, it turned out: five hundred each to Varian and Percival for the insults to their persons in Durrës and five hundred to Ali for the insult to his authority. In addition, Ismal would give Ali and Varian each an Arabian stallion, and Percival a colt of equally good blood.

Lastly, Ismal took up a jewel-encrusted silver box that lay near Ali's divan.

"These baubles I give to my intended bride, in token of our betrothal."

He handed Varian the box. The "baubles" consisted of emeralds, sapphires, rubies, pearls, and other such gimcracks.

Varian gave them one bored glance and Ismal another.

"Naturally, my bride will receive proper jewels when we are wed," the golden prince said. There was a faint note of impatience in his tone.

"Naturally." Proper jewels. Oh, yes. Diamonds, of course, and miles of those gold coin necklaces and hair adornments Byron had described. Hundreds of silken gowns, and slippers embroidered with gold and silver. Esme would never lift a finger again all the rest of her life. Her brown, strong hands would grow as soft and white as the rest of her. She'd be pampered, her every whim a command. She'd dine on rare delicacies, and her slight form would blossom into lush womanhood.

If she lived that long.

Which she wouldn't if she tried to kill her husband. But she couldn't be planning that, Varian tried to persuade himself. His suspicion, surely, was nothing more than feverish fancy, sparked by jealous delirium.

She is not right in the head.

She was not in her right mind.

If Percival and Petro had diagnosed accurately, the only sensible thing to do was get clear of her, as far away as possible, as fast as possible. Percival could well do without a homicidal lunatic for a cousin. England could well do without her as a subject. Let Albania deal with her.

The room was silent, waiting. Ali's expression was inscrutable. Percival's countenance was pale, his green eyes wide and anxious. The golden prince watched Esme. Varian wondered what he saw there, but refused to look at her.

He closed the cover of the jewel box. "A most generous reparation," he said calmly. "I shall be honored to convey your *request* to her uncle."

Ismal's guileless expression never faltered. He was good at this, very good, Varian thought, or else very much in earnest. He ruthlessly crushed the doubt. He was in no state to consider consequences, not those, not now.

"I beg your pardon," Ismal said. "My English has failed me. I do not comprehend."

"I shall be happy to communicate your proposal to the head of Esme's English family," Varian clarified, "when I take her to him."

Silence.

Ali looked to Esme, but no translation was forthcoming.

He directed a question at Ismal, who feigned incomprehension.

It was left to Varian to translate in his wretched schoolboy Greek and explain he'd no right to dispose of a female to whom he was unrelated. If he did so without

Sir Gerald's written consent, Varian claimed, he might be charged with abduction and slave trading, both grave offenses under English law.

"But she is not English." Ismal's voice was angelically patient. "She is Albanian, his highness' subject."

"She most certainly is not!" Percival burst out.

All eyes turned to him. He reddened. "I do beg your pardon. I don't mean to be impolite, but unless I've misunderstood dreadfully, it can't possibly be so."

"Percival, if you don't mind—"

"But, sir—"

"Dëgjoni!" Ali ordered. *"Dëgjoni djali."*

"We are to listen to the boy," Ismal said, smiling faintly. "It is my royal cousin's whim."

Ali patted the boy on the shoulder. "You. Speak."

Percival eyed him nervously. "Thank you, sir." His frightened glance darted to Ismal, then Esme, and settled at last on Varian, who gave a curt nod.

Percival drew a steadying breath. "The mother's side doesn't count," he said. "Mustafa explained it to me. It's as though her bloodline doesn't exist. Therefore, Cousin Esme is British, not Albanian. There can't be any doubt about that, in any case. When Uncle Jason got married, he went to all the trouble of going to Italy and finding an Anglican clergyman and getting it done properly. I know, because he kept all his private papers with his banker in Venice. He had copies made for Mama to send to England, and I saw them all: the marriage lines, and papers for Esme's birth in 1800, and Uncle Jason's will. He said he didn't want any legal problems for Esme. He said—"

"It is nonsense!" Esme cried. "The child makes it all up. My parents were wed in Janina, not Italy."

"They had an Albanian ceremony in Janina," Percival said, "but they were married again with English rites in Italy."

"No!"

Varian looked at her. "So you know a bit about English law, do you?"

"Aye, and I am a bastard by that law," she spat out. "Percival tells this falsehood to persuade everyone I am not. But I am not British. I'm no subject of your lunatic king!"

"It makes no matter, my heart," Ismal said soothingly. "Your father was disowned by his family, and he became an Albanian. You are Albanian." He turned to Varian, whose jaw ached with the effort to maintain his mask of composure.

"You know her kin do not want her," Ismal went on, his silky voice reproachful now. "Why do you wish to take her to an uncle who will only discard her, as he discarded his own brother? Why make her suffer such shame, when she will only be returned to me in the end? You know it is so, my lord. All Albania knows it is so."

"If you knew it," Varian returned coolly, "why did you bother to seek my permission?"

"Out of respect," Esme snapped. "Out of courtesy, which you do not comprehend. You do not understand the honor he does you, and how he humbles himself. Five hundred pounds and a stallion for your trouble he offers, when the law decrees much less. In answer, you insult him. You are a mannerless barbarian!"

"Nay, my little one," Ismal chided gently. "My feelings are of no account. Do not distress yourself on my behalf."

Damn them both, Varian thought. You'd think they'd rehearsed the whole scene. Did they expect him to believe this star-crossed lovers gibberish? What sort of lackwit did they take him for? Or was it for someone else's benefit?

Varian look at Percival, who appeared near tears. A few more minutes of this and the boy, too, would be pleading on behalf of Romeo and Juliet here.

Varian rose. "Come, Percival. I see no reason to linger for more of this farce. I had thought my opinion and assistance were solicited. I was mistaken."

Ali barked something to Ismal, who answered reluctantly.

Varian began walking toward the doorway. "Come, Percival," he ordered, still without raising his voice.

The boy bit his lip but rose obediently and hurried to his side. "I do hope this is not a mistake," he muttered.

Varian hoped so, too. Behind him, the two Albanian men were still talking. Would they let him stalk out? If they did, he couldn't turn back, he knew. He knew as well that Ali had taken his measure and had surely assessed him accurately. The Vizier was near eighty. He'd never have lived so long if he couldn't recognize a blackguard when he met one.

"Varian *Shenjt Gjergj.*" Ali's voice. "Lorrrd Ee-deemund."

Varian paused, his face a mask of boredom, his heart hammering with dread.

"Please to remain," his highness continued in Greek. "The others will return to their own chambers. They grow tiresome, these children." He waved his hand at Ismal. "You, fetch my secretary. I want an interpreter in his right mind."

Chapter 16

One of the guards who had escorted Esme and Percival to Varian's apartment lingered yet, just inside the door. Esme sat on the *sofa,* scowling at her cousin. Percival—his rock-filled leather pouch hugged to his chest—was pacing the room. They had awaited Lord Edenmont's return nearly two hours, arguing most of the time and getting nowhere. Each had proved to be fully as obstinate as the other. Esme's sole satisfaction was that the endless debate frustrated the hateful guard, who understood not a syllable of English.

"I do wish you'd not vexed Lord Edenmont," Percival reproached. "If he's angry enough to leave you here, I can't think what I'll tell Grandmama. She'll speak to the Prime Minister, I know she will—or to the Regent himself, even though she hates him—and the next thing you know, we'll be at war with Albania."

"That is nonsense. Governments scarcely admit that women exist. They certainly don't go to war over them."

"They most certainly do. What about Helen of Troy?"

"Y'Allah, my face would not launch so much as a fishing boat, let alone a thousand ships. I think you have read too many fairy tales. You are always inventing troubles and catastrophes. You invent conversations that never occurred except in your own head. You hear my father speak of a small disturbance—in a place where there is always disturbance—and you imagine plots of revolution."

"I did not. It was just as I told you."

"You saw my suitor with your own eyes, heard him with your own ears. He is even more spoiled and lazy than the arrogant lord who brought you here," she said scornfully. "Ismal nearly wept when his request was answered so insolently. You think this tender-hearted creature would—"

"Whited sepulchres," Percival said.

"What?"

"I shall find the passage for you in the family Bible when we get home. *If* we get home. Oh, I do wish you'd been a boy," he added crossly. "You are ever so unreasonable. No wonder you make his lordship lose his temper. If I hadn't seen it with my own eyes, I wouldn't believe it. He's always so amiable and remarkably understanding. He hasn't even scolded me for taking him here and getting myself abducted."

"He may beat you if he finds out how you lied and tricked him."

Percival stopped short and stared at her, his eyes wide with shock. "You *wouldn't* carry tales. You *promised.*"

Esme leaned back and folded her arms across her chest. "Ismal offered five hundred pounds and a stallion, but that was not enough. Perhaps a chess piece worth a thousand pounds will prove a more satisfactory bribe."

"It—it's not yours to bribe him with."

"I shall tell him it is. I shall say Jason gave it to me, and I asked you to guard it with your rocks. If you can tell lies, why shouldn't I?"

Percival considered. Then his eyes narrowed to two nasty green slits. "If you so much as *hint* at it," he warned, "I shall tell Lord Edenmont—"

"What, that it's a falsehood? And who will he believe?"

"I shall tell him you made that horrid scene tonight to make him *jealous.*"

The accusation was merely a boy's obnoxious taunt, yet heat rose in Esme's face all the same. She *had* wanted to prove something. She'd wanted to show Varian that another man, as beautiful as himself, desired her. And this other man did not think her a lunatic, or a sarcastic know-it-all, or any of the other hateful names his lordship had called her.

Ismal had most obligingly accommodated her. He'd sounded so devotedly tender that she had almost believed he did love her. Until her father's image flashed before her: shot in the back, denied the glory of a hero's burial, his brave body battered against the cruel rocks of the torrent.

Percival studied her with frank curiosity. "You're blushing," he said. "Good heavens. Is it true? Is that what it was about? Really, girls are very strange. I'd not thought—"

The door crashed open, narrowly missing the guard, who hastily scrambled aside. As soon as Lord Edenmont entered, the guard slipped out.

Percival glanced from him to Esme, then yawned. "Good heavens, how late it is," he said. He rubbed his eyes. "Such an interesting conversation, Cousin Esme. The time flew by, really it did." He headed for the bedchamber stairs, oblivious to Lord Edenmont's astonished gaze.

"Percival."

"Sir?" Turning back to him, the boy yawned again.

"Am I to believe you are not remotely interested in what transpired between Ali and me?"

"I'm sure you had a most interesting discussion, sir, but I do believe I've had sufficient stimulation for one evening."

His lordship turned to Esme. "What have you done to him? What insane rubbish have you been filling his head with?"

Percival bridled. "She's not filled my head with anything. I should hardly listen to anything a silly *girl* had to say."

"I, silly?" Esme bolted up from the *sofa.* "It is you who jabber nothing but nonsense. Trojans and white supper curse and—"

"White what?" Varian asked.

"Sepulchres," Percival snapped. "Whited sepulchres. But it's no use telling *her.* It's no use telling her anything. She's got about as much sense as a—as a *fish!*"

"I, at least, do not converse with rocks," she retorted.

"I don't talk to them!"

"Children," Lord Edenmont chided. They ignored him.

"You do! You mutter under your breath, but it is talking all the same. This is sense? To talk to rocks?"

"I don't, you horrid, horrid—you *girl,* you silly *girl.* I never—oh, what's the use?" Percival shook his head. "Please, sir, may I go to bed now? I've got a dreadful headache."

Lord Edenmont waved him off. Percival walked stiffly to the entryway, paused to stick his tongue out at Esme, then marched loudly out.

Esme stood glaring after him until he disappeared from sight. Then she glared at the ceiling, while he stomped about overhead. At last there was silence.

And a low chuckle behind her.

She swung around to glower at Lord Edenmont. His face was blank, but the corner of his wicked mouth twitched.

Esme didn't want to look at his mouth. She didn't want to look at any part of him. She'd thought Fate would at last be kind and spare her from ever having to see him again. But Fate was worse than unkind, and now that dreadful boy believed—

"White supper curse?" he said.

"Go to the devil!" she cried. "May a host of jackals rip out your entrails while your heart still beats. May you fall into black water and a thousand leeches feast upon you. May the mother of vermin fasten herself upon you and breed lice in your eyes and nose and—"

"Ah, an Albanian love song. And you composed it just for me, romantic creature that you are. Very well. I yield." He opened his arms. "Come. You may cover my adorable face with kisses."

Unfortunately, that was just what Esme wanted to do. She was tired and angry and frightened. In a kinder world, she might hide in his arms. In that kinder world, his invitation would not be cruel sarcasm, and she might let his burning kisses shut all else out. She might let herself drown in the hot, dark passion he'd shown her in

Poshnja. He was beautiful and strong, and his splendid body would give her shelter . . . and release.

Only for a short while, true, but she'd have no other chance. No other man. Only Ismal, whom she hated with all her heart, the man she'd kill—then die for killing. What sort of revenge was that? He'd seem a martyr, the innocent victim of a mad female. No one believed him guilty.

Except Percival.

Who claimed Ismal was a traitor, and Risto the go-between who traveled to Italy for weapons for his master. In Berat, Percival had insisted he recognized Risto's voice . . . had said the man spoke bad Italian and worse English. The recollection sent Esme's head whirring like a spinning wheel, and all her consciousness fixed upon the thread she drew from it.

Risto *did* speak Italian. And English. Neither well, but enough to get by. How could Percival know that, when in Berat, and all through the journey, Risto had spoken only Albanian? There was only one way Percival could have known: the way he told her. God help her, how could she have been so unforgivably stupid?

A cold flood of dismay woke Esme from her trance and to the awareness that she was staring blankly at Varian. How long had she stood thus while her mind spun out its revelations?

He had lowered his arms and was watching her, his head tipped slightly to one side, his gray eyes perplexed . . . and sad? No, not sad. He hated her. She'd made her cousin hate her as well. They'd held out a life rope to her and she'd thrust it away. They'd leave her here to kill and die because she'd forced them to, because she'd been too obsessed with revenge to listen to anybody.

The back of her throat began to burn, and her chest hurt, making her breath come in hard, painful gasps. Her lower lip started to tremble uncontrollably. Oh, no. She would *not* cry. She *never* wept, and she'd rather be torn to pieces by wild boars than break down before this man. Her eyes were itching. Esme rubbed them hard.

"Don't you *dare,*" Varian whispered fiercely. "Don't you dare cry."

Esme bit her lip.

"Damnation. You are going to be the death of me, Esme." He swiftly closed the distance between them, gathered her in his arms, and pressed her face to his chest.

"I'm sorry," she gasped against his chest.

"Sorry. Christ."

He was stroking her hair. Not very gently, but then, he had every reason to dash her head against the wall, Esme thought miserably.

"I know," she said. "It's too late to be sorry. I'm not afraid. I only wished . . . I wished to say it to you, aloud." She swallowed. The burning in her throat had subsided. She would not break down now. She had herself in hand. She raised her head.

Varian's black lashes lowered to veil the expression in his eyes. He smiled faintly, without warmth. "And what am I to believe you're sorry for?" he softly inquired.

"All. From the beginning. The terrible things I have said. But worse, the terrible things I have done."

"Ah, well, you can't help it, can you? You're crazy—or Albanian. Come to think of it, they're much the same. I really don't understand how your father lived here twenty years and retained his sanity. I lost all claim to mine in less than twenty *days*."

"I'm sorry," she said. "It is all my fault. I was very confused. I understood nothing . . . until a moment ago."

Varian gave a heavy sigh, and his hands dropped to her shoulders. He stood back, holding her at arm's length while he studied her face. "Esme repentant. That is nearly as disconcerting a sight as Esme in a frock. The combination is devastating. Perhaps I'd better sit down."

He released her, but did not sit down, only backed away to lean against the door. He still looked at her in that studying way. Esme became painfully aware of the silken gown she wore, which had made her feel ridiculous before. Now she felt too female, terribly exposed. He gazed at her as though she were some curious specimen in a cage. She wanted to hide. Her feet carried her toward him instead.

"No!" he warned.

Esme stopped short and flushed.

"You are not to use your arts on me, madam," he said. "Unburden your conscience if you will, but at a distance. Like Percival, I have had quite enough *stimulation* for one day, thank you."

She didn't blame him, not one bit, though it was so mortifying to be ordered to keep away as if she carried a vile disease. But that wasn't why. He was being civilized. He didn't want to be tempted to hit her, or throttle her. Another man, goaded as he had been, would have knocked her clear across the room the instant he walked through the door, and she would not have blamed him. What an unspeakable harridan she'd been! Detestable, stupid, ugly, rude, vicious. An animal.

But she wasn't. She had some honor. She owed an apology. And the truth. Not all, for she couldn't bear that. But some, at least.

She folded her hands and directed her gaze to the carpet. Near her right foot she saw a tiny colored maze of intertwined squares, vivid against the maroon background. She fixed on it.

"I lied to you," she said, "Repeatedly. I exaggerated how long it would take to repair the ship and understated the difficulties in reaching Tepelena. Though I'd have gone alone if I had to, I knew I would encounter fewer problems traveling with an Englishman."

"You used me," he said.

She winced, "Yes."

"You might have used me more kindly."

The reproach made her look up guiltily. His eyes were dark, filled with shadows.

"I did not want you to like me," she said, wringing her hands. "I did not want to like you. That would make everything so much more difficult for me . . . for what I had to do."

"What did you have to do?" he asked quietly.

His dark gaze caught and held her, while her heart pumped crazily. Dear heaven, why did he ask that? Didn't he believe the reason she'd given him in Berat—

that she must wed Ismal? Hadn't she feigned well enough a few hours ago?

"Be-because of Is-Ismal," she said.

"What about him? What had you to do?"

It didn't matter how gently he asked. There was only one way to answer—with the lie she had so carefully contrived. This man would abandon her here. She'd made it impossible for him to do otherwise. She'd no need to tell him the whole truth, to watch his expression harden into revulsion, his soft voice chill with disgust. Yet her soul cried out for truth, for it cried out to him, to release her, punish her—she didn't know what she needed. All she knew at this moment was that she was sick with despair, and the lie would surely kill her.

"I had . . . I had . . ." The words stuck in her throat. She wasn't a coward, yet she was so afraid. Of what? Losing him, when he'd been lost to her from the start?

"Tell me, Esme."

She closed her eyes. "I had to kill Ismal." She said it quickly, and though the words came out in a strained whisper, it was not so fast or so low he couldn't hear it. The sound was too loud in her own ears. She felt cold and ashamed, though to seek revenge was no shame. That, however, he couldn't understand. He'd see her as a cold-blooded monster who mindlessly pursued a man all believed innocent—a man they all believed loved her and wanted desperately to wed her. Oh, why had she said those terrible words?

"Little fool." His voice, too, was low, but it lashed her. "Reckless, passionate little fool."

"Varian—"

"Hajde," he said.

Her gaze snapped to him. He held out his hand. *"Hajde,"* he repeated.

Her heart slammed hard against her chest, and her whole frame shuddered in response. But his low, beckoning voice called to her in her own tongue, and body and spirit answered at once, though tremblingly. Slowly, Esme moved to him and put her hand in his. His long fingers closed over hers, and he drew her nearer. Capturing her other hand, he tugged until she stood intimately close, her silken skirt brushing his trousers. Her breath came in short, strained gasps.

"You can't kill him, Esme," he said, "and I can't kill him for you."

Her heart seemed to splinter into a thousand shards. "Oh, Varian." She pulled free of his hands, threw her arms about him, and buried her face in the warmth of his coat. "Don't hate me," she pleaded. "Please don't hate me."

Strong arms wrapped round her, crushing her against his hard body. He pressed his mouth to her neck for one long, achingly warm moment. Then he lifted her up and carried her to the *sofa,* where he gathered her onto his lap. "Hate you. Oh, yes," he growled. Then his mouth sank down upon hers.

She had expected rage and revulsion, but his kiss was shatteringly tender, for all its heat. She wept within at its sweetness, just as she wept for the heart he had stolen from her so easily. She'd been a fool to imagine she could keep it from him, just as she'd been a fool about everything else.

When he raised his head at last, Esme hid her face against his shoulder. His fingers played in her hair, then slipped down to caress her breast, lightly, barely touching the thin silk. Even under this feather touch, her flesh stirred in aching answer. She shivered. His hand moved to her hip, only to rest there, yet its warmth washed through her belly.

"Ah, Esme, what's to be done with you?"

His voice was as gentle as his touch, and she answered helplessly, just as her body had. "Don't leave me." It was but a tiny, muffled cry against his coat, yet too audible in the room's stillness.

A long silence.

"You're upset," he said at last, "and I am taking advantage. Gad, what a blackhearted swine I am—and the boy just upstairs." He kissed the top of her head. "Thank you for telling me the truth. I wish . . . I wish I were the sort of man you could have told it to sooner. 'My lord,' you'd have said, 'I must avenge my father's murder. Would you be kind enough to offer me your protection en route?' "

Esme peeked up doubtfully at him from her hiding place. "And what would you have answered?"

He smiled. "I should not have answered, but leapt immediately upon my white charger and gone out to slay the evil prince. If I were that other man. But I'm not. I'm Edenmont, lazy, selfish, and utterly useless. I can do nothing but take you away."

This was more than Esme could bear. He not only seemed to understand and would not abandon her, but also blamed himself. "You are none of those things," she said. She sat up fully, her eyes filled with all the admiration and gratitude she felt. "You tried to do what was right—what everyone knew was right, except me. This night Ismal offered you an immense bribe to abandon me, yet you refused it."

He shook his head, and one thick black lock shook loose to dangle rakishly at his eyebrow. "Don't make me out to be noble, Esme. I'm not. Just stubborn, and exceedingly selfish. Percival may be furious with you at the moment, but he's made up his mind you're leaving with him. If you don't, he'll plague me to death. In any case, Ali has made his position very clear: you're leaving tomorrow for Corfu, one way or another. If I chose not to take you, he said he'd send you with an army. I agreed to take you, though I warned I might need the army to accomplish the feat. He expressed his sympathy. He said you reminded him of his *mother.*"

"Ali?" This was incomprehensible. "He *wants* me gone—yet he let Ismal—"

"Make his touching speech, just as he let me make an ass of myself. Ali Pasha has a peculiar sense of humor—and a terrifying gift for judging character." While he spoke, Varian absently stroked her hair. "For the first time, I could understand why your father stayed to work for him. The Vizier is half mad, a sadistic fiend by all accounts, yet he has Satan's own gift for manipulation. And he knows what he's about."

He fell silent, while his long fingers continued their

soothing caress, drawing the tension from her scalp, from her very being.

"I'm sorry about your father," he said after a moment. "It's clear you loved him very much. I wish I could have met him. I wish he were here for you—instead of a numskull knave of a lord and a confused twelve-year-old boy."

Esme forced her voice past the burning obstruction in her throat. "You are not a numskull," she said, "and Percival is much less confused than I have been. You have both been far kinder than I deserve, but I shall try to make it up, I promise. I shall be so obedient and good all the way to Corfu that you will not recognize me."

"By heaven, you do go to extremes, don't you?" He smiled.

So sweet that smile was, warm as the sun. When he looked so, he could make a dying weed blossom into brilliant blooms. His touch could do the same. In the shelter of his arms, her tormented brain had quieted.

"I *want* to go with you," she blurted out. "I would go anywhere you say, Varian. This night I thought you'd leave me. I thought you would go from my life—and worse, that we would part in misunderstanding and anger and lies. Instead, you were patient and helped me unburden my heart. Now it is filled with gratitude. Those are merely words, but I shall prove it. Only wait and see." She swallowed. "No wonder all the women love you."

Varian stared at her most oddly, his beautiful eyes again filled with shadows, like shifting smoke. Then he scooped her up and set her on her feet before him. "I'm no good at resisting temptation," he said. "Go to bed, please, before the strain of everlasting kindness and nobility proves too much for me."

Esme would have preferred to remain in his lap. During their journey, he had kissed and caressed her in lust. He'd once held her nearly naked in his arms and set her aflame. Never before, however, had he touched her in affection or spoken directly to her heart. Never before had she felt so close to him. She wanted to stay as close as she could.

But she'd promised to be good, hadn't she? He'd told her to go to bed, and so she would. "Where do you want me to sleep?"

He gave a short laugh. "Where I *want* you to sleep is not the question. You'd best share Percival's room. Petro is out with his cronies, drinking himself to stupefaction. We'll probably find him sprawled in the courtyard tomorrow."

He glanced at the *sofa,* and his lip curled. "I shall make my bed here. It's a great deal softer than what I've become accustomed to."

"I shall bring you blankets," Esme said dutifully.

"Thank you, but I am quite warm. My thoughts shall keep me so, curse them. Good night, little warrior."

She gave him a hasty kiss on the cheek, but drew away quickly, so she'd not be tempted to seek more. *"Natën e mirë, Varian Shenjt Gjergj,"* she whispered. *I love you,* her grateful heart added.

Chapter 17

Two hours later, Esme was creeping through the quiet darkness of the harem.

Percival had been sound asleep when she'd reached the bedchamber. She'd had to wait, though, until Lord Edenmont was asleep as well. She'd sat listening at the top of the stairs until the restless rustling below had ceased and a light snoring assured her Varian had at last succumbed.

Then she had climbed out the window, made her way to the gallery, and hurried on to the harem. The sleepy guards at the entrance had let her pass without question. When, however, she reached the small doorway leading to the passage she sought—the one Jason had described to her—the mound of blubber nodding there suddenly jerked full awake to raise hissing objection.

"Ali has sent for me," she hissed back. "You'd best let me pass or both our heads shall be offered to his highness on a tray."

"I had no such message," the eunuch said. "How do I know you do not go to assassinate him?"

"I, the Red Lion's daughter? Even if I went on such an errand, with what weapon would I dispatch him? Think you I swallowed a sword and mean to vomit it up when I need it? Where am I to hide weapons in this flimsy garb?" With an exasperated sigh, Esme offered to strip naked if he didn't believe her, though she advised him to check her quickly, for Ali was not the most patient of men.

As she'd expected, the eunuch declined the honor. He checked for concealed weapons by giving her body a few unenthusiastic pats and, grumbling all the while, let her pass. Naturally. What had the Vizier to fear from a skinny little girl?

Now Esme need only pray Ali was in the private chamber she headed for and that he was still awake. It was only a bit after midnight, and he often stayed up well into the early morning, either browbeating exhausted counselors or amusing himself with an attractive object of either gender. If the latter was the case, Esme hoped he'd chosen a female this night. She had no idea what methods men used to enjoy each other and was not eager at the moment for enlightenment. She'd enough to keep clear in her mind without being distracted by new forms of depravity.

A generous Providence had granted her a reprieve, and she would make noble use of it. She would get her revenge, but this time in a way even Jason would have approved, for she would carry out his heroic mission. Even Percival would be proud of her and greatly relieved when his secret was put properly to work. It would be. She knew what to do and was not afraid. She was the Red Lion's daughter, and before she left her beloved country forever, she'd save it.

Though Ali wouldn't believe her at first, he was too wise to discount her accusations entirely. He'd investigate, and his spies would soon discover the truth. In a very short time, Ismal would find himself in the hands of skilled torturers. Then he'd die horribly, just as he deserved, but her own hands would not be stained with his blood. She'd be far away, lonely and unwanted, perhaps, but with her soul wiped clean. In Albania, she might even be praised as a brave heroine. That would be enough for her, Esme told herself. That and satisfying visions of Ismal's slow, agonizing death.

These agreeable fantasies sped her to the door of Ali's private chamber. She was trying to decide whether to knock politely or just creep in when she heard Ismal's voice, sweet and mellifluous as always. With a silent oath, Esme sank down upon the cold floor to wait. She hoped he'd not be all night.

"I should hold my tongue," Ismal was saying, "and not risk your displeasure. Yet though you'll kill me for it, I must speak what is in my heart. My love for you is too great to do otherwise."

Ali chuckled. "I do believe the English lord's beauty has addled your wits, little cousin. The girl has to go. She should have gone long ago, along with her half-brother. This is no time to annoy the British. They're already testy about those villainous Parghiots I slaughtered, and they're bound to give me trouble about the Suliots, too. I'm going to have the Devil's own time softening them as it is. I want our visitors safe in British custody before negotiations begin."

"They won't negotiate at all if you give the girl a chance to poison their minds first. You saw how she abused the English lord and his king. Send her into exile among those she hates, expose her to their scorn, and *you* will become her enemy."

"Yes, a terrible thing that would be," Ali answered. "I'm shaking in my slippers at the thought of her displeasure. What ghastly thing will she do, I wonder? Weep? Curse me? Stamp her tiny foot? Allah, preserve me. It's too dreadful to contemplate, the wrath of this little girl." He roared with laughter.

Esme scowled at the door.

"She may seek revenge." Ismal's voice betrayed no hint of irritation. "She knows how badly you want English artillery and advisers. She's also aware that the more liberal of the English strive to turn their government against you. She can help them, and they'll be happy to use her. It won't be hard for her to twist the truth and make you appear a greater threat to the civilized world than the Corsican, Bonaparte."

Esme's eyes widened. She'd never trusted Ismal. Never had she doubted he was guilty. All the same, she could not believe the filth he uttered—or that Ali remained quiet, as though he was seriously considering the snake's warnings.

Yet wasn't this the sort of threat Ali might heed? He

was always quick to imagine he was being persecuted. He also understood revenge. He was a master of it, a most patient one. He never forgot an injury, though he might wait half a century to collect payment. Damn, but Ismal knew what he was doing; he played the Vizier's weaknesses as though they were the strings of his *çiftelia.*

Ali's roar of laughter broke the silence. Evidently, he was not to be played so easily. Esme relaxed.

"Really, Ismal, you're most entertaining this evening," the Vizier chortled. "If I didn't know your sober habits, I'd think you were drunk. Certainly you're blind. Perhaps she doesn't want to go. But revenge? You forget the handsome English stallion. Do you think he can't keep her mind off her grievances?"

"She despises him."

"Indeed. That's why, of all the places she might have chosen, she took her seat beside him. Very close beside him."

Esme winced.

"And when I asked her whether his English sword struck slow and steady, or quick and fierce, she turned the color of ripe cherries."

"Any maiden would blush at such speech," Ismal said.

"A *maiden* wouldn't have comprehended it or accused me of heeding filthy gossip."

Esme covered her hot face with her hands. She might have known Ali had good reason for speaking so to her. She should have known she'd betray herself to him. Everyone did.

"She understood because she's felt his thrust—or wants to," Ali went on. "Her anger's only the fire of love, as I explained to him. She's young, poor child. She hardly comprehends the passion she feels for him. And, naturally, grief for her father confuses her mind. She's like a wounded creature who strikes out blindly at those who try to help her. But the English lord will doctor her. I advised him how: with sweet words and a gentle touch."

Esme closed her eyes. Sweet words. Gentle caresses. Not affection, but "doctoring." Manipulation.

"You think he'll take your advice?" Ismal asked. "You think this insolent nobleman will trouble himself to keep her quiet with his lovemaking? Just for your sake—or hers? You've extraordinary faith in a man everyone knows is a whore."

"I don't need faith," came the confident answer. "I've paid him well to make certain she goes with him willingly. It's what the boy wants, you see, and the boy is the real problem, as the lord so astutely recognizes."

"The boy? I do not . . ."

A short pause, then Ali laughed. "At last you perceive why your generous offer was so coldly refused. The poor man had no choice, with the boy there. What would happen, do you think, if that intelligent lad told his elders that Lord Ee-dee-mund sold another lord's niece to a heathen barbarian?"

"They'd probably hang him," Ismal answered softly. "Yet you *paid* him to do what he must do in any case?"

"Ah, there I had no choice." Ali's voice was rueful. "The man's abominably cunning. He said he couldn't sell her outright. On the other hand, he pointed out, he couldn't help it if she ran away. He said she's tried that before. I saw I'd better make certain she didn't run away. So I offered him five hundred English pounds to wed her. We settled at a thousand. It'll make the boy happy, and the lord's in desperate need of money. For a thousand pounds, I think he'd even marry *you.*" Ali laughed again.

Esme thrust her fist into her mouth to keep from crying out. Ismal was speaking again, but it was mere sound, drowned in the sea of humiliated rage that engulfed her.

Don't make me out to be noble.

Hadn't she known from the start Varian's heart was black and selfish? Hadn't he told her—as Petro did—that he'd lived by his wits for years, and on his charm and beauty? He'd come for a chess piece worth a thousand pounds. Though he'd not got the chess piece, his wits, charm, and beauty had got him the thousand pounds directly.

He'd also obtained a fine revenge for all the trouble Esme had given him. He'd never wanted her; he'd only played a game. When she'd offered herself, he'd declined—because all he wanted was to torment her, to get even by making her fall in love with him. He'd succeeded admirably. Ali had seen instantly how besotted she was.

Varian had used them all, used her infatuation, her cousin's loneliness, Ali's fears and greed. Varian had turned their weaknesses to his own profit. This man she'd thought stupid and childish had extorted a thousand pounds from Ali Pasha—the greatest miser in the Ottoman Empire—and turned the Red Lion's daughter into a sniveling, mindless wanton who begged to be dishonored.

Drawing a deep breath, Esme forced herself to stand up and return the way she'd come. It was best, she told herself, always best to know the truth. No one wanted her. She was a joke to everyone. Very well. Let them have their joke and all their lies and machinations. Let them play their men's games. It was nothing to her. She was a woman. Now, at last, she understood exactly what that meant. Jason should have told her, long ago. But that was so like him. Always, he left out the most important part.

Shortly after sunrise, Fejzi arrived to escort Varian to the Vizier. He found Lord Edenmont broad awake, washed though not yet shaven, and touchy.

Varian's troubled sleep had been punctuated by a series of dreams, each of which had begun lewdly and ended in the most grisly fashion. In the last, a naked Esme had held in one hand a bloodstained knife and in the other a slimy piece of throbbing flesh. "You have no heart," she'd said, smiling. "No heart, no heart, no heart." He'd awakened to find his own still safe in his bosom, hammering wildly. It set up another racket now at the unexpected and thoroughly unwelcome summons.

Varian raised no objection, however. The last thing he wanted at present was to antagonize Ali. After last night's confrontation, it was a miracle Lord Edenmont's head remained secured to his neck. Five hundred pounds he'd rejected—for the second time—to leave Esme behind. His reasons had been closely examined. So closely that Varian had felt he'd been turned inside out, scrubbed clean of every secret, and wrung thoroughly dry.

Oh, he'd won in the end—about the time he'd begun to suspect Ali had intended that all along, and the bribe was merely part of some convoluted Oriental game, or a test of some sort. Then Varian could have kicked himself for refusing the money. What would Ali have done had he accepted? What would the old fiend do with a girl he knew wanted to cut his cousin's throat? Or did the Vizier *want* her to kill Ismal?

No. Varian would not attempt to comprehend the labyrinthine mind of Ali Pasha. That way madness lay.

The Lion of Janina was standing when Lord Edenmont entered—a promising sign of royal condescension. Much to his lordship's astonishment, the Lion hastened forward to embrace him.

Via Fejzi, Lord Edenmont learned he was as dear to his highness as a son, and were circumstances otherwise, the Vizier would give half his realm to keep this wise and brave lord by him always. Alas, one could not keep him even another day. Ali could not, either, accompany his lordship to Corfu, for duty called him elsewhere. There appeared to be some difficulties in the southern realm; a little war may be necessary to bring peace. Still, there was no need for alarm. Lord Edenmont would depart this morning and reach Corfu speedily. He would not wish to endanger the young ones by remaining.

Ali spoke casually, as though he mentioned negligible matters. Hearing Fejzi stammer through the translation, however, Varian experienced a chill, as though an icy finger traced its way down his spine.

"I told his highness last night I had no intention of lingering. What's the meaning of this ominous hint?" he asked Fejzi.

"His highness is concerned the Red Lion's daughter will continue to raise difficulties that might slow your progress. At another time, her waywardness would be amusing. At present, it could prove perilous. Ismal is deeply disappointed. It is possible his friends will take advantage of the Vizier's preoccupation with internal troubles. Ismal one may easily lock in a dungeon. His friends, regrettably, are everywhere. It could take months to find them all. You see, my lord? His highness cannot properly attend to his realms until you are safe among the British."

"You may assure him Miss Brentmor will not raise difficulties of any sort," Varian said tightly. "I'm aware she appeared agitated when he last saw her. She has since recovered her composure. She has promised to go peaceably with us, and I've no doubt whatever that her word is as good as that of any gentleman. What the devil is that racket?"

The next room had erupted into cries and shouts, crashes and thumps. The words were hardly out of Varian's mouth when Percival hurtled through the door, and two burly guards after him. One managed to get hold of the boy's arm, but let go abruptly at Ali's sharp command.

Percival scowled at the guard, straightened his coat, and marched up to Varian. "I apologize for the disturbance," he said somewhat breathlessly, "but it couldn't be helped. Something most vexatious has happened." He withdrew a piece of paper from his breast pocket and, his hand shaking, gave it to Varian.

Varian gave the note a swift glance, though he didn't need to. Percival's white, stiffly composed countenance told him all he needed.

His own features rigid, Lord Edenmont turned to Fejzi. "Would you be kind enough to express to his highness my admiration for his perspicacity?"

"I beg your pardon, my lord?"

"It would appear there will be a delay, after all," Varian said, his voice deadly calm. "The young lady has bolted. Please convey my apologies for the imposition, but I must ask his assistance. I am obliged to locate her . . . and wring her deceitful neck."

Risto slipped noiselessly into the luxurious chamber and hurried to the *divan,* where Ismal lay sulking.

"The girl's fled Tepelena," Risto said without preamble. With his master, he rarely wasted words.

Ismal slowly drew himself upright, his blue eyes jewel-bright with interest. "Has she, indeed? You're certain?"

"Aye. She took off, in a rage with the English lord about who knows what. They've been looking for her since early morn, very quietly. You wouldn't know anything was amiss—unless you saw the parade of poor devils marched in and out of Ali's apartments. They've only just finished with me. You were next on the list, but luck's with you this time. They've found the guard she knocked unconscious. They found him gagged, bound with his own belt, and stuffed into the chest she climbed on to get out the window."

"She overpowered a guard?" Ismal mouth curved into a reluctant smile. "There's not one under six feet, and all are well over twice her weight. Still, if she was in a great temper . . . she's very quick, stronger than she looks, and clever besides."

"It hardly matters how she did it. She's gone, beyond a doubt."

"And no one knows why?"

"Fejzi said she left a note for the boy. She wrote that every man but you had deceived her."

The blue brightness intensified. "Did she, indeed? I wonder, then, why Ali didn't summon me instantly, to accuse me of enticing the girl away."

"I don't know. There was more to the note, but all else Fejzi would tell me was that she'd warned the boy not to let himself be used as she had been. The English lord wouldn't let anyone else read it. I'm sure the rest was all abuse of him. He seemed calm and insolent as usual, but he wasn't so within. One felt it."

"Doubtless he was contemplating murder. I wish you'd heard how she berated him last night."

"I don't know what he contemplated," Risto said tightly. "I don't trust him. He's not what we thought."

"Nothing is." Ismal turned his gaze to the fire. "So much gone awry," he said. "So many complications. I don't know who killed Jason or why. I don't know what brought the baron here—with that boy, of all boys. I know only that they've upset my plans. From the moment the chess piece left my hands, my beautiful schemes became so many tangled threads, and one by one, I see them slip from my grasp. Now I wonder how and when the black queen will appear . . . to seal my doom, perhaps."

"You've been brooding. You let your mind turn everything dark," Risto chided. "The chess piece is at the bottom of the sea or a river, or in Serbia with those incompetents who couldn't tell a boy from a girl. We've searched everywhere for it. Even if the girl or her friends ever did have it, they couldn't know what to make of it."

"I've told myself the same, yet my instincts answer otherwise. I should have heeded them and left Tepelena while I had the chance."

"You hadn't a chance. The instant you stir from this room, you're followed."

"*She* got away—a mere female."

"A she-devil's more like it," Risto said angrily. "She's nothing but trouble. Now at least you won't have to keep pretending you're dying of love for her. Humiliating, it must have been, to beg for that ugly bitch."

"Not at all. It was most entertaining. Unfortunately, it was also very expensive. A thousand pounds last night's performance cost me. I could have bought rifles, men—the aid of the Sultan himself." Ismal paused, his blue eyes clouding. "At the very least, I could have got the girl."

"You don't want her," came the hasty answer. "A scrawny witch with a vicious tongue. I'd as soon bed a cobra."

Ismal smiled, ever so faintly, at the fire. "Ah, well, you have no taste for women."

"You're not overly fond of them yourself."

"That doesn't mean I share your appetites. Were I capable of desiring a man, I'd have bought the beautiful English whore. An intriguing specimen, is he not, with his coal-black hair and white skin and silver eyes. Should I have bought him for *you,* perhaps? From all one hears, there's little he won't do, for a price."

Risto's olive countenance darkened. "He wouldn't

give up the little demon—yet he got your money anyhow, in the end.''

Ismal shrugged. ''As soon as I learned they were coming to Tepelena, I realized it would cost me. Even when Lord Edenmont rejected my offer, I knew I'd pay. As I expected, Ali generously offered to ease my troubled conscience last night by relieving me of the thousand pounds. He said he needed it to bribe the Englishman. That I greatly doubt. I lied to him; he lied to me, and I ended by paying, as one always does. Still, you'd think he'd at least let me have the girl.''

''Again, the girl,'' Risto said impatiently. ''She's gone and good riddance. Why do you go on and on about that red-haired scarecrow?''

''On and on?'' Ismal turned to his servant and arched one well-shaped eyebrow. ''So much hostility, Risto? Very strange. One would think you were jealous.''

Pain flashed briefly in the servant's dark eyes. ''You please to mock me,'' he said. ''You've always done so—since you were a babe.''

''Would you rather I lied to you, as I do to everyone else?'' Ismal asked softly. ''Shall I wear my pretty mask for you, too?''

''Nay, I couldn't bear it.''

''Then stop acting like a jealous wife. You never did so before.''

''You never behaved so strangely before.'' Risto hesitated a moment, then went on, in aggrieved tones. ''Last night you called out her name in your sleep.''

Ismal calmly studied his servant's face for a long, tense while. ''I see. And this morning, she vanished. I hope you didn't make her vanish, Risto.''

''Y'Allah, I should have known. You have been playing with me.'' Risto closed his eyes. ''I did not kill her, I swear it.''

''What, then?''

''You know,'' the servant said miserably. ''Always you know.''

''I know I woke before the sun rose and found you gone from the room. I know a few moments ago when you brought me news of Esme's departure, your black eyes shone with delight."

Risto winced.

"Her disappearance endangers *me,* Risto, yet you're pleased. Most strange in a devoted servant . . . and friend."

Risto fell to his knees before the *divan.* "Listen to me," he pleaded. "You can't stir a step toward the south while they're headed that way. If the weather turns bad again, they could be traveling for weeks. You must leave for Prevesa within days, but you scarcely think of that. While the girl's within reach, all your mind fixes on her—and that filthy Englishman. You said yourself last night you were trapped by your own scheme. Had you but waited another few days, you said, Jason would have disposed of himself. Now his curst daughter has disposed of *her*self, and it will be Ali who's distracted chasing after her. This is your chance to get away—"

"*Has* she disposed of herself, Risto?"

"May the Almighty strike me dead this instant if I lie to you," the servant said. Tears trickled down his hard, dark face. "I did not touch her. I saw her go, that is all."

"And told no one. And did not try to stop her."

"I followed her a ways. That is all. I did nothing."

Ismal leaned toward his servant, his blue eyes innocent as a babe's, kind as an angel's. "Which way did she go?" he whispered.

Chapter 18

For once, luck was with Esme. Saranda's tiny population had swelled to thrice its size for the festivities, and she'd managed to arrive a day before Donika's wedding. She had spotted Donika's brother Branko shortly after her arrival but waited until nightfall to reveal herself. By then, most of the men were in the early states of intoxication and the women in a frenzy of preparation. They wouldn't have noticed an elephant stampede, let alone the bedraggled boy Esme appeared to be.

Branko wasn't pleased to hear her story. Still, though he said she was a thousand times a fool and a hothead, he wasn't entirely without sympathy. Besides, he owed her. She'd saved his life two years ago and taken a bullet in her leg in the process.

All she wanted, she told him, was a boat to take her north, beyond Ali's territories, to Shkodra. There, Ali had no power, and she might stay safely with the old man who'd years before taught her healing.

"You needn't tell anyone else I'm here," she assured him. "Only help me find a hiding place for now. I won't stir until you tell me so."

Branko reflected. "I don't know the town," he said at last, in his slow, considering way. "The only safe place I know is with our family. Hush," he chided when she began to protest about endangering them. "You say no one will think to come here looking for you. Maybe so. Maybe they won't guess you'd hide so close to Corfu.

Still, word may come any hour—and the officials will be looking for a small female in boy's garb."

"With green eyes," she reminded him. "I must hide. There's no way I can disguise the color of my eyes."

"That won't be necessary if we make you appear a foreigner. A gypsy, maybe. Donika will think of something," he said. "But first I must get you to the house without arousing notice."

He thought again for a long while. Esme tried to think, too, but her brain wouldn't cooperate. It was as exhausted as her body.

"Yes, easy enough," Branko said, eyeing her thoughtfully. "For now, you'll be a weary boy I found. I'll carry you over my shoulder to the house. Only keep your eyes closed until I tell you to open them."

He could not have devised a more appealing plan. She'd spent three days endlessly thinking, planning ahead, while trying to keep panic and misery from addling her reason. She'd sold the fancy rifle she'd stolen from the guard and bought a horse with the money. Thereafter, she'd made excellent progress, for the weather had held fair. Nonetheless, Esme was tired to the bone. For a few minutes, it would be so good to let someone else do the thinking for her. Branko's manner might be slow, but his wits were not. Jason had always thought highly of Donika's elder brother.

Esme handed over her weapons and travel bags. Branko hoisted these over one broad shoulder and Esme over the other. Her body immediately slumped in relief, and her heavy lids fell closed. The rest was a dull awareness of motion, voices, noise. By the time they reached the house, even that awareness vanished. Esme was lost in black, blissful oblivion.

From the top of the rocky hill above the straggling wood, Varian watched the two riders approach the crossroads. They didn't pause as they reached it, but smoothly took the right branch.

"I can't believe it." He turned to Fejzi, who stood behind him.

"I do not understand," the secretary said, but I believe it. Ismal knows what he's about. Such a wise young man. And so kind of him to spare us the trouble of tracking her.'' He signaled to the men waiting below, who quickly gathered up their weapons and mounted.

''We will wait until they collect Ismal and Risto,'' Fejzi went on. ''Then your men will take you and Master Percival to the town. It is a small place. She will not be difficult to find.''

''If she's there.''

''She will be there.''

So everyone said. Varian didn't believe them; he was simply outnumbered. What he believed—or feared . . . but he wouldn't think about that. Not now.

''You're not coming with us?'' he asked.

''I must escort naughty Ismal to his cousin.''

''You've two score men to escort him, and I need a competent interpreter,'' Varian said tightly.

''You do not know Ismal. Forty men is nothing to him. In an hour he would have those brave fighters weeping. When Ismal makes men weep, they always do as he so sweetly asks. Fortunately, I am not a brave fighter but a great coward. Also, I was his tutor for many years and am immune to his arts. Fear of Ali keeps me so.''

''You make that spoiled lordling sound like a sorcerer.''

''Some say his mother was descended from Olympias, the mother of Alexander. They say she was an enchantress, with hair the color of dark fire—the Red Lion's color. They say she took gods as her lovers and it is of such the beautiful Ismal is made. Of course, everyone would like to claim kinship with Alexander. Still, even I believe there is something inhuman about him.''

''Something insane, more likely.'' Varian's gaze returned to the two riders.

''Perhaps,'' Fejzi said. ''The do say desire makes men mad.''

A muscle twitched in Varian's jaw. ''What romantics you Albanians seem to be. Even Ali puts all his faith in Ismal's desperate passion for Miss Brentmor. Or so he'd have one believe.''

''You do not believe it, Lord Edenmont?''

"What I believe appears to be of as little moment as does anything I do or say."

Below, Ali's troops spilled onto the road. As they picked up speed, they swiftly surged into order. In less than a minute, the mass of men and beasts had shaped itself into a broad galloping wedge, racing inexorably toward the crossroads.

Fejzi drew nearer. "You see," he said. "Wherever he turns, Ali's men will be waiting for him. He cannot escape."

"He should have known he'd be followed. He's not stupid. I'll wager he did know—and he's only led us on a wild goose chase." Varian's voice tightened with rage. "They probably planned it, the two of them. She couldn't have got away without his help."

Fejzi shrugged. "Perhaps. Perhaps not. The whole matter is beyond my comprehension. It seems Ali plays some deep game with his cousin, but what it is I do not know. Perhaps Ismal has guessed. Or perhaps he, too, has been misled. Still, our court intrigues are not your concern, my lord. In a short while, you shall find the girl and take her away."

"I wonder if I shall." Varian glanced past the secretary at Percival, who sat on a boulder some yards away, his eyes fixed upon the road. "I wonder if I should."

"You will do what is right, my lord. I have no doubt of that."

"Then you're a fool," Varian muttered. He turned and strode down the narrow path.

Donika's wedding day had dawned bright and warm, the sun beaming kindly upon the new bride and sparkling upon the gold coins that adorned her dark hair. Now, though the afternoon was waning, it beat down fiercely, making Esme wish her accomplices had devised a lighter disguise. Her face was sticky with paint and her body damp under the heavy layers of her gypsy costume.

She'd no idea what had transpired last night. Esme knew only that she'd been roused well before dawn to find herself in a room crammed with Donika's sisters, aunts, cousins, mother . . . and her own grandmother, Qeriba.

Had she not been so weary the night before, Esme would have realized Qeriba would be here, for she was both the groom's cousin and a friend of the bride's family. She was not, she soon made clear, Esme's friend at present.

From the day Esme had begun menstruating, Qeriba had been obsessed with getting her married. Thus, the instant Esme had finished her tale, the old woman began berating her—not for endangering herself or her friends, but for running away from a perfectly good *bachelor*.

She scolded while the others dressed Esme, and all during the hasty breakfast. She muttered throughout the wedding and was still grumbling hours after, while they sat with a large group of women in the terraced garden behind the bridegroom's house. He was inside with the men, listening to indelicate songs and even more indelicate advice, all very loud. The women were singing, too, though with rather less volume and far more subtlety. Only Qeriba ventured the occasional immodest suggestion—when, that is, she could spare a moment from haranguing her granddaughter.

"A fine-looking Englishman, of noble blood, and you ran away from him," she was saying for the thousandth time. "Why should he not take money from Ali? Are you such a treasure that you think a man—even a Christian—would take you for nothing?"

"Grandmama, how many times must I tell you? It has nothing to do with wedding me. He wanted only—"

"Men don't know what they want. Women must show them." Qeriba gestured about her. "Any of these girls could have shown him. But not you. You can read and write. You're more clever than any dozen of them together, but this you couldn't do."

"Any *one* of them is twelve times prettier than I, Grandmama."

"Men don't know what's pretty and what isn't. Make a man happy to look at you, and he believes you're Aphrodite. God give me patience. These things you of all girls should understand."

"I don't want to understand," Esme whispered irritably. "This has nothing to do with ensnaring men—as if I could. I just want to be left in peace."

"And die a virgin." Qeriba sighed. "You won't get a husband in Shkodra."

"I don't want—"

"A terrible place. Barbarians, all of them. Jason kept you there too long. You learned savage ways."

"Then it's best I return. There at least I'll belong." Esme rubbed her face. The thick paint made her skin itch, and she was perspiring heavily, though they sat in the shade. It wasn't just the heat and the six layers of clothing she staggered under, but increasing nervousness as the time for her departure neared.

Branko had found a boatman who'd agreed to take her to Shkodra, but not until nightfall, because he was in no hurry to leave the festivities. Esme could only hope he wouldn't drink too much. She'd never handled a boat on her own.

"You belong with your father's kin," Qeriba said. "It was Jason's wish." She gazed at Esme in vexation. "A little while ago, you played at telling fortunes. Shall I tell you yours? In all that's happened, I see clearly the hand of Fate. You cannot escape your *kismet* by sailing away on a boat. But it's no use to tell you. Never was there a child so obstinate."

"*Aman*, grandmama, grant me peace," Esme begged. "What's done is done. In a few hours, I'll be gone. Must we quarrel and say farewell in anger? May I not have a few hours' respite among those I love before I go?"

Qeriba studied her granddaughter's face, her own countenance softening. "Ah, well, it's bad luck to part in anger." She glanced about. "Song and laughter are good things, but hard on an old woman's ears. The sun beats too strong, and no wind comes to ease its heat. Also, I'm hungry. Let's take a bite to eat, then I'll go with you to the harbor. It's been many years since I walked along the shores of Saranda. Let's stroll there together, and let the sea quiet our spirits, eh?"

* * *

While his men spread through Saranda, Varian waited on a hill overlooking the town. He'd fretted one interminable hour, pacing restlessly, when Agimi returned with his report.

Saranda, it turned out, was in a state of roaring chaos. The son of one of its more prosperous citizens had just got himself leg-shackled, and the entire population was celebrating. The streets near the bridegroom's house were mobbed with men. The only way to get through without trampling drunken wedding guests was on foot. In short, Lord Edenmont could not expect to make his way unnoticed, and word of his presence would spread quickly through the crowd.

"I take it Agimi considers that a problem," Varian said to Petro.

The dragoman scowled. "What else is to be expected? Where *she* goes, always there is trouble. Agimi says the bride is the good friend of the little witch. They will not help us. We shall all be killed."

"Don't be silly," said Percival. "There's always general *besa* at weddings. They won't even kill their own worst enemy. Mustafa said—"

"I don't care what Mustafa said," Varian snapped. "The whole town's drunk. A mob of drunken men could take it into their heads to do anything. You'll stay here with Petro and make sure he keeps away from the *raki* bottle. I've got problems enough without worrying about you."

"But, sir, I promise I—"

"You'll *stay here,* Percival."

"But you need Petro to—"

"There's bound to be someone who knows Greek or Italian. At the least, the priest must know Latin. I'll manage."

"They're not Papists, sir, not in the south. They're—"

"Damnation. Will you hold your tongue for once and just do as you're told? I warn you, Percival, if you so much as *think* of stirring from this spot, I'll give you the birching I should have done weeks ago."

Percival hastily sank back down upon the stone he'd been sitting on. "Yes, sir," he said meekly.

Varian threw one warning look at Petro, then quickly mounted and followed Agimi down the hillside.

Donika squeezed Esme's hand. "No, you cannot go so soon," she said. "You promised you would sing to me, gypsy girl."

Esme looked at Qeriba.

"Well, what harm?" the old woman said. "Sing to the bride and bring her good luck. The bride's wishes come first. Later, the whims of an old woman."

Esme smiled faintly. A substantial meal had radically improved Qeriba's temper. When she'd done eating, she'd even patted Esme's hand. "The air cools at last," she'd said. "A good wind comes. Can you feel it?"

Esme felt no breeze, even now. Though the sun was slowly sinking toward the sea, the garden still seemed stifling. She wasn't sure this was entirely on account of her thick clothing. Perhaps the feeling was inside her. She felt suffocated by Donika's glowing happiness. That was ill-natured and selfish, Esme chided herself.

She returned Donika's hand squeeze and said, "I shall give you my best love song. A plaintive melody, but the end is a happy one."

She sank down on the cobblestones at the bride's feet, arranged her heavy skirts elegantly about her, accepted the lutelike *çiftelia* from another girl, and began to sing.

This was truly a mournful melody, a story of a peasant girl wooed and abandoned by a rich man's son. By the second verse, she saw tears in more than one pair of feminine eyes. Even Donika's were misting, but she smiled, and those tears seemed radiant beams of joy.

It wasn't until the third verse—when the peasant girl plucked a poppy from the spot where her lover had first embraced her—that Esme sensed something amiss. Her audience seemed entirely captivated by her performance; several women were weeping openly. Whatever was wrong, they were too taken up with the sad song to notice.

Esme's glance darted to Qeriba. The old woman's attention was not fixed upon her granddaughter but upon the house, and her narrowed eyes glinted.

Then Esme realized what it was. The men's noise had subsided. No shouts, no boisterous singing, only a buzz of voices. Her flesh chilled. She glanced behind her. Nobody. Nothing. Only the too-subdued house.

The chill had seeped inside her now, and a cold feeling seized her belly. Her tongue stumbled over the next line of the song, then failed her entirely as raw panic engulfed her. She leapt up, dropping her instrument, heedless of everything but the need to escape. She was dimly aware of the women moving about her, of shrill voices sharp with anxiety and questions. Esme heeded none of it. She was already hurrying toward the path, all her being fixed on the gate beyond.

Varian had heard her. He was sure he'd heard her voice. He hurried out to the garden . . . and found himself facing a wall of women.

"Where is she?" he demanded in Albanian.

Silence.

His glance darted over the terraces and stopped at the narrow gate. He'd no sooner begun heading for the path that led to it than the feminine wall surged into motion, blocking his way. He looked behind him. The men had followed him out of the house. Now they stood, unmoving, another wall of sullen faces. Agimi tried to struggle through, but two of the men caught him and held him back. No one would hinder the English lord; no one would be allowed to help him, either.

Swearing under his breath, Varian turned back to the women. There must be fifty at least, and more were streaming into the garden. They wouldn't let him by, that much was obvious. His predicament was equally plain. They stood packed close together, so that to get through, he must touch them. If even his coat sleeve brushed against any of them, the men would be upon him in an instant. Most were the worse for drink and could easily forget that he was English, a guest in their country. They had not been particularly hospitable to begin with. Esme must have made him out a monster—the Devil incarnate, no doubt. It didn't matter. He was not about to retreat.

The Devil flashed his most disarming smile. "So much

beauty in one place,'' he said softly. ''It takes my breath away.''

A few of the younger women stirred uneasily, as he'd hoped. Women didn't need to understand his language. They responded to his tone and his eyes. Whatever they'd believed a moment before, they were confused now. The dark-eyed bride, who stood in the forefront of her army, looked puzzled and anxious. Beside her, a tiny old woman clad entirely in black muttered something. The comment elicited a few giggles. Also, a few irritated responses.

Varian focused on the old lady. ''You understand English?'' he asked.

She shrugged. *''Pak.''* A little.

Thank heaven. ''Please tell them then that never have I beheld so beautiful a bride, a blooming rose in a bouquet of beauty. The men cannot move because they're struck helpless by this sight. They wonder how I dare approach so near, for surely so much sweetness will kill me.''

The old woman gravely translated this for the company. Their uneasiness increased. He heard several nervous giggles.

''I dare because my heart is gone,'' Varian went on coaxingly. ''A little bird has taken it and flown from me. I heard her singing a moment ago. Or did I merely dream this? If she were near, such sweet flowers would not keep me from her. They could not be so unkind.''

Tears were trickling down the bride's face even before the old woman had finished translating. The bride looked enquiringly at the crone. The latter shrugged, then waved her bony hand impatiently. The bride stepped aside, and the others with her.

''Go, Varian *Shenjt Gjergj,*'' said the old woman.

Varian swept her a bow. *''Faleminderit,''* he said. God help me, he thought. Clearly, no one else would.

He strode rapidly toward the gate.

He didn't know where he was going, or that Esme had gone this way. But the garden walls were high, and this appeared to be the only speedy exit from the place.

Beyond the gate, he discovered a vast orchard rising

on the hillside—and not a living soul in sight. He stared despairingly about him. "Esme!" he called. Only the wind answered, brisker than before, coming from the southwest. He could search the orchard or go the other way, west, to the bay. He glanced at the waning sun and headed for the stonier part of the hill, the side facing the water.

After stumbling about blindly for a while, he found at last a well-worn path. As he left the orchard behind, the way grew rockier and narrower, coiling tortuously about the brown marble of the hillside. Hours seemed to pass while he felt he traveled in circles and got no nearer the bay. He reminded himself the ways were always like this in Albania: roundabout and agonizingly slow as they detoured round the unforgiving terrain. Which meant that Esme could go no faster than he . . . if this was the way she had gone. It must be. He could not consider the alternative.

At long last, when he felt certain he'd circled the entire mountain, Varian struggled through the thorns and grasping vines of some unfamiliar vegetation to find the view open at last. Below him sprawled the bay of Santi Quaranta: Forty Saints. He hastened down the slope and across the rough road to the beach. To his right, a mole jutted out into the harbor. Like a great arm bent at the elbow, the stone breakwater held a cluster of small boats in its embrace. West, where the sun dipped treacherously near the horizon, he discerned the dark mass of Corfu rising in the midnight blue of the Ionian Sea.

He took all this in at a glance, along with the disquieting awareness that he had about half an hour—an hour at most—to find Esme before night fell. His feet, meanwhile, carried him on, down to the boat rest, while he scanned the vessels for signs of life.

The tiny harbor within a harbor lay ghostly still. He heard only the waves lapping and the faint creak of wood. He must be the only soul in Saranda who wasn't at the wedding. Except for Esme, wherever she was. Not here, he thought, as despair washed over him. Nothing stirred here.

"Esme!" he shouted. He ran along the breakwater. "Esme!"

The boats—fishing vessels, most of them—gave him no answer. They lay mute, huddled together within the great stone arm. Sullen reddish glints danced upon mast and deck, the only light in the deepening shadows. The boats appeared empty, and he told himself he'd erred grievously to come this way. Then he answered that she was small and might lay hidden under a blanket or behind a heap of ropes and nets. The sun was low, and most of the boats rested in the breakwater's shade. He couldn't be certain until he searched . . . every last, dratted one of them.

He scrambled down over the slippery stones. "Esme!"

He leapt aboard the nearest boat, a tiny vessel. A quick examination turned up nothing. He went on to the next, and the next. No life. No human sound here except his own furious breathing and the pounding of his heart.

He was aware of sound behind him—from the town—as though the merrymakers were advancing to the harbor. It was only a buzz of voices, punctuated now and again by a shout, but he'd no interest in the town and scarcely heeded it.

His senses strained instead to discern life here. One life, one small being who *must* be here. He could not be wrong. He could not have lost her, not this time, for this time, his heart told him, it would be for good.

"Esme!" The next boat was too far away to jump to. He leapt to the stones again instead, stumbled and fell, and cursed. "Esme!" he bellowed. "Don't make me hunt you down!" He scrambled up. "You won't get away from me! You won't, you little witch!"

Something stirred amid the shadowy shapes to his right.

Then he spotted her, on the very last boat of all: a small, dark shape moving clumsily, struggling with something.

"Esme!" He raced toward her, his feet slipping on the wet stones. She was fighting with the sails, and the wind was still rising. If she succeeded, it would sweep her out into the bay in minutes.

"Esme, stop!"

She turned sharply, then away again, and bent to fumble with something.

Varian tripped and nearly slid into the water. As he regained his balance, he saw her boat, free of its mooring now, drifting out toward the narrow neck that opened into the harbor. The tide, or some infernal current, must be carrying her, for the sails still hung raggedly. In the blink of an eye, she had slipped clear of the other boats. For one panic-stricken instant, Varian stood watching the small figure as it battled with the ragged sheets. Then the gusting wind caught and filled them, tearing them from her hands. The boat tilted abruptly. She stumbled and grabbed at the sail.

Sweet Jesus. She didn't know what she was doing.

"Esme!" he shouted. "Don't!"

But she would. She knew she couldn't master the boat, yet she wouldn't yield. Varian didn't stop to think further. He hadn't time—any more than he had time to make off with one of the other vessels. He knew nothing of boats, either. He tore off his coat and boots, ran blindly across the deck, and dove into the water.

When he looked up again, she'd passed the narrow opening, but her motion had slowed. Her vessel was turning, dipping crazily, its partly unfurled sails caught by the wind, then released. He struggled on, forcing his muscles to heed his mind, not their own strength or skill.

He heard a scream and an ominous splash. An answering scream rose within him, and he drove himself harder, though his muscles were shrieking now, his lungs burning.

A lifetime passed or minutes or seconds, then he was close enough to hear her wild thrashing. He looked up in time to see her go under. He kept on moving. He heard death rushing toward her, faster than he, like a roaring wind.

Leave her. Please. Leave her to me. Please. Anything.

"Varian!" One choking cry, so weak amid the great relentless blackness bearing down upon them both.

No. Wait. I'm coming. Wait for me.

Beyond, the sun plummeted to the horizon, red as hellfire. The masterless boat drifted swiftly toward it. Nearer, though still beyond his reach, Varian saw her head sucked down again into the hungry blue maw of the sea. He cried out her name, then plunged into the roaring darkness.

Chapter 19

Varian was aware of the sound before he came fully awake: tenor voices mourning, and with them, the low wail of a pipe.

He opened his eyes to find himself slumped on a stool beside a bed. A few candles flickered fitfully in the darkness, showing him the slight form buried under the bedclothes. A tangled mass of dark red hair framed her pale, still face. Esme stirred slightly, as though she felt his gaze even while she slept. Only sleeping, he assured himself as he lightly stroked her hair. He'd not lost her. The men of Saranda had come to their rescue.

Varian had not made it easy for them. He'd fought like a madman, though even in the madness he'd known he couldn't get her to shore on his own. The heavy garments that had dragged her down had slowed his progress. As he grew weaker, they'd threatened to pull him down with her.

The rest was hazy. Voices, movement. All Varian's being had been riveted upon the girl in his arms, whom he refused to relinquish. He must have collapsed. He didn't recall reaching the house, wherever it was.

Now he realized the voices were coming from outside, and their wailing was merely the usual Albanian melody in minor key, like the one he'd heard Esme singing.

He rose stiffly. His numb muscles awoke with a protest, prickling painfully in his arms and legs as he moved to the open window. Beneath lay a wide terrace where a group of men sang. Below them and beyond, the bay glistened innocently in the moonlight, as though it had not sought to take Esme from him only a few hours before.

From the bed came a moan, then a flurried rustling of bedclothes and a panicked stream of Albanian. Varian hurried back to the bed and gently drew her into his arms. "It's all right," he said. "You're safe."

He felt a shudder run through her thin frame, then another. Then her chest was heaving, wracked with low, terrible sobs she struggled to contain. But they broke from her at last, and when Varian heard her cry her father's name, his heart broke with hers.

He who was so clever with words sought them now, only to find he'd nothing of value. "I'm sorry, sweetheart." He forced the worthless syllables past the constriction in his throat and knew it was futile to try for better. He pulled her close, stroked her hair, tried to give comfort, and found again he'd none to give. All her pent-up grief ripped free in ragged cries, half Albanian, half English. Hot tears spilled down her face while the sobs shook her small body, and he was helpless.

Women's tears had never frightened him as they did other men, but this was different. This was his strong, brave Esme weeping. She was helpless and broken, and he couldn't bear it. His heart ached for her, grieving for her grief and despairing at his own uselessness.

"I'm sorry," he said, over and over. One futile phrase in answer to her misery.

I want my father.

I'm sorry.

So it went, endlessly, yet in fact only a short while. In spite of his ineptness—or perhaps because of it—Esme soon recovered. She did so sharply, pushing away from him, then angrily rubbing her nose.

Varian reached for his handkerchief and realized he hadn't one. They'd taken his sopping garments away. He wore only a robe. He searched the room and found a towel which he wordlessly gave her. She wiped her face.

"I never cry," she said shakily. "I hate it."

"I know."

She muttered to herself a moment, then announced clearly, "You should not have come after me."

"I had no choice."

Esme shot him a look of unalloyed contempt.

In that instant, pure, blessed relief washed through him. She was well and truly angry, therefore herself once more. Her own unreasonable, temperamental self.

She was mortified because she'd broken down. Of course she'd take it out on him. Let her. Her rage Varian could deal with, more or less. Her tears paralyzed him.

"Esme," he began, "you didn't think I'd let you—"

"I didn't think even *you* could be so greedy. I could not believe my eyes when I saw you leap into the water. You could have drowned! For a thousand pounds! What good would money do you at the bottom of the sea?"

"I beg your pardon?" Varian said. "I don't believe I heard aright. Something about a thousand pounds?"

"Something? Do not play games with me. I know that is why you chased me—you, the laziest idler on three continents. But for money, you will stir yourself."

"Indeed I will," he replied, "in moderation. To attempt to swim the Ionian is hardly moderate." He gave her a puzzled glance. "Are you telling me you had a thousand pounds on your person? I thought it was the costume that made you so heavy."

"Do not pretend to be stupid. I know what Ali offered and what you agreed to do. I hope he gave you the money already. If he did not, you shall never see it, I promise you."

Varian rubbed his head. "Ali, apparently, offered me a thousand pounds to do something. Please forgive me, but my mind is muddled at present. Perhaps I was struck by an oar. I cannot for the life of me recollect what I agreed to do."

Her stormy green eyes clouded with confusion. She moved uneasily in the bed. It was a large bed with a feather mattress, decidedly European—"Frankish," the Albanians would say. All westerners were Franks to them, Varian thought absently while he waited. And he would wait until Doomsday if he must. It appeared Esme had not run away for love of Ismal, as she'd scrawled in her cruel note, but because of this thousand-pounds matter concerning himself. Varian's offense, whatever it was, must be a grievous one if she could fly into a tantrum after what she'd just endured. Any other young woman would have wanted weeks to recover.

"No one struck you," came her sullen voice at last. "You are ashamed. That's why you pretend you don't remember."

"I don't feel the least ashamed," Varian said lightly. "If you think the recollection will make me so, I pray you will not mention it. We shall speak of something else."

Once more he took his seat upon the bed. Esme retreated, flushing hotly. "No! You shall not use your arts on me. I shall not marry you. Never! I would throw myself from a mountain first."

"Marry me?" He drew back in alarm. "I should say not. Whatever put such a ghastly idea into your head?"

"Ghastly?" Her voice rose shrilly. "You did not tell Ali it was ghastly."

"I should hope I am not so tactless as to say so to a man possessing several hundred wives. I might hurt his feelings."

"Aye, but *mine* are of no account. I knew it," she grumbled. "I knew he'd not paid you yet. You'd not say such a thing to me if he had. No, you would pretend it was the dearest wish of your heart."

"Good heavens, you do think I come cheap, don't you? That wounds me, Esme, truly it does. You think I agreed to wed you for a mere thousand pounds? My dear girl, I should not agree to shackle myself to Aphrodite herself for anything less than twenty thousand. In gold," he said. "And I should test every coin with my teeth."

"I *heard* Ali say it. I heard him tell Ismal."

"Then you heard him lying. A whore I may be, but a precious expensive one, I promise you." Varian looked toward the window and frowned. "A thousand pounds. The very idea. I have never been so insulted in all my life."

Esme didn't respond. Obviously, she was turning the matter over in her mind. Just as well. Varian had his own riddle to solve, and it had to do with tomorrow. And the next day. And the day after. His mind recoiled automatically, as it always did from that gloomy prospect, the future.

He gave his attention to the window instead, to the sounds coming from below. He'd heard laughter a short while ago, when she was berating him. The laughter had stopped, and the singing had recommenced. A stringed instrument of some sort now accompanied the pipe.

He heard Esme sigh.

"What are they singing?" he asked.

"Nothing. A love song."

"I understand *hajde,*" he said. "But none of the rest. What is the chorus? Shpee-mee—"

"*Shpirti im.* My spirit, soul. 'Come, my . . . my heart.' " She made a small, weary gesture. "The man—he—oh, he calls to the girl in love."

"Ah, well, love. Men will say anything, won't they?"

A taut pause.

"Varian."

He didn't look around. He felt the mattress move as she crept toward him. She stopped abruptly part way.

"Varian, will you swear you did not agree to wed me—for any price?"

"Don't be silly. A gentleman swears on his honor. I haven't any."

"Then why did you risk your life for me? If the men had not come, we would both have died. Why did you do it?"

"I don't know. I wasn't thinking at the time. I assume I was seized by a fit of insanity. They seem to occur frequently in your vicinity."

She crept closer. Varian felt her light touch on his shoulder. He turned his head slowly. Esme was on her knees beside him. The skirt of her thin night rail had hiked up past her knees. Varian hastily looked up and locked with her intent green gaze.

"Tell me something," she said. "Anything. Lie to me, please."

"I'd better not," he answered softly. "You're so overset at present, you're likely to believe anything."

"Yes. I will."

"You'll even believe I love you."

Her hand tightened on his shoulder. Varian quickly pulled it away, wanting to break free and flee from the terrible words he'd uttered. From her, before he destroyed her. He didn't move, didn't release her hand.

Her fingers slid between his, and she brought their twined hands to her bared knee. The room grew fearfully hot, stifling.

"I'd better leave," he said thickly.

Her lower lip trembled. "You always say that. You always go."

"For your own good."

"Nay. You do not want me." She extracted her hand from his. "I am so ashamed."

"You're tired and overwrought. You've had a terrible experience."

"This is terrible." Her voice was low and unsteady. "Always I find death before me. I stare at him fearlessly, because I am a warrior. If I set my mind to it, I could kill you. But I cannot win this struggle. I cannot make you touch me as a man touches a woman."

"Don't be so cruelly absurd," he said tightly. "I've touched you that way far too many times."

Too many times . . . and never enough.

Varian's gaze trailed from her trembling mouth to the smooth white skin above the neckline of her night rail, down to the small curve of her breasts to her tiny waist . . . down to his own hand, still resting upon her knee and itching to stroke, caress.

He drew in a painful breath. "I want you. I *need* you. I'm sick with it. Oh, God, don't listen to me. Don't . . . don't do this, Esme." The flesh beneath his hand was so smooth, so firm. Even as he warned her, his fingers moved longingly up her thigh.

Her head bent closer. The scent of the sea yet clung to her hair. It was sweet and fresh, like her silken skin. "You're so beautiful," he said softly. "It's not fair."

She murmured in her own tongue.

Varian told himself to leave. Just stand up and *walk*

away. Instead, he caught her by the waist and drew her to him.

He gazed into eyes dark and deep as an evergreen forest. "Just one kiss," he breathed. "Just one."

Her slender arms wrapped about his shoulders. "Yes. Just one."

He wanted only one sweet taste of his fierce, innocent nymph. He'd nearly lost her. A kiss was all he asked. It would be enough. It must be, he told himself as his mouth gently covered hers.

Her body swiftly melted against him. Her taut breasts pressed against the silk of his robe. Her mouth was parting for him, so warm, calling him into her depths.

All the world he knew became fragrant with the sea, sweet with the taste of her. She was young and fiercely alive as he'd never been. He tasted the rushing river and the evergreen forest in her kiss, and the turbulence, too, of the mountains where the gods yet lived. He wanted to possess that vibrant spirit and be renewed . . . and he knew he was wrong. It wouldn't be that way. He'd taint and weaken her.

He broke free of her mouth, only to find he was too base to break free entirely. Her scent, irresistible, called him back. He trailed hot, needy kisses to her throat and felt her body yearn toward his, promising rapture. He heard muslin whisper coaxingly against silk, and he answered, yes, because he was weak.

He found the ribbons of her gown, swiftly loosened them and pressed his mouth to the fragrant warmth of her breast. She gasped softly, then twined her fingers in his hair and pressed him closer. He trailed his tongue lingeringly along the taut flesh, to the hard, trembling peak, where he tasted and teased, letting the heat build in him as he felt it build in her. Her breath came faster, uneven.

He was hungry, and the wicked heat within urged him to haste, but he wanted to burn forever. He was aware he must stop soon, too soon. But not yet. He'd make this too-brief moment feel like forever. He'd make her forget her grief and anger, and for that short time he'd forget, too: fear and shame and the dreary haze of tomorrows stretching out before him.

"Only you," he whispered against her skin. "Only *now.*"

"Yes."

Varian looked up. Her eyes were dark, lost. Her hair streamed over her shoulders, garnet gleaming against the pearl of her skin. The gown had slipped down past her waist.

He'd seen her so before, and the memory had taunted him ever since: slight and pale and so achingly fragile outside, so strong and passionate inside. She was wild and young and shatteringly beautiful. How could he not hold her close, possess her just for this moment, when at any moment she might slip through his hands? Yet everything precious he'd ever held had slipped through his hands . . . to lay shattered, forgotten as he raced heedlessly on to the next moment. The next and the next . . . tomorrow.

"I don't want to hurt you," he whispered.

"You won't." Her full mouth curved into a hint of a smile. "Try. See if you can."

"No. Tell me "no" instead."

"Yes." Esme kissed his forehead, then his cheek. He turned his head to capture her mouth. She eluded him, and he gasped when he felt her warm lips at the nape of his neck. She pushed his robe aside and made a tantalizing path to his shoulders, then down. Her fingers strayed to his chest, teasing where his heart beat crazily, and her touch sent heat roaring to his vitals. He tore her hands away and swiftly bore her down.

In an instant the night rail lay upon the floor by the bed. His robe speedily followed.

Outside, the plaintive melody rose in aching cries, subsided, and cried again. Inside, he cried out for the woman he crushed in his embrace. Life was her soft flesh against his, her supple limbs entwined with his. Here the world was warm and rich with her drugging scent. Here it called him in her low, breathless voice. She spoke his name, and all his being answered, desperate to be lost inside her and kept safe, where he belonged.

He knew it was only lust's madness. He knew he didn't belong. He was an intruder, seeking only for himself. He heard the faint, shrill warning at the furthest edges of consciousness.

I need her, Varian answered silently, while he murmured love against her mouth, her neck, her breast. She answered with urgent caresses. They claimed him instantly, and the warning voice sank and died.

His hungry hands found her silky nest of curls and the damp softness they sheltered. She tensed, gripping his shoulders, but this time he didn't pause. It was beyond him. His conscience shrilled again, weakly and unheeded, because her damp innocence was too sweet. Gentle despite his ravening need, he stroked and coaxed and urged, and she moved restlessly against his hand. He felt the tremors run through her, each stronger than the one before, felt her fighting them . . . and the rush of warmth as they overcame her.

"Varian." A small, ragged cry. "Oh, *peren . . . di.*"

She clawed at his shoulders and pulled him toward her, demanding his mouth. He gave what she commanded while his fingers stole deeper. She groaned and jerked away from his driving kiss, frantic and impatient in the storm wracking her body. She turned her face into the pillow and moaned helplessly, while her body surged and shuddered against him, wildly seeking release.

His own frame vibrated with impatience, urging him to the place he'd readied and into the storm of ecstasy he'd meant to give only her . . . selflessly . . . for once in his life. To give the one joy he could without taking as well. To give lovingly, only to her, his wild beautiful girl. He'd meant only that, truly, minutes, years ago. But he found he couldn't give her release, not as he'd meant. Her ferocious hunger would not yield to his hands.

She groaned and cursed, then caught at his wrist and pulled him away. *"Hajde,"* she ordered. She raked her strong fingers down his rigid torso, down, inexorably, to the swollen betrayal below.

"Don't," he gasped. Too late.

A lightning bolt shot through him, blasting reason and will into scorched nothingness.

He pushed her full onto her back and quickly thrust himself between her thighs. Esme lay trembling beneath him, her breath coming in shallow pants. He stared for one desperate moment into the wild green depths of her eyes. Then his hands dragged possessively down her body, over her tight belly, and on to the hot, dark passage.

He poised himself at the entrance, then thrust inward. She was swollen, wet, but her innocence tightened against him, and he grasped her hips as she recoiled instinctively.

Though all his being throbbed to conquer, possess, Varian willed himself to slow down. Yet even as he felt the way easing for him, he felt her pleasure fading and knew the rest would be no joy to her, only pain. Not all his arts could make that fragile shield of innocence vanish, magically, without pain. Then worse: corruption, dishonor . . . her destruction. He could stop. It would kill him, but he could do it.

As Varian bent to kiss her, her hands caught in his hair. "I want you," she said, her voice low, fierce.

"Don't," he whispered. "I don't want to hurt you any more."

"I want you," she repeated. "My body will not heed me. Make it obey you. Make me *yours,* Varian."

Don't listen to her. She doesn't understand. She's innocent.

But his corrupt self wanted to heed her command. It was the beast in him, the lowest of his nature, frantic to conclude what had begun. Varian ordered himself to draw away. He couldn't. Sweat trickled down his back.

"I'll hurt you," he said hoarsely, as he gazed despairingly into her great, stormy eyes.

Her nails dug into his scalp. "Someone must. You, this night, Varian . . . or another."

He tried to tell himself she didn't know what she was saying, yet the words tore through him, taunting, unbearable. Ismal's image flashed before him.

"No," Varian growled. "You're mine, damn you."

She shook her head.

He answered with his hands and mouth, rousing her

more ruthlessly than before. He was beyond patience or gentleness, and her quick, hot response told him she wanted none. She was as fierce and fearless in passion as in all else. Wild and sweet and beautiful . . . *his*.

"Mine," he said savagely. In one mindless instant, he drove himself into her. An instant of animal triumph . . . possession . . . conquest. He heard her gasp, felt her tense against the pain. Then remorse knifed through him. Too late.

"I'm sorry," he gasped. "Oh, love, I'm sorry." Blood pounded in his temples as it thundered in his veins, urging him to release, but he willed himself to pause. His hands moved soothingly over her shocked, stiffened frame. "Let me love you, sweet. Forgive me, and let me love you. I need you, Esme."

Her eyes flew open. "There is more?" she asked shakily.

Oh, Lord, she'd had enough. She wanted it to be over, poor darling. Varian drew his hand longingly over her taut breast, and his flesh stirred, moving him within her. Yes, his body wanted it to be done as well, brute that it was. But he needed more. He wanted her entirely, soul and body, for himself. Selfish. But so he was.

"More," he said. "As much as you'll give me." He let himself move again, slowly, while he stroked her belly.

She caught her breath. *"Varian."*

But it wasn't pain, not now. Surprise, perhaps, and then, as she moved cautiously in response, a soft sound of pleasure.

"Yes," he whispered. "Like this, sweet. All the world goes away, doesn't it?"

He felt it, felt the world leaving her, as it did him. He felt her pleasure growing as her body yielded to him, learning to match his rhythm. Her pain was forgotten, like his regret. He could feel no remorse now, not while he was surging back to life within her. There was only this moment, and Esme, and sweet, dark rapture as she yielded to the storm.

His body pounded with her life, her being. He was lost inside her, racing with her on a furious torrent that clawed and pulled him into eternity. He felt her shattering around him and heard the cry rising in her throat. He sank down to her, caught her tight in his arms, and covered her mouth with his.

Chapter 20

Esme knew he was gone before she opened her eyes to the bright morning light. She had felt the chill of his absence in her last dream. Other dreams had preceded it, but those had been filled with warmth and a delirious gladness.

She could never have dreamed such joy before. She could never have imagined what happened when a man joined his body to a woman's. She'd understood there must be pleasure in it. She'd tasted pleasure weeks before, in Poshnja, when Varian had kissed and caressed her so intimately. But last night's pleasure was darker, more turbulent. It was as though a powerful demon became trapped inside one's body, where it made a terrible but beautiful struggle, like an unearthly thunderstorm, until at last it was released. And with release came the sweetest peace.

But not for long, Esme discovered. She touched the pillow where Varian's head had been and remembered how tenderly he'd smiled as he held her in his arms in that rapturous peace.

Still, he'd surely smiled at all his women so. He'd know how to drive away every doubt and twinge of conscience. He'd know how to keep his women quiet. He didn't like turmoil. He'd leave them, and that must cause unpleasantness, but later. He'd prefer to leave them to be unpleasant all by themselves.

Certainly it was better he had left, Esme told herself. She hoped he was already on his way to Corfu. She didn't know how she could ever look him in the eye again. She'd begged him to take her, and then—oh, how clumsy she'd been. Her childish body had been so awkward, inept. No wonder he'd tried to stop, repeatedly. What a chore it must have been to appease her lust.

She covered her face. She'd behaved like a bitch in heat. She was disgusting.

"Ah, the morning after."

Esme dropped her hands and stared in horrified disbelief at the doorway.

Varian stood there for a moment, a faint smile curving his beautiful mouth as he studied her. Then he closed the door as quietly as he'd opened it, crossed the room, and picked up her nightgown.

"You'd better put something on," he said. "Otherwise, I may be tempted to reacquaint myself with what's under the blankets, and I had rather not wrinkle my trousers." He dropped the gown on the bed.

Her face blazed.

Varian retired to the window and turned away.

His dark coat fit as though it had been sculpted to him, emphasizing his broad shoulders and narrow waist, and his trousers hugged the muscles of his long legs. Last night she'd shamelessly wrapped herself about his naked, sweating body; this morning, he seemed a stranger. Esme wanted desperately to dash out the door while his back was turned and run far, far away.

Instead, she sat up and clumsily yanked the night rail over her head. Her fingers trembled so badly that she tied the ribbons in knots.

"I—I thought you had gone," she choked out.

"Did you? And where did you think I'd go?" He was still looking out the window.

"To Corfu."

"Ah, yes. Without you." He turned around. "Seduced and abandoned, that's what you thought—along with heaven knows what else. I don't especially want to know what else. The morning after, as I said. It's tomorrow, Esme."

The ominous tone in his voice sent a chill through her. Instinctively, she pulled the bedclothes up to her chest.

"Of course it is tomorrow. There is no need to make it sound like Judgment Day."

"Is that what it sounds like to you? How interesting. Because it is, in a way. For you, that is."

Varian leaned back against the window frame and folded his arms across his chest. His face was expressionless as stone, his voice cool and clipped. "I woke early this morning. Among other concerns, I wondered where Percival had got to. I found him downstairs with Qeriba and learned it was he who saved our lives."

Qeriba. In this house. Esme gazed at the bedclothes in despair.

"Your loyal friends were determined I should have no assistance whatsoever, not even that of my own escort," Varian went on. "They were convinced I was Beelzebub, apparently. Luckily, Percival disobeyed my orders and was on the spot to reassure them. Unluckily, they refused to trust a translator. Your cousin was obliged to explain our situation in Albanian."

Imagining her poor cousin struggling with an unfamiliar language while surrounded by a crowd of hostile strangers, Esme winced. "He is a very brave boy. He saved not only us but all my friends as well. Ali would have punished them cruelly if you had drowned."

"Percival didn't know," Varian continued as though she hadn't spoken, "that in Albanian, the word for 'friend' can also mean 'spouse,' just as the word for 'man' can mean 'husband.' He thought he was telling them I was a good man, a friend, and that you'd run away because of a misunderstanding. What your friends heard was that you'd run away from your *husband.* That's why, after rescuing us, they left us to sort out our differences in the time-honored fashion of wedded couples."

Esme tried to read his expression, but he gave her nothing. She raised her chin. "It was a simple mistake. Everyone will understand when it is explained. besides, it can be no secret that I shared your tent many times. If you are worried that my cousin will be shamed by such a thing," she went on stiffly, "then you can leave me here. I never wished to go to Corfu, as I have told you countless times."

Varian's expression chilled. "I hoped that is not why you ordered me to ruin you, Esme."

"I did not *order* you!" But that was a lie. She had insisted. *Demanded.* Her entire body burned with shame.

"I told you "no," didn't I?"

"Yes, but—"

"But you wouldn't listen." He approached the bed. "I've warned you repeatedly. I *begged* you last night. You had only to say "no." But you wouldn't. You know the sort of man I am. A girl as clever as you must have known the instant you clapped eyes on me. You were clever enough, certainly, to manipulate me in other ways. And you'd sense enough to encourage me to believe you were a child. Regrettably, that is about all the sense of self-preservation you've demonstrated."

He heaved a great sigh and sat down upon the bed.

Esme knew well enough how badly she'd behaved. All the same, she did feel it was unkind of him to add his sarcastic reproaches to what was rapidly becoming the most humiliating morning of her life. But as she surreptitiously studied him, her conscience gave a painful jab.

Now that he was near, she saw he was not nearly so composed as he'd appeared. There were deep shadows under his eyes, and his skin was unusually pale. He looked as though he hadn't slept a wink.

"You are upset about last night," she said. It was a stupid, awkward thing to say, but it was out as soon as she thought it. "I am—I am sorry it was—it is not pleasant for you to think about."

Varian turned his gaze full upon her, his face still blank. "Not pleasant?"

Esme looked away. "I didn't realize—oh, I wasn't thinking, or maybe I would have realized that—that it could not be pleasurable with an ignorant girl. I could not understand why you kept wanting to stop. I was not thinking how wearisome it must be for you. Worse—after swimming across the harbor and nearly drowning, too. But it is all of a piece, isn't it?" she said sadly. "I made you go through the swamps and up and down the mountains and endure all the filth and vermin and—''

''Esme, are you quite well?'' he asked in a queer, strangled voice.

''I am much better than I deserve,'' she muttered. ''I deserve to be *shot*. I should not be allowed among civilized people. I belong in the mountains, with the wild beasts.''

He cleared his throat. ''I did indicate the day of reckoning had arrived, my dear. I had something a bit more drastic in mind, however.''

Her eyes opened very wide. She'd not meant to be taken literally. ''M-more drastic?''

''You may well look frightened, Esme. It's about time you did.'' He pried her hand from the blanket and clasped it firmly between his. ''Miss Brentmor, like it or not, you are going to do me the very great honor of becoming Lady Edenmont.''

Esme stared blindly at her trapped hand. ''What?''

''My wife,'' he said. ''Marriage. You can't seduce me and expect to get away scot-free.''

She tried without success to extricate her hand. ''Varian, this is not amusing.''

''The knell of doom rarely is.''

''You talk nonsense,'' she said. ''It is a spiteful joke—to get even, because you are angry with me. Or else you lied to me about Ali. Or else . . .''

Esme paused as another, far more disquieting possibility came to her. ''Oh, Varian, it cannot be because I was a maiden. Surely I was not the first—'' She stopped dead then, because he stiffened. A shadow crossed his features.

''I am not yet thirty years old,'' he said. ''I'd not yet got round to ravishing virgins. Not that I blame you for believing otherwise.''

''It does not matter,'' she said quickly. ''You cannot be so foolish as to tie yourself to a female on that account. You said you would not wed for a thousand pounds, yet you will do so because of a small piece of flesh? That makes no sense. How many girls lose their maidenheads by accident? It may happen on a horse or in a host of ways. I do not understand why nature created such a thing at all. It only makes trouble."

Varian shook his head. "I might have known. Esme logic, that's what it is. I should not have left you this morning. I should not have given you one instant to think. I knew you'd need looking after. But so did other people—and I've not had much practice looking after anybody."

"I do not need—"

"Yes, you do. Come here." He released her hand.

"Where?"

"Where do you think? Where would your lover want you but in his arms?"

"You are not my—"

"Yes, I am. Stop being silly, Esme. *Hajde.*"

He was her lover—or had been—and in any case, she could no more resist his invitation than night could resist the sunrise. Sheepishly, she crept onto his lap. His arms tightened possessively about her, and her heart gave a mad leap of relief. She buried her face in his coat.

"That's better, isn't it?" His voice was gentler.

"Yes."

"Because we're excessively infatuated with each other, aren't we?"

"Yes. At least I am, Varian," she mumbled to the wool.

"That is why we made love," he said. "I did not find it wearisome. My only trouble was guilt. I am very fond of you. You make me insane, but that's simply part of it. I did not want to dishonor you. You're brave and strong and beautiful, and a great many of my countrymen will fall head over ears in love with you. If I'd left you untouched, you could marry one of them. I had good intentions, you see. Unfortunately, those were no match for my lust and selfishness—and when you wouldn't say 'no,' you quite finished them. I want you to understand that you're a little to blame in this, Esme. I've not much honor left to me, but I would have heeded a 'no' . . . I hope."

She drew back to look at him. "Of course you would. Why do you think I would not say it? And do not talk of a *little* blame. I am sure I would have tried to kill you if you had refused me."

"Then perhaps you'll understand why I shall kill you if you refuse to wed me."

Esme closed her eyes. Every time she had tried to run away from him, she'd felt so wretched she wanted to die. But to tie him to her in the eyes of all the world and God Himself?

She was a rude, ungovernable hoyden, he an English lord . . . and a libertine. His nature could not tolerate the shackles of marriage. And when his desire for her faded—as it must—he'd abandon her, in spirit if not in fact. His gaze would turn cold, disgusted . . . How would she bear it? Better, far better, to break away now.

"I can hear you thinking," he said grimly. "It's bound to lead to trouble."

"Varian—"

"Try thinking about *this.*" He tilted her face back and brought his mouth to within an inch of hers.

Automatically, her head snaked round his neck to bring him to her.

"No," he said. "If you won't marry me, I shall never kiss you again."

His breath was warm on her face, his body strong and sheltering. His hands were so gentle, tenderly stroking her jaw. Her pulse was racing.

"This is not fair, Varian," she said shakily.

"I don't play fair. Yes or no?"

And so he won.

She *was* doomed, Varian told himself an hour later, as he pressed a kiss to her neck. She'd been doomed from the moment she met him. Not content with killing her father, Fate had sent Varian St. George along to kill her future.

All the same, he'd found it difficult to feel guilty while this beautiful, wayward creature lay in his arms, begging to be loved. Heaven knew she needn't beg. He'd wanted to make love to her from the instant he'd awakened. He'd just done so, and wanted to again.

But he couldn't spend the entire day in bed with her.

Percival and Qeriba were downstairs, waiting to be assured Esme would not create difficulties about getting married. More disturbing was the thought of Ismal, who could be waiting as well . . . anywhere.

This latter anxiety drove Varian from the bed to gather up his clothes.

"I'll send your grandmother up with some garments for you," he said as he thrust himself into his trousers. "She's already seen to the packing."

Esme burrowed under the bedclothes. "Aye, she's eager for me to be wed. This is all her doing, isn't it?"

"It's all *my* doing." Varian pulled on his shirt. "Qeriba simply cooperated. Whether I'd found her and Percival downstairs this morning or not, the result would have been the same. Do not begin imagining anyone has forced me to marry you, or that I'm acting out of some absurd notion of nobility."

He moved back to the bed and gazed sternly down at her. "I am not noble. I have wanted to make you mine practically from the start. Since you neglected to forestall me, you shall be. It's quite simple, Esme. Don't make it complicated."

Reproachful green eyes peered up at him. "I see how it is. You make me drunk with lovemaking, so I cannot think, and so I will say, 'Yes, Varian. No, Varian. As you wish, oh great light of the heavens.' "

He smiled in spite of himself. "Just so."

"Just wait," she warned, "until I become more accustomed to your tricks."

"Then it will be too late, because we'll be wed." Varian shrugged into his coat, avoiding her gaze as he continued, "There'll be no more tumbling about together until then. We leave for Corfu in a few hours. Once there, you'll be chaperoned."

That shot her up from the blankets. "Chaperoned? You cannot be serious!"

"You ought to know that Percival had prepared himself for a duel this morning, to avenge your honor. You cannot wish to shock his youthful sensibilities further by living in sin with your betrothed."

Varian headed for the door, then paused. "You won't

be entirely among strangers. Qeriba has agreed to come as chaperon, and I am given to understand Donika's family will provide a suitable Albanian celebration before we're properly wed in a proper Anglican ceremony by a proper Anglican minister." He threw her a guilty glance. "You needn't fear you'll be without friends on your wedding day."

He didn't wait for an answer and was already through the door when Esme called him back. He stood just at the threshold, bracing himself for the outburst.

"Thank you, Varian," she said softly.

He relaxed and smiled. *"S'ka gjë."*

Chapter 21

Sir Gerald glared at the letter he'd only just received, though Lord Edenmont had written it more than a fortnight ago. The delay was Percival's doing, no doubt, as was everything else. The wedding was only two days away. With cooperative winds, one might reach Corfu in a day—but to do what?

Sir Gerald raised his scowl from the letter and directed it across the Bay of Otranto. What in blazes was going on over there?

Jason had gone and got himself killed, heaven be praised, but heaven granted precious small favors. The curst fool had left a byblow behind, and Edenmont claimed he meant to wed her.

"Bloody blackguard," Sir Gerald muttered. "Probably thinks I'll buy him off. Hah! Let him have Jason's bastard—and the plaguey one my false bitch of a wife saddled me with as well. Ten years to conceive a child," he grumbled as he began to pace the terrace. " 'A miracle,' Diana called it. As if I couldn't count."

He'd counted. Nine months before Percival's birth, Sir Gerald had been abroad. Not for a moment had he believed that Percival had arrived prematurely.

The old outrage hadn't cooled with time. The mere sight of the boy was enough to set it ablaze. Now there was another of Jason's bastards to deal with.

The baronet stormed back into the house and on to his study, composing along the way a scathing reply to his lordship. As Sir Gerald took up his pen, however, his eye fell upon the chess set, minus a queen. He ground his teeth.

The Queen of Midnight, he'd learned, had been seized by British authorities days before it reached Prevesa. Shortly thereafter, two more ships had been intercepted, and word had spread quickly. Several customers had shied off, and it was very likely the rest would soon do the same. He'd put a great deal of money out; at present, he'd no hope of any coming in.

He might very well have to apply to his mother for funds, a ghastly prospect. The old witch was sure to cross-examine him. Though his records were creative enough to protect his secret, the process would be humiliating all the same. The dowager would find fault with him, because she always did. It was Jason, the prodigal son, she'd always doted on, though she feigned otherwise. Even now, were Jason alive, the senile old harridan would give him . . . whatever he wanted. As she'd always done, except that last time. Now there was this girl Edenmont claimed was Jason's.

Putting his pen aside, Sir Gerald took up the letter once more. The girl had written a note, but there was nothing in that. The baronet flung down the sheet covered with her illegible scrawl and re-examined Edenmont's.

"Hopes for my blessing . . . no, here. Aye, plain enough now. Take her to England, will you, and Percival too, if I like?"

That was what it was all about. Edenmont meant to take the girl to her witless old grandmama and use Percival, too, if he could, to soften the old hag's heart and brain.

"Oh, no, you don't," Sir Gerald growled. "Not *my* inheritance. Not one groat, Edenmont. The crone may be in her dotage, but I'm not."

The weeks before the wedding passed like a long, bewildering dream, filled with strange faces and strange voices with their clipped English accents. Though in the center of it, Esme felt she was looking in from another world, watching herself do as the dream required of her.

Varian had lodged her and Qeriba with the clergyman, Mr. Enquith, and his wife. They were both kindly people, but strangers. Varian and Percival's visits were so rare that they seemed strangers as well. While they bustled about Corfu, arranging the proper English wedding Varian was so determined to have, Esme undertook the more daunting task of making herself into a proper English bride.

Her regrets and anxieties she banished to the depths of her heart. Her father's murder remained unavenged, her homeland on the brink of disaster, but it was too late for her to act heroically. Her betrothed was a foreigner, a lord, a penniless debauchee, but it was too late for her to act wisely. Esme had given her heart as well as her virtue and could call neither back.

She would be his baroness, which meant she must at least appear a lady. Upon this, consequently, she fixed her mind. She made herself take interest in the fashion books Mrs. Enquith displayed and dutifully helped the two older women translate patterns into frocks. Esme took her lessons in English manners with the same singleminded concentration. It had to be done, she told herself. There was no choice.

A few days before the wedding, Donika—along with most of her relations—arrived, and Esme entered the prenuptial celebrations with the same resolve to do what must be done. She feared for the future, but it was merely heartbreak she feared, she told herself. That was just unhappiness, and life was unhappy for most human beings. What she felt inside, therefore, she kept locked within, showing others nothing but confidence and smiles.

In this way the strange dream time came to her wedding day, which dawned warm and bright.

Standing in the morning sunlight, Esme patiently endured her friend's fussing with her hair and frock. At last Donika stepped away. As she scrutinized the sea green gown, her anxious frown smoothed into a smile.

"What will your bridegroom think when he sees you now?" she asked. "His little bird he called you—but today you are a princess."

Esme resisted the urge to smooth the folds of her skirt. They were smooth enough, and her palms were damp. "L-little b-bird?"

Donika laughed. "Y-yes. How you stammer. He called you his little bird that day in Saranda and said you'd flown away with his heart. I wept to look at his sad eyes and hear the grief in his voice. All the women wept then—and later, when they heard how he'd leapt into the water after you. So beautiful a man, so strong and tall, and filled with so much love. How could we deny him?"

"No woman can deny him." Esme's voice sounded high, thready. "I could not even try, and now . . ."

"Now you shall make each other happy."

"*Happy*. God have mercy on me." Esme pressed her fist to her breast, as though this would stifle the violent thrashing of her heart. "Oh, Donika, I cannot—"

Donika grabbed her hand and yanked her to the door. "Yes, drag your feet and I shall push you on, and you shall appear a properly modest bride. But you *shall* be wed, my friend."

Though Donika led her, it was the dream that carried Esme along. Uncomprehending, she was swept through a blur of faces and buzz of voices until she stood before the clergyman. Then the fog lifted. Esme looked up to find her beautiful god smiling tenderly down upon her. All about him seemed to shimmer. Glistening jet framed the smooth marble of his face, and his eyes gleamed silver. Even his voice seemed to glow, within her, as he said the words, and the warmth drew a tremulous smile from her in answer.

Then there was movement, and the blur and buzz closed in once more. "My lady," the strange English voices called her. It made no sense, yet she answered unhesitatingly, by rote, with the polite phrases she'd been taught.

Hours later, the dream carried her to the harbor. She was aware of Petro, sobbing as he embraced Percival, then cheering considerably when Varian pressed a bag of coins into his hands. Then there were Donika, Qeriba, friends . . . the sounds of farewell in her own language.

Esme felt Varian's arm about her, steadying her as she watched the boat sail away, yet it all remained unreal, incomprehensible.

The haze did not lift fully until she stood at the bedroom window of the house Varian had rented. The house was his surprise for her: a large whitewashed structure on the Bay of Kouloura, on Corfu's northeast coast. The window looked toward her homeland. The vanishing sun burnt faint copper sparks upon the deep blue-green of the Ionian.

She'd already lit the candles. She'd changed into the lacy night rail Mrs. Enquith had so lovingly sewn, and taken the pins from her hair. She'd brushed it until it shone, using the silver-handled brush from the set Percival had given her. The room boasted a large looking glass, in which Esme had studied herself.

She'd seen reflected one small, scrawny girl, utterly alone.

Now, painfully awake, she stared out the window.

That was not her homeland across the narrow stretch of water. She was not Albanian any more. She was a girl without a country, without family.

Her uncle had not come to the wedding, doubtless because he couldn't bear acknowledging her, not even to get his own son back. But Percival must return to him somehow, sometime, and Esme would be shut out, as her father had been.

She had nobody, *was* nobody, only Lord Edenmont's wife. Not even a proper lady. She'd mastered the rudiments and performed and recited as any schoolboy might recite Latin. She, too, could recite Cicero and Catullus and the rest. That didn't make her a Roman.

She started at the light knock on the door, and her heart hammered painfully. She could barely choke out the words to bid her husband enter.

The door was flung open, revealing the tall, splendidly formed lord who'd made her his—and nothing but his . . . and Esme burst into tears.

In an instant, Varian was across the room. Without a word, he scooped her up and carried her to the bed. He didn't put her down but kept her cradled in his lap, while Esme clung to him, sobbing helplessly.

He held her, lightly resting his chin on her head while he stroked her back. Gradually, his quiet transmitted itself to her, and she began to quiet as well. When at last the horrible sobbing eased, he found his handkerchief, which he wordlessly gave her.

She'd always hated crying. Until she'd met him, tears had been alien to her, a contemptible weakness. Appalled with herself, she rubbed her wet face vengefully, as though to punish it.

"It is nothing," she told him, glaring at his lapel. "It was stupid. I have only made myself look hideous." She pulled away, but he wouldn't release her.

"No, Esme, that will not do, and I will not be driven mad, wondering what the trouble is."

His gray eyes searched her face far too intently. It made her want to squirm, which vexed her as much as crying had.

"I told you it was nothing," she said. "I am tired, that is all. I am weary with pretending to be a lady."

"You don't have to pretend anything—not on my account."

"Indeed. I might have done as I pleased, and looked a fool and a barbarian to your countrymen, and made them pity you while they laughed at me. You know as well as I how they were all waiting for me to err—to shame you and my cousin. That is why you kept away until this day," she accused. "For one day, at least you hoped I might contrive not to disgrace you."

Varian looked down at her clenched fists. "I see," he said. "What a silly creature you are, to be sure."

"Silly?" She dug her nails into his hands and pulled at his fingers, but she might as well have clawed at iron manacles for all the good it did.

"You know I'm stronger than you," he said. "Even if I weren't, you wouldn't get far if I did release you. It would be a deal more productive to scratch my eyes out, don't you think?"

Esme knew—or the reasoning part of her did, at least—

that he was goading her. It didn't matter. Pure, mindless fury coursed through her.

"I hate you!" she cried. "I *would* scratch out your eyes—but then you would be blind as well as stupid and crazy—and I have no one but *you!*" She slammed her fist against his chest, making him gasp. "I wish I were dead!"

"No, you don't." Before she could strike again, Varian caught her hand and kissed it. "You wish *I* were dead. Or had never been born."

Releasing her hand, he lifted her from his lap and stood her before him. "Why don't you look about you? Perhaps you'll find something larger and harder to hit me with." He looked toward the washstand. "The stone pitcher, for instance. I daresay a sharp rap with that would put me out for several hours."

Taken entirely aback, Esme followed his gaze. "The pitcher?" When she turned back to him, his eyes were glittering strangely. "It would break your skull."

"Oh, I much doubt that. You'd want an axe, I expect, to do the job properly. English lords, you know. Skulls of oak."

She let out a heavy sigh. Her rage had dissipated as swiftly as it had arisen, and she could not call it back, badly as she needed it. Anger was so easy, so familiar. It made her feel strong. Despair made her weak. "Oh, Varian. I cannot do that. You know I cannot."

"I suppose not. I'm a pitiable enough specimen as it is, and all you've got, unfortunately. Nowhere to go, no one to turn to. Only stupid, crazy Varian—who abandoned you for near three weeks to strangers. All for propriety, which makes no sense to you, because you are not a hypocrite, as I am. And you're angry as well, because you've had no say, no choice, all these weeks."

Esme stiffened.

His glittering silver gaze traveled slowly from the top of her head to the toes of her silk slippers. "Now I am to be punished," he added softly. "On my wedding night. Tears first, to frighten me half to death—"

"You were not frightened," she said. "Do not make a game of me. And do not accuse me of weak, womanish tricks. As though such things could ever move you. How many women have wept on your account? And how many more will weep, I wonder."

"Was it on my account, love?"

"No!" She turned away, toward the window, dark now. "Oh, what is the use? Yes. Yes! Because of you."

His hand closed round her wrist, and he drew her round again to face him. "That's what I suspected. That's what frightened me. That's my punishment, too. Lord, I hate it when you cry. Even when you look as though you might." He caught her other hand and gently pulled her nearer. "But you don't hate me, do you, sweet?"

"Yes. No."

He studied her left hand for a long moment, while he lightly traced the gold band circling her finger. Then, bringing the unresisting hand to his lips, he kissed the soft flesh of her palm. Esme trembled, with longing, with fear. To give her body was easy. She'd done so gladly and would again, if it were only that. But to give all her will, all she was . . .

She drew her hand away.

Varian looked up. His eyes still glittered in that troubling way, but darker now. "Will you make me beg, Esme?" he asked, so very softly. He slipped his hands about her waist. "I've missed you dreadfully."

"Don't." She didn't try to push him away. She'd no right to deny him. She was his wife. It was her fault she was. Yet she couldn't bear to be made drunk and helpless. She was lost, and in his arms, maddened by his lovemaking, she'd never find her way.

"I know," he said. "I knew long before you did. To take me as a lover was merely dishonor. But to take me as a husband . . . Ah, well. That is very dangerous."

She swallowed a gasp. It was not fair that he could read her heart so easily, when his was the darkest mystery to her.

"I know what I am, Esme," he said. "But you gave yourself to me, and now I need you. Beyond bearing, and so, beyond conscience." His hands tightened on her waist. "And I shall win you all over again, this night, however I must. Without scruple."

Esme understood the glitter then, saw the danger in it, but before she could back away, he brought his leg behind hers, pulling her off balance. She stumbled toward him, and he fell back with her onto the bed.

She fought him in blind panic, aware only that he must not win, not this night, not so easily. She needed to find some part of herself that was still truly her, not what he'd made her. She couldn't surrender, not yet.

But he was too quick, too clever, too strong, and in moments she lay beneath him, gasping and filled with despair because the hard weight upon her was so warm and achingly familiar. She'd not realized until this moment how deeply, terribly lonely she'd been. She hated herself for the loneliness, just as she hated herself for wanting his shelter, though it was a prison.

His hand closed over her breast, and she wanted to weep. "No, Varian," she begged.

"Yes, Varian," he returned in soft command. He pressed a warm kiss to her temple and made a path of lingering kisses to her ear and down to her throat. Her pulse was racing, an instant betrayal. He found the throbbing place and lingered there, and she felt his triumph in that long, savoring kiss. She felt it in his touch, lazily kneading her tautened breast, while yearning heat coursed through her, deep, to ache in her womb.

"Yes," he repeated. "Because you want me. Tell me."

She bit her lip.

He slid the gown down past her shoulders and down, exposing her tight, aching breasts. "Tell me." He teased with his hands and with his tongue, and the slow fire built, against her will, against her reason.

"No," she moaned, stirring helplessly under his caresses. The gown slid lower, to her hips. His mouth and hands followed, lazily, deliberately.

"Yes." There was laughter in his voice, and though her heart, surely, was breaking, she wanted to laugh, too. Madness.

"No," she gasped. "I will die first."

"Then you shall surely die, love . . . beautifully."

He moved down over her, and Esme trembled as his

head bent. The silken tendrils of his hair brushed her skin, making her shiver. Then soft kisses heated her belly, and she strangled a moan.

She clenched and unclenched her hands, but it was no use. Closing her eyes, she let her fingers slide into his hair. She wanted to crush him to her, but she would not. He knew he was torturing her and reveled in it. But she wouldn't give in, no, not so easily.

Lightly she combed her fingers through his hair, as though she needed no more, as though her muscles were not thrumming with tension. As though she weren't desperate to have him inside her.

Then his mouth moved lower, and a rapturous shock vibrated through her, wrenching a cry from deep within. In that hammering moment, her will swept away in a stream of delirium. *"Varian.* No . . . oh, *no."* She dug her nails into his scalp and cursed in every tongue she knew. It was not her own voice but a demon's, low and harsh. His wicked mouth and tongue set demons dancing within her. They answered to his will, not hers. She had none.

"Varian . . . no . . . no . . . oh, *please."*

He lifted his head and laughed.

His fingers glided up and down her inner thighs, and she felt his rigid flesh throb hot against her skin. She wanted to scream.

"Say yes," he commanded. "Tell me."

"Yes. Yes. I want you."

"Yes," he repeated. "I want you." And he drove himself into her at last.

Varian had been dimly aware of the rain beginning, hours before. He'd heard the soft pattering in the world beyond while he had caressed his bride and roused her again. It had been again, and again, because she made him hungry, fearfully so. He'd been miserable without her these last infernal weeks, and utterly wretched when he'd found her weeping and understood he was the cause. She'd come to her senses at last, poor darling. Too late.

"It can't be undone," Varian had told her. But not until after they'd made delirious love, when he'd given and taken pleasure, showing her how it was, how it would be, for both of them. "I won't let you go. I won't let you draw away from me. In this, I'll always win, Esme. Believe you've sold your soul to the Devil, if you like, because in this I shall be the very Devil."

"Only wait," she'd warned, stubborn as ever. "Only wait until I become accustomed."

He'd laughed. "I shall see you never become 'accustomed,' my lady." Then he'd taken her again, happily. He'd been wickedly happy from the moment the clergyman had united them. When Varian yearned for her, Esme would be there, his, and it was right and proper, the bargain solemnly sealed before God and two score mortal witnesses.

Now he looked toward the window, where the gloomy morning loomed. His hand glided over her smooth shoulders and along her arm, pausing briefly to stroke the scar more tenderly yet. She was oblivious. She slept trustingly in his arms.

"Dear God, how I love you," he murmured. "And damn me if I know what I'm to do."

He'd ten pounds left to his name, nowhere to find more on this wretched island, and they had the house only for a week. He'd heard nothing from Sir Gerald, though the letter had gone more than a fortnight ago. Percival must be taken back, but where? Otranto? Venice? Where was his blasted father?

And Esme—where would he take her? They could live in Italy, perhaps. For a while at least. One could get by on so little, and Varian did have ways. But no, not those ways, not any more, not with a wife. He'd not drag her through that sordid existence.

Nonetheless, they must go somewhere. He couldn't keep her on this curst rock forever—not even a week, not with Ismal so perilously near. Corfu's governor was not at all easy about Albania. The populace was being armed. Some ships had been seized, but who knew how many others had reached their destinations? Esme must be got away, far away. That much was clear.

There was only a week in which to do it. Varian had heard the *pielago* had been repaired and was on its way to Corfu. It could arrive any day now, if reports were to be believed. He wasn't sure he could believe them. He had left the captain more than enough money for repairs and paid a high price in the first place. Furthermore, most of his and Percival's belongings were still aboard. These factors might weigh for something. On the other hand, he'd engaged the vessel for just a fortnight, not two months, and its owner might easily decide the contract was fulfilled and return to Italy.

Then what?

Esme stirred and mumbled, as though she felt his agitation. Varian kissed her ear. "Sleep, love," he whispered. "Just sleep."

She snuggled closer, her small backside warm against him. He looked at her, then to the window again.

It was just the sort of damp, dreary morning meant to be slept away. The girl who'd driven him mad these two months and more lay safely in his arms, as sweet and passionate a lover as any man could wish. This was no time to brood on the future, Varian told himself. It was time to savor the present, to lie at peace for once and enjoy his rare happiness. He kissed her shoulder, then closed his eyes.

The Fates allowed him one hour of semi-dozing tranquility. Then there was the thumping of hurried footsteps and a louder thumping on the door.

"Drat you, Percival. Can't a man—"

"Oh, please, sir, I'm so very sorry." The boy's voice was abnormally high-pitched.

"You'll be a deal sorrier when I—"

"Please, sir. He's come. It's Papa!"

Chapter 22

Fifteen frantic minutes later, washed, haphazardly shaven, and dressed, Varian escorted his bride to the parlor and presented her to her uncle. Esme was very tense, Varian knew, though the inexperienced eye would have detected no more than aristocratic reserve. Three weeks in Mrs. Enquith's company had simply given polish to a young woman possessing sufficient natural pride for an empress.

As he politely accepted Sir Gerald's terse, rigidly polite congratulations, Varian thought the business might pass smoothly enough, so long as Esme kept her temper. This would not be easy. She couldn't be pleased with the cool glance her uncle treated her to before dismissing her from his mind as he returned his attention to Varian.

Yet Esme contained her indignation, just as she held her tongue, and Varian silently vowed to kiss her from the top of her head to the tip of her toes when this cursed moment was over. Her future hinged on the interview. Sir Gerald must be handled delicately, and that would require all Varian's presence of mind.

Sir Gerald, unfortunately, had no idea of delicacy. When he'd got through the social niceties, he barged to the point. "I can't stay long. Press of business. You understand, Edenmont, I'm sure. I only came to take the boy off your hands." He bent a black look upon his son. "Pack up your belongings, Percival—and be quick about it."

"N-now, P-papa?"

"Surely not now." Esme put her arm about her cousin's thin shoulders. "You have only just come, and—"

"Percival—pack!"

"Y-yes, Papa." The boy fled the room.

Varian's face remained politely blank. "Certainly I would not wish to keep you from business," he began smoothly, "but—"

"You won't keep me," said Sir Gerald, just as smoothly. "Nor the boy, either. I don't mean to let him out of my sight until we're in England. And then not until he's safe in school, where he might learn his duty at last at the end of a birch rod."

"As to duty—"

"He knew it was his duty to go with you to Venice, sir."

"That he did not was entirely my fault, as I explained in my letter."

Sir Gerald smiled coldly. "I won't call you a liar, my lord. You'd feel obliged to call me out, and I'm not such a fool as to duel over a boy's nonsense—even if I believed in that medieval claptrap, which I don't. Nonetheless, I know perfectly well it was no Italian who talked you into a cruise across the Adriatic. It was that blasted child, his head stuffed with his mother's sentimental twaddle."

Varian caught the blaze in Esme's eyes, but she saw his quick warning glance, and said nothing.

"In any case, events have come out happily enough," Varian said, his voice quite cool and easy. "Our detour brought me my lady wife . . . your *niece*. An occasion for celebration and forgiveness, I hope."

Sir Gerald shook his head. "You may hope all you like, Edenmont, but the forgiveness you want isn't in my power to give. You want at least ten thousand pounds of forgiveness if you hope to appease your creditors."

Varian's spine went rigid.

The baronet briskly continued, "I hope she brought you at least that much dowry, my lord, because I don't see anywhere else on earth you're to get it."

The rage these words sparked came so fast and furious that Varian couldn't trust his tongue. While he was fighting for control, his visitor turned his cold gaze upon Esme.

"Meaning no offense, *my lady,* but you know how family matters stand, even if your lord doesn't."

"I know well enough," Esme answered icily. "I have told him. I have told him as well, that I should sooner die than seek your charity."

Annoyance flickered in Sir Gerald's eyes, but he answered with false amiability. "Properly and sensibly said. Because there's no charity to be got, is there? Not in my mother's case."

His glance slid back to Varian. "Won't be moved, not she, not an inch. Won't allow the matter to be mentioned. Tried, I did, countless times. Especially after Percival was born. Thought a grandson would soften her. She told me she'd cut the boy off without a groat if I ever spoke my brother's name again." He shook his head sadly. "My hands are tied."

He'd certainly tied Varian's. "I see," Varian said. "You would like nothing better than the family's reconciliation. For your son's sake, however, you dare not attempt it. Certainly, I should not dream of asking you to do so. Esme and I are fond of Percival. We should not wish to cause him difficulties. It would appear you've no choice but to take him home yourself. Were my wife and I to accompany him, his grandmama would take it ill, I collect."

"Exactly, my lord." Sir Gerald rubbed his hands. "A regrettable situation, indeed. Dirty linen and all that. So good of you to understand."

"I understand," Varian said, "quite well."

Ali glared at the filthy beggar who stood before him. "Miserable wretch," he said. "The grief you've caused me. I should let the lions make a breakfast of you. But my heart's too soft. It tells me you're not to blame that Allah gave you the brains of a jackass." He looked to Fejzi. "Yet this deluded fellow thinks *he's* the clever one and Ali the jackass. Because I'm old and sick, he thinks I'm blind and stupid as well. What say you, Fejzi? What should be done with this faithless dog?"

"I would not presume to advise your highness," Fejzi answered. "Yet it would appear the man should be fed—and bathed—else the lions will turn up their noses."

"Then go see about it," Ali snapped. "And let me speak to this dirty creature in private."

Fejzi silently withdrew.

As Fejzi's footsteps faded away, Ali turned a reproachful gaze upon the beggar. "I won't embrace you, Red Lion. I'm deeply offended."

"I suppose it's the stench," Jason said. He dropped down to the carpet and arranged himself, cross-legged, at the low table. "Couldn't be helped. When one hunts rats, one must go among them." He calmly poured a cup of *kafe* for the Vizier, then another for himself.

"You might have let me hunt with you," Ali grumbled. "But no. How many years have we known each other? Yet in this, you couldn't trust me."

"This was too personal. You've invested so much in your cousin. You'd great plans for him."

Ali shrugged. "Ismal's an ingrate. A European education he had. A complete waste. He still thinks like a barbarian. It's a great pity, with those looks and winning ways. He was formed by nature for diplomacy. He could have made all the rulers of Europe weep for our plight and aid us against the Turks. So much he could have done for his people. He might have been a hero greater than Skanderbeg. It's most disappointing. Where shall I find another such?"

"You've risen above many disappointments, highness."

"So I have, and got my revenge as well." Ali sipped his coffee and smiled. "This particular revenge will be especially amusing."

Jason pushed his own cup away, untasted. "I won't ask. I've done what I could to avert bloodshed. If you mean to strew the countryside with dead bodies, I can't stop you."

"Aye, why don't you just drive your dagger into my heart while you're about it? Twenty years and some—and this is your opinion of my intelligence?" Ali gave a reproving click of his tongue. "My cousin is confined to the finest apartments of the Janina palace. He's gravely ill. The physicians grieve because he's dying of love for the Red Lion's daughter, and there's no cure. One physician is so low in spirits I fear he'll die soon after my cousin does."

"The one you've paid to poison him, I take it?" Jason asked, his voice barely a whisper.

Ali's silence was answer enough.

"It's a pity," Jason said after a moment. "A sad waste. Had matters fallen out differently, I could have wished . . ." He trailed off, frowning.

"I know what you wished. The same I wished, once. But I saw with my own eyes, Red Lion. Your daughter gave her heart elsewhere."

"Fejzi tells me she wed the cur a week ago." Jason's frown deepened. "I'd no idea. I was at sea—"

"That's just as well," Ali said quickly. "You needed your wits about you. And you couldn't have interfered without risking your life and those of many others."

"*Someone* should have interfered. The man's a—"

"Whore. Aye, so they say. But he's good-looking and strong. He'll give your daughter tall, handsome sons. Even now, she may be carrying your grandson."

"Dear God, I hope not."

"A grandson, Jason, who'll be an English lord one day."

"And a lot of good that'll do him—or my daughter. What the devil's Edenmont to do with another mouth to feed? Where's he going to keep her? *How's* he going to keep her?"

Ali shrugged. "I offered him money to leave her here. He refused. She ran away from him. He chased after her—even risked his life, I'm told. He'll find a way to keep her, my friend. Don't trouble yourself. When you meet him, you'll see I'm right."

"When I meet him," Jason growled, "I'll thrash him within an inch of his sorry life. I've more than one score to settle with that worthless piece of aristocratic depravity."

"Then you mean to pursue them. You mean to abandon me, Red Lion."

"I'd intended to leave when this business was finished."

"It's not finished. You haven't told me who provided those ships."

"I don't know who provided them." Jason looked the Vizier square in the eye. "And if I did, I wouldn't—"

"Highness, a thousand pardons." An ashen-faced Fejzi burst into the room and threw himself at Ali's feet. "A message from Janina, most urgent—"

Jason swore violently in English and leapt up.

Fejzi winced. "Ismal—"

"Yes, yes," Ali snapped. "He's escaped. Obviously. What other urgent message from Janina would make you hurry your fat carcass so?" He, too, rose, but slowly and painfully. "Only hurry to the point. When did it happen, and which direction did my accursed cousin take?"

Ismal knocked the bowl of gruel away with the back of his hand, splashing the contents over the already-damp blanket. "This rathole of a vessel pitches so," he muttered. "What's the good of swallowing when I can't keep it down? Unless you mean to choke me to death, you black whoreson."

Risto picked up the bowl. "Ali's poison left you weak," he said. "You must try to eat something, else you'll be dead long before we reach Venice."

"I won't die," came the grim answer. "Not until I've settled my score with that English swine."

"You don't know it was him." Risto found a rag and scrubbed at the blanket. "You've no proof he betrayed you. Even if he did, you'd be far wiser to let it go."

"And hide in Constantinople, for who knows how long, with no money and only two blackguard servants to lend me countenance? The Sultan would laugh in my face—most likely while it lay upon a silver tray."

"You've money still," Risto said. "More than I'd ever see in three lifetimes."

"Sir Gerald Brentmor took thousands from me—then cheated me of the goods. Who else knew each and every ship, each and every route and destination? One, even two shipments lost, I might believe an accident of Fate. But *all?*"

Risto flung the rag to the floor. "Ships! Guns! For what? To rule a wretched piece of land, nothing but rocks and swamps? To waste your youth and beauty fighting every marauder who wants those same filthy rocks and swamps? To spend your life kissing foreigners' fat behinds, for yet more guns to defend your precious *pashalik?* God gave you beauty and wit. Your own cousin sent you among the Franks to learn their ways, so you might go freely among them and win honor and respect. Aye, and bend them to your will. Yet you wish to dirty your fine white hands with the blood of ignorant savages."

"My people need me to lead them out of savagery."

"It's not your *kismet,*" Risto said stubbornly. "The Almighty warns you, time and again, but you won't heed. Like a hotheaded boy, you chased after that red-haired whore—and nearly died for it."

"I paid for her," Ismal ground out. "She was mine by right."

"She was never yours, and you only wanted to keep her from the English lord. Ali played cat and mouse with you, but the cat kills the mouse in the end, doesn't he? As Ali nearly killed you. You better than anyone know his games, yet you played into his hands. If I hadn't found Mehmet, you'd be dead. Without his help, I could never have saved you. For what? That you may risk your neck again—for revenge on a low English smuggler? What curse is on me that I love such a madman?"

"I don't want your love." Ismal's eyes were blue-black with rage. "I never wanted it. Your love is vile, disloyal. You're glad I failed. You wish I'd lost everything, so I'd need you. I don't need you! Run away to Constantinople. To the devil if you like. Find yourself some weak boy to pamper. I'm not your boy. I've never been, never will be."

Risto whipped out his dagger.

"Yes, do it!" Ismal taunted. "Kill me, my loving Risto. I shall die with Esme's image in my heart, her name on my lips. I'll die smiling, thinking of her firm white breasts and the red curls of her—"

The cabin door swung open, and Mehmet's big, ugly form filled the doorway. "Peace, I beg you, master. All the crew can hear you." He stepped inside and calmly took the shaking Risto's dagger. "Though Greek, they might understand a word or two of our tongue. Besides, this arguing and shouting agitates them. Tsk, tsk, Risto." He put an arm about Risto's shoulders and led him to the door. "Why do you vex the master?"

"Keep him away from me," Ismal said, as he sank back down onto the narrow bunk. "He hovers over me like a nagging grandmother."

Mehmet grinned over his shoulder. "Aye, master, and you'd rather a pretty young nurse. In Venice, we shall find you three: one dark, one fair, one red fire, eh? Sleep now, and dream of them."

Leading Risto to the upper deck, Mehmet ordered him to breathe deeply of the brisk sea air to calm his angry spirit. "The trouble with you is, you don't understand human nature," he told the miserable servant.

"He's not human," Risto grumbled. "The Devil gave him that tongue to lash me with—while he throws sweet honey at everyone else."

"Because he trusts no one else. It's a sad burden for you, my friend. Still, you should pity him. It's a hard thing to be half god, half man—and more boy than man, at that. What good humor can you expect when he's been crossed in everything he's attempted?"

"He's been crossed because he attempts the wrong things."

"Satan makes work for idle hands. Lord Ismal has a busy mind and spirit and wishes to conquer the world. But he's not that kind of conqueror. I see this, as you do." Mehmet stared out at the sea. "It's a pity he didn't get the girl."

"That whore of a hellcat—"

"You can't keep him from women."

"Do you think I didn't learn that long ago? It isn't women. It's *her*," Risto spat out. "A cutthroat who acts like a man, even reads and writes. She's bad-tempered and willful. And a foreigner's slut besides."

"You fear this prodigy of a female will enslave him, do you?" Mehmet laughed. "Better for you if she does. Her heart's brave like a fighter's, but just and generous, too. Were she his wife, and you treated her kindly, she'd make him treat you kindly, too, in justice. She has brains enough, as well, to see the rightness of your wishes for him. If you made her your friend, she might well help you."

"I want no female's *help.*"

"What do you care who he obeys, so long as the result's what you want? You're a clever enough man, Risto. Cleverer than I, surely. Yet even ignorant Mehmet can see the value of a wife the master dotes upon."

Risto looked closely at his companion. "Why do you tell me this?"

Mehmet turned his gaze to the sea. "It's something to ponder. The British found all the ships and confiscated their cargos. For this, the master blames the English smuggler. And so, we pursue him to Venice. If we don't reach Venice in time, where shall we go next, I wonder?"

"Not England," Risto whispered, aghast. "You can't believe he'd go so far for revenge."

"He might, especially if he learns the girl goes there as well—"

"Then we must take care he doesn't learn."

"You've known him since he was a boy. When have you ever succeeded in keeping any secret from him?"

"Never," Risto answered gloomily. "Even the one locked in my heart he knows—and mocks me with."

"And so he knows you'll follow where he goes." Mehmet shrugged. "For my part, I'm glad enough to go. I don't mind travel and the farther from Ali and his spies, I say, the better. Wherever Ismal goes, and whether he goes for revenge or money or a female, I don't object to going with him." He turned his gaze to Risto's anxious countenance. "If he succeeds, we'll prosper with him. If he fails—well, what's the difference where a man dies?"

Chapter 23

The house was enormous, a great stone fortress, except that no sensible fortress builder would have designed such large windows, or so many of them. Row after row of gray rectangles stonily confronted the sunless January day. The steadily falling snow had blanketed the flat stretch of land about the house and dressed the dark, naked trees in ribbons of white.

Esme had seen snow before, but never so much as in England on this last day of traveling to her grandmother's house. Still, snow was preferable to the bitter cold which had preceded it. The countryside, with its squat, fat hills, did not look nearly so somber and dull under the white carpet.

Here there were no mountains, only farmland broken by a patch of woodland now and then, and miles of stone walls, twisting about and crisscrossing the hills. Varian had said there were fine, beautiful mountains to the north, surrounding lovely looking-glass lakes. Esme would have liked to go there. Anywhere but here.

As she climbed the front steps with Varian, she glanced behind her at the battered old coach that had brought them. In minutes, it might well be ordered to carry them right back. That would be fine with her—except they hadn't any more money. They'd spent their last coins to get here.

Esme winced as Varian slammed the knocker for the second time. This time, however, the door was opened by a very small, thin man with a very long, sharp nose.

He looked without expression first at Varian, then at Esme. Then he blinked his round black eyes very hard.

"Lady Brentmor's granddaughter to see her," Varian said curtly.

The man made a sound, quite incomprehensible, and let them in as far as the foyer. "I shall ascertain whether her ladyship is at home," he whispered. Immediately he turned his back and marched away, his shiny shoes clicking upon the marble floor.

"Where else would an old woman be on such a day?" Esme muttered. "How rude he is, to leave guests at the door. He did not greet us, or welcome us, or ask after our health."

"Servants are usually discouraged from making inquiries of so personal a nature, love. Especially when they're unsure of a visitor's welcome. At least he didn't turn us out directly. That's something." Varian drew her arm through his. "I hope you're not too chilled. Still, I expect the temperature will go up very shortly."

A full ten minutes later, the servant returned, relieved them of their wraps, and led them down a maze of hallways to an immense set of doors, thickly carved and painted gold. He quietly opened them and nodded Esme and Varian inside. Not sure if it was correct to thank him, Esme made do with a tight smile. To her surprise, the servant flashed one in return, but so quickly was it gone, she wondered if she'd imagined it.

An instant later, she was inside the lion's den. Lioness, rather, and this was hardly a den.

The room, in keeping with the house's exterior, was immense. Every stick of furniture from a dozen large Albanian towns would have fit inside easily, with room to spare for fifty people besides. All the same, some determined individual had managed to fill it nearly to bursting. The draperies, rugs, and most of the furniture were green and gold. Every solid material ornately carved, every fabric thickly trimmed or embroidered with gold, the great, heavy room seemed determined to press Esme down and squash her flat.

As the great mass of *things* resolved into individual

objects, Esme discovered the other living being in the place.

An old woman stood straight as a pike by the windows, glaring down at her visitors, though she wasn't much taller than Esme. Her hair was thick, gray with streaks of faded brown, and elegantly arranged. She was sumptuously dressed in dark green velvet with gold lace at her neck and wrists.

"Well, what are you gaping at?" she barked, making Esme start. "Come here where I can get a look at you. It's black as Hades in here, and those lazy fools ain't lit the candles. Come here, gel."

"My lady," Varian said. "Lady Edenmont, my wife."

"Did I ask you, coxcomb?" the old woman cried. "I know who you are. Let me see the chit who calls herself my granddaughter."

Esme yanked her hand from Varian's, marched to the windows, dropped a deep curtsy, then rose to glare at her father's mother, who glared back.

"There," Esme snapped. "You see me. Call me what you like. It is nothing to me. You did not wish to see me. I did not wish to come. But my husband said it was my duty. And so I have done it. Goodbye."

"I ain't excused you, Miss High and Mighty. You just hold your tongue and show some respect for your elders. Damnation, Edenmont," the insufferable creature went on, still scowling at Esme, "she's but a child! What the devil was you thinking of?"

"I am not a child! I shall be nineteen in—"

"And cold and wet and half-starved to boot," her grandmother went on, heeding her not a whit. "I've seen more promising specimens in a workhouse."

She backed away a few steps and, her eyes still fixed on Esme, yanked violently on the bell pull. "What a man thinks of, I don't know I'm sure, except I much doubt he's got the equipment for it. And you less than most, Edenmont. But you've brazenness enough to make up for brains, I collect. Drays! Blast the scurvy rogue! What's keeping him?"

The doors opened once more, and the beaky-nosed little man entered. "My lady?"

"Take the gel to Mrs. Munden and tell her to order a hot bath, and then—"

"Take?" Esme echoed incredulously. "Bath? I am not—"

"And tell Cook to send her up a good hot curry and a pot of strong tea with plenty of sugar and a heap of them biscuits and a bowl of—"

"I do not—"

"No one asked you. Go along with Drays, now, and get out of them rags. Disgraceful's what *I* call it."

Esme's glance darted from her obviously insane grandmother to her husband. Varian smiled, very faintly. She couldn't tell what it meant. "Varian?"

"Your grandmother is most gracious," he said.

"You want me to do as she says?" Esme asked, bewildered.

"It would be best. I believe she wishes to speak with me in private."

"I most certainly do," the old lady said darkly.

Reading his expression was always difficult. Varian assumed masks so easily, and they all appeared so genuine. Still, as she moved reluctantly to the doors, Esme thought there was an easing of some kind, in his stance if not in his cool gray eyes. She lightly touched his hand. He caught hers and squeezed it briefly. "It's all right, dear," he murmured.

Nothing seemed all right to her, but Esme gave him a weak smile and her grandmother a great flounce of a curtsy and, lifting her chin, left the room with Drays.

"Jason's gel," Lady Brentmor said, when Esme was well out of hearing range. "If I was blind and deaf, I could deny it, but I ain't, so I won't. I've heard all about this business—from that incompetent son of mine and his lunatic boy."

She waved at a large gilt-legged marble table. "There's brandy in that decanter on the what-you-call-it. Get me a fistful, will you? Yes, and yourself as well. You ain't no Methodist, I know."

As Varian moved to obey her orders, she dropped into a chair. "Devil take the chit. Of all the imbecilic, worthless rogues in all of God's creation, she had to shackle herself to *you.* No more sense than her father. Got himself killed, didn't he?—and by a pack of heathens, of all things. Which he wouldn't have done if he'd been where he belonged. But he wasn't. No sense at all. A pack of fools, men are. Every last dratted one of them."

Varian wordlessly gave her the glass he'd generously filled. His great-aunt Sophy had been of this species: a woman of the last century, a hard living, blunt spoken breed. Great-Aunt Sophy could drink most of the men in the family under the table, and her oaths could redden the countenance of a marine.

"Sit, sit." Lady Brentmor gestured impatiently at a large chair opposite. "I'll get a rheumatic in my neck looking up at your sneaking, lying face."

"I assure you, my lady, I've not come to deceive." Varian sat, and immediately suspected his hostess had ordered the chair upholstered in macadam and painted over. "You'd given your son Jason permission to call on you, I was told. I hoped the permission would apply to his offspring."

"We won't speak of that numskull, if you please," she said sharply. "As to deceiving me, you couldn't. I ain't a green gel, and I ain't cozened easy by pretty words or pretty faces. Handsome is as handsome does, I say—and what *you've* done don't bear repeating. I know all about you, Edenmont." Her shrewd hazel eyes bored into him. "You and Davies and Byron and the rest. Birds of a feather, and you the blackest magpie of them all."

"Wild oats, madam. The follies of youth."

"Not six months ago you cuckolded two Italian counts, one banker, and a pastry baker. A pastry baker!" she repeated. "Haven't you any discrimination at all?"

"My misspent youth, as I said. But I am a wedded man now, my lady, and cognizant of my responsibilities."

She leaned toward him. "Are you *cognizant* as well that you're miles up the River Tick and got no prospect of an oar to paddle you out of it? Because I won't paddle you out, my lord. If you thought I would, you'd best think again, with whatever it is you've got passes for brains."

"I assure you, I had no illusions on that score." Varian turned the brandy glass in his hands. This was not going to be easy. And later would be worse. "I've a good idea what you suspect—what anyone aware of my reputation would suspect. I can only assure you I did not bring Esme in hopes of coaxing a dowry from you. I didn't wed her because she had a wealthy grandmother."

"But you knew she had one, didn't you?"

"Esme has never claimed to be an heiress. Quite the contrary. Furthermore, nothing I knew of your family inclined me to imagine otherwise. I've gambled often enough to recognize exceedingly poor odds."

"Yet you wed her."

"Yes."

"With no thought to your interests, I'm to believe."

"I wed her because . . ." Varian stared into his glass, as though he might find the words written there, clearer than in his own heart. "Because I am much attached to her," he finished tightly.

The dowager gave a loud snort. "This is not *my* notion of attachment, sir, any more than it's my notion of practical sense. You wed her, though you *knew* you couldn't feed or dress or house her. A mere child—and you put a ring on her finger so you could take her direct to the sponging house?"

"You tell me nothing I haven't berated myself with a thousand times. The damage is done, and can't be undone."

"There ain't many ties can't be untied," she said, her tone brisk, "if a body's willing to pay. I'd not give *you* a groat. But an annulment of this abominable marriage I'd consider a wise, very sound investment."

His fingers tightened about the crystal stem. "That is out of the question."

"Why? Don't tell me the poor child's breeding already?"

"Good God, no!" The glass jerked in his hand, splashing brandy onto the carpet. Only a few drops. A few tiny blots, that was all. Varian drew a steadying breath. "I mean that's not the reason. I mean I should never consent to such a thing."

She watched him with hard, pitiless eyes. Not that he'd expected or wanted pity. Nothing she'd said was truly unjust. "Poor child," she had called Esme. That was what mattered. Like the bath and the food, it meant there was hope. A chance.

"What do you want from me?" she demanded. "Tell me straight. I won't be sweet-talked to the point. I've never cared for roundaboutation, and I'm too old to learn to like it now."

He met her gaze straight on. "I want you to look after her for a while. I want her safe and—and well. I can't risk taking her to London. My title protects me to some extent—from the sponging house, at least. But I don't want Esme exposed to harassment. That's why I brought her here."

"I won't support an idle rogue, I tell you."

"Only Esme, only for a while," he said. "I must go to London, bailiffs or not. There's no other way to deal with my affairs."

"And just how do you propose to deal with 'em?"

"I don't know."

The dowager leaned back in her chair and heaved a sigh. "Ain't that just typical? Men never know, but they always 'must,' mustn't they? They never know, not one blessed thing. Not a prayer of coming to the rightabout, yet you won't let the poor girl go, will you?"

"No."

"Want to have her safe in the country with her old grandmama, do you? For how long? Weeks, months, years? The rest of her life? No Season for her, no beaux, no chance for a proper match. Damnation, Edenmont, if you had to bed her, why couldn't you have left it at that? I'd have found her a mate. Not every man *has* to have a virgin bride, whatever they say. Not that they've any business saying it, selfish hypocrites."

Varian rose. "It's no good telling me," he said coldly. "She won't wed another while I'm alive. If dissolving the marriage is your condition, then say so, and I shall take my offensive self—and my wife—out of your way."

"You're a base and selfish man," she said, rising as well. "But I won't have Jason's gel starving or sleeping in alleys. She'll stay. And *you,* my lord, may go to blazes."

The bath was everything Varian had described to Esme that morning so many months ago: the great, steaming tub, the scented soap, the soft towels. Even the servant.

In response to Drays' summons, Mrs. Munden had come chugging down the hallway like a tugboat, aimed straight for Esme, and towed her away, all the while tooting orders to various lesser servants who came rushing in from every direction. The halls quickly began to resemble the River Thames, with a host of vessels coming and going, carrying their diverse goods: buckets of coal for the fire, buckets of steaming water for the bath, valises, linens, and heaven knew what else.

All the bustle made Esme dizzy, tired, and anxious. Everything was done for her and to her, and nothing was under her control. From the moment she had entered this house, she'd been swept into its power. Her grandmother's power.

The feeling did not lessen at dinner, though Varian was there, regaling the dowager with gossip from Corfu and Malta, Gibraltar and Cadiz—all the places they'd so briefly stopped at on their hectic voyage to England. Less than two months it had taken them. But that was because the schooner was racing a sister vessel.

The owners of both were rich, idle lords—Varian's former schoolfellows. They had been touring the Greek islands when they heard the rumors of Lord Edenmont's marriage. One believed it, the other didn't. The result was a wager—and a mad dash to Corfu to settle it. The result of that, for Varian and Esme, was free passage to England.

As Varian was now pointing out to Lady Brentmor, his rakehell reputation had rescued them. Had he lived a life of rectitude, he and Esme would probably be in Corfu yet. The old lady was amused. She laughed loudly, as she had at the gossip he'd shared—in between berating Varian for proceeding in such a lackwit, harum-scarum way with a new bride.

After dinner, they returned to the green and gold room. The drawing room it was called. There Varian gave an edited account of their adventures in Albania. Lady Brentmor did not laugh so much then, or scold as much either, but stared into the fire, shaking her head from time to time. At last she called for her port and brusquely sent Varian and Esme away.

Though the dowager had made it clear she disapproved of Varian and viewed the marriage as an unmitigated catastrophe, she'd assigned the couple adjoining rooms.

The maid, Molly, had just left when Varian entered through the connecting door. He took up the brush Molly had minutes before laid down upon the dressing table, stared at it for a long while, then put it down. He placed his hands on Esme's shoulders and gazed at her reflection in the looking glass. Then, in a few quiet sentences, he told her what he'd arranged with her grandmother.

When he was done, Esme jerked away from him and walked stiffly to the window.

"There's no alternative, Esme," he said. "If there were, I swear to you—"

"There's no need to make vows," she said, trying to keep her voice steady. "I understand. I believe you."

"You're distressed all the same."

"Only for a moment. It is not agreeable. My grandmother is a cross, rude old woman, but I have met worse, and worse could befall me. In Albania, the bride goes to her husband's kin. As the newest of the family, she is lowest in precedence. All the women—mother, sisters, aunts, grandmothers—order her about. If they wish to be disagreeable, they can make her life wretched, and she must endure it, because she is outnumbered. Here, it is only one vexatious woman—and the maid tells me my cousin is coming."

She had managed to compose herself while she spoke. She turned now, able to meet Varian's anxious gaze with a reassuring smile. "Percival has been expelled from school—again—and my uncle is banishing him to the old lady, because he cannot be bothered with his troublesome son."

"Esme, it's not like that with me. You must know that, surely."

"I know. I was not comparing you to my ignorant uncle. I only tell you I am glad Sir Gerald is so, for Percival will soon be here and I shall have an ally. You may go about your affairs with an easy heart. He and I shall outnumber her."

Varian came to her then, put his arms about her, and crushed her close. "I'm sorry, darling. You can't know how sorry. But I'll be back soon. A few weeks. No more."

A few weeks. In London. Among his old friends, like those idle men who'd brought them to England. Laughing, gambling, drinking, whoring.

Esme closed her eyes.

"Only a very short while," he said.

She believed he meant it, for now at least, and now was all that mattered to him. Now, this night, was all she had. Then he'd go, and all would change. She'd not quarrel or complain, not this last night, the last one in which she might be sure of him.

Because she was sure, for this moment, she eased back in his arms and reached up to cup his beautiful face in her hands.

"Make love to me," she said. "Enough to keep me these few weeks . . . until you come back . . . and make love to me again."

It was still dark when Varian left the room. Esme was asleep, deep in dreamless sleep, he knew. He had shared her bed long enough now and lain awake often enough—watching, listening, thinking—to know. He left while she was sleeping because he couldn't bear a farewell. They'd said it without words last night, in those long aching hours of lovemaking. Then he'd drunk in her scent and her soft cries of passion, and loved her. Needily. And angrily. And desperately. He'd wanted to memorize her. He'd wanted to burn her into his heart, not so he wouldn't forget, but that he might take her with him in some way.

He not been able to let her go since the night he'd first touched her. This time, he must let go. That "must" meant he dared not wake her, dared not say goodbye. If he did, his resolve would fail . . . and he'd fail her.

He'd made everything ready in his own room the night before, while the maid had helped Esme prepare for bed. He'd even written the note.

Varian had only to dress, take up his bag, and leave. He did so without looking back.

Eager to be rid of him, Lady Brentmor had apparently sent word to the stables. Though the sun was only beginning to rise, Varian found one stable man brightly awake and prepared to accommodate his lordship.

Less than half an hour after he'd left the warmth of his wife's bed, Varian was on his way to London.

Chapter 24

Varian made a detour round Eden Green, deliberately avoiding its homey public house. He was in no mood for local gossip, especially when he would be the focus of it. The afternoon was waning under thickening gray clouds, and his horse was tired. Mount Eden's stables were merely two miles away, and the deserted estate would offer all the privacy one wanted. Unfortunately, it would offer nothing else.

He headed down the overgrown path that skirted the village and ended back on the main road a safe distance away. As he rounded a turn, he saw smoke rising from the chimneys of the Black Bramble inn and breathed a sigh of relief. Unlike Eden Green's Jolly Bear, the Bramble catered to travelers. On this bitter winter day, the yard was empty of carriages, as he'd hoped. Few would journey on such a day if they could help it.

Upon giving his mount into the hostler's care, however, Varian saw the stables were not entirely empty. Two sorry-looking hacks were munching disconsolately in their stalls.

Moments later, he found their riders in the public dining room. They, too, were eating, but with greater enthusiasm.

One was a slim, dark-haired fellow who talked excitedly in between stuffing hunks of meat pie into his mouth. The other said little, only nodded now and then while he applied himself to his plate with steady determination. He was bulkier in build, and his light brown hair was not so fashionably styled as his companion's. Though their backs were to him, Varian recognized them quickly enough.

By the time they heard him enter and looked round he'd already collected himself.

Two pairs of eyes—one brown, one dark blue—widened. Varian calmly crossed the room to them.

"If you must gape, Damon," he said, "you might at least swallow your food first. What a rude fellow you've become."

The younger of the pair, whom he'd addressed, leapt up. "I say, it *is* you, isn't it? By heaven—of all that's—but I said so, Gideon, didn't I? Didn't I say we'd find him?" He started to move toward Varian, then hesitated and stood, unsure, looking at him.

Gideon had risen as well, but with more dignity, first putting his utensils aside. "Sir, I am delighted to see you." He held out his hand. "Welcome home, my lord."

A mist obscured Varian's vision for an instant, but he blinked it away and grasped his brother's hand. "Well, met, Gilly." He turned and gave his hand to Damon. "And you, too, Dervish."

Damon's uneasy expression brightened into a grin. "There, isn't it just like him?" he asked Gideon. "Walks in cool as you please and tells me to mind my manners—as though he'd last seen us four hours ago, not four years. But come, you're right. I've no manners. Do sit down. You look fagged to death. No, there, closer to the fire. We've had hours to warm up. I was all for keeping on to Mount Eden, but Gideon still keeps country hours and must have his dinner, and we couldn't be sure to find any there, not on short notice. But now I'm glad he's such a piece of clockwork, because we might have missed you—" He broke off. "But you're alone. Where is she?"

While Damon had been chattering, Varian had taken off his cloak and put on his guard. He was preparing for the "she" before the question was out of Damon's mouth. Now their hostess bustled in and curtsied herself breathless. While she regathered her wind, Varian calmly ordered his dinner. Not until she'd left the room did he return his attention to Damon. "Where is whom?"

"Oh, don't tease, Varian. We've—"

"Damon refers to Lady Edenmont," Gideon interrupted, flicking a warning glance at their youngest sibling. "At least, we were informed there exists such an entity."

"I see," said Varian. "Lackliffe and Sellowby made direct for London, I take it?"

"I'm told they did not even change out of traveling garb, but raced to Brooks' club. Within two hours, the news was all over the west end. It was the talk of Almack's that very night, and the next day I was summoned to Carlton House to satisfy His Highness' curiosity."

"I do beg your pardon, Gilly. My mind was taken up with other matters, else I'd have given you some warning. I'm sorry I placed you in so awkward a predicament."

"Oh, Gideon wasn't the least discomfited," said Damon. "He gave one of his explanations, and by the end of it, Prinny no longer cared what day of the week it was. He sent for his physician and demanded to be bled. But you *have* returned, Varian, so that much of the tale is true. Not that I doubted them. It was only the rest that was so hard to take in. But you will tell us, won't you? Have we got a sister at last, and is her hair truly red, and are her eyes as green as Lackliffe says?"

"Her eyes," Varian said, "are quite . . . green."

"I see," said Gideon. He carefully lined up the handles of his fork and knife, then made a long, careful business of arranging his napkin.

Damon sat back in his chair, his deep blue gaze fixed on his eldest brother's face.

"And so you set out from London in pursuit, I collect," Varian said as the silence lengthened uncomfortably. "You thought I'd take Lady Edenmont to the ancestral . . . ruins."

"*I* did not think so," Gideon answered. "I only accompanied Damon out of concern that he'd otherwise wander about the kingdom for years, searching for his brother—as though you were the Holy Grail."

Damon flushed. "We did find you, though, didn't we? Dash it, Varian, I don't wish to be indelicate—but where the devil *is* she?"

"With her grandmother." There was a tightening in Varian's chest, followed by a fierce shaft of pain. He stared hard at a gravy stain near Damon's plate. "Don't let your dinner cool on my account, gentlemen. I shall tell you all about it, once our hostess returns with the wine."

They went with Varian to Mount Eden the next morning, despite his frigid objections. He'd thought he'd told his tale well, with just the right note of coolly detached amusement. Yet at the end, they'd both looked very grave, and he'd glimpsed something horribly like pity in Damon's eyes.

Still, Damon was young and excessively romantic, and he'd always idolized his oldest brother—heaven only knew why. Gideon's feelings were not so blatant. He'd always been the sober one. Quiet, occasionally priggish, but always thoughtful, calm . . . discreet.

Nonetheless, their feelings were plain enough to Varian. They didn't think he could bear seeing Mount Eden without moral support, and *that* was unbearable: to find his brothers determined to support him in what they believed to be his hour of need . . . when he'd never, not once, given their needs, their problems, more than a second's thought.

They stood at present in what had once been a sumptuous library.

Not a book remained, not so much as a tract. The walls were stripped bare, and the floors were thick with dust, debris, and mouse droppings.

It was an old house, needing constant upkeep. Varian's father had been conscientious in that regard—as in every other—until Varian had begun getting himself into difficulties, which soon mounted to tens of thousands in debts. Though the family was well off, their resources weren't limitless. To rescue his heir, the late Lord Edenmont had to put off rescuing the house. After his death, Varian had abandoned the estate entirely.

What he now observed was the result of at least ten years' neglect, all his own doing.

"There's something to be thankful for," Varian said as he looked up. "At least I can put a roof over my lady's head."

"Stewards are a selfish lot," Gideon said. "They *will* insist on wages. Still, it might be worse, considering no one's looked after the place these last years. There's a great deal of dirt, certainly, and the paint wants to be renewed. It's not nearly so bad as it appears, however."

"Certainly not. All it wants is money—and a staff—and more money." Varian moved to the fireplace. Broken bits of mortar lay within. "This chimney has its mind on tumbling, I believe."

"It's obliged to respect the laws of gravity."

"You'd better tell me about the tenants," Varian said, his eyes still upon the chimney fragments. "For your sake, I won't visit them just yet. If I were stoned by an angry mob, you'd inherit, poor fellow, and I know you'd far rather be hanged."

"Oh, Gideon's lived in terror you'd get yourself killed on the Continent." Damon was standing by the French doors, and his voice echoed across the cavernous room. "He's so thrilled you're shackled at last, I daresay he'll rebuild the entire estate for you, singlehanded—and the nursery first of all."

There was that cruel tightening again in Varian's chest and the dart of pain.

"Excuse me," he said.

They watched him leave, but didn't speak or try to follow him. Varian heard no sound but his own footsteps as he left the library and climbed the stairs. He saw nothing of the stairs or hallways, thick with dirt and cobwebs. He heard nothing of the small, wild creatures scrambling in panic at the sound of human footfalls. Varian knew nothing of his surroundings until he opened the door he sought, heard it squeal painfully, and stood on its threshold, staring into the nursery.

Then he saw, all of it. He leaned against the door frame.

Don't tell me the poor child's breeding already.

"God forgive me," he breathed. "Oh, Esme, what have I done?"

. . . children. If God is generous . . .

He closed his eyes against the shattering grief. He'd been away from her not even three days and he was lost, sick with loneliness. but that was nothing to this. He'd no one else to blame. He'd shaped and carved this day for himself these past ten years. Now at last, when he'd learned to love, when he wanted to love and look after one brave, beautiful girl and give her children they might love and care for together . . . now the Devil laughed and demanded payment. Now Lord Edenmont understood that fire and brimstone were not wanted, nor even death. Hell was regret.

It was tomorrow.

And Varian pressed his face to his arm and wept.

The room Lady Brentmor called "the counting house" was originally the master's study. All the world knew her late husband, however, had never been master of anything. His wife was the brains behind the Brentmor fortune. It was she who'd hauled her spouse up from a middling tradesman to a titled man of property.

Immediately upon his death, all pretense of his mastery was abandoned. The dowager banished his cozy masculine bric-a-brac to the attics, painted the walls a brooding maroon, and lined them with stern shelves for her massive ledgers. The furniture at present comprised a few exceedingly hard chairs and the large desk behind which she sat, intimidating bankers, brokers, and lawyers alike while she singlehandedly ruled her formidable financial empire.

It was to this room she took her grandchildren four days after Lord Edenmont's departure and less than ten minutes after Percival's arrival.

Percival and Esme sat upon two rocklike chairs watching Lady Brentmor peruse the letter Percival's tutor had delivered along with the boy.

"An explosion." She looked up from the closely written sheets. "Who do you think you are—Guy Fawkes?"

"No, Grandmother," Percival answered meekly.

"Blew up the hen coop, he says. I suppose it's too much to hope the hens weren't in it?"

"I'm afraid they were."

"That'll cost me. Lud, you always cost me."

"They were sick, Grandmama." Percival's green eyes flashed with indignation. "One of the boys told me that's why we were forever getting chicken soup. They weren't laying hens, I promise you. I never saw an egg all the weeks I was there. But there was a good deal of soup, with the most disagreeable odor."

"I'll be damned if I'll pay for diseased fowls." She gave him a piercing look. "Are you sure they were sick?"

"Oh, yes, Grandmama." Percival's face brightened. "I dissected one, and I've got the intestines in a jar. I can fetch it for you if you'd like to examine it yourself."

"No, thank you." Her gaze grew sharper still. "I'd like to know what's to be done with you. Your pa told me you was to be shipped to that school in Bombay the instant you kicked up one of your larks."

Esme reached for her cousin's hand and glared at her grandmother. "You will do no such thing," she said. "If the fowls were sick, then it is the schoolmaster who should be sent to Bombay. To poison little boys with diseased animals—Y'Allah, they should be poisoned themselves."

"I didn't ask you, did I?" Lady Brentmor snapped. "And none of that heathen talk, if you please."

" 'Y'Allah' only means 'dear God,' Grandmama," Percival pointed out.

"Then why don't she say what she means?"

"I said it plain enough." Esme met her grandmother's stare fearlessly. "You shall not send him away. God knows such a course is monstrously unjust, even if you do not. But you wish to frighten him—as though the boy has not suffered enough."

"I know what he's 'suffered' and what he's done. And

I aim to make it clear there'll be no more of it. I won't have children poking their noses in their elders' affairs.''

A small box lay upon the desk to her right. She opened the box, took out the object that lay within, and placed it on the desk. It was a chess piece. A queen, to be precise.

''Oh, dear,'' said Percival.

''I collect you know what it is,'' the dowager said to Esme.

''I have seen chess pieces before. The game is not unknown in my country.'' Esme did not so much as glance at Percival.

''Never mind trying to protect *him.* It don't take a prophet to work this matter out.'' Lady Brentmor bent a black look upon her grandson. ''You hid your bag of rocks in your room that day you come with your pa, which was a fool thing to do. Don't you know we always turn your things inside out? You're forever leaving corpses behind. Last time it was a reptile. The time before, a rodent. You was told time and again not to dissect your creatures in the house, but you never listen.''

''Yes, Grandmama, I'm dreadfully sorry.''

''Never mind sorry. I know what you done. You *stole* this chess piece. You guessed your pa would offer a reward, didn't you? And you used that to lure Edenmont to Albania. Very clever, Percival. Now your cousin's wed to the blackguard, and it's all your fault.''

''Varian is not a blackguard!'' Esme cried. ''And nothing is my cousin's fault. He brought Varian to me, and for that I am grateful, and shall be so, all my days.''

''You ain't half started your days, my gel. I daresay there'll come a time not too far ahead when you'll eat them words, and they won't go down so easy, either. Left without so much as a fare-thee-well, didn't he?''

''He left a note. A very kind note. You understand nothing about him.''

''I know a bad bargain when I see one, and I know more about him than I want.'' Her eyes narrowed to slits, the dowager leaned forward. ''He's been in money scrapes since he was eighteen years old, and his father was forever digging him out. By the time Edenmont came into the title, he'd already pissed away half the family fortune. It took him less than five years to run through the rest."

"Varian is extravagant. I know that," Esme said. She didn't want to hear more.

"He let his estate go to pieces," Lady Brentmor went on. "He made paupers of his two brothers. In a few years he destroyed what it took generations to build. Thanks to his soft-hearted pa, he'd never had to face the consequences, and so he never learned to think of 'em. Never thought of anybody but himself. So he goes to the Devil—which is fair enough—only it ain't fair he takes his kin with him."

Esme's head jerked back as though her grandmother had slapped her. She'd simply thought of Varian as a penniless pleasure lover. Flawed, yes, deeply flawed. She loved him, but she wasn't blind. She hadn't thought, however, of the damage he'd done. Unintentionally—but that only showed his thoughtlessness. This was his great crime in her grandmother's eyes: Varian was not simply a libertine and wastrel, but a destructive man. This was why she'd taken Esme in—to protect her from him.

The dowager was watching her. Esme straightened her posture but said nothing. She didn't know what to say.

"I suppose you think I was too hard on him, just like you think I was too hard on your pa. Percival thinks so, too, don't you, Master Ignoramus?"

"Well . . . y-yes . . . rather . . . that is—"

"Because you don't know a blessed thing. Because you're both ignorant babies." She fixed her scowl on Esme. "The path Edenmont took was the same I'd seen your father starting on. Lots of men go that way, and take their families with 'em. I could have fixed your father's mess easy enough, and I can fix Edenmont's—though that's a good deal worse. But I won't do for him what I wouldn't do for my own son. I won't lift a finger, not when it'll only help him make paupers of us all."

"But, Grandmama," Percival began.

"He got himself in, now let him dig himself out," Lady Brentmor said grimly. "If he cares as much for Esme as he claims—and if he's got any self-respect—

he'll try at least." As she turned back to Esme, her stern countenance softened a fraction. "But I must tell you fair and straight I don't think he's got it in him. Best face it now, I say."

"You mean he is not coming back," Esme said. She folded her hands. "I am not amazed. There is no welcome for him here, and he cannot take me with him. I am only a burden. I can do nothing for him."

She met her grandmother's gaze. "I understand your reasons, Grandmother. Still, he saved my life, more than once. He is not evil. He has tried to be kind to me, in his way. He even warned me against him, many times. I shall not try to change your mind, but I ask you to reflect upon these things. And pray for him, if nothing else."

Percival, who'd been fidgeting upon the unforgiving chair through this exchange, darted his grandmother an anxious glance. "But, Grandmama, you must give her the dowry."

"Don't tell me what I must. I don't take orders from ignorant children."

Esme sighed. "Oh, cousin. Do not vex our grandmother. I understand that she does what she believes is best. There will be nothing for Varian." She started to rise.

"But there *is*. Mama left you the chess set, for your dowry. It's worth a great deal. Five thousand, at least. Twice that, if you find the right buyer."

"Five thousand?" Esme repeated. "My dowry?"

Her grandmother stiffened. "You mean to say you didn't know?"

"I'm sorry," Percival said to Esme. "But I was afraid to tell you, in case Papa—"

The old woman swore at the room at large, then sank back wearily in her chair. "Devil take me for a fool. Talk myself hoarse—and all the while you'd no idea. Now we're in for it, and it's all my own curst fault."

"Twelve thousand pounds," Varian repeated. He appeared to be studying the document his solicitor had given him. In fact, his lordship saw only a blur of lines.

"But of course you knew about your great-aunt's will, my lord. I sent you a letter while you were in Spain." Mr. Willoughby took up another piece of paper. "I have your answer here. In it you indicated—"

"I remember. But there was a time limit, was there not? Twelve thousand pounds, *if* I were wed within—what was it, three years? Surely it's been longer than that."

"Three years from the date of her death. She passed on late in December of '15. You were wed this past November, according to your documents—which are fully in order, I'm happy to say." Mr. Willoughby essayed a thin smile. "Therefore, you are now twelve thousand pounds to the good."

"That depends on one's point of view." Varian put down the copy of the will. "What is the sum of my debts?

"I cannot name the precise figure at present. What with interest and Fortier's bankruptcy and other such variables—"

"An approximation will do." Varian's heart was pounding furiously.

"Something in the vicinity of twelve thousand pounds, my lord."

The pounding stopped dead, as though an immense weight had fallen upon it, then recommenced, slow as a funeral drumbeat.

"What an amusing coincidence," Varian murmured.

"I am sorry, my lord. Still, it might be worse. The estate is in no danger, as I explained."

"I've recently viewed the . . . remains. I collect the reason it's in no danger is that no creditor would be fool enough to want it."

"Perhaps not. Still, I flatter myself I have placed sufficient obstacles to discourage even the most daring of speculators."

"I thank you for that, Willoughby." Varian looked toward the grimy window. "I suppose you think I ought to use this windfall to pay my creditors."

"So I would advise, yes." Mr. Willoughby carefully

lined up a small pile of documents and moved them a few inches to his left.

"That would leave me with nothing."

The solicitor cleared his throat. "We may be able to preserve a small sum. As I mentioned, I should want some time—a few weeks—to ascertain the precise amount. However, if you owe a man twelve hundred pounds, I may be able to satisfy him with eleven hundred, or even one thousand. Admittedly, they don't like to settle in that way, since it disallows any future action for the remainder. On the other hand, legal actions are costly and, when undertaken against members of the peerage, so often disappointing."

"Disappointed creditors can make one's life exceedingly disagreeable all the same," Varian said. "I should not wish my wife to be annoyed."

"Naturally not, my lord. I quite understand. That is why I suggest you clear the slate, so to speak. And I should undertake to preserve a small sum. With that, and her ladyship's dowry—"

"Her ladyship has no dowry."

Mr. Willoughby blinked. "Does she not? How very odd. I was led to understand—"

"Nothing," Varian told him firmly. "Not a shilling."

"If you say so, my lord. Yet, if you will not object, I should wish to pursue certain inquiries."

"I should *not* like, particularly if you intend to question her family. They hold me in the greatest dislike. Even if her father managed to set something aside for her—which is highly improbable—they'll make certain I can't so much as look at it." Varian shrugged. "One can hardly blame them."

"But if anything is owing to you—"

"Whatever might be owing to me, I can't possibly collect. Would you have me spend my windfall in a Chancery suit? I'd stand a better chance at the faro tables. There, at least, one has a chance of doubling one's winnings. Or tripling them." Varian frowned.

Mr. Willoughby uttered a small sigh but said nothing.

"I cannot restore Mount Eden if I pay my creditors,"

Varian said stiffly. "I must have something, Willoughby."

"I do understand, my lord. Still, I might be able to preserve as much as a thousand pounds."

"I might make twelve thousand into twenty-four this very night."

Willoughby said nothing. His face had lost color in the last few minutes, and the expression in his eyes had grown bleak. He appeared some decades older than the fortyish man who had greeted Varian a short while before.

Varian rose. "If there is nothing else, I'd best be on my way."

"Yes, my lord. I imagine you would wish an advance on the sum, since the paperwork will take some time. Will a hundred do for the present?"

Chapter 25

After leaving the solicitor's office, Varian proceeded unhurriedly toward Oxford Street. At this early hour, he stood little risk of encountering any of his acquaintances. Glancing down at his threadbare cuffs, he thought ruefully that his friends wouldn't recognize him anyway.

His appearance, however, could be quickly amended, now that he'd a few pounds in his pocket. One of his favorite tailors would surely have something on hand. With a few alterations, Lord Edenmont would be presentable by nightfall. He'd take his brothers to dinner, and perhaps they'd look in at Brooks' club. Then he'd try a hand or two at the card tables, just to make sure he still knew what he was about.

His mind busy with plans for transforming his windfall into a vast fortune, Varian turned a corner, then stopped.

An elegant bow window jutted over the sidewalk. Within it stood a gathering of tiny mannequins dressed in the latest modes. One miniature lady, garbed in a walking dress, caught his eye. Her white muslin petticoat boasted four rows of ruffles round the bottom. Over it she wore a richly worked open robe. A green spencer tightly encased her upper torso. Matching green shoes and a plumed headdress completed the ensemble. The green was very much like the color of Esme's eyes.

As he studied the other figures, Varian could easily picture Esme dressed in a sumptuous ball gown, whirling to the lush strains of a waltz. He imagined as well an elegant carriage lined in green velvet, and his lady wife upon the seat, smiling up at him as they rolled down the Champs Elysées. Paris. They could run away and live like royalty on his inheritance. For years, perhaps.

He had no sooner closed his eyes to savor the glorious image than it dissolved into numbers: £12,000 per annum, a thousand a month. He could spend as much in minutes at *rouge et noir.* But no. He'd double his windfall, triple it. Yet his mind's eye offered only heaps of IOUs and small stacks of coins upon a green baize gaming table. Meanwhile, his brain tolled out that ghastly cliché about lucky at cards . . .

"But I must have something," he muttered as he opened his eyes again.

. . . children. If God is generous . . .

Twelve thousand pounds today. But tomorrow?

As he looked down again at the tiny lady in green, Varian's expression softened.

He strolled into the shop and asked the *modiste* for a piece of paper and a pen. His sensually indolent countenance did the rest.

Varian had only to smile—which he did, rather shyly—and Madame would have burned down her shop if he asked her to. Without a word she got the materials he requested. Then she stood, her fingers unconsciously covering the racing pulse at her throat, and stared at his face in a sort of delirium while he wrote.

It took not a minute. Varian folded the note and placed a coin on the counter beside the pen.

"I'm much obliged," he said. "It couldn't wait, you see."

"Non, m'lord. Certainement, m'lord," she said breathlessly. She was about to offer to carry the message for him—to China, if he wished—when she recollected some fragment of her dignity and offered to send one of her assistants with it instead.

The note was put into Mr. Willoughby's hands not fifteen minutes later.

"Pay them," read the slashing black script. Beneath sprawled a large, hasty, "E."

* * *

Lady Brentmor flung open the copy of *Ackermann's Repository* Esme had just slammed shut. "If you won't pick out your frocks, I'll pick 'em for you," she said.

"I want no gowns," Esme ground out. "I want my dowry."

"By gad, you're as obstinate as your pa—and without half his wits. How in the name of all that's holy did he beget such a ninnyhammer?"

Lady Brentmor bolted up from the sofa and took a furious turn about the room. Then she sailed at her granddaughter again. "For the hundredth time, you haven't *got* a dowry. Not until I say you do."

"Then I shall write a letter to the *Times,*" Esme said. "I shall tell the world what you have done."

"The *Times? THE TIMES?*" the dowager shrieked.

"Yes, and all the other newspapers as well. Also, I shall stand up in church on Sunday and tell everyone how my husband is forced to desert me because my family does not fulfill the marriage contract."

Lady Brentmor opened her mouth, then shut it. She sat down again and stared at Esme.

Esme sat poker straight, her hands tightly folded, her mouth set in a stubborn line.

There was a long silence.

Then the dowager's sharp crack of laughter.

"Plague take you! Stand up before the congregation, will you? A letter to the *Times?* 'Pon my honor that's good. Did Percival help you think of it?"

"He suggested the newspaper, but the announcement in the church was my own idea," Esme stiffly admitted.

"I thought you took it too quiet yesterday. Damme but you're pigheaded. I told you it wouldn't do any good. Edenmont won't be running back to collect you. You can't buy his company, child. He'll only spend what he gets on gaming, liquor, and tarts."

The words stabbed deep, but Esme answered doggedly, "It is Varian's decision how he spends it. If he does not wish to come for me, I cannot force him to. I did not beg him to keep me with him, and shall not. I brought nothing to my marriage. Now at least I have a dowry and may hold my head up. My honor demands it be paid."

"Blast and botheration! You talk just like a *man!*" Lady Brentmor again bounced up. "Very well, my *honorable* lady, if you wish to manage everybody, and think you know better than your elders."

She moved to the library door. "Come along with me to the counting house, and I'll show you the Pandora's box you want to open."

Mystified, yet firm in her resolve, Esme marched after her grandmother to the gloomy study.

There the dowager unlocked a desk drawer, took out a sheaf of letters, and thrust them into Esme's hands. Then she sat, waiting in silence, but for her index finger tapping impatiently upon the desk.

After a few minutes, Esme looked up from the endless rows of figures and explanatory notes. "You had this man spy upon my uncle?"

"I had him look into Gerald's accounts. I only wish I had a proper spy, to find out how Gerald managed it." The old lady gestured at the letters. "He told me he'd had 'a few setbacks'—but what those figures amount to is near ruin. How, I ask you, could he come to a crash with such sound investments? I ought to know. That's where I've been investing my funds these last thirty years."

"I do not understand these matters," Esme said. "Yet I have heard of speculations in which men lose fortunes."

"He's been up to something worse than that, or he'd have admitted he was under the hatches."

Esme handed back the letters. "His money concerns are his problem. I do not see what this has to do with my dowry."

"Oh, don't you?" The dowager locked away the letters. "Then *think*, child."

After giving Esme exactly three seconds to do so, she went on, "Gerald is desperate for money. Even without knowing how bad it was, I wouldn't give him any. Not until I could be sure his troubles weren't his own stupidity. I don't throw good money after bad, as I hope you understand by now."

"Yes, Grandmother, but—"

"The chess set," Lady Brentmor said impatiently. "Worth thousands—complete, that is. That's why Percival kept the queen hid from his pa. The boy had that much sense at least. He knows Gerald can't be trusted."

This Esme did not find difficult to believe. In Corfu, not only had her uncle been cold and insulting, but he'd lied about her grandmother. All that talk about trying to soften her toward Jason and about her threats to disown Percival—all lies.

"Gerald must know about Diana's bequest, but he ain't mentioned it," the dowager continued, "though the set's worth little to any buyer with a piece missing. That tells me he ain't given up hope of getting the queen back, and won't give the set up easy if he does. Soon as he finds out we've got the queen, there'll be trouble. For one, he'll surely threaten to contest Diana's will in Chancery."

Esme frowned. "I have heard these lawsuits are very expensive. Also, Percival told me some Chancery suits have continued for generations. How can my uncle—"

"When he's got next to no money? He don't need to actually go through with it. Only threaten. Or maybe just spend a few quid to get things started. Then what's Edenmont to do, when *he's* got less than nothing? I'll tell you what. Settle out of court for some measly sum. Or, if he's wise enough to call Gerald's bluff . . ." Lady Brentmor shook her head.

"No," Esme said firmly. "No ominous hints and shaking your head at me. Tell me plain what you suspect."

"Ain't you seen enough among them heathens to work it out for yourself?" Her grandmother gestured at the ledgers lining the room's walls. "Any business that can't be writ down plain for all the world to see is dirty business, in my experience. Which means one's dealing with dirty people. If Gerald's sunk to that and he's desperate, he could sink deeper."

It required little imagination to take the hint. Esme felt

chilled. "You mean violence. Like hiring these dirty people to—to put Varian out of the way. You truly believe my uncle would do such a thing?"

"When I smell something bad, I usually find rottenness at the bottom of it. There's a stench about Gerald since he come back. Worse than usual. Now you know as much as I do. Now *you* can think about it, like I've been doing, since the curst day I found that be-damned chess piece."

Esme didn't need to think. She'd seen the evil men could do, for lust, for greed, even for the pettiest reasons or no reason at all. Her father had been murdered on her account. She would not tempt another villain to rid her of her husband.

She looked at her grandmother. "Will you tell me one thing?"

"That depends what it is."

"Do you believe the chess set is rightfully mine, for my dowry, and must be given to my husband?"

"Bother the child!" The old lady's scowl was fearsome. "D'y' think I've no conscience at all? Of course it's yours—or that pretty-faced lackwit's, if you insist. I only wish you wasn't so moony about him. I wish you could've been sensible and listened to me and said, 'Yes, Grandmother. Whatever you think is best.' "

"I am sorry, truly, Grandmother."

The scowl eased ever so slightly. "It ain't right for a young gel to be dragged into these filthy doings. It ain't right for you to know anything about 'em. You got enough trouble, with that paperskulled debauchee roistering in the cesspits of London. Damn and blast that son of mine! If he hadn't gone and got himself killed, none of this would have happened. If he wasn't dead already, I'd throttle him myself."

Esme rose and walked round the desk. She bent and dropped a kiss on her grandmother's papery cheek.

Lady Brentmor's eyes widened. As Esme straightened, she discerned a glitter in those eyes. Tears?

But her grandmother gave an indignant snort, and the glitter vanished. "I'm forgiven, I take it," she grumbled.

"It's I who should seek forgiveness," Esme said. "To tell you frankly, I did not wish to give Varian money he would be tempted to spend on women. I am very jealous, and the women would vex me more than drunkenness or gaming. Still, I believed it was my duty."

"So it was," the dowager grudgingly agreed.

"Also, I must have some faith in him. I told you yesterday how he has been good to me. And brave. Perhaps you see this, too—else you would not care what my uncle might do to him. Yet you see a great deal else in my husband that troubles you, and you wish to spare me. I am not certain you are altogether correct, but I must believe in you, too."

This earned Esme a sharp look. "Does this mean you'll hold your tongue about your dratted dowry? And stop plaguing me?"

"For now, yes, because you think there is a chance my uncle will harm Varian. Still, you are very clever—and I am not altogether brainless. We will think of something."

Another snort. "*We,* indeed."

"Yes. We two. In the meantime, I shall cease my 'moping' and choose gowns, if that will please you. Also, I will have the dancing master—and whatever else you believe will help make a lady of me."

Esme straightened her shoulders and walked away from the desk. "If—*when* Varian returns to me, he must have no cause to be ashamed. And if—*when* he mends his troubles, he must have a worthy baroness beside him."

Lord Edenmont gazed unhappily about him at the shabby interior of the small cottage. He had left London the day after he'd sent Willoughby the brief note. He'd been at Mount Eden for five days, and this was the first cottage he'd mustered the courage to enter.

It was tidy, despite its shabbiness, as were the six children—ranging in age from thirteen to two. This brood stood behind their noticeably pregnant mama and gazed at him in unblinking wonder.

"Gravity again," said Gideon, coming away from inspection of the chimney. "It's pulling down the chimney and the roof."

The mother of the brood flushed. "John's not had a chance to mend the roof, my lord. He's had to take work where he can get it, and that's took—taken—him to Aylesbury this month."

Varian suppressed a sigh. John Gillis was only one of many who'd been forced to abandon the land his family had worked for generations.

While Varian considered how to respond, he saw Annie give her eldest—a lanky, tow-haired boy—a sharp nudge. When the boy didn't react, she whispered something. The boy backed out of the room.

"Well . . ." Varian glanced uneasily at his brother. "Well, Annie, there's not much to be got out of farming . . . here. I cannot . . ." He trailed off as the lanky boy re-entered, bearing a small earthenware jar.

As the boy gave it to his mother, his shoulders sagged, but he shuffled back into position beside her without a word.

Annie emptied the jar's contents into her hand. "It's all here," she said. "Every last farthing for the past five years' rent. No one ever come—came—for it, and there was nobody at the great house to give it to. So we put it aside."

"The rent?" Varian repeated numbly. "Five years?"

"Aye." She held it out to him, a pitifully small pile of coins. Judging by the chagrin on the eldest boy's face, however, she might have been offering up a fortune.

So it was, Varian reflected. To them. To take it was criminal. To refuse would insult her, and she was proud. She and John would not have saved those precious funds if they were not. Varian thought quickly.

He accepted the money with polite thanks. "It must be properly invested, of course. In the estate."

"Yes, my lord."

"Which at present means it must be invested in people. The land is worthless unfarmed. If men must go away to work, they're not farming it. We must persuade them—and make it worth their while—to return. It would appear my income would be most wisely invested in that way. Don't you agree, Gideon?"

"Very wise," came the stolid answer.

"Then it's settled." Varian carefully counted out the coins and gave all but one shilling back to the bewildered Mrs. Gillis.

"These constitute John's advance wages," he said, "to make it worth his while to work my land again. When he returns, perhaps he'll be so good as to call on Gideon, who'll discuss the practical details with him and put the agreement in writing."

Gideon nodded composedly, just as though he was fully prepared, at any given moment, to provide every sort of detail about everything under the sun.

Annie stared at the coins in her hand.

Varian turned his attention to the lanky boy. "You are old enough to work, and strong enough, I'd say."

Annie tore her gaze from the money. "Oh, yes, my lord," she said eagerly. "He's the man of the house while John's away. Does what he's told, Bertie—Albert—does, and quick, too. And he can read and write as well," she added with pride. "I learned—taught him."

Varian remembered that his mother had devoted a good deal of time to seeing local young people educated. She'd insisted both sexes must be taught, despite strong opposition to education, not only among her peers but among the older tenantry as well. Yet the people had loved her for it, and his father, too, for other reasons. The heap of coins was proof of that affection and loyalty. Certainly Varian had never earned it.

Aloud, he said, "If Albert can be spared, I should welcome his help at the house. Mount Eden must be made presentable for its mistress, and we are all at sixes and sevens." Varian held up the coin. "I should like to engage you to help us make a start, Albert."

"Indeed he will," Annie answered for the dumbstruck boy. "This cold weather will put the planting back, and John can manage well enough without him, and anyhow . . ." She hesitated a moment. "It'll be good to have the family among us again, my lord."

After naming a time tomorrow for Albert to report for

work, Varian took his leave of the Gillises and set out with Gideon through the new-fallen snow.

They trudged a ways in silence, each brother reflecting in his own way upon the scene they'd just left.

"That was well done," Gideon said finally. "By sunrise, we'll find a line of tenants at the door, ready to strike their own bargains with us."

"I'll let you do the bargaining, if you don't mind. I've no head for these matters."

"You did well enough on the spur of the moment. I shall follow your lead. Those as honest as John Gillis and his wife will come with their rent and get the same offer. The others I'll persuade to work on speculation or some sort of trade arrangement. Or perhaps a reduction in rent. We won't see much income at the end of the year, but the land will be worked at least and, as you said, it's no good unfarmed."

"Good heavens. Was I really so sensible? I had better lie down the instant we get home. On second thought, I'd better not. Gad, I do wish we might have salvaged a few beds at least." Varian laughed in spite of himself. "Do you know how often I dreamed of home and a soft bed? I slept on the bare ground, and wet it was, and on wooden floors. How Esme will laugh when I tell her . . ."

His humor faded. "No, I can't tell her, can I?" He paused. "I told her 'a few weeks,' Gideon."

"You said she was levelheaded. She'll understand."

"Will she understand when I tell her it must be months—years, perhaps? Damnation." Varian gazed bleakly about him. "That cottage was probably the best of them. I must do something for the Gillises, and the others. They can't live in hovels. But how the devil am I to repair the cottages when my own roof is ready to drop on my head?"

"Mount Eden's roof will endure a while," said Gideon. "As to the other essential repairs, including the cottages—the cost of materials is negligible. It's the labor and skill we need."

"We've no money to hire anybody." Varian resumed walking. "Still, I helped repair a mill in Albania, and it didn't kill me.'' He glanced at Gideon. ''I don't suppose you know how to mend a roof or a chimney?''

''I understand the principles.''

''Will you stay long enough to tell me how to go about it—and watch the first time to be sure I do it correctly?''

Gideon exhaled a sigh. ''I daresay you've never listened to a word Damon and I have uttered on this topic. We are not returning to London. Only tell us what we're to do and we'll do it—so long as it's sensible. If we think it isn't, we'll tell you. What you propose appears the only sensible course, in the present circumstances.''

''Dammit, Gilly, I told you—''

''You don't understand, do you?'' Gideon's stiff-set countenance eased into a grin. ''It isn't for you, my lord, but for the fascinating creature we're so eager to meet. The sooner we repair the ancestral ruin, the sooner we get a glimpse of the young lady you want so desperately to impress.''

Varian's face grew hot.

''Good grief. Edenmont blushing. Lord Alvanley would give a pony to see it.''

''Devil take you, Gideon!''

Gideon laughed. ''You said you owed us a great deal, did you not? Mayhap we'll take it out in plaguing you about your bride. For your own good, of course. It'll keep your wits sharp, and then you shan't be sinking into melancholy.'' Gideon gave his lordship an avuncular pat on the shoulder. ''For your own good, my noble brother. Can't have you blowing your brains out. Not until you've got an heir at least.''

Chapter 26

April arrived in a drizzle, to launch in earnest the London Season's annual round of gaiety. But Sir Gerald Brentmor took no interest in society's profitless amusements. At midnight, while the Beau Monde danced and gossiped, he was neatly tucked in his bed, dreaming of annuities, cent-per-cents, and promissory notes.

Though a sound sleeper, he bolted up from the pillow the instant the hot wax splattered on his forehead. He'd no time to scream, scarce time to open his mouth before he felt the cold blade of a dagger against his throat.

"Cry out, and your soul flies to hell," a low voice warned.

The voice was disagreeably familiar. Despite the panic that froze his brain as well as his heart, Sir Gerald retained sufficient reason to identify its owner: Risto.

The dripping candle retreated and was returned to the bedstand. By someone else. Good God, there were two of them.

Risto's companion, encased in a hooded cloak, drew a chair up beside the bed, sat down, and threw the hood back. The candlelight revealed the face of a young man.

"Risto you recall, I see," said the stranger. "I am his master." His voice was gentle and his sweet smile that of an innocent youth. These qualities did not quiet Sir Gerald's fears in the least.

"Is-Ismal," he gasped.

The young man bowed his head in acknowledgement. "You'll forgive our unceremonious entry. I thought it best the servants not see me. Servants of all races like to talk, and neither you nor I would wish my arrival made known to certain individuals. I have come merely to settle a small matter of business. Then I shall be gone, I promise.''

Ismal calmly removed the cloak and leaned back, utterly at his ease. He was dressed in English garb, complete to the elaborate knot of his neckcloth. Except for the faint accent, he might have passed as an English gentleman.

''Before you vex your brain contriving some way to escape me, I will explain your position.'' He gracefully draped one arm upon the back of the chair. ''In Venice, I found a man named Bridgeburton.''

Sir Gerald felt the blood draining from his face.

''This man has been a partner in your enterprises for many years—since the night, some twenty-odd years ago, he helped you cheat your brother out of a valuable property.''

Ismal withdrew from his inner coat pocket a thick letter. ''He was persuaded to write a confession of all your mutual crimes.'' He dropped the letter onto Sir Gerald's lap. ''That is a copy. The original is to be delivered to a member of your ministry in the event I am inconvenienced in any way. If you think to trick or betray me, you will only betray yourself.''

The dagger withdrew just enough to let Sir Gerald take up the letter. He needed only to skim it to understand how much danger he was in. No one but Bridgeburton knew these particular details.

He set his jaw. ''I suppose he's dead.''

''I fear your partner was so incautious as to fall into the canal.'' Ismal examined his smooth nails. ''May Risto put away his dagger now? If his hand grows too tired, it may slip.''

''You know I daren't raise any alarm.'' Sir Gerald handed back the letter. ''I've no more inclination for the gallows than for your servant's blade.''

When the dagger was withdrawn, he gingerly touched his throat. It was wet. Perspiration, perhaps, or blood. It hardly mattered. He wasn't dead yet.

What mattered was the young man sitting by the bed. Ismal had got this damning confession out of the immovable Bridgeburton, killed him, and come all the way to England. That was more than persistence. Madness?

"What do you want from me?" Sir Gerald demanded, more boldly than he felt. "I dealt squarely with you. It wasn't my fault—"

"It was not a deliberate betrayal, I admit," Ismal amiably agreed, "though I thought so at first. I have since learned that not only have my dreams crumbled, but your empire as well. I cannot believe you'd deliberately destroy yourself. Nonetheless you were careless, Sir Gerald, else no one could have known about every single ship, every single destination."

"It could have been one of your own people."

"Only Risto knew all—or nearly all—and he would not be with me now had he betrayed me. It was you, of course."

"I swear to you—"

"You were incautious in some way, and this error nearly resulted in my death." Tipping his head to one side, Ismal softly enquired, "Have you ever been poisoned, Sir Gerald? My cousin, Ali, prefers the slow poisons. I did not find the experience at all to my taste. Yet as I recovered on a filthy fishing vessel, I began to appreciate the method's charms. I should enjoy, very much, watching one who's played me false die . . . very, very slowly . . . in great agony."

Definitely mad, Sir Gerald decided grimly. But the first shock had passed, and his powers of self-preservation were returning. "I suppose it's no use trying to convince you I'm not your enemy, or even that I never spoke a word to anyone or within anyone's hearing. It hardly matters anyhow. You know I must have the original of Bridgeburton's letter. What's your price?"

"The sum I paid for weapons I never received, plus a thousand pounds to repay what my cousin extorted from me—because of your niece and her pig of a lover." An edge had crept into Ismal's mellifluous voice. He must have heard it, too, for he smiled more sweetly. "And another thousand for my travel expenses,'' he continued in gentler tones. ''All to be paid in two days.''

Utterly deranged. This, regrettably, did not make a man any the less dangerous. Still, Sir Gerald had strong objections to being blackmailed and a keen sense of the injustice of Ismal's demands. Moreover, the baronet hadn't yet met the man he couldn't get the better of, sooner or later. He thought quickly.

''I can't raise such a sum in only two days,'' he said. ''If you know so much about me, you must be aware I've already sold off my remaining investments, not to mention half my possessions.''

''Then you will give me the chess set.''

Sir Gerald stared at him.

Ismal's smile grew reproachful. ''Or have you sold that, too—your niece's dowry?''

Indignation instantly submerged Sir Gerald's alarm. ''Sold it?'' he repeated. ''And get but a fraction of its worth? Most of the value was in its being complete, with every piece intact, every gemstone the original. Collectors may be eccentric, some of them, and they might, just possibly, overlook a missing pawn—but a *queen?''*

Ismal's arm came away from the back of the chair. The false smile had broadened, and his eyes gleamed.

With amusement? Sir Gerald wondered. What the devil was so funny?

Ismal leaned toward him. ''Sir Gerald,'' he said, ''you are in deeper trouble than you know. I am not the only one in possession of your dirty secrets.''

''What in blazes are you talking about?''

''The black queen.''

''Which this backguard said he was going to give you—''

''And which was soon thereafter given to your son. With your message still inside.''

Esme's lips were twitching as she gave the letter back to her grandmother.

''It ain't funny,'' the old lady growled.

''Not only amusing but imaginative,'' Esme said. ''They say I have tattoos on my hands, wear a ring in my nose, and in this garb—and nothing else—I dance lewd dances in your rose garden. By the light of the full moon. Mrs. Stockwell-Hume does not mention my howling at the moon as well, but perhaps her London friends will think of that in time."

"It don't matter if it's ridiculous. Most of London gossip is. That don't make it any the less damaging. What do you think Edenmont's going to say—no, better—*feel,* when he hears of it?"

Esme quickly sobered. The rumors Lady Brentmor's friend reported were preposterous, blatant examples of English society's provincialism and ignorance. All the same, to have one's wife an object of mockery, and oneself an object of pity . . .

"Quite," said the dowager. "We must go to London. Tomorrow."

"London? Tomorrow?"

"You ain't an echo, so don't act like one. I'd leave this minute if I could, but we'll want all the day to pack. And the young brute must come, too, unless I want to come back and find he's blown up the house."

"But, Grandmother, I am not ready. You said yourself my manners—"

"They're better than what them fools expect. Besides, we ain't staying the whole Season. Just a week or so. Enough to set 'em straight. Bloody lot of nincompoops."

London. Tomorrow. Esme suppressed a shudder. All those women. *His* women. They'd pick her to pieces, and she lacked the art to defend herself. She wouldn't have the heart, either, when she saw her rivals. They'd be more beautiful than she'd imagined, more graceful, and she'd feel uglier, utterly worthless. Two months without Varian had already weakened her confidence. She needed time to regather her strength if she hoped to make sensible decisions about the future . . . without him.

"No," she said. "This gossip is no more than a joke. But if I am there, they will see what is truly wrong, and that will be worse."

"It'll be a deal worse if he takes it into his head to start issuing challenges. A man's obliged to defend his wife's good name—even if he loathes her. Gad, men are such jackasses," the dowager grumbled. "We spend half our lives trying to save the bloody idiots from themselves."

"You cannot expect me to believe—"

"If you won't go," her grandmother went on heedlessly, "you'd best hope he's cleverer with a pistol than he is with finances."

"God have mercy." Esme rubbed her head. "And the English claim *Albania* is dangerous. Varian would have been safer there. Here, his uncle will kill him for a chess set, his friends will kill him for gossip . . . Y'Allah, even Ali Pasha could not survive among these people. They are insane, all of them."

The dowager was not attending. Her abstracted gaze wandered about the sitting room. "Of course, there is the bright side. Once he makes you a widow, you might find something vaguely resembling a proper husband." Her attention settled upon a small watercolor hanging near the mantel. "Dunham's a widower, and he's got an heir already. Saxonby's wife's ailing, but there's two brothers between him and the title. Herriot—or is it the other one? Damnation, I must find my Debrett's—no, I can ask Lady Seales. She'll know to the minute what's on the market."

Esme stared at her grandmother. "What market? What are you talking about?"

"The husband market. Your next. You ain't meaning to mourn the halfwit all the rest of your days, are you?"

"Heaven grant me patience," Esme cried. "He is not even dead and you are planning my next husband? You are worse than Qeriba. She at least did not wish him ill. But you are much the same as she. 'Do this. Do that.' And I am not to think. I am to have no say."

"Then why'n't you try saying something intelligent?"

"Why do you not give me a moment to think? Only *you* say Varian will fight duels on my account. Why should I believe he would risk his neck for such small cause? He's more likely to laugh."

"I told you how men are."

"Yes, and you told me as well that many men leave their wives in the country while they amuse themselves in town. If he wishes to return to London, and I am there—"

"Yes, most inconvenient for him, I'm sure."

"Also," Esme went on doggedly, "you do not think what the talk will be like if I remain with my grandmother in London while my husband lives under another roof."

"That would be his doing. I didn't separate you when he was here, and I wouldn't do so there. But you're just making excuses. The reason you don't want to go to London is simple enough. You're a coward."

In this particular case, the words struck very near the mark. Esme had admitted as much to herself the instant she thought of the women. All the same, her temper flared at the taunt. "You are completely impossible!" she cried. "You will do and say anything to have your way. But you make a mistake in me. Like it or not, your blood runs in my veins, and I shall have *my* way. Yes, Grandmother, we shall set out tomorrow, as you wish. No, Grandmother, we do not go to London—not until I know my husband's opinion. Then I can judge sensibly."

Lady Brentmor's scowl was truly ferocious. Esme quaked not a whit. She scowled back.

"You want to go to Mount Eden?" the dowager demanded. "And get the sapskull's *permission* first?"

"I shall not race to London to rescue him from duels, only to find I've made a fool of myself. I've heard your opinion of what must be done. Now I will hear his. *Then* I will decide. For myself."

"Very well," said her grandmother. "As you wish, *my lady.*"

"And no tricks," Esme warned. "Percival has shown me the maps. If the carriage goes anywhere but to Mount Eden I shall jump out of it."

"I wouldn't dream of tricking you," came the sardonic reply. "I'm only too happy to drop in on his lordship without warning. About time you saw for yourself. Let him introduce you to his drink—and opium-sotted friends, and his whores. I should like that above all things.'' Lady Brentmor moved to the door. ''I wouldn't miss it for the world.''

Percival had already scuttled down the hall to the backstairs when his grandmother emerged from Esme's sitting room. He knew he shouldn't have been listening at the door. He'd spied on his papa just the once, and look what that had led to. He could hardly bear to think about chess any more because that led his mind to the black queen, which led to Papa's shameful secret, and thinking about that made Percival feel very sick. He felt rather sick now, as he had from the moment he'd seen the letter on the table at breakfast.

After opening it, Grandmama had got all stiff and purplish in the face. Which she'd every reason to do, as Percival had just learned. And it had nothing to do with Papa, he told himself. It was just a lot of horrid, ignorant gossip.

Frowning, he sat down on the topmost step. The part about the nose ring, for example. Lots of people were aware it was a common form of adornment in several exotic cultures, just as in some cultures it was common to go about unclothed. The gossips couldn't know these weren't Albanian practices—nor were any of the other things they'd made up about Cousin Esme.

Except for the tatoos. In some Albanian tribes, women did tatoo their hands. It was very odd that a lot of English gossips had accidently got the one very obscure practice right and everything else so ludicrously wrong. One couldn't help wondering how anyone but an Albanian would even imagine a *woman* having tatoos. On her *hands*.

But it wasn't impossible, he told himself. It could be a coincidence.

Like the letter's stationery. Papa surely wasn't the only one who used that particular kind. It didn't seem the sort a woman would use, but Mrs. Stockwell-Hume might have borrowed her husband's. Except he'd died ten years ago.

Percival closed his eyes. It *couldn't* be Papa's stationery. It certainly wasn't Papa's handwriting or anyone else's but Mrs. Stockwell-Hume's, or Grandmama would have noticed. It couldn't be a forgery, either. If Papa knew how to disguise his handwriting, he'd have done that with the black queen's message.

But someone else might know how to forge a letter, his worried brain pointed out. Someone very, very clever. Someone Albanian.

"No," Percival whispered. "It can't be. Please, Mama. I'm just imagining things, aren't I?"

Chapter 27

Damon was on Mount Eden's roof patching a chimney, and Gideon was down in the kitchen attempting to assemble a luncheon. Varian was finishing his morning task of sweeping the bedrooms clean, mainly of mouse droppings. Though the cat did her best, she was only one against a legion, and her offspring were too young to be of much assistance. Judging from the volume of the droppings, some of the mice must be twice the size of her children.

He swore when he heard the door knocker. Broom in hand, he raced down the stairs and very nearly crushed the tortoiseshell kitten crouching at the bottom, waiting to pounce.

"Dash it, you've only got nine lives." Varian scooped up the kitten. "Don't use them all up in one week."

The kitten clawed free of his hand and tore its way up his shirt. Varion was trying to pry it loose when he reached the door. Hissing, the feline dug its claws in.

Varian gave up, flung the broom aside, and jerked the door open.

He blinked once, and all thought, all the world vanished in that instant. All he saw or knew was Esme, staring up, open-mouthed, at him.

"Esme." In the next breath, he'd yanked her over the threshold and crushed her in his arms. "Darling, I—Ow!"

He grabbed for the murderous kitten, but Esme pushed his hand away. "You will hurt him," she said sharply.

"He is too frightened to let go." Murmuring in Albanian, she stroked the hissing cat. It promptly succumbed and went willingly into her hands.

By this time, reality had returned. Varian looked past his wife through the open doorway. He saw the carriage and the dowager alighting from it, then Percival jumping down after her.

Varian raked his fingers through his hair. He felt grit. As he took his hand away, he saw it was black. He saw as well he'd marred Esme's elegant cloak with dirt and soot.

Heat rose from his neck to simmer in his face. He looked at Esme, then away at the dowager who was marching purposefully toward them. Percival had evidently caught sight of Damon on the roof, because the boy was running round to the side of the house for a better view.

Though acutely aware his face was crimson, Varian squared his shoulders. When the dowager reached the doorstep, he bowed. "My lady. This is a pleasant surprise."

"Don't talk to me," she snapped, pushing past him. "It ain't my doing, but *hers.*" She looked about her and sniffed. "Tell my servants to bring the baskets. It's plain you ain't prepared for hospitality, and I'm thirsty." She sailed on down the hall, muttering to herself.

Very soon thereafter, following a hasty washing-up, Damon and Gideon were moving cautiously through the main corridor. They'd already peeped into the morning room, where a small, fierce old woman was perched upon a valise shouting orders to a small army of harassed-looking servants.

In the drawing room, a red-haired adolescent boy lay on his belly before a mouse hole, patiently lecturing a kitten that was swatting at his nose.

Though intriguing in themselves, neither of these visions could be spared more than a glance. Damon and Gideon had one particular quarry in mind and, resisting these lesser temptations, continued their search.

They paused at the partly open library doors and peered

in. Then Damon looked at his brother. "It can't be that little girl," he whispered.

"It most assuredly is not the mature lady in the morning room."

"But she's no more than a child. Varian couldn't possibly—"

He broke off as the low voices within grew louder. Cautiously, Damon opened the door another fraction of an inch. At that instant, the little girl hurled her reticule at his brother. Varian ducked aside, and the reticule bounced against the mantel, then onto the floor. The girl began pacing furiously, in a whirl of green skirts, and her voice burst out at full volume.

"I shall *never* forgive you!" she raged. "You are impossible. Your stupidity is immense beyond belief. Also, you are a great, filthy *liar!*"

"Esme, I did not—"

"You *lied!* There, I have said it. Will you defend your honor? Go ahead, find your pistols. And I shall find my own and shoot you through your black heart. And with better reason. It is *I* who am dishonored. You have shamed me. All the world will laugh at me—more loudly than they do now."

She spat out something in a foreign language, and Varian started to move toward her. Her hand went up, waving him back. "Do not come near me," she warned. "Do not tempt me. I shall strangle you."

Varian subsided, to lean against the mantel once more and watch her march to and fro, her heels making a steady drumbeat on the bare floor.

She went on with another stream of what could only be vituperation, then recommenced in English. "Three letters every week you send me, and never once do you tell me the truth. Only stories and jokes—as though I am a child, to be amused. Your debts were paid. There was no more of the danger you spoke of—as though I care about danger. But you tell me nothing. You leave me with my grandmother, which is a great disgrace in my country, but I bear it because this is another country and all the English are crazy."

"Darling, I hadn't any way to keep you."

"I do not need keeping! I am not a sheep or an ox. How do you think I have lived in my country with no money? I have slept in caves and under bushes. But I know what it is." She stopped short. "I am not a child, nor yet a weak woman. You could have told me the truth, that you did not want me with you. But your conceit is even more vast than your stupidity. Did you think I would die of grief?" She marched up to him and folded her hands across her bosom. "Hah!"

Though her back was turned to him now, Damon had no doubt of her expression. Her small, rigid frame vibrated defiance.

"We oughtn't be eavesdropping," Gideon murmured.

"Yes, it's vulgar, but ever so interesting."

With a reproving glance at his brother, Gideon loudly cleared his throat.

The girl was again belaying Varian in her own tongue and evidently didn't notice the sound. Varian did. He looked toward the doors.

Gideon pushed them fully open.

"Ah, here they are," Varian said in a strained voice.

The girl swung round. A becoming shade of pink washed her high-boned cheeks, and her eyes opened very wide.

"Quite green," Damon said under his breath.

Varian moved to take her arm. "May I present my brothers, my dear? This sturdy fellow is Gideon."

Gideon made a courtly bow.

"And this one with his mouth hanging open is Damon."

Damon's bow was rather less graceful. This was due to a temporary disarrangement of his wits. Now that he saw her up close, it was clear she was by no means a child, but a young woman. An astoundingly appealing young woman. Also exceedingly cross at present, but that only made her the more attractive. He'd never seen anything quite like the green fire in her eyes. Evidently, Varian never had, either. That must explain it.

"They've been perishing to meet you," Varian said.

Her ladyship eyed the two brothers with patent suspicion. "Then you should have brought them to see me," she said curtly. "At least my grandmother would have fed them."

"I say, we don't look as bad as all that, surely?" Damon protested with an abashed smile.

She clicked her tongue. "It is disgraceful. It is plain you do not eat or sleep properly." She stepped a bit closer to Damon, making his heart thump oddly. "You are much too thin," she told him. "Who cooks for you?"

"I have been delegated the position of chef, my lady," said Gideon.

"Yes, and he's a dab hand with boiled eggs," Damon assured her, "though I'm afraid he hasn't quite got the knack of—"

"I shall beat you senseless," she told Varian. "You are a great idiot."

"Oh, but it isn't Varian's—"

She gave Damon a withering look. He shut his mouth. Clearly, he would not be allowed to complete a sentence.

"*He* is head of the family," she said austerely. "It is his responsibility. Unfortunately, he has no sense. But the mistress is here now. I shall make a proper meal for you."

Varian began to say something, received a deadly shaft from the green eyes, and also decided to hold his tongue.

"Go have a bath," she told him. "You make me ashamed."

Then she marched past them, her half-boots tapping an ominous tattoo, and swept through the doors.

Damon looked at his oldest brother. "I say, Varian, she won't really beat you, will she?"

"I had better have a bath," Varian said. And left.

Following a surprisingly amiable luncheon, the dowager spent several hours minutely examining the house. Gideon followed her, dutifully jotting down her comments in a notebook. Damon, much to Varian's annoyance, trailed Esme about like a lovesick puppy. Nonetheless, his lordship knew better than to go with them on their tour of the grounds. Esme needed time to calm down. Meanwhile, he could occupy himself in doing something about the shambles in the master bedroom.

He had thought he'd rather die than let her see him in this state, in this squalid house which so loudly proclaimed all his villainies. And he *had* died, a hundred small deaths of shame and guilt. Having endured the worst, however, he knew he could certainly endure rejection of his amorous advances.

He knew well enough he'd no right to make any, and was mad to even consider it, let alone hope. He just couldn't help himself. After the first stunned—and short-lived—embrace, he hadn't found another chance to touch her. Not with strange servants scurrying about, and his brothers or Percival or Lady Brentmor popping in at inopportune moments—and Esme all this while in an awesome state of temper.

God help him, he'd even missed her demented rages.

Varian smiled bleakly as he smoothed the shabby bed linens. Today's display had shown a new imperiousness. Not that it wasn't to be expected, after two months of her grandmother's tutelage. By now, his brothers must think him thoroughly henpecked. That was because they didn't understand. Nor had Varian any intention of explaining.

He knew Esme was deeply hurt, and it was he who'd hurt her.

He didn't know how to undo it. She'd shown him the letter from Mrs. Stockwell-Hume—the reason for the unexpected visit—and found his response thoroughly unsatisfactory. Varian had tried to explain that until his fellows saw her for themselves, they'd kept on creating their own solutions to the mystery of Lady Edenmont.

He knew this was his fault, and said so: his scandalous reputation, a bride from a little-known land—wild stories were bound to result. Yet he hadn't the means to introduce her properly, which meant, at present, that the dowager must do so. That was when Esme had exploded.

He understood now that she believed his miserable condition reflected upon her as an inadequate wife. That was merely a cultural difference. What troubled him was her certainty that *he* believed her inadequate. She thought he was ashamed of her, or tired of her.

Which was perfectly insane. Unfortunately, insane beliefs are by definition not amenable to reason. She refused to believe a word he said.

Varian stuffed his dirty clothes into the wardrobe and looked about him. The furnishings had been salvaged from the discards of a partially-burnt house in Aylesbury. Only the bedroom furniture had been usable. Or so he and his brothers had believed.

Now, he noticed a faint odor of firedamp, despite the hours of scrubbing and diligent application of herbs and oils. The bed linens, too, were second—or more likely, third or fourth—hand, shabby and gray, though Annie Gillis had scrubbed them mercilessly. The draperies were even worse. Ancient and moth-eaten to start with, they were rapidly crumbling, thanks to the kittens' busy attentions.

Varian groaned and sat upon the bed. What the devil had he been thinking of, to even consider seducing his baroness in this sordid cell?

"Varian?"

It was Esme's voice outside the door.

Varian experienced a cowardly urge to scramble under the bed. Instead, he gripped the edge of the mattress and prayed she'd look elsewhere, so he might slip out before she caught sight of his ghastly room.

The door swung open with a protesting squeal.

He closed his eyes.

"I thought you would be hiding from me," she said. "You *ought* to hide. But I have promised your brothers I will not kill you. They say they cannot afford the funeral."

He opened his eyes. She stood in the doorway, her arms folded across her chest.

"Also," she said, "Gideon does not wish to be baron. He says he would rather be hanged."

After staring at him for a moment, she abandoned her defiant pose, stepped into the room, and gazed casually about her. "This is a very large room. All my house in

Durrës would fit inside. But it is the same with my grandmother's house, and so I am not amazed."

Varian rose. "It's a dreadful room, though it was elegant once, in an old-fashioned way. I wish you could have seen it then—the entire house."

She shrugged. "It is not so bad. With a few women to help, I might have made it very clean in a week, perhaps a bit more. You must get another mouser, my grandmother says, and I agree. Though what the poor mice find to eat, I cannot tell." She threw him an accusing glance. "Damon tells me you work very hard. He thinks I am blind, perhaps."

"For ten years, I never worked at all. I've a good deal to make up for."

"He says you do this for me. He thinks I am stupid, too."

"You *are* stupid if you don't believe him. What other reason could I have, Esme?"

She answered with another shrug. "My grandmother wishes to spend the night at the inn."

"The Black Bramble."

"Yes. She did not bring food enough to make the evening meal. I am sent to invite you to dine with us. She has invited your brothers, also."

Varian swallowed his pride in a painful gulp. "Is that where you plan to spend the night?"

A long silence. He waited.

No answer came. Finally, she turned to the door.

"Esme, please."

"Please, *what?*" Her voice was taut, like her posture.

"I've missed you, darling."

She turned back to him, her eyes wary.

"I . . . I wish you'd stay."

Her glance darted to the bed, then back to him. "You told me I must go to London."

"That doesn't mean I don't want you! Goddammit, Esme—" Varian caught himself up short. "I'm sorry. I promised myself . . . but it's no use, never is. I've tried to explain, but I just can't make you understand. Why is it so difficult, love? I know you want to help me—but if my peers were to hear my wife was slaving for me, I could never look them in the eye again. Nor could I live with myself."

She said nothing, only watched him.

Varian gazed helplessly about him while his mind frantically sought the right words.

"I would be *disgraced,*" he said at last. "Worse than I am at present. Far worse. I know it sounds crazy to you, but that's the way of my world. Ask anybody."

Esme considered for a frustratingly long while.

"Ask anybody," Varian repeated, "when you get to London. If even one member of the Beau Monde tells you different, you may tell your grandmother to send you right back to me."

She folded her hands tightly in front of her. "Do you promise this?"

"Yes. I promise."

She studied the grimy floor a moment. "I do not like this country," she said. "The people have no sense."

"So it would appear."

Her brow furrowed. "I have a dancing master, you know. And a maid of my own. She thinks I do not know how to dress myself, and so I must pretend I do not or I will hurt her feelings. It is tiresome sometimes to be a lady, and I become cross. I told your brothers I was sorry for my rudeness. I told them my temper is very ugly, and it cannot be helped." She flushed, and his heart gave a desperate lurch in answer.

"I love your temper," he said. "They did, too. It was the most excitement any of us have had in weeks."

"I do not wish to be exciting. It is not ladylike."

"I like you just the way you are."

"Tsk."

"I do," he said firmly. "Very much. I've missed you very much. I'm not happy without you, Esme."

"I—I am glad," she said. "You *should* be unhappy."

Varian moved past her and shut the door.

"They are waiting for us, Varian." Her voice was low, shaky.

"I never dine before eight o'clock." His eyes fell upon the shabby counterpane. It was wrong, he told himself, and he was selfish and base. But he was also desperate.

He caught Esme by the waist and deposited her upon the bed, then knelt before her. "In any case, I've two months of conjugal duty to make up for."

Her beautiful eyes were filled with doubt . . . hurt as well.

Varian looked down. He'd make it better, he told himself. He knew how. It was the one thing he did well.

He removed one ridiculously tiny half-boot and stroked her foot. "Silk," he said softly. "Only a concubine would wear silk upon her feet." He looked up at her. "I wanted you then."

"Because you are wicked."

"Yes." Varian removed the other boot. Then, very slowly, he slid his hand up her leg and unfastened the lacy garter. Slowly again, he inched the stocking down. Her toes curled. He dealt with the other garter and stocking with the same deliberation. She shivered.

He trailed his hands up her bare legs, drawing her muslin frock up over her knees. He kissed each knee. Her scent swam in his head. His fingers tightened on her thighs. He looked up into eyes dark as the forest depths. Watchful. Waiting.

Varian shivered. His trembling hands moved swiftly to the fastenings at her back. Then he took his time again, letting his fingers trail along her creamy skin while he eased the frock down to her waist and past her hips until it sank to the floor.

She wore a gossamer-thin chemise, embroidered in a lacy pattern of twining rosebuds. The rosy peaks of her firm breasts were already hard, trembling against the fragile fabric. His breathing grew labored.

His fingers stiff with the effort *not* to hurry, Varian slowly removed the pins from her hair. Rippling over his fingers, the loosened tresses tumbled to her shoulders. "Garnet and pearls," he murmured. His voice seemed to come through a fog. "How I've missed looking at you. And touching you."

"I have not missed you so much." Her voice, too, was muffled. "I have been very busy."

Varian watched the rapid rise and fall of her bosom. "Liar."

"Tsk." But her eyes told more even than her quickened breathing. Longing shimmered in their green depths, making his heart ache.

He wanted to throw her down and have her there and then, that instant, and let anguish burn up in the savage fury of passion.

Instead, he stood and, his gaze locked with hers, pulled off his clothes. Her darkening glance slid the length of his lean torso, pausing for one dazed instant where his desire was so blatantly evident.

"As you observe," he said hoarsely, "your husband is prepared to do his duty."

A small, choked sound escaped her.

Varian silenced it with a kiss, quick and hungry. Then he drew the chemise up over her head and impatiently tossed the flimsy garment aside.

"*Eager* to do his duty," he amended. He nudged her, and Esme inched back upon the bed. Kneeling between her legs, he bent over her and took her mouth in a deep, fierce kiss that drove her down onto the mattress. He drew away to nuzzle her breasts. He heard her catch her breath, but she made no attempt to hurry him or even touch him. He teased with his tongue and with his hands. Esme simply accepted, her response a breath of a sigh.

He lifted his head to look at her. Her eyes were sleepy, unfocused, yet he discerned the glint in them.

"Esme."

"Tell me."

"I want you."

"Yes. Want me." Closing her eyes, she gave a throaty sigh.

Varian's hand tightened over her breast. She moved sinuously, and the faintest of smiles curved her mouth.

"I want you *now,*" he said hoarsely.

Slowly she slid her hand over her sleek body until it rested at the bottom of her belly. "No. Not yet."

He swallowed a groan. "No, first you want to drive me insane."

"Yes."

"Revenge."

"No. Yes."

"Very well, my lady," he growled.

Ravaging her mouth with needy kisses, he stroked and caressed, infusing her with his heat. She gave him soft moans and sighs, and stirred under his touch, but unhurriedly. Yet he felt pleasure vibrating within her, felt it growing into urgency while he kissed every inch of her silken skin.

Every art he'd ever learned became part of one tormenting search to make her fully wild as only she could be, and as he wanted. Then, even when she reached for him at last, her strong hands dragging him down to her, he wanted still more. Even when she was maddened fully, sobbing and laughing at once, he wanted more. Then, as she wrapped her hot, supple body tightly about him, his words spilled out. Not the easy endearments of a practiced lover but harder truths: of regret and shame and loneliness . . . and something else. It was this last he uttered most painfully of all, the words tearing his throat.

"I love you, Esme."

She pulled his mouth to hers, as though to take the words inside her.

"I love you," he repeated. The sounds trembled in the darkening room. Again and again he told her, and the words hung in the air as he surged into her . . . and carried her to rapture . . . then spilled his love upon the ragged sheets.

Chapter 28

Esme lay in her husband's arms, listening while his breathing slowed. She felt the tension growing between them even as their bodies quieted.

The words he'd uttered had made her drunk with happiness. Now she understood she'd heard only the madness of passion. She tried to persuade herself passion was enough; it was a miracle he still wanted her, this man for whom desire was but the whim of a moment.

Even if she wasn't a whim, she must represent an aberration. She was without beauty, grace, or lover's skill. Coming of a race he viewed as savage, she had brought into his life everything he most disliked and avoided: hardship, confrontation, violence.

He'd stumbled into wedding her only because lust had wiped out reason. In these last two months away from her, though, he'd surely had second thoughts. While she was his wife, like it or not, she need not be the mother of his children. He'd not pollute the noble blood of the St. Georges with that of a foul-tempered barbarian.

When he nuzzled her shoulder, she tensed.

Varian raised his head to look at her. She fixed her gaze upon the ceiling.

"Esme."

"Go to sleep," she said. "You are weary."

"You're upset." He sighed. "I'd hoped you wouldn't notice. That was stupid of me, wasn't it?"

"I have no idea what you are talking about. Go to sleep, Varian."

"No. We'll discuss it, as we should have done long ago if I'd possessed a grain of forethought. But I didn't."

Wrapping his arms about her, he pulled her round to face him. "I've two younger brothers to carry on the line," he said. "I'd always assumed they would, for obvious reasons. You're not obliged to give me an heir, Esme."

"I understand. You do not want children."

"It isn't that. Our situation is difficult enough—nigh impossible, in fact." Bitterness edged his voice. "In fairy tales, the prince and princess wed and live happily every after. But I'm not one of those pure-hearted princes. I took your innocence, knowing it was criminal, then wed you, which was more criminal still. Now we're both paying. I won't make an innocent babe pay as well."

He held her too tightly, and his voice betrayed too much pain. The words he meant as reassurance only confirmed her fears. He blamed himself, blamed desire. But it was she, its object, who'd spoiled everything for him, made his life ugly and weary. With each passing day, his unhappiness would erode his desire for her. In time, he'd come to hate her for what she'd done for him . . . and she'd have no child. She'd have no permanent remembrance of their passion, no babe conceived in love, no child for her to love when its father turned away from her.

"I'm sorry," she said. "We have only this night together, and I cause you distress."

"It's my own doing." He brought her hand to his lips. His mouth was warm, so gentle upon her fingers. "I didn't want you to see this moldering ruin I live in. I didn't want to make love to you in this tawdry room."

"I do not care where we make love, Varian. I do not care where I am, so long as I am with you. Even for a short time," she added hastily.

"But you care about children, very much."

Yes, she wanted to cry. *Your children.*

"I am not even nineteen years old," she made herself answer. "There is time. Many years. It is not as though my only chance is now, this once." Her heart rapped sharply with anxiety.

He smiled. "Of course not. I certainly don't wish to keep repeating that nerve-wracking experience all the rest of my life. You've a talent for putting good intentions to naught, my dear. Behaving responsibly nearly killed me."

"It—it was not the most agreeable way of—of ending." Her countenance heated.

He touched her burning face. "There are other methods, but equally disagreeable, I'm afraid. Shall I embarrass my delicate flower with the gruesome details?"

She *was* deeply embarrassed, because preventing conception seemed a most unnatural act. All the same, she was aware he was trying to distract her, trying to be kind. "How gruesome?" she asked.

He chuckled, and as he went on to describe sheaths made of sheep bladders or fish skin, Esme giggled in spite of herself.

"You tie it with a string?" she asked incredulously. "Where? How?"

"Don't be stupid. Where do you think?"

"It does not sound comfortable. You must not do it, Varian. If you tie the string too tight—"

His roar of laughter lightened her heart. He was made to laugh, to amuse and be amused. Because it amused him, Esme encouraged him to tell all he knew—of the sponges women were being urged by certain radical reformers to use, and of the various herbal concoctions some resorted to. Men dosed themselves as well, some with honeysuckle juice or rue, others with castor oil. There was an endless assortment of potions to be drunk or applied.

"There are also some benighted persons who believe violent lovemaking prevents conception," he said, grinning.

"They are not logical," she said. "How many children have resulted from rape? How can the civilized English believe such nonsense?"

"Wishful thinking, perhaps. Speaking of which . . ." His hand slid down her spine to cup her bottom.

"Oh, Varian, you've no need to *wish.*"

"But it's not as you want, is it, love?" His hands

moved over her so tenderly. Yet even the gentlest of his caresses was magic, making her crave more, crave all.

"It's you I want," she said.

She needed him. It was more, she knew, than her body's hunger. She wanted all that he was: the lazy charm, the careless grace and easy laughter . . . the sin as well, the shadows darkening his soul. He was the Devil's gift—and snare as well, for a woman. But she was glad to be so ensnared. He taught her pleasure, and his grace touched her earthbound warrior's soul, to lighten it with dreams and delight.

She wanted all he was and to be his entirely. When he was inside her, in that long moment of joining, she could believe it was so, eternally so. She knew she'd no right to forever. She had this moment, though.

"Just love me, Varian," she whispered. "Love me beautifully, as you do."

No one disturbed them. The others, it appeared, had given up waiting and gone to the Black Bramble without them. The house was still, and night had long since fallen. In the darkness, Varian made love to his wife once more. Afterward, unwilling to waste their precious hours together in sleep, they talked.

Esme told him of her dancing master, her coiffeur, her dressmaker, and of Percival, who was always by to lend moral support. While her stories made Varian laugh, he hurt inside as well. It should have been her husband, not her young cousin, with whom Esme practiced her dance steps. It should have been Varian to whom she complained of hairpins and corsets, and Varian who unraveled the baffling intricacies of English etiquette.

At least, he consoled himself as he lay beside her, she was here to tell him. At least he could listen in the darkness to her faintly accented voice. He'd missed her voice, just as he'd missed the tumultuous intensity of her presence. He would have been happy to spend the night so, but sometime near midnight he remembered he'd kept Esme from dinner.

He gave her his shirt to wear, donned his trousers, and found an oil lamp—for candles were a luxury at present.

In its yellow light and reeking fumes he led her down to the kitchen. There they ransacked the dowager's remaining travel stores, devised a meal of sorts, and settled down by the vast empty hearth to eat. While they ate, Varian found himself telling her of his own activities. Though the details of patching together his ravaged estate were dreary at best, mortifying at worst, it was better, he found, to tell her. In trying to shelter Esme from the truth these last months, he'd only made her feel shut out.

Watching her face while he talked, he saw the unhappiness fade, and that eased his own. Later, when they went upstairs together, she thanked him in her own way.

"I am glad you have told me all these things," she said when they entered the bedchamber. "I like your letters with their amusing stories and clever nonsense, but I wish as well to know your troubles." She looked up at him. "You never had a wife before, and so you are confused, but I will explain. A wife is not like a concubine, only for amusement and pleasure. A wife is to quarrel with and complain to as well—to ease your heart as well as your body."

He shut the door. "Very well. Every other letter from now on shall be filled with nothing but my grievances. However, you must do the same. You scarcely write me at all, you know," he chided.

"Because no one can read my hand. Jason said he could write better with his feet."

"I have no trouble deciphering. If you want reams of the ugly truth from me, you must provide the same. I shall expect lengthy, detailed epistles from London. You must at least tear yourself away from your flirts long enough to boast of them."

Frowning, she crept onto the bed. "I did not know I must flirt as well. No one told me. They have taught me to dance and how to eat with twenty different spoons and what to say to this one and that. But no one has taught me to flirt."

"Not even the all-knowing Percival?" He slipped in beside her and arranged the pillows so they might sit comfortably. "Then it's a good thing you came to

Mount Eden first, my dear. Tonight you shall learn from a master."

The following day, about the time Lady Brentmor's carriage left Mount Eden, Sir Gerald Brentmor, sick with anxiety, was pacing his study.

As soon as he'd realized the black queen was under his mother's roof, he'd offered to go after it. He'd even offered to take the distrustful Ismal with him.

"I beg you not to mistake me for a fool," Ismal had answered amiably. "It is nearly three days' journey from London to your mother's house. You might easily be rid of me on the way, get the queen for yourself, and flee abroad. This would be a stupid and needless risk for me. No, Sir Gerald, you will remain with me in London, and we shall lure the queen to us."

After a frustrating discussion, Sir Gerald had been obliged to unearth an invitation from Mrs. Stockwell-Hume, his mother's closest friend. Not only had Ismal imitated her lavish script beautifully, but the forged letter's contents could not have been better calculated to send the dowager thundering into London forthwith.

It had been futile to remind Ismal there was no assurance the black queen would arrive with her, that for all they knew, Percival or Esme—whichever of them had it—might have buried it in Corfu or in her ladyship's garden.

"The night of her arrival, we shall have several hours to search thoroughly," Ismal had replied, "because you will see that all your household lies in drugged slumber. If we do not find the queen, rest assured you will compensate me another way. There are several alternatives, Sir Gerald. All, I regret to say, will prove much more awkward for you than this simple matter of finding the black queen."

The baronet paused in his pacing to gaze despairingly at the chess set. Rest assured, indeed. He'd blackmailed enough men and women to know extortion never ended. Worse, he feared that even a copy of Bridgeburton's letter might destroy him. The words alone were damning enough to trigger an investigation . . . at the end of which he'd hang.

He took out his pocket watch. One o'clock. His mother had written that she'd arrive before nightfall. Time was running out, and he had not yet devised a way to extricate himself from Ismal's nets. He couldn't even leave his own house. Every time he'd tried, a huge ugly fellow had promptly appeared in his path. It was no use explaining that one had business appointments. The brute understood no English and spoke only the five words he'd evidently memorized: "You go home now, please."

The man always appeared, whether it was early morn or the small hours of the night. Sir Gerald had finally given up trying.

With a low moan, he sat down at the chess table. Every night since the first terrifying one, Ismal had slipped into the house when the skeleton staff was in bed. He came for conversation, he'd said. And chess. Every night they'd played, and ever night Ismal had won. He played brilliantly. One could almost believe he could read his opponent's mind.

Jason had been like that, Sir Gerald remembered. Frighteningly perceptive—except, of course, on one occasion a quarter of a century ago.

But if his ghost was about, he must be laughing now. A fine revenge this would seem to him: six days of purgatory Sir Gerald had endured, and there was hell to come.

Taking up the black queen's humble substitute, he cursed himself for the moment of panic in which he'd given up the original to Risto. If not for that, the set could have been sold by now, and he'd have at least five thousand pounds to start fresh with abroad.

If he survived this night, he'd have to flee England with next to nothing. His countrymen would soon know him for a criminal, a traitor. The shock would likely kill his mother. Small comfort in that, when he'd never be able to put his hands on her money. The family would be disgraced, and Edenmont as well, having wed into it. Sir Gerald shook his head. Another poor consolation.

Edenmont had been putting on a fine show of saintliness—an obvious ruse to win the dowager over. After denying the modest loan her own son had requested, she'd turned around to throw away a fortune on a mannerless, barbarous little whore of a granddaughter. Oh, Jason in his grave must be delighted. All the trouble Gerald had taken to cut the black sheep out of the family had been for naught. Jason's offspring—Percival and the little whore, along with her dissolute baron—would get all the dowager's money.

"Laugh then, you filthy bastard," Sir Gerald growled. "You always got everything: the looks, the cleverness, the charm. And the women, all of them. You had scores, but you have to have *her* as well. Even when she was mine, you got to her, and got your bastard on her."

Low as he'd spoken, the words seemed to echo in the still room. He was talking to himself. Worse, to a dead man.

His hand shaking, Sir Gerald returned the queen to her place. He was not finished yet, he told himself. He'd been a match for his brother when Jason was Ismal's age. And Jason was burning in hell, where no one laughed but the Devil.

One must be calm, focus on priorities. The highest at present was getting out of this debacle alive.

He sat staring at the chess set, his mind working furiously, until four o'clock when the butler announced that Lady Brentmor's carriage had arrived.

By five o'clock, the baronet was closeted with his mother in the study.

"Someone will *see* us," Percival objected.

Esme glanced about the narrow, walled garden of Sir Gerald's townhouse. "Not from the outside, unless they can see through walls. And the servants are all busy inside." She removed her shoes.

"You can't stand on the ledge. I've tried it. You can't keep your balance. It's too narrow."

"I shall keep one foot on your shoulder."

"You won't hear any better than we could inside. The window's closed."

"Not completely."

Moving back a few paces, Percival looked up. Though the curtains were drawn, the window was open a very little. With a sigh, he came back to Esme, linked his hands, and bent.

"We will not be caught," she promised as she accepted the boost up. "You must trust me."

Ismal had no need to see through walls. He'd only to peer through the narrow slit of the garden gate.

Smiling, he turned to Risto. "She spies upon her uncle and makes his son help her. She entertains me vastly."

Risto scowled. "It will not be entertaining if she calls attention to the open window. What if she demands the chess set be locked up securely?"

"Then Sir Gerald must un-secure it while she sleeps," his master answered.

"I don't like it. The old hag brought too many servants with her."

"And all will partake of a feast as fine as their betters'. The greedy ones will sleep very soundly. The others will be too heavy-headed to think or act. We, meanwhile, *shall* act, quick and silent as death."

"Second thoughts, indeed," the dowager said coldly. "You had plenty of chances to be kind to the gel before. But you left 'em stranded on that godforsaken island and come home and tried to poison my mind against her. Not that I was surprised. You've ever resented anything Jason had. You was always jealous of him."

She had taken over the big chair behind the desk. Sir Gerald stood by the chess table. He'd just raised his wine glass to his mouth. Now he paused. "Jealous, indeed. *I* wasn't the one who insisted Papa cut him off. *I* wasn't the one who made Diana break off her engagement."

"I did it for her own good, as the rest was for the good of the family. He'd have dragged us to ruin."

"You did it to punish him, because your precious baby wanted no part of your plans for him. You thought he'd come crawling back, begging forgiveness, promising to be a good boy. But he didn't, and now he's dead. And you've learned nothing."

"I've learned dredging up the past don't mend anything." Eyeing him with dislike, she took a swallow of wine. "And it won't win you no favors from me, Gerald."

He calmly set down his own glass. "I never won a favor from you in my life, though I always did what you wanted. Stayed with the business, while you planned a Parliamentary career and an earl's daughter for Jason, and stayed with it after he was gone. Stayed with Diana, and had to wed her at last because you didn't care to do better for me. I even held my tongue through her infidelities—even the most intolerable of all."

"She was never unfaithful," the dowager snapped. "You made her wretched, yet she stuck it out, even after I told her she needn't."

"She certainly stuck it out, Mama. Presented me with my brother's bas—"

"I'll never believe that." Lady Brentmor shook her head. "I've learned the hard way never to believe you at all. Always blaming someone else for your troubles. Now you blame what happened twenty-five years ago?"

Her son approached, to lean over the desk. "It's you who's dredging up the past. Bound to keep Jason's girl to yourself, aren't you, though she belongs with her husband."

"He can't keep her. He's next to penniless."

"And you'll see he remains so, won't you? I do wonder how you managed it. Don't tell me Percival never told either of them about the chess set. He knew of Diana's bequest before I did, I've no doubt. She kept few secrets from him. Only one, perhaps," he added bitterly.

"Edenmont don't know about the set, and it's going to stay that way." Her eyes flashed a warning. "There's no point telling him anyhow since it won't do him no good."

"Certainly not." Sir Gerald drew back. "No more good than it does me, with a piece missing."

He flung himself into the chair at the chess table. "Might as well let him have it. At least then I won't be responsible for the curst thing."

You'll do *nothing*. I'll handle this my own way."

He looked away, lest she see the triumph in his face. She'd just told him all he wanted to know. She was so determined to keep Jason's girl that she wouldn't let Esme have the dowry Edenmont so desperately needed. Yet why should the crone care, when the set was nigh worthless with a piece missing? She cared, he answered himself, because she knew the queen wasn't missing. She had it, or knew where it was. That's why she hadn't demanded the set long since. That's why she wouldn't let him give it to Esme now. Selfish, ruthless old bitch.

"I know your way," he said. "Keep us all tied like puppets to your purse strings. But not me, not any more, my dearest Mama. I'm ruined. I've nothing to lose now."

Her eyes narrowed. "You'd better not be threatening me."

Sir Gerald took up the black queen's substitute. "I think my niece should be told the truth."

"You mean your twisted version of it. She won't believe you."

"Maybe not." He smiled at the chess piece. "It hardly matters. I've nothing to lose, as I said."

Lady Brentmor put down her own glass and folded her hands upon the desk. "I figured you was up to something. How much do you want?"

Though they'd kept their voices low, Esme had heard all she needed: it was her grandmother who kept back the dowry, and all those grim warnings about Sir Gerald were nothing but lies. The reason was obvious. Esme had wed a man Lady Brentmor disapproved of. Since the willful old woman couldn't dissolve the marriage, she'd tried to do the next best thing. She'd probably hoped Varian would drink himself into an early grave or come to any of the host of untimely ends fast-living men were prone to. The dowager must have been highly annoyed with his efforts to rebuild and restore his inheritance.

Luckily, Percival had heard nothing. He appeared satisfied with Esme's brief summary and her pretense of disappointment. "He only wanted money," she said, "and at last our grandmother agreed to give him some."

"As she should have done in the first place." Rubbing

his shoulder, Percival staggered to the narrow terrace leading to the salon and collapsed onto a bench.

Esme sat beside him and took over the task of massaging his aching shoulder. "I did wonder why she would not bribe him. She told me he was desperate for money. But I supposed bribery was against her principles."

Percival frowned. "I shouldn't think so—though one can never be sure about Grandmama . . . or Papa." His worried gaze met Esme's. "Neither of them mentioned the chess set? It was there, right under their noses. I saw it when the footman went in with the wine."

"Perhaps they discussed it before I got to the window," Esme calmly answered. She wanted to get away and think. On the other hand, she suspected Percival knew more about his elders' secrets than he let on. He had seemed very uneasy since they'd reached London.

"Not that it matters," he said. "Grandmama would never give him the black queen. If he'd had it, Papa would have sold the set by now."

"That it is legally mine would not stop him."

"Not when it meant so much money. He might make off with it and pretend it was stolen and . . ." Coloring, Percival, added hurriedly, "But he doesn't have the queen, so it's perfectly safe, and I expect Grandmama won't let him know she's got it until she can make sure he can't touch the set at all."

Esme's hand paused. "Yes, I imagine she has hidden it very cleverly. Somewhere in the country house."

"Oh, yes, yes. Certainly. It's miles away. Quite safe from Papa," came the hasty response.

Too hasty. The wretched child knew it was not miles away. Now she did, too. Esme rose, her expression revealing only cousinly affection. "Then we've nothing to worry about," she said.

Percival stared at his shoes. "Certainly not. Nothing at all to worry about."

Chapter 29

"Cook will be disappointed," Sir Gerald told his niece. "You've taken no more than a spoonful of her famous syllabub. Or perhaps you find it too rich? I find it so, but then, I've never had a sweet tooth."

He'd been sickeningly genial from the instant Esme had entered his London townhouse, and more so after meeting with his mother. She must have paid him handsomely, Esme thought.

She manufactured an apologetic smile. "I like syllabub very much, Uncle, and I hope you will tell your cook this is the best I've ever tasted. Every dish has been delicious. But my headache weakens my appetite. Tomorrow I shall be well again and make the cook happy."

Percival gazed longingly at her dessert.

"Don't stare like a begging puppy," the dowager grumbled. "May as well eat that, too. You've finished everything else for her."

Percival had, in fact, eaten as though he expected to be hanged first thing in the morning. He'd taken at least two enormous helpings of every dish, then disposed of everything Esme had left on her plate. She'd noticed before that his appetite grew in proportion to his anxiety. His conscience was troubling him. As it ought.

Sir Gerald bestowed a fatherly glance of approval upon his son. "He's a growing boy, after all."

The growing boy blinked once at this display of paternal affection, then snatched up Esme's dessert and speedily disposed of it.

Sir Gerald's kindly gaze returned to Esme. "I'm sorry you're ill. Headaches can be dreadful. I suffer them myself. You'll want some laudanum, perhaps?"

Esme accepted the offer and politely excused herself shortly thereafter.

While the others adjourned to the drawing room for tea, she went upstairs and made a rapid inspection of her grandmother's bedroom. Having already thought the matter through, she wasted no time. Unless the chess piece was upon the dowager's person, it must be hidden where even servants were unlikely to come across it. Which meant no place that was dusted daily. Not a locked place either, like a drawer or jewel box, for any determined person could pick a lock. And no place so obvious as under the mattress.

Thus it took Esme mere minutes to locate the little box wedged in a corner of the underside of the bedstand. She only made sure the chess piece was actually inside before putting the box back. She dared not take it now. The dowager might check before she went to bed. It was enough to know where it was.

Esme quickly slipped out and reached her own room minutes before Molly arrived, bearing a small pitcher of lemonade and the laudanum bottle.

The maid appeared so sluggish and stupid that Esme wondered if she'd been drinking. Not that Esme minded. She was perfectly happy to see the drowsy maid depart as soon as she'd prepared her mistress for bed.

When Molly had gone, Esme dumped all the lemonade and a small amount of the laudanum into the chamber pot. If anyone checked, it would appear she'd taken her medicine like a good girl. She opened the door just a crack, then slipped under the bedclothes and prepared for a long wait.

After what seemed like many hours, she heard Percival mumbling to the servant accompanying him. Soon thereafter, a grumbling Lady Brentmor passed the door. A while later, Esme heard her uncle's voice. He must have stopped only to say good night to his mother, because his footsteps soon faded as he went on to his own room. That was on the other side of the house, thank heaven.

Esme continued to wait, though the house had already sunk into silence. It seemed she waited hours, yet when the hall clock struck, she was very surprised to count only ten chimes.

It was odd that the house should be so still at such an early hour. In the country, the dowager rarely retired before midnight, and the servants were always about some while after.

Then Esme recalled that the footmen who'd waited at dinner had seemed as sluggish as Molly had. Sir Gerald had ordered a feast for dinner, to celebrate his niece's arrival, he'd said. Evidently, the servants had decided to celebrate, too. Not that they'd need to drink much if they ate any of the syllabub, Esme thought. It had contained a great deal more wine than any she'd tasted before. Even Percival was probably drunk after three helpings of it, plus the glass of unwatered wine his father had allowed the boy at dinner.

All the better, Esme told herself as she got up and pulled on her dressing gown. The family would sleep the more heavily for their overindulgence. This would not only simplify her task, but give her an earlier start.

Esme opened the door fully and listened. The house was utterly silent.

She padded quietly down the hall and opened Percival's door first. She heard no stirring from his bed, only the sound of steady breathing. In the faint moonlight, she spied his trousers and shirt set out neatly on a chair by the window. After considering for a moment, she slipped in, took the clothes, and quickly slipped out again, noiselessly closing the door behind her.

The dowager's room was as peaceful as Percival's. From the bed came the low burr of heavy slumber. Esme got down on all fours, crept to the bedstand, quickly freed the container, removed the black queen, then returned the box to its hiding place.

In less than a minute, she was back in her room. After covering the narrow opening at the threshold with pillows, she lit a candle. Though she'd little packing to do, she'd rather not fumble about in the dark.

With steady hands, she braided her hair and pinned it into a coil about her head. Then she donned Percival's shirt and trousers, wishing she'd brought her own. His were rather thin, and more snug than she liked. Still, they were preferable to a frock. In England, lone females were subject to every sort of annoyance.

Her packing took little time. The small heap of garments rolled up easily in a shawl. The queen and several hairpins she wrapped in a handkerchief, which she stuffed in her waistband. After arranging the pillows under the bedclothes to resemble a sleeping form, she put out the candle. A moment later, she was creeping down the back stairs, her boots under one arm, her bundle under the other.

Despite the darkness and an unfamiliar house, it was not so difficult to find the study door. It was the only one Esme expected to find locked. The Brentmor's studies, Percival had told her, were constructed like vaults, with walls and doors of double thickness. When she and Percival had tried to eavesdrop from within the house, they'd been unable to make out more than a murmur, even with their ears pressed to the door or to the wall of the adjoining salon. Had the study window been securely closed, Esme would never have learned the truth about her wicked, selfish grandmother.

Kneeling at the study door, Esme felt no qualms or pricks of conscience whatsoever. The chess set was rightfully hers. Soon, she would put it into Varian's hands. Then she'd learn for certain whether it was simply his poverty that kept them apart. If the truth turned out to be painful, she would endure it. Always, it was better to know the truth.

The lock yielded at last. Esme opened the door . . . and froze, her fingers still on the handle. There was light in the room.

A quick glance assured her there was no one within. The candle had been forgotten, that was all. It was a wonder if this was all the drunken servants had neglected.

Esme studied the door for a moment, then closed it again. Yes, it was the same at the country house: the bottom fit snugly against the threshold. No wonder she'd not seen any light. Yet how careless of her uncle to leave a candle burning in a locked room. The house might have burnt down about his ears . . . unless he had meant to return here.

She'd hear him coming, she told herself. He was a large man with a heavy footfall. Leaving the door open a crack, she made for the chess set.

She unknotted the shawl and began wrapping the chess pieces in the assortment of garments she'd brought. She didn't want a single piece damaged in transit. She was about to knot up the shawl again when she remembered the black queen, which she'd stuffed in her waistband after getting the hairpins.

As she was pulling the chess piece out, one of the gemstones at the base caught on the wool. Esme eased it free very gently. All the same, she must have damaged it, for the base was coming loose.

Swallowing an oath, she brought the queen nearer the light. Then she stood a while, frowning at what looked like threads in the metal. She turned the base. It unscrewed smoothly.

It was very clever, she thought. She'd never have guessed the queen was made of two pieces. Wondering why anyone would bother, she turned the queen upside down. She was hollow. Or would have been, if a twist of paper weren't wedged in the cavity.

Even while telling herself she hadn't time for idle curiosity, she was removing the scrap and smoothing it out. Then she stared at the four lines in bafflement.

It wasn't possible, she told herself. Even if it was possible, it made no sense.

She looked up and listened. The house was still as a crypt, and she'd need only a minute or two to learn if she'd guessed correctly.

Moving to the desk, she found a pen and paper, and quickly began replacing the letters with their counterparts, as Jason had shown her years ago. The code had been one of his games to make her Latin lessons more interesting. In his own boyhood, he'd learned the game from his tutor.

This was the same game, she saw, for the letters did form a few words of ungrammatical Latin:

Navis oneraria
Regina media nox
Novus November Prevesa
Tēli incendere M

Merchant ship. Queen . . . midnight. New November . . . but 'Prevesa' wasn't Latin. It was a port in southern Albania. *Tēli* were javelins, darts, or just offensive weapons of some sort. *Incendere* was 'to burn, to fire.' Burn a thousand weapons?

She clicked her tongue impatiently. Then something clicked in her mind. In Corfu, she'd heard that in late October or early November British authorities had captured several ships en route to Albania. Ships bearing stolen British weapons.

This was the conspiracy Percival had told her about. Ismal's conspiracy. The last line referred to firing weapons, like rifles or cannon. A thousand of them.

But Ismal couldn't have obtained weapons on his own, not so many. He'd had help. Esme had only to glance about the desk, strewn with samples of Sir Gerald's handwriting, to realize who the helper was.

There's a stench about Gerald since he come back.

Had the dowager known? Perhaps. Perhaps not. But Percival must know.

Esme stuffed the message back into its hiding place, screwed the queen back together, and wrapped it up with the other pieces. She'd have plenty of time to solve the remaining riddles on the way home.

She held to the candle the paper on which she'd decoded the message and tossed the burning sheet in the empty grate. When nothing remained but ashes, she put out the candle and left the room.

* * *

Ismal frowned when the light in the study window went out. ''He signals trouble, yet there should be none. Every other room is dark.''

''Perhaps it's a trick,'' Risto answered.

''He can't be fool enough to try to betray me now. Stay here and keep watch. I'll speak to Mehmet.''

Ismal slipped out of the garden and into the street. Moments later, he found Mehmet at his post near the servants' entrance.

''Ah, master, you answer my prayers,'' Mehmet whispered. ''You told me to remain, yet—''

''What's wrong?''

Mehmet gestured upwards. ''Her window was dark. Then, some while ago, there was light for a brief time. Then darkness again.''

''No light elsewhere?''

''None. The servants scarcely waited for the family to retire. I looked in, right after I saw the light in her window. Several never reached their beds. Two lie upon the floor in the dining hall, and one sits with his head upon the table. Another lies curled like a babe upon the rug by his bed.'' Mehmet chuckled softly.

''Yet something is amiss.'' Ismal gazed at Esme's bedroom window. ''She was listening at the study window earlier. I wonder what she heard.''

Mehmet shrugged. ''The servants will be helpless for hours. No strangers have entered. That leaves only one fearful man, an old woman, a boy, and the little warrior. Even if the four of them set upon us at once, the battle would be amusing, that's all.'' He looked at Ismal. ''You'd like to do battle with her, perhaps.''

''Tsk. Even to look at her window . . .'' Ismal tore his gaze away. ''Best I keep far from her. She makes me stupid.''

''We might steal her easily and be gone from England long before the others wake.''

''Nay. I'll not risk everything for a female. Not a second time. She—'' Breaking off, he waved Mehmet back and flattened himself against the wall of the house.

A moment later, they heard the click of the door handle. The door opened, and a small figure stepped into the shadows. Esme, curse her . . . with a leather pouch slung over her shoulder. Clothes only . . . or the chess set? There was but one way to find out. He waited until she pulled the door closed. Then, drawing his pistol, Ismal leapt.

It was only a nightmare, Percival assured himself. That huge ugly man had not bashed out his eyes with an immense stone in the shape of a chess piece.

All the same, Percival's eyes would not open. Slowly he lifted his hand, which seemed to be made of lead, and tried to find an eye. After some searching, he located one and pried the lids apart.

Dark as the room was, it seemed to be moving. He'd rather not see that. He let his hand drop to the bed and tried to make his sluggish brain think. He found it only wanted to think about how horribly sick he was. It wanted to think about vomiting. That would be fine, except it was too much work.

His throat felt as though someone had left a torch burning in it. Dragging his hand up again, he flung it at the bedstand. Water. It was there somewhere. But he couldn't reach it. He dragged himself closer to the edge of the mattress and tried again. This time, his leaden hand knocked the pitcher over. Water dribbled onto his face. He tried to lick at it, but his tongue refused to budge. He groaned.

He wanted to be very, very still and go back to sleep, but the nightmare was waiting for him. And there was something important he had to do.

Inching down from the pillow, he flung a leg over the edge of the mattress. Then another leg. Then he was falling, sinking, a very long way. He landed on something hard. The floor.

Immediately, he felt hideously sick. He clawed under the bed, pulled out the chamber pot, and vomited.

His body did not feel much better after the exercise, but the fog in his brain cleared somewhat.

Percival lay on his side, his cheek against the cool floor, and tried to think. He'd got drunk once before, when one of his schoolmates had stolen several bottles of port from Mr. Saper's secret hoard. The physical sensations had been altogether different.

If he was not drunk, he might very well be ill. His brain suggested that someone had made him ill. It offered two choices: he'd been (a) drugged or (b) poisoned. Which confirmed his suspicions. Only at the moment, he couldn't remember what his suspicions were, exactly.

The effort to remember triggered another wave of nausea, and Percival had a second discussion with the chamber pot.

His brain gave signs of approval. It offered to cooperate. It reminded him of Mrs. Stockwell-Hume's letter, which he'd found crumpled in the empty grate of Mount Eden's library. It reminded him of the nasty feeling he'd had in the garden that someone was watching him. There was probably more, but this was enough to help Percival recall that he'd decided to do something. This very night, before It happened. He didn't know what It was, exactly. Only that It seemed to be happening already. He had to stop It.

He tried to get up, but couldn't. The effort led him back to the chamber pot. After this, his brain cleared sufficiently to suggest that, if a fellow couldn't walk, he might very well crawl. Then it warned him not to tumble down the stairs.

Varian tethered his weary horse to the lamppost and took the shabby carpetbag from the saddlebag. He didn't expect to be invited to spend the night. He doubted he'd be let in at all. Though it wasn't yet midnight, the Brentmor townhouse was dark. Still, the streets were filled with carriages hastening from one festivity to the next, and there were always loiterers about, not to mention idle bucks looking for mischief. The nag they might have with his lordship's blessing. The carpetbag, however, contained his pistols, and he'd not be able to afford another pair of Manton's finest in the near future.

Glancing up at the gloomy house, Varian wished he'd not come so late. He wished he'd possessed the will not to come at all. Wed or not, Esme wasn't even nineteen. She ought to experience all the gaiety of the London

Season, just as any other young English lady might. He couldn't give her the treat. He couldn't even appear in public with her. He looked like a ragpicker.

He still wasn't altogether certain why he had come. He'd watched Esme leave Mount Eden, watched the carriage rattle down the weedy drive, then re-entered his house . . . to find it haunted. He had taken up task after task, only to find he couldn't keep himself fixed to anything. A thought would come to him, and he'd look up to tell her or pause, about to call her . . . then remember she wasn't there. He'd done it a score of times, and each time the realization was a shock. He'd not experienced anything like it since the time after his mother's death. More than a year had passed before he gave up looking for her.

He was no boy of sixteen, Varian had chided himself. Esme was not his mother and not dead, gone forever. She was only a few hours away in London, where she'd have a wonderful time, because they'd all fall in love with her. She'd flirt, as he'd taught her just last night.

Then he'd wondered whether teaching her had been a mistake. He wouldn't be by to warn off the rogues and rakes, and she was so inexperienced. It was ridiculously easy to take advantage of a lonely young bride. Varian had done it himself, more than once. If his own wife betrayed him, it would be a fitting punishment.

Yet now he suspected it wasn't betrayal he feared, and it wasn't altogether jealousy that had driven him to London in the middle of the night. It was loneliness, and the cold bleakness of looking for her and realizing she was gone, and feeling she was somehow lost to him forever.

As he climbed the townhouse steps, he told himself his imagination had grown altogether gothic. He'd simply worked himself into a state, because he was abominably selfish. He didn't want Esme anywhere but with him.

Now he'd wake them all up, and he'd no excuse that wouldn't make him look an utter fool.

Cursing himself, he dashed the knocker against the door, waited what seemed an eternity, then did it again. After he'd repeated the action several times, his self-disgust quickened into disquiet. Someone should have heard him by now.

At the country house, a porter's chair stood by the door. The lower servants took turns spending the night there, so that the family might be quickly roused if a neighbor reported any sort of emergency or danger. A sleepy, shivering footboy had been there to open the door for Varian the morning he'd left.

Someone should have been at this door, or at least within hearing range. Suppose a riot broke out nearby? Suppose the house took fire? London being far more dangerous than the country, servants should be doubly vigilant.

Varian hurried down the steps and turned into the passageway separating the Brentmor townhouse from its neighbor. Near the back was what must be the tradesmen's entrance.

Varian pounded on the door. No response. He tried the handle. The door opened, and a chill shot down his spine.

Sir Gerald stood by his window, scowling into the dark garden. The clock had just tolled midnight, and the drunken fool had at last left off pounding at the door. For a few ghastly moments, the baronet had thought it was the constable, but that was only foolish panic. Ismal wouldn't have alerted the authorities until he had obtained what he'd come for, and he needed some help from Sir Gerald for that.

He should have been here by now, Sir Gerald fretted. Would have been, but for the curst drunkard at the door. Still, it wouldn't be long now, and the whole business would be over quickly.

His desperate gamble with his mother had paid off. Five hundred in coin and bank drafts totalling a thousand she'd paid to keep him quiet. While this wasn't nearly enough, it was more than Sir Gerald could have hoped for several hours ago. That, and the bit he'd got from the last visit to the pawnshop, would get him to the Continent and set him up adequately. Once he was safe abroad, he'd easily contrive ways to get more.

His spirits soothed by the infusion of money, he felt reasonably certain he would get away alive. Ismal wouldn't murder a blackmail victim. That was short-sighted, and Ismal was the type who thought ahead. He was also the type, the baronet thought resentfully, who enjoyed tormenting his victims. One must take care he found no future opportunity to do so.

But he would worry about that later, when he was safely across the Channel. At present, all Sir Gerald wanted was to have the matter done and his tormentors gone.

When he heard the approaching footsteps in the hall, he almost felt relieved. Though his heart rate doubled, he was outwardly composed, his hands quite, quite steady.

Until the door crashed open.

After more than an hour in utter darkness, the candle-light burst upon him like a lightning bolt, and for a moment he could only stare uncomprehendingly at the dark figure at the door. He blinked once, twice, but the vision didn't change. The candlelight glinted upon the sleek barrel of a pistol, and holding it aimed straight and steady at Sir Gerald's heart was Lord Edenmont.

Chapter 30

"I know exactly what happened," Sir Gerald blustered. "They planned it together, the three of them, to make me the scapegoat." He rubbed his throat, where the marks of Varian's fingers remained. "If anyone wants throttling, it's that wretched boy."

Varian had dashed up the stairs just as Percival was about to pitch headlong down them. Though sick and frightened, the boy had communicated enough to send Varian charging into Sir Gerald's room—only to hear the man stubbornly insist he knew nothing.

It had taken a frantic quarter hour to verify that Esme, the chess set, and the black queen were gone, and everyone else in the household was in various stages of drugged stupefaction.

That was when Percival finally blurted out his suspicions that Ismal was involved. Not at all disconcerted, Sir Gerald had declared Esme had eloped with her Albanian lover. He'd scarcely got the words out before Varian hurled him against the study wall and nearly choked the life from him.

Varian was calmer now. He could not afford panic or rage. He'd no idea how long Esme had been gone or where she might be headed. He needed help, mainly Sir Gerald's, and he needed it quickly.

He took out the crumpled letter Percival had given him and placed it on the chess table in front of Sir Gerald. "I know Mrs. Stockwell-Hume. If necessary, we'll go to her house presently and ascertain the truth. If she declares the letter a forgery, I shall escort you—with the aid of her servants—to the nearest magistrate and let him interrogate you." He folded his arms. "Or you may tell me the truth, in as few words as possible."

Sir Gerald stared at the letter for a long moment, then looked up at Varian. "Blackmail," he said. "You're no better than that filthy foreigner."

Varian said nothing.

"Ismal knew things about me," the baronet said angrily, "and he had damaging proof. He wanted money, and I hadn't nearly enough, so he settled on the chess set. He knew Percival or Esme had the black queen. All I did this night was make sure Ismal could obtain the complete chess set safely and easily. I had nothing to do with the girl's disappearance. I would have, if he'd asked." He glared defiantly at Varian. "He didn't ask. Maybe he didn't need to. Maybe he'd arranged it with her. It would appear they found the queen easily enough without my help."

"Never mind how they found it," Varian said. "I only want—"

"And that boy helped them. He's plotted against me all along," Sir Gerald snarled. "Spying and interfering. Manipulated you as well, didn't he? And neither he nor your *loyal* wife told you they had the chess piece."

Percival, who had been sitting at the desk watching his father in silent misery, found his voice. "Of course I couldn't tell him Papa, He might have found out what you'd done."

"Indeed. Protecting my honor, were you? As if you ever showed a glimmer of loyalty in your life."

"Sir Gerald," Varian began.

"Not that I expect any loyalty," the baronet went on. "My brother didn't show much, did he, when he got you on your lying whore of a mother."

"That's enough!" Varian glanced anxiously at Percival, but the boy did not appear in the least distressed. On the contrary, his countenance brightened several degrees, and his green eyes widened with interest.

"Good heavens, Papa, what a curious thing to say.

Even I know conception requires very close contact, and the gestation period for humans is nine months.''

''Percival,'' Varian put in hastily, ''this is no time for scientific theories.''

The boy's brow furrowed. ''I cannot think how Uncle Jason could have done it. He was escorting Colonel Leake through Albania from late eighteen hundred four until well past the eleventh of January, eighteen hundred six, when I was born.'' He shook his head. ''What you propose, Papa, is a physical impossibility.''

''Impossibility!'' Sir Gerald cried. ''Is that what your fool mother told you?''

''Not exactly, Papa. She only let me read the letter Colonel Leake had written Uncle Jason. When we were in Venice last spring Uncle Jason showed Mama his marriage lines and the other papers he kept safe there. Colonel William Leake, as you know, is an antiquarian topographer. He plans to publish accounts of his travels and wrote for permission to mention Uncle Jason. He knew Uncle Jason was involved in certain secret activities, and did not want to endanger him inadvertently.''

Sir Gerald turned very red, then very white, and slumped back in his chair.

''I do wish you'd mentioned this sooner, Papa,'' the boy said. ''I could have suggested you write Colonel Leake.''

Sir Gerald's mouth worked, but no identifiable words came out.

''My father has always fascinated me,'' Percival confided softly to Varian. ''An intriguing study in human nature, is he not?''

Varian leaned over the desk. ''Let's study someone else's nature, Percival. If you were Ismal, for instance, where would you go?''

Esme rubbed her sore wrists and stared out the carriage window into the night. Though only Ismal was inside with her, and apparently unarmed, she knew escape was out of the question. The carriage lanterns showed her Mehmet's large form riding beside the vehicle. Risto, she knew, rode on the other side. If she so much as raised her voice, they'd kill her. Though the prospect of death would scarcely deter her, she did not plan to die before she took revenge on Ismal.

That was not going to be easy. In addition to the murderous bodyguards, Ismal possessed several forged or stolen documents attesting to his diplomatic status. In his present garb, he looked like an English gentleman. Only the most discerning ear would catch his faint accent, which he might easily explain as the result of years spent abroad. He could as easily concoct a lie explaining Esme's presence. He could claim she was a spy, a runway servant—anything he liked.

He'd little to fear from her. They had stopped a short while before to change horses, and he'd untied her so she might use the inn's privy without causing comment. Esme had meditated escape then, but not for long. This was not simply because Ismal had escorted her and stuck close, but because she'd finally got a good look at Risto. His entire being vibrated with hatred. Then she'd understood that all that stood between her and his dagger was Ismal.

Turning her head from the window, Esme found Ismal staring at her hands. She folded them in her lap.

"The rope hurt you," he said in English. She'd not heard a word of Albanian from him yet. "Risto perhaps tied it too tightly."

"I'm sure he'd rather have tied it around my neck," she said, "and tighter still."

Ismal shook his head in agreement. "Very likely that would have been the wiser course, but I abhor violence. It distressed me greatly to strike you with my pistol, but it could not be helped." His gaze lifted to her face. "Does your head still pain you very much?"

"Only when I try to think."

"Since you are bound to think nothing pleasant, I advise you not to try. You will only produce various plans for injuring me, and the consequences would distress you. Very much."

He spoke sweetly, as usual. He was incapable of registering an honest emotion. He'd probably ordered her father's murder in the same musical tones.

Esme realized she was digging her nails into her palms. She shifted into her customary cross-legged position and let her hands rest casually upon her knees.

Ismal narrowly watched her movements—on the alert, no doubt, for a sudden assault. When he understood she was only making herself comfortable, he went on. "I have told you why I came, and so it must be clear I did not plan for you. On the contrary, I promised myself I'd have nothing to do with you."

"Then you should have left me unconscious in the garden," she said. "You got the chess set from me. You had already made sure no one would pursue you. And I would not have known who attacked me."

"It was a difficult decision. Perhaps I chose wrongly. Yet you fell into my hands—it was none of my doing—and so I thought it was Allah's will."

"Or Satan's."

Ismal considered. "Perhaps. I cannot be sure which of them rules me."

"I can."

He treated her to an odd sort of smile. In another man, Esme would have called it shy, but "shy" and "Ismal" simply didn't go together.

"Do you think I am entirely evil?" he asked. "A tool of the Devil?"

"You tried to destroy our country, you did destroy my father, you have stolen not only my dowry but me as well, shaming all my family." She heard her voice rising. Lowering it, she added, "At the moment, you do not appear to possess any redeeming qualities."

He thought this over, too. "What you say is true in its way," he said, "except for the part about your father, for I had nothing to do with his death. Despite my many faults, I am not a cold-blooded assassin. Also, killing him was stupid and exceedingly dangerous." He shrugged. "But you don't wish to believe that, because you are a hothead and must blame somebody. As to my other 'crimes,' I cannot contradict you. I can only explain my perspective. Sometime soon, I will do so, but not now. You are too agitated to pay proper attention."

"I am not agitated! No man could be so calm in the

circumstances. Also, I very much dislike being humored as though I were a child—and I am not a hothead!"

He made a graceful, dismissive gesture. "Indeed you are—strong-willed, stubborn, and bloodthirsty. It is very strange that I should want such a female," he said thoughtfully, "but so it has happened. It did not begin so. All I sought at first was a hostage, to keep Jason quiet. Once he was dead, you were of no use to me. Unfortunately, my cousin had a whim to meet your companions. And so, in Tepelena, I was obliged to feign passion. I do not recall the precise instant it ceased to be feigning. I know only that when you raged at the pig English lord, some poison must have entered my heart, for I grew very jealous. I wished it were me you lashed with your cruel tongue. I wished I might have the quieting of you, though I knew you meant to kill me."

Esme moved uneasily. He was lying, of course. He'd made off with her for revenge and would, if he could, rape her for the same reason. All the while his voice would remain sweet, gentle.

"You don't believe me." He gave her another faintly abashed smile. "I do not believe it myself. I have been well-educated and do not believe in demons, yet I find myself behaving as though I were possessed. When you fled Tepelena, I knew if I pursued you, Ali would have me followed—yet I could not stop myself. And so they caught me and took me to Janina, where Ali's doctors began poisoning me. By then, you see, he had learned somehow of my disloyalty. I lay upon my lonely bed, dying by inches, and saw all my hopes destroyed, because a woman had made me stupid and reckless."

"Your vanity made you stupid," she said. "You only wanted what you could not have—Ali's kingdom, a woman who hates you."

"Nay, I am merely your scapegoat. You have persuaded yourself to hate me. I shall persuade you otherwise."

She wished he'd lose his temper, show some sign of hostility, because his gentle patience was disquieting. His soft voice was like the silken threads of a dangerous net.

He looked down. "Listen to me." He took her hand

and closed his lightly around it. "I was raised, educated for intrigue. I can make men—and women—do almost anything but see into my heart. The Almighty gave me an attractive form and intelligence. These I learned to use as tools, always with calculation. You know this of me."

"I know it well enough." His nearness bothered her a great deal more than it ought. He was only a man, and this was skill only, as he said, a gift for making others do as he wished. Yet Esme couldn't help recalling the superstitions about him: that he was not quite human. The graceful fingers closed about hers disturbed her too much. She had not been able to resist Varian. It was possible she was weak-minded about men, or certain kinds of men. It was possible—nay, likely—that Ismal possessed even greater skill and fewer principles than her husband. Esme told herself she loved Varian and hated Ismal with all her heart. All the same, Ismal's nearness, his touch, his scent . . . filled her with dread.

"Don't be afraid of me," he said, making her heart hammer.

She hastily assured herself he couldn't read her mind. It was only her body that betrayed her: the chill clamminess of the hand he held and the hurried pace of her breathing. "If you don't want me to be afraid, then don't play your games," she said.

"You want me to speak and act plain, as you do?" Ismal gave a small sigh before lifting his gaze once more to hers. "I lost that skill long ago. To live in Ali's court is to live an endless chess game: to mislead and feign, always alert for traps ahead. Always, I played the game well, until you came to Tepelena and sickened my mind. But you shall cure me, little warrior. When we lie together, I shall be part of you and you shall be part of me. In this way, you will know me, and in time you will take pity."

Esme drew back, but didn't try to pull her hand away. She didn't want to trigger a physical struggle she was all to likely to lose. "I don't want you," she said, "and it is monstrous to imagine I could ever pity you."

"You don't understand. Later, you will."

"I understand well enough. You mean to rape me. You talk this nonsense only to amuse yourself."

He clicked his tongue. "I abhor violence. If you wish violence, I shall give you to my crew. When they are done with you, I think you will find yourself in a more accommodating temper. Then I shall give you a second chance, perhaps a third. I am not without patience."

Esme felt the blood draining from her face.

"It would be much simpler to accept me," he said. "I cannot expect you to show eagerness for my embrace, but because you are stoical, I can ask that you endure."

"Endure? Dishonor my wedding vows, cuckold my hus—"

"*I* am your husband, by right," he said calmly. "I paid your bride-price and was cheated. When I tried to claim you, I nearly paid with my life."

"That is nonsense. You have the chess set. You have reclaimed this so-called bride-price many, many times over." Esme kept her voice as low and calm as his. "You are a savage, no better than Ali."

His hand tightened about hers, and his blue eyes flashed briefly, but that was all. His control was formidable. "That may be so, for Ali made me what I am. If you want a better man, Esme, you must make me one. Before this new day is ended, I will show you how."

Dawn did nothing so decisive as break that day. Lumberingly it rolled upon Newhaven in a heavy blanket of low clouds, a somber light slowly penetrating the blackness of night.

As he'd done countless times before, Jason—currently in the guise of ship's surgeon, wearing a black wig and spectacles—scanned the vessels in the harbor. He didn't allow himself to think, only to see and let his instincts do the rest.

He had let reason overrule his instincts at Gibraltar and wound up in Cadiz, on board the wrong ship with an irate foreign minister. The man loudly objected to having his vessel searched and thereafter accused Jason of stealing valuable government documents. The consequent complications had trapped Jason in Cadiz for more than a week, and Ismal, who'd been mere hours ahead at that point, had eluded him again.

Jason had sent word ahead to Falmouth. Thence it should have traveled England's coast. It should, as well, have reached London by now. Unfortunately, Ismal had already obtained more than a week's lead. In that time he might have done anything, gone anywhere. Jason swore under his breath.

The hands were making his small craft fast when he became aware of a bustle on a nearby vessel. He stared hard at the ship, a small American-made schooner. Sleek and fast, ships like this—though usually larger—had harassed British shipping to a frustrating degree during the last war with the Americans.

Jason glanced at Bajo. The Albanian's attention was fixed on the same vessel. Before Jason could consult him, their captain approached and gestured shoreward. A naval officer was hurrying down the quay toward them.

Jason hastened from the ship to intercept him and, without a word, handed over his papers.

"Yes, sir, I've been expecting you," said the officer. "Captain Nolcott, at your service. I regret I've no news for you."

Jason indicated the vessel which had alerted his instincts. "Tell me about that little schooner," he said.

"The *Olympias?*"

Bajo approached. When Jason repeated the vessel's name, the bearlike man smiled.

"The man we seek fancies himself a descendant of the mother of Alexander," Jason explained to Captain Nolcott. "That was her name."

"Can't be the same man," the captain said. "The owner's an Englishman named Bridgeburton, and the ship's papers were all in order. They're awaiting a foreign trade official they're taking to Cadiz."

"Bridgeburton's body was pulled from a Venice canal a few months ago," said Jason. While the captain gazed at him in consternation, he went on to explain that Bridgeburton was reputedly addicted to a particularly lethal combination, absinthe and wine. Since no marks were found upon the body, it was supposed he'd fallen into the canal in a state of delirium. Jason's Venice contacts had told him of the matter because Bridgeburton had recently come under suspicion of smuggling and slave trading. They'd assumed he was Ismal's source of weapons.

Jason didn't tell Captain Nolcott and hadn't told his associates in Venice that Bridgeburton had once been a friend. It was Bridgeburton who had lent Jason the money to continue the endless game of hazard long, long ago: the game Jason had scarcely remembered when he woke, violently ill, late the next day . . . woke to find himself owing Bridgeburton a fortune.

Jason supposed he'd get the remaining answers soon enough, no matter how much he dreaded having them.

At present, however, Captain Nolcott was awaiting instructions. Jason studied the harbor and quays. Newhaven had boasted a thriving shipping trade early in the last century but, as the paltry collection of vessels—mostly fishing boats—sadly proclaimed, the trade had gone elsewhere. One who wished to depart with a minimum of annoyance might consider it an ideal site. It was a shorter distance from London than Dover was. Dover's other disadvantage was the busy traffic of post chaises racing to catch the packets to Calais. Bridgeburton's name fully settled the matter.

"The *Olympias* looks ready to be leaving soon," Jason said. "If this wind holds, there's nothing to stop her."

"You want her taken?"

Jason was about to answer when he heard the clatter of wheels and hooves on the cobblestones. He'd no need to look toward the sound. Bajo's countenance and hasty retreat out of sight told him all he needed to know.

Chapter 31

As the carriage was slowing, Ismal moved to sit beside Esme. "Do nothing foolish when we disembark," he warned. "You cannot know who is in my pay and who is not. You will do as I request or prepare to satisfy the lusts of my crew. Do you understand?"

Esme looked bleakly out the window. He'd already explained sufficiently, all the way from Lewes. Besides, she understood the British well enough to see how minute were her chances of finding a sympathetic rescuer. She was dressed in boy's clothes, and her accent was noticeably foreign, despite Jason's efforts. No one would believe she was a lord's wife, or any sort of lady. She bore no marks of ill usage to prove she'd been taken against her will—while Ismal possessed a heap of official-looking documents.

Any attempt to escape now promised only failure . . . and finding herself in the hands of Ismal's men. He'd not offer idle threats, or futile ones. Death she could face courageously, he well knew. What he'd threatened instead thoroughly terrified her, as he must also know. As the bile rose in her throat, she cursed herself for being a coward. "I hate you," she said.

"*Shpirti im,*" he whispered, "you lie to yourself." He began removing the pins from her hair.

Esme remembered the bedroom at Mount Eden. Was it only two nights ago that Varian had taken the pins from her hair? She remembered his urgent hands upon her, inflaming her, and the aching tenderness of his words of love.

She should have heeded him. All he'd done was try to spare her discomfort while he worked to redeem himself and make a life for them both. She should have told him she loved him, believed in him, was proud of him. Now he'd learn only of her shame. That was why Ismal loosened her hair. He wanted the bystanders to notice the young red-haired woman. Eventually, Varian would be told.

She stared blindly out the window while Ismal finished his work.

"In Tepelena, you so beautifully feigned your love for me," he said. "Now you will do so again, and those who watch will understand you leave happily with me. Did you know Englishmen are greatly aroused by the sight of a woman in trousers?" He smiled tenderly. "You will wish to keep close to me, for protection."

Soon enough, she knew, she'd be as near as female could be to male. But she'd endure what she must until her time came. Then he'd pay.

As they alit from the carriage, Esme covertly studied her surroundings. The village of Newhaven lay about half a mile behind them. If she tried to run, she'd be caught long before she reached it. Upon the cluttered wharves she spied several possible avenues of escape as well as numerous places wherein she might be hopelessly trapped.

The nearest and most formidable dead ends, however, lived and breathed in the shape of Risto and Mehmet. Without a weapon, she had no chance at all. Still, Ismal had armed himself before they left the carriage. The pistol would be awkward at close quarters and clumsy to get in the first place. The dagger, though . . . . . . one stab only . . . and she'd cry "Murder!" But how would this crowd react?

Esme saw sailors and fishermen, mainly. Two men in naval uniforms were talking to another man who wore a beaten old tricorn and equally ancient knee breeches. He carried what looked like a surgeon's bag.

None of those watching Ismal's party approach the

boats looked particularly friendly. On the other hand, none seemed obviously hostile. They were all staring, but then, the likes of Risto and Mehmet would not appear in this small port every day, nor yet the elegant likes of the mad but beautiful Ismal in his English garb. No matter where he went, he attracted attention.

"Didn't I warn you'd arouse their lust?" Smiling, Ismal wrapped a protective arm about her shoulders. "You will wish them to understand you are mine."

Esme lifted her eyes with what she hoped was an expression of adoration and forced her mouth into a besotted smile.

Ismal drew her closer and slowed their pace. "Soon you will look upon me in this way without feigning." His mouth brushed her ear.

"So you keep telling me." Esme's sidelong glance took in the line of vessels ahead. Though he'd not described his ship, she discerned two reasonable possibilities. Both were very near now. There was little time.

She added sweetly, "I always thought a man assured of his skills would have no need to boast."

He laughed. "You are trying to provoke me, I think."

"You said I must not show my true feelings. You did not say I may not speak them, even in a whisper. Must I tell pretty lies as well as make pretty faces for you?" She gave him another infatuated look. "Once, years ago, you kissed me, and I spit the taste of you from my mouth. Do you think your lips will taste less vile to me now?"

"That may be easily settled." He paused, his blue eyes sparkling with amusement. A few feet away, Risto scowled horribly.

"Shall I kiss you before all this rabble?" Ismal asked.

Esme shrugged. "They all believe I'm your whore. Soon I shall be in truth. I'm already sick with shame. Nothing you could do would make it worse."

Risto was beside himself with impatience. "Master!" he hissed.

Ignoring him, Ismal lazily gathered Esme into his arms. She heard Mehmet's chuckle and Risto's curses and raucous shouts from sailors nearby. She was aware of Ismal's hand at the back of her neck and the warmth of his breath as his face lowered to hers. She was aware, too, as his mouth slanted sensuously over hers, that his boasts had not been idle. In spite of herself Esme was taken aback by his skill, and her lips parted without her ordering them to. He was annoyingly good at it, to confuse her at all, but it was only for a moment. Cold resolve quickly dispelled the fog in her mind.

She let her hands slide caressingly to his waist. Her heart beat fast but steady while her fingers inched toward the dagger under his cloak.

He began to draw back, and Esme's hand paused. "This was not wise, little one," he murmured against her lips. "I shall not be able to wait all the long day for more."

"Curse her!" Risto snarled, moving nearer. "Half the town comes to watch. How long will you dally here?"

Even Mehmet murmured a warning, but Ismal wasn't listening. He had turned out to be a man like other men, Esme thought grimly, as his mouth sought hers for a deeper kiss. His brain was not doing all the thinking at present. Hers, on the other hand, was fully alert. She was aware of the onlookers' scattered cheering and vulgar advice. She felt the building heat of his kiss and the growing tension in his slim frame. Arching against him, she reached cautiously toward the dagger.

Every nerve tingling, every sense painfully acute, Esme heard the gulls' cries, the waves' pounding against the sea wall, and a distant pounding from the shore. Hoofbeats . . . hurried footsteps . . . new shouts among the cheers. She heard, yet it all seemed lifetimes beyond. The present was revenge . . . a hairsbreadth away.

She'd just touched the dagger's hilt when Ismal's body stiffened. In the next instant, he'd wrenched her about and the blade lay against her throat.

All the quay went very still. The bystanders came into sharp focus: ten, twenty, no, at least fifty men, and not one moved. Every eye was on the blade.

Including Varian's.

Esme blinked, but the vision remained.

She wanted to shake her head, to clear it. The faint scratch against her throat told her she was awake.

It *was* Varian who stood not twenty paces away. He held a pistol. Why the devil did he not fire it? Ismal was a full head taller than she. A babe could have put the bullet through his evil brain. Surely Varian could. Twenty paces, she thought wildly. Only dueling distance. Why did he not shoot?

"Ah, you prefer not to test your skill, my Lord Edenmont," Ismal said amiably. "Very wise. If you wish your wife to go on living, you must also tell this rabble not to hinder me. And put your weapon down, if you please."

Varian lowered his pistol, but didn't drop it. "Let her go," he said.

Ismal ignored him. "You may come out now, Sir Gerald. What strange allies you make—but you are too fat to hide behind his lordship."

Holding his own weapon pointed downward, the baronet emerged from the crowd gathered behind Varian.

Ismal began backing toward his ship, and his bodyguards quickly moved to shield him. No one else moved. They wouldn't, Esme thought despairingly. Ismal had let them know she was the lord's wife. No one would risk getting her killed.

No one, however, had to get on some accursed ship with Ismal and submit body and soul to him. Esme reminded herself that hundreds of Albanian women had thrown themselves from cliffs rather than submit to their enemies. She was as brave as any of them. She'd not go with this man, not alive. Varian had come for her. She'd not leave shame behind to haunt him.

"Kill him!" she screamed. "Avenge Jason! Avenge *me,* Varian!"

The blade nicked her throat, and she saw Varian's pistol go up. *I love you,* she told him silently. Then she bashed her head back against Ismal's windpipe.

Just as his grip slackened, something exploded nearby and Mehmet stumbled. Esme drove her elbow into Ismal's groin. He staggered back, dropping the knife. Mehmet lurched toward her. Esme dove for the knife and there was another explosion. For an instant, the world flashed with blinding color. She heard Varian's cry, fa away . . . and her father's voice, somewhere in the black wave surging toward her. *I'm dying,* she thought, and the wave sucked her down.

Oblivious to the crew swarming from Ismal's ship and those rushing forward to oppose them, Varian raced toward his fallen wife. He'd seen the small dark man aim his pistol at her just as Varian had fired his own at the big, ugly one. But someone had got hold of the smaller bastard already, and all Varian cared about was Esme.

Though pandemonium raged about him, all he knew when he bent over her still form was terror, sharp as the blade that had rested against her throat a moment before. As he laid his shaking hand against that throat, tears started to his eyes. A pulse throbbed faintly under his fingers.

Just as he began to gather her up, a hand ripped into his scalp, violently jerking him back.

"No!" Ismal screamed. He swung his pistol at Varian's head. Varian's arm shot up, and the weapon struck his elbow. Pain shrieked the length of his arm. Rolling sideways, he grabbed Ismal's leg and brought him down. Ismal kicked free and flung himself at Varian, sending him sprawling back. Varian's skull struck the wharf with devastating force. His ears rang, and the sky spun crazily above him. Yet he saw the pistol swinging toward him again. He grabbed Ismal's wrist and slammed it against the wharf's edge. Ismal only grunted, but his grip loosened, and the weapon skidded away.

"You fight me for a whore," he gasped. "*My* whore."

Yanking his hand free, he slammed his fist into Varian's jaw, sending him reeling back. Varian saw black for an instant, then blood red. Then all sense of pain vanished.

He struck, was struck in turn, and it was nothing. All that existed was Ismal, to be killed. They struggled furiously, more evenly matched than Varian could have guessed. Slight as he appeared, Ismal was powerful and quick. Blow after blow seemed to have little effect, and as they rolled toward the quay's edge, his knee drove into Varian's gut with the force of a cannonball. In the next moment, he was on his back, staring up into Ismal's contorted face, fighting for breath and consciousness while he struggled futilely with the powerful hands squeezing his throat. Through the darkness slowly suffocating him, Varian saw Ismal's smile. "My whore," he panted. "My Esme."

The words raged through Varian like hellfire. Grasping Ismal's wrist, he dug his nails in. With all his remaining strength, he wrenched the hand away and dashed it against the pier's edge. There was a crack and a low animal howl, and Ismal jerked away, his face twisted in agony. Varian lunged up and knocked him aside. Ismal tried to scramble free, but his useless hand made him slow. Varian caught him and began pounding his head against the pier. The once beautiful face was smeared with dirt and blood. Ismal's head lolled helplessly, but a glitter lingered in his half-closed eyes.

"My whore." The words oozed from his bloodied lips "My Esme."

Just as Varian raised his fist, he was shoved backward He looked up in time to see a blade flash toward him.

With a painful effort, Jason thrust Mehmet's lifeless body aside and struggled to his knees. The chess pieces lay strewn about him, along with his wig and spectacles

He was getting too old for this nonsense, he thought He'd lost his taste for waterfront brawls long ago, and this one ought never have begun. It was that sapskull Edenmont, dashing to the rescue, and that fool girl, with her own heroics.

Esme was at least safely out of the way. Bajo had hauled her clear of the fray before returning to help Jason clear a path to the main part of the riot, where Edenmont battled Ismal. Ismal's crew, unfortunately, had got the same idea, along with Mehmet, and flailing bodies now blocked Jason's view of the place he'd last seen the two men struggling. Rising to his feet, he saw his brother knock one man aside with the butt of his pistol. Another attacked, taking Gerald down, but Gerald flung him off and scrambled to his feet. Furiously he fought his way out of the press of battling men.

The sight was so incredibly out of character that Jason was momentarily distracted. He came abruptly back to the present as a bloodied sailor sprang from the crowd at him. But not quickly enough. The sailor's fist crashed into his chest, and Jason staggered back, perilously near the edge of the quay. A hand pulled him to safety, and the sailor, swinging wildly into the air, toppled over the edge.

Jason turned to his rescuer, and the words of thanks died on his lips as he met his brother's grim gaze.

Clenching his teeth against the agony of his crushed wrist, Ismal crawled to the shelter of a heap of casks. He'd taken up the pistol Risto had dropped when he attacked the English lord. It was nearly impossible to reload the weapon with one hand, but Ismal refused to acknowledge impossibility. He was certain a few men remained aboard the *Olympias*. With luck, he might still get away.

The vicious throbbing of his hand was making him violently ill. Afraid he'd lose consciousness, he focused his being on reloading. Though it seemed to take lifetimes, he managed at last and peered out from his hiding place.

Two figures stood between him and the *Olympias:* Sir Gerald . . . and a man who was supposed to be dead.

If his mouth had not been swollen and caked with blood, Ismal would have smiled. All became stunningly clear, all the Red Lion had done, and why. Ismal admired him for it, because he must admire a man who could outwit him. Had he realized . . . oh, much would have been different, and certainly he'd never have walked into what he saw now was a trap: Edenmont and Sir Gerald on one side, the Red Lion on the other.

At present, however, only the two brothers blocked his way, and they were quarreling, oblivious to all else.

Though he'd only the one bullet, the decision was easily made. Ismal stood and, mustering every iota of will to make his left hand obey, aimed. Smiling inwardly, his heart light as an angel's, he pulled the trigger. The second report followed the first so quickly that they seemed but one ringing vibration. But suddenly fire was raging through his flesh, and a black pit yawned before him, flames licking in its depths.

"Esme," he gasped . . . and fell.

Slowly, Varian lowered the pistol. The wharf seemed unearthly quiet. Or perhaps the buzzing in his ears drowned out all else. He didn't know, didn't care. He'd driven a knife into one man's gut and just fired a bullet into another. Risto lay dead at his feet . . . Ismal was an unmoving heap not ten yards away . . . and beyond, Sir Gerald—fallen, too, because Varian had pulled the trigger an instant too late to save him.

He turned away. So much blood. The world stank of it. He was stained with it and stank, too.

Through the buzzing and the rising wave of nausea, he heard someone call his name. He turned back toward the sound. The red-haired man kneeling by Sir Gerald beckoned. Varian drew a deep breath, squared his shoulders, and went to him.

"Shut up," Jason warned Gerald. "Edenmont's here."

Edenmont knelt on the other side, his eyes fixed on the crimson stain spreading through Gerald's shirt.

Gerald's eyes moved to him. "Look who's . . . back. From the dead. A joker, he is, my brother. Like me. What a . . . trick I played, eh, Jason?"

Edenmont's head snapped up as though he'd been struck. Repeating the name, he scanned Jason's face.

"Yes, I'm alive," Jason snapped. "Get that bag behind you. There's whiskey in it, and bandages."

Gerald clutched his arm. "Tricked you. To get her. Diana for me. The land for Bridgeburton."

Jason had hoped Edenmont's presence would stop his brother's tongue, but nothing would. Gasping and choking between words, Gerald babbled on while Jason changed the bandages. But the bleeding wouldn't stop any more than the rasping voice would. Boasting. Of how they'd plied Jason with absinthe and wine that night so long ago. That's why he remembered so little of the game, couldn't recall signing the heaps of IOUs. He thought he'd borrowed a fortune from Bridgeburton because Gerald, the brother he'd trusted, said so and held the notes as proof.

"Never mind," Jason gritted out. "You haven't the breath to spare—and anyhow, I know."

"Diana told you."

Jason shook his head.

"She found out," Gerald went on. "The baby came . . . early. Your eyes. Hair. Lost my . . . temper. Said things. Not much, but she . . . guessed. And I had to be . . . good . . . to the boy. Let her do . . . as she pleased. Or she'd tell . . . Mama. Twelve years, Jason."

This Jason didn't know and didn't want to believe. Yet he remembered that last time, how Diana had urged him to hurry back to England. What had she said? *I fear when I'm gone* . . . When she was gone, there'd be no one to protect Percival from his father. As she had. From his wrath, from his pernicious influence. By blackmailing Gerald with his vile secret.

Gerald turned his head toward Edenmont, who knelt there yet, his rigid face betraying nothing.

"Never guessed, did you?" Gerald gasped. "The bitch Diana was. She let me believe . . . my son . . . was Jason's. Years . . . in my gut . . . gnawing. I couldn't say . . . a word." He drew in a rattling breath. "Twelve years. Punished." His eyes closed. "Loved her." A last, rattling gasp, and he was gone.

Jason pulled off his coat and covered his brother's face.

"He was delirious," Edenmont said stiffly. "Poor devil."

Jason looked at him. "He was a filthy, treacherous swine, and she managed him the only way she could. Lovely family you've married into, isn't it?"

Esme raced back toward the quay, the cabin boy charged with guarding her in hot pursuit. Though she didn't know how long she'd lain unconscious, she feared it had been too long. The din of battle had subsided, and the damp air bore a sharp tang of gunpowder. As the wharf came into view, she saw sailors gathering up the fallen. Searching the crowd of strange faces, she lit upon a large, oddly familiar figure. Esme passed her hand over her eyes. Bajo? He lifted one of the wounded men in his burly arms.

"My lady, if you please." The boy was beside her, panting. "Captain Nolcott will have my head—"

Esme waved him back. "My husband. Where is Lord Edenmont?"

"I'm sure he's all right, m'lady. If you'd just—"

He broke off, apparently transfixed by the same grim sight that had just caught her attention: a litter, borne by sailors, its human burden covered by a bloody cloak.

"No!" she cried. She ran toward the litter, thrusting aside those in her way until someone caught her arm. Esme looked up into the countenance of one of the naval officers she'd seen earlier. "Please," she said weakly.

"My lady, there's nothing you can do for your uncle. The wound was mortal. I'm sorry."

Her uncle. A wave of sick giddiness washed through her, and she swayed. The officer caught her. "You'd better sit down, my lady."

Esme nodded sharply. "No. *No.*" She pulled herself free. "I must . . ."

Then she saw him. Blood and dirt caked his face, and at this distance she couldn't make out the color of his eyes. His hair, too, was thick with the filth of recent battle, and the dull copper gleam could well have been blood. His head bowed, he was wiping his face with a dirty kerchief. She knew him, all the same.

Tears stung her eyes. Angrily rubbing them away, she moved on unsteady legs toward him. The officer was saying something, but it was only noise to her.

Esme saw the kerchief pause, then drop from her father's hand. He didn't move, only watched her approach, his mouth creasing slowly into a smile. The smile made her hurt inside.

Pausing several feet from where he stood, she set her clenched fists upon her hips. "I hate you." Her voice came out high and reedy. "I shall *never* forgive you."

Jason's smile broadened into a grin. "Ah, now, there's

my little girl.'' He opened his arms and with a strangled sob, Esme shot into them.

Her father hugged her briefly, then broke away, cursing and staring at his hands. ''Deuce take you, Esme, you're bleeding!''

Chapter 32

Unmoving, unnoticed, Varian stood by the *Olympias*. He'd started toward Esme, then checked himself when he saw where she was heading. An involuntary smile curved his bruised mouth as he watched her stop, take up an indignant pose, and hurl some epithet at her father. But when she flung herself at Jason, the smile cracked, and something within as well.

Avenge Jason, she'd cried. She'd been ready to die to avenge him, just as she'd have sacrificed herself in Tepelena for the same cause. Now the father she loved so fiercely was alive . . .

Varian tried to strangle the unworthy thought, but it gnawed at him. He'd lost her . . . she was never his to lose. He'd loved her and wed her against her will. She'd gone with him only because she'd no choice, no one else. She'd said so on their wedding night. *I have no one but you.* Now, though . . .

She was his wife, Varian told himself. No one—not even her father—could take her away. Yet he hung back because her face would tell him the truth, and he doubted he could bear it.

Then he heard Jason's angry cry and saw Esme sag in her father's arms.

Panic surged, swamping all else, to drive Varian across the wharf in the space of a heartbeat. He wrenched Esme's dead weight from her staggering father and lifted her in his arms. Her shirt was sticky with blood, and

Jason was bellowing for a doctor. Varian cradled his wife closer and hurried toward the village.

In minutes a crowd was swarming about him, everyone talking at once, advising, warning. He paid them no heed.

As they neared the buildings, Esme's eyes fluttered open, and she mumbled in Albanian.

"It's all right, love," Varian said thickly. "You'll be all right. Don't try to talk. I'll take care of you."

"Put me down," she said.

Relief tightened his chest. He dropped a kiss on her forehead. "Shut up," he said. "You're bleeding."

He made direct for the nearest respectable-looking establishment, which belonged to a shipping agent. Varian kicked open the door. "Get a doctor," he told the startled man at the desk. "My wife's hurt."

Esme closed her eyes and muttered under her breath. The man hastily opened the door to his private parlor, and Varian carried Esme inside.

As the shipping agent was hustling out, Jason stormed in, dragging a doctor with him.

Varian very tenderly placed his swooning wife on the sofa. When the physician entered, however, she became sharply alert and ordered him away.

It took both Jason and Varian to keep her still while Mr. Fern examined her. She swore while he cleaned the mercifully shallow path Risto's bullet had torn at the back of her shoulder, and cursed the doctor in acutely personal terms while he wrapped her in bandages.

Mr. Fern stoically endured her abuse, merely remarking that her ladyship was wonderfully high-spirited. "I'd simply suggest one watch for signs of concussion. The wound is minor, as you quite rightly point out, my lady," he said soothingly. "Still, you have two nasty lumps—"

"*Three,*" she corrected. "Three stupid men fussing like old women."

Mr. Fern made her a polite bow. With equal courtesy he described the symptoms to watch for and what to do about them. He then courteously accepted the coins Jason pressed into his hand and bowed himself out.

"I certainly feel old at this moment," Jason told his daughter. "Altogether too ancient for these high jinks."

"You are also dirty and disgusting." Esme's glance flicked uneasily over Varian. "Both of you. And do not tell me it is all my fault. I know well enough."

"Of course it's not your fault," Varian said hastily.

"Certainly not," said Jason. "She'd not have been here in the first place if she hadn't wed a selfish reprobate who can't be bothered to look after his own wife properly."

Varian's face heated. *"In the first place,* if you'd bothered to look after your daughter properly, she'd never have met me."

"Don't tell me my duty, you insolent degenerate!"

"I, at least, did not leave her to a pack of murderous sodomites and pederasts!"

Esme scrambled up from the sofa and planted herself between them. *"Aman,* have we not shed blood enough, but you must make blood feud between you? You will not call my husband names," she told her father. "Again and again he has saved my life, and all he gets is trouble. You will make no more for him, Jason. I am trouble enough."

When she turned to Varian, the fire went out of her eyes. "I am sorry, Varian. I am not a good wife." Her voice broke, and she buried her face in his battered coat.

His arms went around her. He forgot his mortified rage, forgot the father-in-law who despised him. All that mattered was that Esme was alive. All he wanted at this moment was to hold her.

Jason cleared his throat. "I think I'll have a wash," he said.

Leaving his son-in-law and daughter to their maudlin reunion, Jason headed for the Bridge Inn. After washing and changing, he dispatched a message to his mother, then arranged with the innkeeper for rooms and a change of clothing for Varian and Esme. Immediately thereafter, Jason met again with Captain Nolcott.

Sir Gerald Brentmor had expressed a wish to be buried

at sea, Jason told the captain. His remains would travel on the same ship with Ismal.

"Two corpses then," said the captain. "That boy won't live out the day."

So Mr. Fern confirmed a short while later, when he exited the room in which Ismal lay. The physician had removed the bullet and set the broken hand, though he was convinced both operations were futile.

Sick at heart, Jason entered the chamber.

Bruises made garish welts of color upon Ismal's ashen face, and his eyes shone with a feverish brightness. Though he'd scarcely the strength to breathe, he, as Gerald had, insisted on talking—but to Captain Nolcott.

"You cannot deny a dying man's last wish." Ismal's once-sweet voice was a cracked whisper.

Jason dragged a chair to the bedside and sat. "Maybe it's not your time to die."

Something like a smile contorted Ismal's swollen lips. "Nay, I must confess. Everything."

"You'll save your breath, my lad. Gerald's dead. You can't do him any more harm, and I won't let you destroy my family's future. Your bullet spared my brother the gallows. Rest assured I'll see my family spared disgrace. I've burned the black queen's message, as well as the letters Risto and Mehmet carried for you."

Another ghastly smile. "To protect your family's honor."

"That, yes." Jason forced an answering smile. "But also for the sake of your immortal soul, or—if you somehow manage to live—your conscience."

Ismal closed his eyes. "Better not to live. You'll send me to Ali. Better to cut my throat, Red Lion. Now, or I will find a way to tell my story."

"Bajo is already making arrangements to take you away. You can be sure we've seen to everything. His Majesty's government wants nothing to do with you."

"You made it so. You are too persuasive, Red Lion. And too clever. Yet, almost, I outwitted you."

"Not at all. You played the game very badly. Astonishingly badly when you followed Esme from Tepelena.

I couldn't believe you could do such an idiotic thing." Jason paused. "Until today."

Ismal's eyes opened slowly. The feverish light was gone, clouded by pain. "What saw you today?"

"It wasn't what I saw, but what I remembered: how young you are."

"Only in years."

"A boy, all the same, infatuated for the first time."

"You understand nothing."

"Of course I do. I too fell in love and made stupid mistakes because I was young, arrogant, and conceited. I didn't take rejection well, either, and nearly destroyed myself as a result."

"It's you who've destroyed me."

"I was trying to save you. You're not Alexander, nor is ours the world of two thousand years ago. You're too young to build empires and far too young to cope with love and politics simultaneously."

"Aye. I am only a foolish boy to you, and you laugh." The foolish boy's eyes filled with tears.

Pity and rage thickened Jason's throat. "You're a bloody fool, and you've thrown your life away. Look at you—not three and twenty, a pathetic heap of useless flesh, and likely to be a corpse before sunset. It's not me you hear laughing, but the Devil you've listened to these last two years."

"I'm not afraid to die."

Yet he was afraid, Jason knew, and helpless for the first time in his short life. All Ismal's cleverness could not mend his failing flesh or keep his young heart beating.

Jason could not help grieving for him, more even than he'd grieved for Gerald, who'd wasted his life in bitterness, greed, and envy, with no love, loyalty, or joy of any kind to lighten his days. At the end, if any trace of good lingered in a heart so corrupt, all it could feel was regret.

Ismal was another case. His soul was only tainted, not yet black with sin. And so Jason grieved the more, and raged as well, at the needless waste of youth and beauty and strength, but above all, of mind.

He smoothed the damp golden hair back from Ismal's burning forehead. Shuddering, the young man turned his face away.

"There are no holy men of your faith here," Jason said in gentler tones. "Shall I fetch an English cleric?"

"No."

The door opened, and Bajo slipped inside. "The boat waits," he told Jason softly. "Your countrymen want him gone."

Ismal wouldn't last an hour at sea. Not that he'd last much longer even if he remained where he was. "Would you rather I came with you?" Jason asked.

"You want so badly to watch me die?"

"If I were you, I'd want a friend beside me."

"Nay. I killed your brother by accident. It was you I was aiming for."

Jason sighed. "I wish you hadn't. Now I'll have to thank Edenmont for saving my life. If he hadn't broken your hand, you'd not have missed."

"I dislike him very much." Ismal grimaced as he turned to face Jason. "But he is a good fighter." He caught his breath, and his face tightened in agony.

"I think you've talked enough," Jason said. "Why didn't that fool doctor give you any laudanum?"

"I would not take it." Another struggle for breath, another ghastly effort at a smile. "It saps the will."

Bajo shifted impatiently. "Red Lion."

Jason rose. "Bajo is obliged to make haste. I'll come with you to the ship."

"Tsk."

From the hall beyond came the sound of hurried footsteps. Bajo moved to the door to bar the way, but Esme thrust past him.

"No!" Ismal cried. He pulled feebly at the blanket, trying to cover his face.

Ignoring the warning look Jason threw her, Esme moved to the bedside. She was shaking, yet she gazed steadily at Ismal. "You are very fortunate that my husband is the noblest of all men," she told him. "He gives me permission to try to save you, and so I shall."

Ruthlessly she pulled back the bedclothes. Ismal went

very still and stared doggedly at the ceiling while she studied the blood-soaked bandages.

"Esme, you're embarrassing the poor—"

"It is too bad for his pride," she said, gesturing her father away. "Listen to me," she told Ismal.

His gaze jerked to her.

"I shall do my best," she said. "And so, if you live, it will be because of *me*—only because of me. You will remember this, Ismal."

"And if I die?" he gasped.

"Then you shall burn in hell."

About an hour after Esme had commenced her dubious errand of mercy, Jason entered the Bridge's private dining parlor, where Varian was doggedly trying to eat breakfast.

Jason set his traveling bag at Varian's feet. "Captain Nolcott gathered up the chess set while we were with Gerald. It's all there, safe and sound."

Varian nodded stiffly.

"I owe you an apology," Jason said. "And thanks."

Before Varian could respond, the innkeeper's wife bustled in.

"Oh, whatever you like, my dear," Jason amiably replied to her inquiry. "So long as there's plenty of it. And bring me the biggest mug of ale you've got."

When she had gone, he turned back to Varian. "You saved my life."

"I wasn't trying to," Varian answered shortly. "I only wanted to kill *him.* I let Esme clean up the mess I'd made only because she was beside herself. She was in agonies of guilt, I believe, because she'd nearly killed him for a crime he never committed. It was no good pointing out those crimes he *had* done. She was certain Ismal would survive out of spite and come back for revenge—on all of us."

"Just so. Now he can't. His pride won't let him." Jason shrugged. "If he lives."

Varian firmly pushed Ismal's battered, bloody image from his mind. "What's going to happen to him, if he lives?"

"He ought to be taken to Newgate and hanged, but that could create diplomatic complications. There's also the question of whether he did the kingdom a favor in ridding it of Sir Gerald Brentmor. Fortunately, I won't have to puzzle the courts with that intriguing problem. I started tidying up some months ago, while I was trailing Ismal," Jason explained. "Gerald's partner, Bridgeburton, was considerate enough to drown in Venice. The authorities already suspected him. I encouraged them to suspect no one else."

"But Ismal?"

"They've left him to me. He's going to New South Wales in the care of friends of mine."

Their hostess arrived with Jason's breakfast, which he set to with enthusiasm. His appetite, unlike Varian's, appeared not at all affected by the morning's events. But Jason was used to violence, Varian reflected.

Jason looked up from his plate. "Gerald's body goes on the same ship with Ismal. I've done enough lying for him. The hypocrisy of a funeral I will not tolerate."

"I'm sure it's none of my affair."

"You feel sorry for the swine, I suppose, and blame yourself for bringing him here. You think it's your fault he's dead."

"If I hadn't bribed him with the chess set," Varian said tautly, "he'd never have come."

Jason shook his head. "One of Ismal's men nearly knocked me into the harbor. Gerald pulled me to safety. That may have been the only decent thing my brother's ever done, intentionally, for anybody. The next minute, he was scrambling for his precious rooks and pawns. I told him to go while he still could. But no, he must have the damned set." He severed a thick slice from the loaf before him. "*Greed* killed him today, Edenmont, as it would have done, sooner or later."

Varian pushed his plate away. "I see."

Jason glanced at Varian's barely touched breakfast. "Lost your appetite?"

"I hadn't much to begin with," Varian said.

"You're too bloody sensitive." Jason buttered his bread. "No wonder Esme's made a wreck of you."

* * *

Jason accompanied his late brother and what was left of Ismal to the ship. Leaving Esme in care of the innkeeper's wife, Varian went with him. He wasn't sure why. Perhaps it was a need to see the thing to its end.

He'd intended to wait on deck while the Red Lion took his leave of Ismal. When Jason was done, however, Ismal had asked to speak to Lord Edenmont.

Varian stood by the narrow bunk. Ismal's blue eyes were swollen nearly shut, and the sensuous mouth was a torn lump on his battered face.

"You fought well," Ismal rasped.

"I'd have performed far more elegantly in a duel," Varian answered coolly. "You might consider duels in future. Much tidier, the rules clearly defined. One knows exactly what to do."

"The English. So polite. I stole your wife."

"I stole her back," Varian said, "and took my revenge. I know you Albanians like to drag your quarrels on for decades, as we do our lawsuits. Nonetheless, I'd much appreciate it if you'd agree our feud is at an end."

"Nay." Ismal tried to lift his head and winced. He lay back again, his good hand plucking fretfully at the coarse blanket. "I called her my whore."

"But she wasn't. You were just being disagreeable."

The swollen mouth twisted. It seemed to mean a smile. "Is this what she told you?"

"She'd not have begged to nurse you if you'd shamed her. She'd no need to tell me, and I'd no need to ask."

"You are not stupid."

"Thank you."

Ismal looked past him, toward the doorway. "Red Lion."

Jason moved to the bed.

"Make my peace for me," said Ismal.

Jason drew out from his coat a small, richly embroidered bag. "Ismal tried to steal your wife and tried even harder to kill you," he said. "Despite these crimes, you allowed your wife to ease his suffering. If he lives, Ismal will owe you his life. These circumstances create a burden he finds intolerable."

"I do not—"

"No interruptions, Edenmont," Jason reproved. "This is a *ceremony.*"

Varian subsided.

"He values your wife more highly than an ordinary woman," Jason went on. "He agrees, with many of his countrymen, that the little warrior is worth two good men. Her great healing skills must also be taken into account, as must your princely status. Finally, as a nobleman himself, his honor must be estimated at a high value. His calculations amount to this." Jason gave him the bag.

Varian looked to the invalid.

"For my honor," Ismal said.

Varian emptied the bag's contents into his hand: diamonds, emeralds, sapphires, rubies. "Good God," he murmured.

"In accepting this fine, Lord Edenmont, you agree that Ismal's shame is wiped away and he no longer owes you. In accepting this, you declare your honor satisfied and your two families at peace. My honor's already been seen to," Jason explained, "much the same way."

Varian stared numbly at the gems in his hand.

"Not enough," Ismal fretted. "I told you, Red Lion, it would not be—"

"No, no, it's enough," Varian said quickly. "I nearly said it was too much—but that would be an insult, I suppose."

"You see?" Jason told Ismal. "He understands better than you think. Not all Englishmen are blockheads."

"I understand the payment," Varian said as he returned the stones to the bag. "There was a time when my own countrymen settled differences in a similar way. Still do, in some cases. What I don't understand is why you came all this way for the chess set when you'd already a fortune in jewels."

"I came for revenge," said Ismal. "On Sir Gerald. The rest . . . Fate, perhaps." He glanced at Jason. "Or my own stupid arrogance."

"I quite understand," said Varian. "Esme's made a wreck of me, too."

Chapter 33

After leaving Ismal, Esme trudged to the chamber Jason had reserved. She managed to wash, change into the frock set out for her, and consume most of her breakfast before she gave up and collapsed on the bed. She didn't waken until mid-afternoon, when Varian and Jason returned to collect her.

Deaf to her pleas that they remain in Newhaven and rest, they briskly bundled her into a carriage. Minutes thereafter, all her attention was riveted upon Jason and the story he told. He began twenty-five years before, when he'd fallen in love with Diana and lost her and his property through Sir Gerald's treachery. He related her uncle's deathbed confession, with its astonishing revelation about Esme's aunt, who'd turned Sir Gerald's vicious mind against him, blackmailing him with his own evil deed and punishing him with his own misconceptions.

"I admire my aunt for the way she managed and punished my uncle," Esme said, interrupting her father, "but that does not change what he did. He destroyed your life."

"I tried to tell you before," Jason answered. "I'd been headed for ruin anyhow. Gerald only hastened the inevitable. I recognized years ago that marrying Diana would have been a disastrous mistake. We were both wayward and selfish. You didn't know me then. You've no idea how Albania—and especially your mama—changed me. Just as Diana's experiences changed her. By the time we came together again last year, we were different people."

"Wayward you may have been, but selfish I cannot believe," Esme said. "You sent her a chess set worth five thousand pounds at a time you so badly needed money."

"My dear girl, I hadn't the remotest notion what it was worth," he said impatiently. "I won the bloody thing in a card game."

Esme didn't open her mouth again until Jason's tale had taken them to this morning, when he'd been waiting to capture Ismal . . . and found the task grossly complicated when Esme emerged from Ismal's carriage.

Then she was obliged to explain how she'd managed to stumble into his clutches. When she'd finished, her father was glaring at her. Varian only stared doggedly out the window.

"Damnation, Esme, don't you know your grandmother better than that?" her father demanded. "Don't you think she knew her own son? I'd stake my life she knew Gerald was desperate and planning to bolt—and she was happy to help him. She'd have done anything to get rid of him."

"Then why not give him the black queen—and let him take the whole chess set?" Esme countered.

"Because he settled easily for less. Though I'm sure she suspected he meant to steal the set as well. She probably meant to do something about that, too—only she was drugged before she could."

"Percival meant to do something," Varian put in quietly. "He even suspected Ismal was involved. The poor boy never dreamed he'd be drugged within a few hours of entering his father's house."

"As you both wish I had been," she said tightly.

Neither man replied, which was answer enough. As usual, everything was all *her* fault. She clamped her mouth shut and did not open it again except to eat, when they stopped at the Dorset Arms in East Grinstead.

Varian felt the tension building all through dinner. Jason must have sensed it, too, because he elected to spend the rest of the journey on the box with the coachman. It was a mild night, he said, and he hadn't seen his homeland in a quarter of a century.

After five silent minutes in the carriage with Esme, Varian began to wish he'd joined his father-in-law. He was in no state to handle any more confrontations. His nerves still jangled after what had been, beyond doubt, the very worst day of his entire misbegotten existence. He could scarcely look at her without seeing the deadly blade at her throat. He stared into the night, praying she'd hold her tongue all the way to London.

"I wanted to be with you," she said in a choked, hurt voice. "I wanted to give you the chess set, so you would not have to work so hard any more and spoil your hands."

"Dear God," he muttered to the window. "My hands."

"Once, they were smooth and white. Now only look. They are brown and hard and calloused and—and bruised and cut as well. It is all my fault, I suppose. Yet you are angry because I tried—"

"Because you nearly got yourself killed!" He swung around to her, and it flashed before him again, for the hundredth time: the blast of fire and smoke, and Esme falling. "Why couldn't you just keep still and leave it to me? For God's sake, did you think I'd let Ismal—anyone—take you away? Do you think I'm so inept?"

"It was you I thought of! I could not let him shame you!"

"*You* couldn't let him. What the hell do you think I was there for? A sea bath?" He closed his eyes. "Why do I ask? *Think.* You never think."

"I'm sorry," she said. "I did not mean to insult you. I know you came to save me."

"You just didn't trust me to do it. 'Avenge Jason. Avenge *me.*' That's all you were willing to leave to me: revenge. You never considered the rest, did you?" he demanded. "Of what it would be like for me, to spend the rest of my days blaming and hating myself because I couldn't find a way to keep you safe."

"Then why would you not keep me with you?" she cried. "I begged you, but you would not listen."

He winced. He should have kept her with him, should have known better than to let her out of his sight. But she wasn't a child, and he would not play nanny the rest of his life. He could not live in constant fear that she'd do something insane if he wasn't by to prevent it.

"I thought I explained everything at Mount Eden," he said levelly. "I thought you understood. Yet you had so little faith in me, you didn't even consult me. You could have written about what you'd overheard. I was only three hours away. Instead, you tried to run away with that cursed chess set. All by yourself, in the dead of night. In England, where a lady doesn't step out the door in broad day without an escort."

She clasped her hands tightly in her lap. "I know that was wrong. But I had lost my temper. And you know how it is with me, Varian."

"Demonic possession."

"Yes," she answered sadly.

She had him at *point non plus.* He couldn't fight the demon in her breast.

Varian thought for a long while, aware of the anxious glances she darted at him. "Very well," he said finally. "If you cannot manage your temper, we can't possibly have children. Ever."

Her gasp was sharp as a shriek. "*No,* you cannot—"

"I can just picture you as a mother. The first time the poor devil tries your patience, you'll lose your temper and drown it. And be dreadfully sorry after, of course. Then you'll promise never to do it again and pester me for another. The next thing I know, the blighter will wake you up in the night—and you'll toss him out the window."

"I would never, *never* harm a child."

"I don't trust you." He folded his arms across his chest. "I can't trust you to come to me and say, 'Varian, the child is making me crazy. What shall we do?' *We,*" he repeated. "As in asking for help. As in consulting my opinion. As in having some fragment of confidence in my judgment. And my honor. And affection."

Her bottom lip began to tremble. "I know what you are telling me. I am sorry, Varian. I only wanted to give you what was rightfully yours." Her voice wavered.

He scooped her up and onto his lap. "You shan't distract me with tears. Tell me the whole truth."

"I have," she mumbled, her face downcast.

"You've told me only half. The other half is that you wanted to test me, didn't you? You wanted to see how I'd react when you took away my excuse for not keeping you at Mount Eden."

Her head shot up. He stared right back into her startled green eyes.

"Just because I'm not as devious as *your* side of the family doesn't mean I'm stupid," he said. "I'll wager you're still wondering what I'll do. Gad, what a little idiot." He crushed her against his chest. "What a stubborn, reckless, passionate little fool."

It might have been worse, Esme told herself. She did not mind being called names, so long as he kept her on his lap. After a while, he even fell asleep so, his arms still wrapped about her. The stream of insults must have quieted his mind, else he'd not have slept. Her mind, too, was quieted, for she'd heard his pain and understood he was angry because she'd frightened and hurt him. He would not have felt so if he cared nothing for her. To feel assured that he did would have been worth even a beating, though she did not think she truly deserved one.

Esme wished she might remain so, snuggled close to him, forever. In a few short hours, though, they were in London, and minutes thereafter, at the Brentmor townhouse.

Percival dashed out into the street, a troop of servants behind him, even before the carriage halted. The Dowager Lady Brentmor, however, did not so much as step into the hallway.

Rigid as a pikestaff, she stood in the salon to await her family in state. She frowned at Varian when he entered with Esme in his arms, glared at Esme as Varian deposited her upon the sofa, and glowered at Percival, who trotted in a step ahead of his uncle. It was upon Jason, the son she'd not seen in two and a half decades, that the dowager bent the blackest scowl of all.

Jason smiled, put down the travel bag containing the chess set, marched up to her, and gave her a hard hug and a noisy kiss on the cheek. Then he drew back to study her with frank admiration. "My dear Mama, how well you look."

Her sharp hazel eyes raked him up and down. "Can't say the same for you. Brawling on the waterfront, was you? With a lot of sailors and godless barbarians. Not to mention the gel shot, and her numskull husband nigh beaten to pudding. And your scapegallows brother gone to Judgment. There's one thing to be thankful for—at least we hadn't to watch him be hanged, drawn, and quartered."

After thus welcoming them, she plunked herself upon a chair, ordered Jason to serve the brandy, and demanded an explanation.

What she got was a highly condensed version of the tale Jason had related in the carriage. It appeared to satisfy her—for the present, she said. Then she turned one of her brimstone looks upon Esme. "Your pa ain't seen me in twenty-five years—yet *he* knew what I was about. What in blazes was you thinking of?"

"I was angry," Esme answered calmly. "I was not thinking clearly."

"If you was angry, you should have come and quarreled with me. Never held your tongue before. Keep you, indeed," the old lady muttered. "I'd as soon keep a flock of jackdaws."

"I know, Grandmama. I am impossible. But if you wish to scold me, at least let the men go to bed. They are both weary, but too proud to tell you so."

The dowager considered her son, seated next to her by the fire, then Varian, who was perched on the sofa arm near Esme. "Not a pretty sight," she grumbled, "neither of you. Get along to bed, then." She nodded curtly at Percival. "You, too. And no dawdling behind to listen at the keyhole. You've done enough of that for one lifetime, I think."

Percival flushed.

Varian fixed his cool gray gaze upon the dowager. "I trust you meant that as a compliment, my lady. Every one of us has reason to be grateful to your grandson."

"Only by the grace of God," she snapped. "Things might have turned out different—"

"But they didn't. Even if they had, no reasonable human being can fault him for trying to do his duty." He rose and approached the boy. "Your uncle's story ought to speak for itself. Since it evidently hasn't, for some parties, I shall elucidate. We are all deeply grateful, Percival, for your courage and intelligence."

Percival's flush deepened. "Oh, dear. Not—oh, but I didn't. That is to say, I did lie to you and keep secrets—and really, I'm very sorry."

"I cannot imagine how you might have done otherwise." Varian put out his hand.

The boy's chagrin eased into relief, and he shook the offered hand.

Thank you, Esme silently told her husband. Even she had forgotten about Percival. She, too, needed reminding how much she owed her cousin: thanks as well as apologies, for she had misjudged him, repeatedly.

She heard her father echo Varian's sentiments, and her grandmother grumbling that the boy had done his best, after all, and a body couldn't ask more than that. All Esme could say would be redundant. Instead, she moved to her cousin and gave him a crushing hug.

Rather shyly, he hugged her in return. "I was monstrous worried last night," he confided softly to her. "But I knew his lordship would find you. Mama told me he was much more intelligent than he pretended. She said—" He blinked twice, then went very still. As she stepped away from him, Esme noticed that Jason and her grandmother had fallen silent as well. They were watching Varian.

He'd taken the chess pieces out of the travel bag and was just setting the last of them upon the low table near the sofa. When he straightened, he returned their stares with a blankly innocent one.

"I thought you was tired," said the dowager. "You ain't meaning to play now, are you?"

"I loathe chess," he said. "It is tediously complicated. Just looking at the set makes me frantic."

"You don't need to like it," Jason said impatiently. "All you need to do is sell it."

Varian raised his eyebrows. "The St. Georges do not engage in *trade*. At any rate, I can't possibly sell Percival's inheritance."

"My—oh dear. But it isn't. It's Esme's dowry, sir. Mama said so, and wrote it in her will."

Varian focused on Esme. He didn't utter a word, didn't need to. She didn't so much as look at the set. "It has nothing to do with me," she said. "The dowry goes to the husband, to dispose of as he chooses."

"As I did, last night," said Varian. "I promised it to Sir Gerald. He kept his end of the bargain, only didn't live to enjoy the reward. Therefore, like the rest of his property, it must go to his heir."

Percival swallowed hard. "Thank you, sir, but I—that is, Papa shouldn't have needed to be bribed. You mustn't think I . . ." He blinked, several times. "Mama wanted Cousin Esme to have it."

"Only to be sure she got a husband. Your mama had no way of knowing Esme would get a husband all by herself. Otherwise she'd have left the set to you."

Percival started to protest, then gave up, perilously near tears. "Th-thank you, sir. It is very—"

"Old," Varian finished briskly. "Why don't you see if you can find a proper container for it? You don't want to wrap it up in Esme's underthings again, I hope."

The boy promptly fled. Just before the door closed behind him, Esme heard his choked sob. Her own throat tightened. She noticed her father's eyes had become suspiciously bright. Beside him, the dowager sniffed, for Varian had reduced even that tough old lady to tears. Two tears, to be precise, which she swatted away indignantly.

Because she understood, as they all did, what the gift meant to Percival. He'd nothing of his beloved mama's to remember her by. His father had seen to that. All that remained of Diana's possessions was the chess set. Worth a fortune.

Brushing away her own tears, Esme met her husband's bored gaze.

His lordship yawned. "I beg your pardon," he said. "It's been a long day. I had better say good night."

"You make me feel ashamed," Esme said.

Varian was leaning back upon the pillows, his hands clasped behind his head. Through half-closed eyes he studied his wife, who sat cross-legged on the bed beside him. "I suppose you can't help it," he said. "I am so noble, so inexpressibly saintly. Naturally, you adore me. Worship the ground I walk upon. I am, after all, the great light of the heavens, your beautiful god."

Her wistful green gaze traveled from his face down over his naked torso, then back to her folded hands. She sighed. "It is true. This is how I feel."

"Sometimes. In your rare moments of tranquility."

"It is not easy to be tranquil about you. I look at you, then I look at myself . . ." She hesitated.

"And?"

She made a small, helpless gesture. "I do not understand why God would put together two people so different."

"You think the Almighty has made some sort of ghastly mistake and, being all-wise, must eventually correct it?"

She moved uneasily. "Yes, I think this sometimes, and it makes me anxious."

"It makes you *crazy* sometimes," he corrected. "It's made you think idiotic things: that I don't want to live with you, for instance, and that I don't want your children. However, I mean to make you see the error of your ways."

She lifted her head. "Then you will take me to Mount Eden?"

He nodded.

"And—and we shall make a family?" She blushed.

He shrugged. "I have no choice. You find all prevention methods thoroughly revolting. I shall not wound your tender sensibilities again—or my own," he added half to himself.

"But do you *want* them?" she persisted. "They may—it is possible they will be like me. I would try my best to prevent that, but there is no recipe. One cannot make children as one does a poultice."

His mouth twitched. "Are you trying to persuade me or talk me out of it?"

"I thought perhaps, when you imagined children, you would picture sons in your own image. Men often do," she said defensively.

He nodded. "I've imagined that. It fills me with inutterable horror. Fortunately, it is scientifically impossible, I believe, to get children *exactly* like me, even if I could make them all by myself, which is an even greater scientific impossibility. Since I must make them with you . . ."

He eyed her consideringly. "You're rather small, and horribly bad-tempered. Still, you did promise to grow, and on the whole, I tend to find your temper exciting. The shouting and vituperation, I mean," he clarified. "Not the homicidal or suicidal aspects. Fortunately, if I keep you very busy breeding and attending to my every whim, you won't have time for violence."

"Do not tease." She nudged him with her knee. "I am not so savage as that."

"I only worry that you'll find domesticity boring."

"Tsk. You do not understand." She edged nearer. "There are other ways besides battle and blood feud to test one's courage. This day you fought like a brave warrior. Yet all the days and weeks before you fought as well, a greater struggle in many ways." She laid her hand over his heart. "That is the battle I truly wished to fight, Varian . . . by your side."

The touch warmed him. The words made him ache. "I know," he said gently. "Unfortunately, I was determined on martyrdom. I went after redemption with a vengeance—trying to prove myself worthy, I suppose, of the wonderful creature I married."

She drew her hand away. "I am not wonderful. Ask my father. All the same, I can—"

"Wonderful," he said firmly. "Why do you find it so easy to face harsh truths and so hard to accept the pleasant ones? When I've anything tender or sentimental to say, you oblige me to camouflage it with witticisms and silly jokes. I wouldn't mind, if only you didn't keep missing the punch line."

"The point of the joke, you mean?"

"The point of everything." Sitting up fully, he took her hands in his. "I love you," he said, *"as you are."*

"Nay, you need not say—"

"Listen to me," he said.

She bowed her head.

"Do you recall the night on the way to Poshnja, when I said you were the flame and I the moth?" he asked.

She started to shake her head, Albanian style, then managed an awkward nod. "Yes, I recall."

The small gesture, toward him, toward the England that was her home now, nearly undid him. But he was determined make her understand, and believe, fully.

"I said you were always bursting into flame." He twined his fingers with hers. "You set things on fire inside me. Wishes, dreams, needs I'd hidden so deep I hardly realized they existed. They were like dead wood, kindling. You set the spark to them."

She kept her gaze fixed on their twined hands. "That night, you meant desire."

"Desire drove me, yes. At the time, that was all I comprehended. It kept me with you when my old self urged me to run away as I always had, from every difficulty. From tomorrow. From life itself, I think."

"You are not the only one who has wished to run away," she said guiltily. "Yet you have not done so once in the time I have known you, while I have, several times."

"Not to escape your problems, but to meet them head on. To fight for honor, independence. Last night, this morning, you were fighting for your rights, your marriage. For me."

"I caused you distress, all the same."

"Perhaps that was necessary." His soft chuckle made her look up. "It seems I can only learn the hard way," he explained. "Because of you, I've learned I can fight not only unscrupulous rivals, but circumstances as well.

Whether I want to or not. Mostly not, it would seem. I've been kicking and screaming the whole way. Because it *has* been horrible, Esme."

"Yes, horrible," she sadly agreed.

"And *glorious,*" he added. "As you are. As life is. You think the Almighty made a mistake. I think some angel sent you." He released her hands and, smiling, stroked her cheek. "One who'd evidently read *Childe Harold* and decided it would do better transformed to comedy."

"Childe Harold?" Esme moved his hand away. "You speak of Lord Byron's poem? The one about Albania?"

"Albania is only part of a long tale about an unhappy wanderer. The night in Bari when Percival lied about the black queen, he'd been reading the first canto."

Closing his eyes, Varian quoted, " 'For he through Sin's long labyrinth had run, / Nor made atonement when he did amiss, / Had sigh'd to many though he loved but one, / And that loved one, alas! could ne'er be his.' " He bent to whisper in her ear, "Who does that sound like to you?"

She shivered and drew away. "Nay, that is not the whole passage. Percival lent me his book weeks ago. I do not recall every word, but I remember it goes on to describe how the man would corrupt the girl he loved and then betray her with others while he spent all her money."

Varian opened his eyes. "You know it, do you? Did you also know that your aunt told Percival I was like Childe Harold?"

"Perhaps she saw you so. But with me you have not wandered aimlessly about, sulking and acting tragically."

"Because the mischievous angel decided my pilgrimage would be different and put Percival in my way. All that's happened since the night he lied about the black queen—every conflict, every fear and heartache—all of it was necessary, all part of a journey of discovery."

Drawing her back onto the pillows with him, he threaded his fingers through her hair. "Most important, on this journey we discovered each other," he went on.

"I want to go on discovering, Esme—children, family, home—all of life, all of love—with you."

"Always I have thought of life as a battle," she said shakily. "A journey, even a difficult one, is better." Her eyes were glistening. She blinked very hard. "And better still that you wish to make your journey with me."

"If you hadn't been distracted by revenge and honor and the rest, you'd have deduced that ages ago." He looked down at her. "Luckily, I'm not a very demanding spouse. I don't mind that my wife is not brilliantly logical in *every* way. Or that my beautifully romantic speech did not move her to tears. One can't have everything."

"You do not wish me to weep," she said. "I become very cross after. And I do not wish to be cross with you. Not tonight—even to make you laugh." She smiled. "For it does please me to make you laugh, you know—even though at the same time I may be vexed."

"Because you accept me just as I am, don't you? You haven't tried to reform me, only to hold onto me. I don't want to reform or tame you, either, only keep you safe with me, always."

He tilted her chin up and let himself be caught, lost in the evergreen depths of her eyes. "I love you," he said. "Just believe it."

"I do," she said. "I will."

"Then tell me something. Anything."

"I love you, Varian *Shenjt Gjergj,*" she whispered, "with all my heart."

He bent and lightly brushed his lips against hers. *"Hajde, shpirti im,"* he said softly. "Come, my heart, and show me."

Author's Note

Colonel William Martin Leake's *Travels in Northern Greece* was eventually published in 1835. This, and John Cam Hobhouse's *A Journey through Albania* (published 1817), were my main sources of information about early nineteenth-century Albania. This is why Janina and Prevesa, for example, are Albanian towns in the novel, though they will not appear within the country's borders on any modern map.

At the time of the story, no Albanian alphabet existed; until recently, even modern phonetic spelling alternated, depending upon the writer, between northern and southern dialects. Consequently, early travel writers spelled Albanian words as they sounded—no easy task for the English ear—or, in the case of place names, took refuge in the Latin, Greek, or Italian versions. For simplicity's sake, I settled, with one or two exceptions, upon contemporary Albanian usage. Thus Esme does not live in Durazzo or Drus or Duratzo or Dyrrachium, but in Durrës.

On the other hand, I did retain a few words of Turkish origin, such as *y'Allah*. Though rarely used in modern Albania, they would have been common in the last century.

For clarification of numerous other linguistic, physical, and historical enigmas, I thank my parents, George and Resha Chekani; my sister, Cynthia Drelinger; my uncles Mentor, Steve, and George Kerxhalli; and my cousins, Skander and Mariana Kerxhalli. The latter spent three months with us early in 1991—among the first Albanian visitors to the U.S. in fifty-odd years.

For constructive criticism, advice, general wisdom and moral support, I am, as always, deeply indebted to my husband, Walter.

Any atrocities herein perpetrated, however, are without question solely my own.